John Cochrane, Leonard Pratt, Frank P. Frisby

Trial for Malpractice

Frank P. Frisby, by his next friend, Pearson Noble, vs. Dr. Leonard Pratt, in the

Circuit Court of Carroll County, State of Illinois, March 7th, 1864

John Cochrane, Leonard Pratt, Frank P. Frisby

Trial for Malpractice

Frank P. Frisby, by his next friend, Pearson Noble, vs. Dr. Leonard Pratt, in the Circuit Court of Carroll County, State of Illinois, March 7th, 1864

ISBN/EAN: 9783337780333

Printed in Europe, USA, Canada, Australia, Japan

Cover: Foto ©Andreas Hilbeck / pixelio.de

More available books at **www.hansebooks.com**

TRIAL

FOR

MAL-PRACTICE.

FRANK P. FRISBY,

BY HIS NEXT FRIEND, PEARSON NOBLE,

vs.

DR. LEONARD PRATT,

IN THE CIRCUIT COURT OF CARROLL COUNTY, STATE OF ILLINOIS,
MARCH 7th, 1864.

Reported by
JOHN S. COCHRANE,
ROCKFORD, ILL.

———————— ◆◆◆ ————————

CHICAGO:
PUBLISHED BY C. S. HALSEY.
JOHN W. DEAN, BOOK AND JOB PRINTER, 148 LAKE STREET.
1864.

PREFACE.

Each discovery in science, and the efforts of the progressive to adapt that science to the uses and wants of mankind is regarded by those who have sanctioned and adopted the more ancient methods, invariably, as an innovation. This is especially true in medicine. The persecution which discoverers in the science and reformers in the art of healing have suffered and experienced, has always been in ratio with the value and success of their efforts. Homœopathy—a form of truth—is no exception to this rule. Beginning with its illustrious founder HAHNEMANN, they have been persecuted from "city to city," and the system has been the victim of public and private abuse and misrepresentation. No opportunity for the villification of its tenets and practitioners has been permitted to pass unimproved. Resorts beneath the notice of honorable gentlemen have been the opening wedge of contumely and scandal. Its relative merits as compared with the ancient system of medical practice, have been tried in courts of justice and verdicts extorted by subterfuge, and every other possible means; with a view to damage the system and ruin its prospects of success.

This volume is the record of another attempt to bring disaster to a reform in medicine, and those who have adopted it. Although it is disclaimed in 'the beginning of this trial, yet the persecutors exhibit in its progress the *real cause* of all their efforts, by compelling an issue between the two schools of Medical practice.

INTRODUCTION.

No one can know the condition of a patient so well as the attending physician or surgeon. A lack of knowledge, coupled, perhaps, with an intention to deceive, led the plaintiff's family to remember facts which did not occur and to mistake others which did really take place.

As this case is put into a tangible shape, justice to myself would seem to demand from me a plain statement of the facts. There may be those who will disbelieve what I state; but those who best know me will know what value to place upon my assertions ; with that estimate I am satisfied. I give the following as the principal facts: Frank Frisby and brother, on the 20th Dec., 1862, in Rock Creek township, were on their way home, in wagons loaded with corn in the ear. The boys, I understood, had been running their teams. The forward end-board of Frank's wagon burst out by the pressure of the corn, in cross-ing a gully. The boy was thereby thrown astride the wagon tongue, and from thence to the frozen ground. His head, right hand and left arm were injured ; the two latter severely. I was called to visit the boy by Mr. Morris, at his house. I found he had fractured the lower third of the humerus in two places. The lower fracture was a little below the entrance of the nutrient artery, and was oblique. The other was above this point, and was transversed. The frac-tured ends of the bone had been thrust through the flesh on the back part of the arm, and I judged that the lower branch of the nutrient artery had been rup-tured, as it bled profusely from this external wound. The muscles of the arm were severely injured.

After reducing the fracture, a roller was applied from the hand to the shoulder. Two splints were then applied, reaching from the axilla and the shoulder to the elbow, with three shorter flexible splints between. The fore-arm was then placed in a sling. There was a wound upon the upper and back part of the head. The thumb and inside of the right hand were much mutilated, and the metacarpal bone was fractured from the outside above the second joint obliquely, extend-ng nearly the whole length of the bone.

The inside fleshy portion of the thumb was literally torn out, laying bare the tendons and vessels near the bone. This laceration extended into the second joint, which was dislocated downwards and inwards. The lower fragment of the bone sliding upwards toward the wrist, prevented the joint from remaining in position unless firmly retained. A shellac splint fitted, to the joint, effected this object. The injuries to the soft portions of the thumb and hand rendered it impossible, at first, to so apply the bandage as to retain the bone precisely in place. But when the wounds had healed sufficiently, I informed the parents and boy that a perfect reduction of the fracture could then be made ; but they refused to permit me to do it, and the thumb is, consequently, a trifle too short.

As to diet, the parents were directed to give the boy light food—toast, crackers, &c.—until the inflammation and fever had subsided ; after that, such food as the family used.

The wounds of the head, arm and hand healed within a reasonable time, and the process of repair went on well. The upper and transverse fracture of the arm became quite firm in six weeks, but the lower, oblique fracture united more slowly. My visits, after the first ten days, were at intervals of from one to two weeks. A careful examination of these injuries was made at nearly every visit. On the 20th Feb'y, I think, I visited the boy with Dr. Wales. The dressings were removed and the fractures were found to be well united.

I thought of leaving off the splints entirely, but Dr. Wales suggested he was a boy, somewhat restless, and I re-adjusted the dressing and splints. The mother's attention was directed to the fact that there was no motion at the site of the fracture. She expressed herself much pleased at the result. The boy raised and elevated his arm himself without aid. After bathing the arm, I replaced the bandages and splints, for the reason above stated.

A few days afterwards I called again. I found the arm " loosened," or refractured, and the angular splint badly split at the joint in two places. The family told me the boy injured his arm in playing ball, by hitting the fore-arm against a post.

The fragments were merely separated, no other displacement. They were again placed in apposition and retained by firm bandaging and splints. A few weeks afterwards the fragments appeared to be uniting, but shortly after this they were again "loose." I informed the parents there was no union.

In April, I think, I used friction. Afterwards, at Mr. Frisby's request, a consultation was had at Milledgeville, with Drs. Belding and Freas. This was in May. Drs. Belding and Freas were informed of the refracture. Dr. Freas examined the elbow splint, and observed it must have taken a severe blow to have split it thus. The mother suggested it was basswood and would split easily. Dr. Freas remarked he could discover a remnant of the provisional callus where the upper fracture had been. The subject matter of remedies was talked over. I was in favor of more stringent measures. Dr. Belding was opposed. Dr. Freas was for resorting to friction once more, and which was finally agreed upon. He rubbed the fractured ends of the bone together, applied the roller and the same splints, and I assisted. Another consultation was to be had at my office two weeks afterwards, but neither Dr. Belding nor Freas came. At this time I examined the arm ; found no union had taken place. I urged the necessity of an operation to restore the arm. The father partially assented to what I said at the time—said he had not friends there, but would determine in a few days what he would do. Subsequently I saw him ; said he had concluded to employ Dr. Miller, and did not longer desire my services. Such is a plain, unvarnished statement of the facts. There may be testimony that conflicts with what I have here stated. If there is such testimony, I can only state it is incorrect. The boy was careless, and the parents, I presume, acting under the advice of some one or more *medical* advisors, are stubbornly bent upon not having that done which is necessary for the boy's complete recovery. The consequence is, he has a bad arm. It is a case where re-section could be used with little danger, and with every probability of success.

Conscious that I have performed my duty faithfully and carefully, in strict accordance with the principles and practice of surgery, as held and practiced by the best authors, I rely upon this for a complete and final vindication of my acts, and without further comment I submit this case to the candid judgment of he public.

L. PRATT.

SUIT FOR MAL-PRACTICE.

FRANK P. FRISBY,
  vs.
DR. LEONARD PRATT. }

Statemeut of the case to the jury, by Col. Turner.

Gentlemen of the jury:—Sometime in Dec. 1862, the plaintiff in this suit, a young, healthy lad, had the misfortune to get his left arm broken. There may be some little question in regard to the wound, whether a simple or compound fracture. Dr. Pratt, the defendant in this suit, was residing in the neighborhood, holding himself out to be a physician and surgeon, and practicing as such, and professed to be competent to do that work. The father of the boy employed Dr. Pratt to treat the case, and as it was a difficult matter, the father had much interest in it, and asked Dr. Pratt if he felt himself competent to take the case. Dr. Pratt assured him that he was competent, and under that assurance he was employed to treat the arm of this boy. Dr. Pratt came to the house, did up the arm and took exclusive charge of it. There was no other physician called; the parents of the boy felt satisfied from the representation of Dr. Pratt, that he was a proper man, to attend to it. It was put in splints and kept there some little time, and I suppose that the plaintiff will show that there were several examinations made of the arm; and after a long period of time had elapsed after the arm ought to have been well, the boy's parents became uneasy and expressed their uneasiness to Dr. Pratt, and he assured them that it was all right and doing well; and he still assured them that it was not necessary to set the arm again, that it was doing well enough. It continued this way for sometime after the splints were taken off, and it was found the arm had not adhered at all. There is what is called the false joint, caused by improper treatment. The truth in regard to the manner of that treatment will be brought out better in the testimony than I can bring it out before you. The boy's arm was never cured. The bone has become shortened to a considerable extent, and at all events, the boy has no use of his arm—cannot lift it. The theory of our case is this, that Dr. Pratt did not treat that arm as it should have been treated, and that the question we submit to you, and the primary point in this case is this,—was it treated in a proper manner? If it was, you must find him not guilty. If, on the contrary, you find that he ought to have been cured, the probabilities are, that he might have been cured if he had had proper treatment in this case, you must find him guilty, and assess the amount of damages the plaintiff sustained.

His thumb was injured, and that was never properly set. I speak more particularly of the arm because that was more serious than the other. I wish to direct your mind to this point. The issue in the case is this,—did Dr. Pratt treat this case properly, and is he a skillful physician, as he ought to be to understand such a case? If he did not treat this right you must find him guilty and assess such damages as will be justifiable from the treatment the boy received and the condition he was in, and we think it is one of those cases that the jury cannot refrain from awarding large damages. This is a case exciting a great deal of interest one way and the other. So far as the plaintiff is concerned, he has no prejudice, one way or the other, as to medical practice. They have no ill feeling against a man because he practices one system of medicine or another. The fact is, the boy has lost an arm, and we must represent the case to you. We have no fault to find with the theory at all, but with Dr. Pratt, as a professional man ; he should have done his work right. The only safety that humanity has in the world is in making surgeons do their work right. If he holds himself out to the world as a doctor, he is bound by the law to be skillful, and the very same thing applies to the lawyers around this bar. When you place a note of $5,000 in a lawyer's hands for collection, he must collect it. If he carelessly manages the case, and gets defeated, and you lose the case, he is bound by law, to pay for that note, because he assumed to do that work for you which you cannot do yourself. You cannot, when you are sick, doctor yourself. When you have a limb broken you cannot set that bone yourself, and consequently it is of very great importance to the people in a community, that when a man holds his name out to the world to do this work, he should do it properly, and if he fail he must pay the damages.

If Dr. Pratt has suffered this boy to lose his arm, when a skillful physician could have saved it, and the thumb is out of order and he has not prevented a bad case, then he should pay for it. We present both cases to you. The boy being a minor, the suit is brought by his next friend.

MR. KNOWLTON'S OPENING FOR THE DEFENDANT.

Gentlemen of the Jury :—I appear before you as one of the counsel for the defendant. At this time it is proper that I should give you our understanding of this case. Most cases have at least two sides—and some have more.

Mr. Turner has given you their theory of this case in behalf of the plaintiff. It will not be necessary for me to take issue with him as to what he has said about the liability of attorneys, and I will only remark, that should he ever be sued on such a state of facts as he has supposed, I have no doubt that he would, upon an examination of authority, change his opinion.

It is proper that I should say to you, that when skill is required of an attorney, surgeon, or other professional character, it is *not* the *utmost* or *highest skill* that is required, but *ordinary* skill. Ordinary skill and care is all that the law requires of a physician or surgeon. If this kind of skill is employed, there is no legal liability. What this skill is, must, to a great degree, be obtained from professional witnesses. As this case involves professional considerations, professional testimony will have a controlling effect as to the proper mode of treatment. Ordinary skill and attention to the plaintiff is what the defendant owed in this case, and upon their exercise *this* case and *your* verdict will depend.

There is a great gradation of skill. The gentleman will not deny that some men have more skill than others. Lawyers are presumed and bound to know enough of law to conduct the business entrusted to them with ordinary skill, care and attention.

A man like Daniel Webster, or Marshall, might have more skill than many other men.

In this case the plaintiff must establish, by competent evidence, that the defendant *did not* exercise ordinary skill and care in treating the injuries of the plaintiff in the particulars complained of in the declaration, and we are not bound to prove that he *did* use this skill and care. The undertaking of the defendant was, that he would treat the plaintiff with ordinary skill and care. This was the obligation on his part, and that in doing this he would resort, if necessary, to all the means that promised success, and recognized as proper by the surgical profession.

The obligation of the plaintiff was, to permit the defendant to resort to all such means, if necessary, to effect a cure, and to pay the defendant such sum as his services were reasonably worth, whether he succeeded in accomplishing the object or failed. The undertaking of the defendant was not that of a guarantor or insurer that a cure should be effected.

In case of fracture, the surgeon is bound (if it can be done) to put the broken fragments of bone in proper place, or in apposition, and bring into requisition such appliances as will keep them in that position. Re-union is the operation of nature, and *not* of the surgeon. When nature refuses to perform this work, where the pieces of bone are put and kept in apposition, no liability attaches to the surgeon. In some cases, means may be used that will aid the operations of nature. This should be resorted to when need demands. The sum total and short of the matter is this: the surgeon must do his part, and *nature* hers. When from past experience it has been ascertained that different modes of treatment are proper and succeed, the pursuit of either is not, in legal contemplation, want of skill or care. When the means most generally resorted to fail, and there are others that promise success, (because they have been successful,) the surgeon should— and has a *right* to—resort to those other means; and if he is not allowed to do so by the patient, or by others who control the matter—as the parent of a child—then we claim that no action can be maintained because a cure was not effected. This is the very state of case that we expect will be developed on this trial.

In this case it will not be denied that the boy's arm was fractured—precisely *how* it was done may not be proved. It is proper that I should say to you that surgeons have designated particular kinds of fractures.

First, there are what are termed simple fractures. These are the least dangerous. In simple fracture only one *bone* is broken at *one* place, and no other injury.

Second, there is what is termed a *compound* fracture. This is where the bone is broken at *more* than *one* place. This is more dangerous than simple fracture.

Third, there is what is termed compound comminuted fracture. This is where the bone is broken at more than one place, and an external wound leading to or connected with the point of fracture. This species is much more dangerous than simple or compound fractures.

Fourth, there is *compound comminuted complicated* fracture. Here the bone is broken at more than one place—an external wound of the flesh communicating with the fracture, and a wound or some injury upon some other part of the body. This is the most dangerous of the whole class.

This last is the kind (as we anticipate the proof will show) with which the plaintiff was afflicted. We expect that the proof will show that the *humerus* of the left arm of the plaintiff was broken in two places, and in its lower third, and that there was an external wound of the flesh communicating with the lowest fracture; and in addition to this, that the right hand was badly lacerated, and one joint of the thumb dislocated.

That Dr. Pratt set these bones and dressed them all in proper manner, and gave them the requisite attention so long as he had charge of the case. That some short time after the injury was inflicted, the defendant, in dressing the hand, discovered that the thumb was not in correct position, and desired to adjust it; but the parents of the boy would not allow him to do it. That in some few weeks after the arm was first dressed, the defendant, in the presence of another physician, examined the arm and found it all right—even to its length by measurement. That in about eight weeks from the time of the injury, the doctor, in the presence of Dr. Wales, again examined the arm and found the bone well united. That it was again, however, re-dressed, and that some short time thereafter, by some improper act of the plaintiff, his arm was refractured. That it was again set, dressed, and properly attended to, but that re-union would not take place.

The roller and splints were applied to the arm in the usual manner, and this angular splint was put on over the dressing. We also expect to prove that some months after the injury, *provisional callus* was perceptible to the touch at the points of fracture. This kind of callus *sometimes* soon entirely disappears, and sometimes it remains a good while. Provisional callus is, as I ought to inform you, a sort of band or hoop thrown around the fractured bone to hold the fragments in place, like the hoop upon a barrel.

If I have made any mistakes in my defining surgical terms, the professional witnesses will correct me when they come to testify.

After Dr. Pratt had treated the case for some months, and wished to resort to other and stronger measures, in order to induce *re-union*, the case was taken from him and placed in charge of Dr. Miller—a brother of one of the attorneys for the plaintiff. I agree with Mr. Turner, that persons who hold themselves out to the world as physicians, surgeons, lawyers, or of other professional character, should possess a certain amount of knowledge and skill, so that they may pursue their legitimate pursuits in a proper manner.

I concede, and Dr. Pratt concedes this, and he does not wish to evade the responsibility of his position in any manner whatever. He is ready and willing, on this and every occasion, to stand up to all that the law requires of a surgeon; and holds himself answerable for any lack of skill on his part. I apprehend that this case will turn mainly upon points of law, but the end can only be known by your verdict upon the testimony. All this talk among the people, which accumulates as it spreads, like a wet snow-ball rolling down hill, you should wholly disregard.

I have now stated to you our theory of this case, and the main points of law which govern it. The facts will be developed by the evidence, as well from non-professional as professional men. I do not believe that you will have any trouble in disposing of the case when you have heard the testimony, although it may be lengthy. It is correctly said, that when a man's life is in danger, no time spent in saving it is too long. This is also true when the reputation of a professional man is at stake, especially when a party claims to have been injured by his neglect.

Listen, gentlemen, to the case as it is developed and get a proper understanding of its merits. I must, in the outset, crave your patient attention. The case cannot be tried in a few moments, like many cases submitted to juries.

I shall take no more time at presentation, but will see what the prosecution has to offer.

IN CARROLL CIRCUIT COURT,

March Term, A. D., 1864.

STATE OF ILLINOIS, CARROLL COUNTY, SS.

FRANK P. FRISBY, a minor, under the age of twenty-one years, by PIERSON NOBLE, his next friend, *vs.* LEONARD PRATT.

BILL OF EXCEPTIONS.

BE it remembered, that on the trial of this case, at the March term, A. D. 1864, of the said Circuit Court, the said Plaintiff, to maintain the issue on his part, gave in evidence to the jury the following testimony, to wit:

Charles Frisby, sworn, says that, I was not along when this boy, the plaintiff, broke his arm. It was in Dec., 1862. I did not see him for one or two hours after he was hurt. I know Dr. Pratt. When I got there the neighbors had got him into Mr. Morris' house and Dr. Pratt had sewed up the wound on his hand. I asked Dr. Pratt if he was a surgeon. He said he was. I asked him if he could set his arm right. He said he could do it as well as anybody else. He came to my house and dressed the arm two or three times. He was treating it, in all, some five months. There was nothing said about paying him anything at that time. I never offered to pay him anything. I told him to attend to the boy at once, without delay, and not to stand about expenses. He said he would do it. He then went on and did the arm up. This was on the 20th of Dec., 1862, that the arm was broken. Dr. Pratt was a stranger to me, was the reason of my asking him if he was a surgeon. I knew he practiced medicine, that is, he held himself out as a *doctor*. It was in Carroll County. I think he treated the arm about five months and ten days. He did not come as often as I wanted him to, and I went after him sometimes. Heard him say the arm bone was all mashed fine, and that the matter to heal the arm was like the white of an egg.

There was a wound on the outside of the arm. I do not know how long before the external wound healed. The thumb was cut some, and I think he said it was out of joint. I don't know that he ever had a fit of sickness in his life. He has always been as healthy as any boy in the country. All the time Dr. Pratt said the boy was doing well, except once. I think it was about the first of May when he dressed the arm and said it was doing well. It was at this time I told Dr. Pratt I wanted some one for counsel. He wanted to know who I wanted. I told him I was not particular. He appointed a day to go to Milledgeville, about one week from that time, and we agreed to meet at Dr. Belding's, and Dr. Belding and Dr. Freas to meet with Dr. Pratt. In two weeks from that time we were to meet at Dr. Pratt's. On this day I took the boy down, and Dr. Pratt undid the arm and said it was not any better. He said he must have very little food. He said he might have toast and gruel and crackers. I don't know for how long a time it was. We begged him to let him have some meat. He said the boy better have a good arm than to eat too much. I think it was three or four weeks before he changed the diet—it might have been more, or less, I cannot tell. I was present sometimes when he dressed the arm ; I cannot tell how long it was before he took off the dressing. He left it longer than I thought he ought. Usually he took the elbow and rested it on the leg; did not move the arm much ; the doctor kept hold of it all the time.

Cross-Examined.—I saw my son first in one or two hours after his arm was broken. It was about four miles from my house where he got hurt. The boy, who was with my boys, came up with one team, and I took one horse out of the harness. I first saw the boy at Morris' house. I found Dr. Pratt there when I got there. The Morris boys were there. I cannot tell whether David Morris assisted Dr. Pratt or not. I cannot tell who assisted. I was so nervous that I cannot tell much about it. Dr. Wales was there and held the chloroform to the boy's nose. I cannot tell who else assisted the doctor. He had sewed up the hand when I got there; I think had completed it. I did not notice in what manner it was done up. The thumb was considerably torn. I cannot tell how the arm was injured. It bled some. I do not know how much. Well, there was considerable blood at the point where the arm was broken. I did not notice a bone protruding. I did not examine the arm so as to know for myself how it was hurt. There was a splint put on. I think he brought that splint afterwards; I cannot tell when it was. He came after breakfast. I do not know whether he brought the *brace* or not. I am under the impression he brought it the next morning. I did not notice the hand much. I did not examine the hand at any time to see how it looked. I do not know when he came again after the next morning. I cannot tell how long it was before he visited the boy. It might have been three or four weeks; it may have been three or four days. I think it was more than that. I remember when Drs. Pratt and Burbank came there. I cannot tell whether I was away much about that time or not. I was not always there when the doctor came. I was sowing grain frequently; it was seed time, and I was busy in the Spring. I cannot have been away more than one or two nights. I was hauling posts, and was away frequently during the day. I cannot tell what I was doing when Dr. Burbank came. I recollect he stopped, but cannot tell precisely when. I think it was some two or three or four weeks. I think there was no person present when Dr. Pratt dressed the arm. I cannot tell how long after Drs. Pratt and Burbank were there. They took off the bandages and *brace* when Dr. Burbank was there, except the bandage next to the arm. The brace was on the outside. He usually did up the arm when he came. There was a string to hold the brace at the lower end and near the wrist, and another near the shoulder, and I don't know but there was another near the elbow. Dr. Pratt took off the bandage. I don't know whether Dr. Burbank felt of the arm or examined it. I do not think he did in my presence. I think they took the bandage off from the thumb. I don't think Dr. Pratt ever told me the thumb was out of place until after the wound was healed. He then said he was ashamed of it and wanted to fix it. I did not hear anything about re-setting it at the time Dr. Burbank was there. It was after that, he put the compresses on it, I think he called them. At the time Dr. Burbank was there the wound on the thumb was not healed. I do not know what dressing he put on to keep the thumb in place. I cannot tell how long after Dr. Burbank was there that the thumb was healed. I cannot tell when that was, that he wanted to fix the thumb. It must have been sometime after Dr. Burbank was there. I cannot tell whether the boy objected to it or not. His mother and I thought he had been hurt about enough, and I told him he needn't fix it. I don't remember whether the boy objected or not. I never blamed him for not putting the thumb in place. I told him he need not fix it. I guess the boy didn't say anything. I don't think he said much about it. I don't recollect that he did. He will be fifteen years old the twenty-fourth day of next May. From that time to the present there has been no surgical treatment of the thumb. I do not recollect of ever seeing the boy whittle, or try to use the arm. He did not use the arm because he could not. We fed the boy until the hand got well enough to hold a knife, I think; I am not positive how long we fed him. It was on the night he broke the arm that he gave us directions about the diet. I think it was over a month that we gave him this kind of food. I don't know exactly what he said. He might have said we might give him a little toast, crackers and gruel. I cannot tell how long the low diet continued; as long as the Dr. required; when he consented to a higher diet we gave the boy such food as we used ourselves·

The brace was broken while the boy had it on. He was at home, out of the house. I did not see it done. (A brace was shown the witness, and he was asked if that was the one.) This may or may not be the brace. It was not broken like this at the time. It was only a small check, but afterwards the boy slept in it, and it was thrown about the house and split worse. The boy told me that in attempting to kick a ball he hit the brace against the fence, and checked it a little, not a quarter as much as it is broken now. The boy never said it hurt his arm. My wife saw the check, and then I told the boy to tell me if he had hurt his arm, because if it was hurt, we must go for the Dr. He said it did not hurt him one particle. A day or two afterwards the Dr. was passing by and I called him in. The Dr. looked at it and said the boy had *loosened* the arm a little. I do not know of his attempting to reset the arm. I think the short end of the brace was up. From the time the arm was first broken until the brace was split, was about two months. The boy never complained of any pain after the brace was split, and never has to this day.

Don't know how long after the injury before the external wound in the arm was healed. I took the boy down to Dr. Pratt several times at the Dr.'s request. Dr. examined the arm at such times. I took the boy down two or three times. The last time, about the first of May. The Dr. never proposed to try any other operation to make the bones unite before I took the case out of his hands. He never had told me the bones were not united. Dr. Freas was the first to tell me that the bones had not united. At Belding's, the 10th or 15th of May, was when Dr. Freas said it was not united. When Freas said that, Pratt said he thought it was united some. They agreed to rub the bones together and see if they could not get up an irritation and make them unite, and did so, and agreed to meet again at Dr. Pratt's in two weeks. I went there with the boy, and only Dr. Pratt was there. He examined the arm and said it was no better. I then took it out of his hands. He did not then propose another mode of treatment. A few days after that I met the Dr. near his house, and told him I had concluded to get somebody else to treat the arm. After that he came to my house and proposed another mode of treatment. He proposed to have me take the boy to Chicago, and let Dr. Beebe operate on the arm, and proposed to go himself, at his own expense. It was, I think, about a week after I took the case out of Pratt's hands that he made the proposal to go to Chicago. I told him I should employ Dr. Miller. Dr. looked at it and said it would have to be operated on. Dr. Miller never did anything except to examine and propose an operation. No operation has ever been performed on the boy. I think Miller said it was not in a healthy condition to operate upon. Dr. Miller set a day to meet McPherson there and examine the arm, but never set a day for an operation. I do not know Isaac Hodgeson. I know Dr. Wales. Have no recollection of Dr. Pratt's proposing an operation in their presence, at his house. He proposed, at my house, to have an operation performed. He might have proposed to have Dr. Beebe perform an operation before that time, at Dr. Belding's. Dr. Belding said he guessed if they would put a couple of shingle nails through the arm it might get well. Heard nothing at Belding's about ivory pegs, or wiring the arm. Dr. Pratt his since spoken of such things.

Direct Resumed.—The boy never said his arm hurt him when the brace was split; did not complain of any pain, and that was about two months after the hurt.

Cross-Examined.—The boy complained of pain in the forearm on account of the tightness of the binding; it was almost black in consequence of the tightness.

Mrs. Charles Frisby, sworn, says: I am the mother of this boy. I went up and saw the boy when he was hurt. The Drs. had gone and the boy was getting over the influence of chloroform. We moved the boy Sunday about noon. The bandage was put around the arm and then splints were put on, and then a bandage was put around them. The injury occurred on Saturday, about 4 o'clock in the afternoon. This outside one was not put on until the second Tuesday after the injury. The first I saw Dr. Pratt was on Sunday; he did nothing to the arm then. On Tuesday he looked at the hand and the arm; he dressed the hand and arm on Tuesday; on Thursday he undone the hand and looked at it. Dr. Burbank came with him the second week after he was hurt. It was six or seven weeks before he removed the bandage. The thumb joint was then out, as it is now. He continued to treat the boy five months and ten days. Said I must give no coffee or tea. The Dr. told us to give the boy very little and very light food, toast and crackers, or a little gruel, and we did just as he directed. It was dressed on Tuesday, the second week; about ten days after the injury he took off the bandages and dressed it; another person held the arm. It was three or four weeks before the wound healed up; it run some matter out of the arm; the arm was not swelled much; the arm looked white and natural, except a small hole. On Wednesday, the third week, he done up his arm, and his hand and arm swelled up and looked black, and the boy complained, and I told the Dr. about it before he left, and he said, "Rub it and it will come right; if it don't, send your elder boy for me;" and we sent the elder boy, and he sent word to loosen the bandages, and I did a little about the hand. The next day Dr. Pratt came and took off the bandage, and put it on again. I did not see where the brace was cracked. I knew when it was checked. It was checked a little on one side. The boy did not complain at all. The Dr. told me the arm was doing well; told me every time he looked at the arm he thought it was doing well, except after the brace was checked he said he thought the boy had loosened it a little. The brace was checked a little over two months after the injury. He did not take off the bandages at the time he said the boy had loosened the arm a little. About two weeks afterwards, he told me the arm was back just about as it was before. All this time Dr. Pratt never intimated there was a false joint. We watched him day and night for two or three weeks; my sister was with me. The directions were carried out in every point. His health was good at the time; was never sick twenty-four hours. His general health has been good since he was hurt. I was there when Dr.

Burbank came there the second week. Dr. Wales was there twice afterwards; was there four times in all, I think.

Cross-Examined.—They did not do anything the first time Dr. Wales was there, but to take the bandage off and put it on. It was some five or six weeks after the hurt, it was dressed in the presence of Dr. Wales. Dr. Pratt did not call my attention to see that the arm was right; never did call my attention to it; never did any such thing. When it was first dressed there were two small flat splints outside of the under bandage, about as wide as between the width of two and three of my fingers; one above and the other on the under side. There were also three narrow splints, not quite as wide as my fingers. I did not observe whether the splint was on the outside the wound, one under and the other upper; there were three small splints about half the length of this elbow splint. He came a week from the next Tuesday and undone it, that was the first time I saw the splints. At first the arm was not swollen; on the third week the arm first swelled; it continued to swell more or less all winter; the swelling would always be worse immediately after dressing. The arm was not bandaged below the elbow much; I never saw there was much swelling, except on the hand; I spoke to the Dr. about it and he said, " Rub the hand, and the swelling would get better when the blood circulated." It would swell up every time. I told him I hated to have him bandage it so tight. He became so used to the splint that we kept it on until after we had discharged the Dr. The boy came in and went up stairs. When he came down stairs he says, "Mother, I believe I have split the splint." He said it did not hurt him much; he never complained. I cannot tell when that piece was split out. I did not notice that little piece out at the time he checked it; I do not think it was out, or I should have seen it. I cannot tell when that was done. I took the outside splint off every day and washed the arm in a wash the Dr. gave me. I cannot tell exactly when this splint was put on. It was about three weeks. There were little blisters along that arm. Some festered matter came out of the wound at the time the splint was split. On Sunday and Tuesday the Dr. dressed the arm and examined it. He said the boy had loosened the arm a little. Nobody ever examined the boy's arm until after he was taken out of Dr. Pratt's hands, in my presence. Dr. Pratt spoke about fixing the arm. Frank did not say much. Dr. Pratt said " I think Frank won't object to my doing it." Mr. Frisby was away more than usual. He was off and on some ten or twelve nights. He was away a good deal of time during the day time. The Dr. was there several times when he was not there. We were moving from Elkhorn at the time of the injury. My husband was hauling from there a good deal that winter. I do not know Mrs. Dr. Belding; I never had any conversation with Mrs. Belding; I don't know the lady; a lady, I supposed was Mrs. Belding, was in and out of the room while we were at Dr. Belding's, but I had no conversation with her about Frank's arm; nor did I speak to her that day. I did not then and there say in her presence and that of Mrs. Pratt's, that Frank had broken his arm over again; nor that I had got Frank to own that he had broken his arm over again. Mrs. Pratt said Frank fell off from the fence and broke the splint and broke his arm over again; and I said Frank did not fall off the fence at all. Dr. Pratt never called my attention to the arm when it was undressed, in the presence of Dr. Wales, to see that it was united. I never told Mrs. Downs that the arm was well. I told that the wound in the flesh was healed up. I may have told Mrs. Downs that the Dr. said the arm was doing well.

Direct Resumed.—The splint was cracked two or three inches. The splint is broke a great deal worse now than it was when the Dr. took it from our house.

Mrs. Jane Moscript, sworn, says: I am a sister of Mrs. Frisby, and the one who helped nurse the boy. The boy was hurt on Saturday, and I went there Monday. That brace was put on the second week after the hurt. The boy was well taken care of, according to the Dr.'s directions. The Dr. came there on Tuesday; Dr. Wales came with him. On Thursday of the same week, Dr. Burbank. I stayed there until after the arm stopped running. If I should say what I thought about the diet, I should say he had no diet at all. He was watched day and night; our eyes were never taken off from him at all, day nor night, for three weeks. He put on the splint so hot he burned the thumb ironing it.

Cross-Examined.—I heard him say he must be kept on toast and some light food. I once toasted him a half slice of bread, and his mother came in and said it was too much, and we divided it. The Dr. told the boy, if he wanted a good arm, he must not eat too much. I cannot tell how often I heard the Dr. say the arm was doing well. I said to the Dr. that it seems to me that the arm is getting along very slow. He said it was doing well and uniting. On the 12th March he said the arm had been hit, and I asked my sister; she told me the splint had been split about two weeks before. The day this splint was brought home the Dr. bandaged the arm too tight, and the next day after he loosened it. I never saw much discharge until he put on the outside splint on the elbow, when it discharged considerable bloody and corrupt matter. It commenced soon after I went there. It was not dressed more than two or three times. I saw the arm every time he undressed it while I was there. I think Dr. Wales was there one day, and then washed his head in arnica. That wound on the head bled some; it had not healed when I left there; it was hurt worse than the arm. There was a separation of the skin on the back side of the head, near the top of the head on the side. I did not dress it; my sister dressed the wounds. When I left it was not healed. Dr. Pratt gave my sister some weeds. I know catnip, but I did not know what it was; the Dr. called it arnica. There was a bandage around his head, and it was taken off and the wash made out of these leaves, steeped in a basin, and put on every day; I frequently saw Mrs. Frisby wash it. He left a phial with some medicine, but it had no color in it. I never saw any medicine of theirs that had any color. Every time Dr. Pratt came there and moved the arm, it would bow out just as much as it does now. When he took hold of the arm to dress it, it bowed out every time just as it does now. I noticed the arm was not in line with the dressing.

He could not move it without lifting it with the other hand. Dr. Pratt brought Dr. Burbank with him on Thursday of the first week I was there. Dr. Pratt took off the three outside shingle splints, and showed the arm to Dr. Burbank, and told him there was two more splints on with the bandages. Dr. Burbank did not examine the arm. Dr. Wales did not examine the arm while I was there. Mrs. Frisby did not want this elbow splint put on again. She said the arm looked crooked, and she did not want it on. The splint on the thumb Dr. Pratt made; it looked like woolen cloth. He dressed the hand every time he came. He took and heated a flat-iron and pressed it on a board, and put it on so hot that it burned him. It had some stuff on it that made it stiff when it got cold. He did not put any splint on the hand, but the woolen cloth-looking article. I do not know that this was gum shellac. When I came back, in March, the head was pretty nearly healed.

Edward S. Shafer: I am thirteen years of age. I have seen

that splint; Frank hit it on the fence post and split it. I was about a rod from him. He was standing on the corner, and hit the post. He went to kick the ball. I did not see that it was split. When he went up stairs and came down, his father and mother talked with him about it. He did not fall down when he kicked the ball; he only hit the fence post.

Cross-Examined: I did not see that the splint was split until he went up stairs. He did not complain of its hurting him. I did not see it was split until I heard him talking with his mother about it.

Francis T. Yeomans says, he is acquainted with this boy, is his grandfather. Was present when Dr. Pratt called to dress the fractures at Mr. Frisby's; it was on the 3rd day of February, A. D. 1863. I remember it well, because it was Mrs. Frisby's birthday, and I went there on a visit. Dr. Pratt took off the bandage of the arm, and I held him at the shoulder, standing behind him, and the Dr. tried to press down the bone in the arm into its place; it stuck up some. He took hold of the arm and pressed down the bone. He wanted me and my wife to pull on the arm, and we did so. I should judge that we pulled a hundred pounds. I stood at the back of the chair and held him in the chair, and my wife took hold of the arm at the elbow, bent up in this way. I think we pulled all of a hundred pounds. The boy had not at that time been out of doors. I have never noticed this splint since until to-day.

Cross-Examined.—I resided at Eagle Point. I knew the arm was broken. He left my house on the morning of the 20th Dec., A. D. 1862. If there is any particular event which occurs in my family or my neighbors' families, I can always remember. I went there on the 2nd day of February, and I remember it for the reason that Mrs. Frisby's birthday was on that day. She was born on the 2d day of February, A. D. 1823. The Dr. came there the next day. There was no external wound at that time, but there was a red spot where there appeared to have been a wound. The arm appeared to be natural when it was straight, but when moved it would bow out as if the bones had not united. There was a little spot which stuck up a little. It was, I should judge, nearer the elbow than the shoulder where it was broke. The Dr. said there was a loose piece of bone. He said he wanted to press it into place. It appeared to be raised some higher than it was below. My wife had hold of the elbow. I think my wife did not let go until we got through. I know I did not let go. I don't know but Mrs. Frisby helped some at last. I know that this was before the splint was split. It was about the first of April I heard of that. Mrs. Moscript told me about the splint being split. These are the splints. I examined them when he took them off. I should think they are about the same width ; there was a widish splint. He put on the splints again and bandaged the arm.

Dr. John Porter, sworn : I am a physician and surgeon ; practice medicine in Carroll County. I graduated on the first of March, A. D. 1843, at the Medical University in the city of Baltimore. I have been regularly and extensively engaged in the practice of my profession, except some two years I devoted to farming. (The witness here examined the plaintiff's arm and took up a bone.) In the first place I would state to the jury, here is a bone called the humerus. This corresponds with the bone broken—that is broken here. Anatomically speaking, this bone is divided into three portions—the head, the shaft and the lower extremity. I doubt whether there is another bone in the human body which is used as much as this bone, and there is no bone, from its anatomical structure, that is so well adapted to perform as great a variety of uses. Here is a bone which is attached to the shoulder, and is calculated to perform all the varied uses which the wants of man may require. You will also observe that here are ridges on this bone, which by the muscles, motion is produced. The structure here is large. We have then, here two varieties of motion. In this arrangement is manifest the wise provisions of nature. These muscles lay along the groove of this bone horizontally, to make them work. If you were to draw a log you would hitch your chain over one side so as to gain a lever power or force. This bone is also spongy, and it increases as you see, at the upper end of the bone. The articulating sur- face is by this means much increased. You see by these two bones, we have points of attachment for these muscles, by means of which they can move the arm. You can readily per- ceive that a joint and bone possessing such a wide range of mus- cular action, must necessarily, in case of accident, require a great deal of force to steady it, and keep it in a quiet position. He has broken what I call the lower third of the humerus. We have what I call an oblique fracture across the bone. We have also what is called a longtitudinal fracture ; it is when one end is fast and is broken on one side. A longtitudinal fracture is generally produced by gunshot wounds. We have what is called a simple fracture, which is when the bone is merely broken and the flesh not bruised or lacerated. If broken more than once, it is a compound fracture. If in addition to this, the flesh be lacerated by the bone being thrust through the tissue, it is a compound comminuted fracture. In this case the fracture is of the lower third. You will discover by the end of these bones, that it was something of an oblique fracture, not exactly oblique either. The bone is rounded by cartilage. I see here a scar which might have been caused by the protrusion of the bone, this may have been a compound fracture caused by violence. You discover here I can make a pressure without causing much pain to the boy. Nature at once throws around that broken bone a fleshy substance to repair the injury. It is said General Scott has two bullets in him now, received in the Mexican war. Nature has thrown around this ball a kind of sack to prevent injury to other parts of the body. So with this, there is thrown around the bone a muscular or cartilagenous substance to shield it. This will continue as *long* as he lives, to prevent the spicula, or cragged ends of bone, from producing too much irritation or nervous sensation.

The first time I saw this boy's arm was in the month of June last; I had been visiting a patient near the red school house. I observed a man rapidly approaching, and motioned me to stop. When he came up I discovered it was Dr. Miller. He asked me if I wished to see a case. I answered I would like to do so. I went with him and he called this boy up to us, and I gave it a partial examination. I have since seen him in Lanark. I examined it carefully. My opinion was, that it was a simple fracture. But the evidence of this small scar shows that if made at the time of the fracture, it may have been a compound fracture.

I did not at the time I made the examination recognize this scar. But I pronounce it a simple fracture. According to my medical reading, a simple fracture is when the bone is broken without injury to the soft parts. Secondly, a compound fracture : in addition to the fracture of the bone, there is a laceration of the soft parts of the flesh. Third, the comminuted fracture : the bone is broken into two or more pieces or spicula. If I were called upon to examine a fracture, there would be a difference, very perceptible, between a simple and a compound fracture. I will state to the jury that if the fracture has, by its violence, produced a laceration of the flesh, the blood vessels around the bone immediately throw a large quantity of blood around the seat of the fracture, which, if I may so speak, is a scaffolding which nature kindly throws around the bone to aid it or protect it in its present injured condition. After a while nature goes into her work of organizing these materials into callus, and in a short time this callus is thrown entirely round the bone a sort of band, and the work is complete.

There is no callus here, and if there ever was one it must have been entirely absorbed, which cannot be; and I see no evidence here that there ever was a comminuted fracture. I think the best writers all agree upon this point as to callus being the proper evidence of a fracture, which always remains. Taking this, then, as true, I cannot find any evidence whatever that there was ever a comminuted fracture. I can discover nothing to indicate it. I think the evidence of such a fracture could not have disappeared so soon as at the time I made that examination.

Question: From what you know of the case, what is your opinion, as a surgeon, as to the necessity of the arm being in its present condition, if it had been properly treated?

Ans. In order to answer that question, I must explain some of the general principles of surgery. If there had been coaptation—by this I mean when bones are broken and united again—when the bones override each other, there is no proper coaptation. From the condition of the boy, as I saw him last June and frequently since, and at the present time, I would state that if there ever had been a proper coaptation of the bone, and it had been properly taken care of, I see no reason why there should not have been proper and perfect union. I have seen similar cases in the course of my practice. There are a variety of causes which will produce the formation of a *false joint*.

In the first place, after a bone is fractured, if there are any soft parts around the broken structure, if they are allowed to remain between the portions of the bone, these will prevent a perfect union. After a bone has been fractured and the surgeon leaves any portion of the flesh to intervene between the fragments, this foreign substance must be first thrown out before the bone will unite. This flesh, if not thrown out, will cause a false joint. There may be a proper coaptation, or bringing of the bones together, and there may be an officious intermeddling of the surgeon, so as to break up, or prevent the formation of provisional callus; or there may be too much motion, however produced. There are very many other causes which would prevent a union and cause a false joint.

I heard the testimony of Mr. Yeomans yesterday. It would not be correct practice to have two persons, after six weeks from the injury, to take hold, one at the shoulder, and the other at the elbow, and to pull with sufficient force to pull a weight equal to one hundred pounds; and it might, and would probably, altogether break up the provisional callus. I say, that under these circumstances it is my opinion that such an unusual force applied to the limb with these manipulations of the surgeon, would break up, if not destroy, the ossific structure there formed. In a boy of this age the circulation is much more active than in one of older years, or an adult, and the ossific repair would be much quicker accomplished than in an older person. I see no reason why this bone would not unite.

There are false joints stated in surgical works, of this kind, but they seldom occur if properly treated. The food should be nutritious; this is one of the means to which the physician resorts to work out some desired end. If a person is accustomed to eat hearty food, and we put him on a low diet, he will become emaciated, the circulation of blood will be feeble, no inflammation will take place, and no ossific matter will be furnished to repair the injury. A generous diet, therefore, is necessary to furnish ossific matter for the repair of the bone; this is in harmony with all the beneficent operations of nature.

Question: Was it proper dietetic treatment to keep the patient upon a small supply of toast, crackers and gruel, in absence of inflammation?

Answer: By no means, sir. The dietetic treatment would be aggravating instead of furnishing the organizing stimuli which nature requires in such a case.

Question: What is that which forms the new bone?

Answer: Permit me, sir, to state to the jury, that the bone is wisely provided with ossific matter to keep it up. Now, this bone in its natural condition, is surrounded with a thin substance, by what we call in surgical terms, the periosteum. It is the medium through which the ossific matter passes around the seat of the injury. It is there massed, and is of a plastic substance, or character. It grows harder and harder, and the blood vessels deposit this ossific matter which is supplied by the blood. This periosteum is thin, and delicate in its formation, and these little blood vessels pass through it. It is thus the bone is supplied with nutriment.

Under ordinary circumstances the first step of nature is to throw around it a kind of shield to protect the bone. It may be in the course of a week; it may be less, or longer, owing to circumstances, the constitution of the patient. Without local inflammation this bone cannot be repaired.

Question: Under these circumstances and in the absence of that inflammation, was a small portion of crackers, toast and gruel sufficient nourishment to furnish ossific matter, necessary for the repair of this fracture.

Answer: By no means, sir.

Question: Doctor, upon the hypothesis that there was a wound produced at the time of fracture, that resulted in a running sore, that was cured in four to six weeks, what was the condition of the health of the boy?

Answer: The condition of the boy's health was good. A wound of that kind healing up in that time is evidence that there was no material derangement in his system.

Question: If there had been any constitutional derangement or disease of the boy, would that wound have healed up directly?

Answer: Perhaps it would if there had been no hidden disease.

Question: If that fracture had been properly reduced, had not the bone time to unite in from four to six weeks?

Answer: Under ordinary circumstances, I should expect the union in bone from four to six weeks. The more a man works the harder the muscles become. The arm of the blacksmith is much harder than the farmer's. These muscles have remained inactive, and by reason of that they have become shriveled up and lost their healthful condition.

Question: What do you find in the right hand and thumb of this boy?

Answer: There appears to have been a dislocation of the thumb, and at present there does not appear to be a union of this thumb; there is a partial dislocation. When the surgeon fails to do his work the beneficent hand of nature does the work for him. There is not a perfect reduction here. The bone is down. There may have been a fracture. There is evidence of a want of proper adjustment.

Question: State the condition of the joints here in the thumb.

Answer: I have already stated there appears to be a partial dislocation of the second joint of the thumb. In this bone, I am of the opinion that there may possibly have been a fracture here sometime. It is made up of three bones. There is a displacement here at the lower joint, also.

Question: Has that fracture been properly reduced?

Answer: It is not in proper position now. My attention was called to the thumb here, and I never examined the point or end above.

Question: Does the boy have any use of that thumb now?

Answer: He has not.

Question: Has this bone been properly set?

Answer: The boney structure of the hand is very complicated and I know not what might have been the condition of the hand. There is now a bad union. Thus you see there is a partial dislo. cation, as I said before.

Question: Dr., is it good surgical practice in the treatment of that wound, three weeks after the fracture, to bandage it so tightly as to produce blackness and swelling of the lower arm and hand?

Answer: By no means, sir; just the opposite, sir.

Question: What produces this blackness and swelling after bandaging?

Answer: I will explain this to the jury. It will not be generally understood by those who are not medically educated. We have the arterial circulation which is going on always from the heart, and we have the venous circulation always returning to the heart. Too much bandaging was applied here, and this when too tightly applied, prevents circulation of the blood in the veins, and if continued would produce mortification, and would tend to retard the union of the bone, and would also produce a high amount of local inflammation.

Question: Would that have a tendency to make a bad structure?

Answer: Undoubtedly it would. The blood is the great fountain by which all this is made perfect, consequently it would prevent all local inflammation. The arterial blood is that which comes out from the heart, and the venous, that which returns back again. This high bandaging would cause them to meet at this point, and would produce too light an amount of local inflammation.

Question: How long would a skillful surgeon treat a fracture of that kind and not discover the bone had not united?

Answer: He would discover it in a week or ten days, that the proper co-adjustment of the parts had not been effected, and a proper deposit of ossific matter.

Question: In this case should not the surgeon know that adhesion had not taken place in five months?

Answer: I see no reason why he should not have found that out four months before that time, unless there should have been some great constitutional defect. I mean by this that the child is the offspring of a parent afflicted with some constitutional disease, as scrofula, or tuberculous affection by which the blood is tainted

If a person is predisposed to consumption, that is a constitutional defect. That is what I mean by constitutional defect. There is no constitutional defect in this boy.

Cross Examined.—I judge, sir, very much of the constitutional defect of the patient, from his general appearance. There may be some hidden disease. I judge from the appearance of the person himself. If there is what we call a scrofulous diathesis, anything in the lungs like tubercles, which is found by a *post mortem* examination. I mean by diathesis that he has a transparent skin, their eyes are watery, we find a flattened chest, which shows a tendency to tuberculous formation. We find in that person a development of weakness—a flush upon the cheek. In case of another disease, these constitutional diseases manifest themselves by retarding—by a slow and tedious union.

You will find, sir, that people who have lungs filled with tuberculous matter, may live to extreme old age, and that scrofula will not be developed until the age of puberty—may be ascertained very early in life. In many instances it may be that a man or woman may have these tubercles in their lungs—their lungs lined with tuberculous matter.

There may be scrofula and yet not have tubercles. If they have tubercles they must be scrofulous. The hip joint disease is nothing but a scrofulous disease. The patient may pass to the grave with this hip joint complaint. It is attendant upon a scrofulous diathesis. I can refer you to Sir Astley Cooper and others. It is the opinion of all physicians, there becomes a wasting of the parts. This wasting and debilitating of the body is the development of the disease from its incipient state. It does not always develop itself in such discharge. When there has been inflammatory disease, this violent action may have been transferred to other organs, what we call metastasis, and the person may pass off with a phthisis pulmonalis. It is spontaneous

2

dislocation of the joint. This spontaneous dislocation takes place when it changes the structure of the body. In some instances it is dislocated by the debilitating process of the disease itself. I do not pretend to say that these are the invariable results. I take the position, sir, that the person must be scrofulous in order to be tuberculous. We discover this by autopsy. I speak of the examination after death. We find in the lungs the scrofulous disease. If a person has gone on with a scrofulous disease, there might be tubercles and they not manifest in the lungs. Tubercles are all over the body. The infant six weeks old may be saturated with tubercles. It is stated that tubercles are found in the brain, and present almost the same appearance as in other parts of the body. This is not a rare thing to find tubercles in the brain and in all parts of the body, and the history of medicine abounds with such instances. I cannot say, sir, as to how you are, but I think I might have that opinion. First, then, is flatness of the chest—small muscular development, and one good reason, we find an uneven articulation. There is no small amount of muscle in you for your size. While a man is developing the brain instead of the muscular system; the development of your muscular system for a man in your occupation is good. I do not see anything in your general formation which would lead to that conclusion. It is not an unerring test. When you find a flattened chest, a small amount of pulmonary capacity, you find shortness of breath, hurried respiration. This is so sometimes, not invariably so. Show me a man with a large chest, and I will show you a man with a good pair of lungs. I claim in consequence of flatness of the chest, that the lungs cannot have the amount of action required. It is utterly impossible for you to inhale the same amount of atmosphere as those whose lungs are more abundantly developed. Medicine is not a mathematical science, sir. You cannot demonstrate it upon the black board. Through the strength of the general system it does. I stated to them that from the blood this peculiar ossific matter, which we term the bony tissue, is derived. Blood contains every element of the human economy. Blood is the pabulum from which all the tissues are made. The flesh of the hand is the result of secretions from the blood, held there by the bony tissue derived from the blood. Every tissue in the animal and in man, even the very hairs of your head, are fed and supported by the blood. When we speak of the tissues we mean the various organs, as the brain, the nerves, lungs, &c., which are made from the blood.

They are all tissues. The nervous tissues and all other tissues—man is made of tissues which is the result or product of *blood*, by the secerning process of the organs adapted to that office. The blood is the result of the assimilating process—the chylific principle. The very moment you receive your breakfast into your stomach, the beefsteak you ate is being assimilated to your nature . It results in the formation of blood, as this circulation of the matter is sent out. When the blood comes in contact with these organs, constituted for that purpose, there is a deposit of this ossific matter. Hence, I repeat it, that bone is not only formed by it, but it is sustained by it, so as to prevent any loss.

No sir ; if a man come from Ireland and eat American food, he would not become thereby an American. But the beef does change itself into my system from the assimilating powers of the digestive organs which send it out into all parts of the system. In animal food we have more fibrin than in vegetable. If we should eat altogether vegetables the fibrin of the blood would grow small. I speak of that theory, sir, that has been handed down from the remotest ages, and taught by the most illustrious men known in history. There are encroachments upon almost every orthodox system. Man living in a cold climate, for comfort and convenience and health, I should claim, must eat a larger amount of animal food than in a warm climate. This I am willing to admit, so far as the theory of the production of animal heat is concerned, animal food is more carbonaceous, and is calorific in its nature. That is the reason why a man living in a cold climate requires more animal food than one living in a warm climate. In living under a vertical sun, man might live almost entirely upon vegetables. Man, by the formation of his teeth, is shown to be an omniverous animal. He is not intended by his Creator to live exclusively on either vegetable or animal food, but upon both. I claim-that from the formation of the teeth man is intended to eat meat. A horse is not intended to live on meat, but the dog is. We base our opinion upon the formation of the teeth. I answer this question, that a hen or turkey does not masticate their food. Mastication is performed in the stomach, hence the hen does not need meat. There are points of insertion of the muscles of the fore-arm upon these condyles. *These muscles* are intended to pronate the hand ; the office of that muscle (the deltoid) is to raise the arm. This bone is used as a lever for the action of the deltoid muscle by which the arm is raised. We have the triceps muscle,

which forms the capsular ligament of the joints. We have the
various muscles so arranged as to work the arm in accordance
with the will. We have the triceps muscle, which is simply for
the purpose of extending the arm. We have the supinators and
pronators; we have in connection with these, the pectoralis
major and minor. We have the lissimus dorsi, which is used
for moving the arm backwards. I cannot, or have not time to,
run over the whole list of these. I state that the *brachialis anti-
cus* is one of the muscles which perform action, which might displace this bone and would prevent the ends of the bones from
being kept in a proper coaptation. The very same muscle would
cause the fragments to separate. This is one reason why an intelligent surgeon will place his bandages over the fore-arm, so as to
confine these muscles to prevent action, and thus prevent the bone
from being displaced. We have the triceps, a three headed muscle, which might possibly have a tendency to displace it. Now
take, for instance, this bone (the humerus). We have on the
front part of the arm the four leading muscles which I have named,
which have a tendency to displace the bone. The triceps extensor cubiti which would have this tendency. We have here two muscles in front and one behind. This behind is attached to the
forearm (radius and ulna). For instance, when we come to the deltoid, the office of which is to *elevate* the arm, it is connected
with the fore-arm in its motion. These muscles which I speak of
would, if they were irritated, have a tendency to displace the
bone. If not irritated, they would not have such a tendency.
We have to put the whole leg in splints and fasten the foot down,
or, in consequence of this spasmodic action, the bone would be
loosed. If the muscles had not been irritated it would not.

The brain is the great sensorium of all nervous action. If there
be any disturbance of the brain, it being the grand sensorium,
it may be from congestion, caused by pain, sorrow, etc. Let a
child go to sleep when this disturbance is in the system, and it will
start and jerk; a *spicula* may cause this irritation. I am of the
opinion, if there was nothing to excite this muscular system, there
would be no such spasmodic action. I was called upon to see a
little child who fell from its chair and broke its thigh. I took hold
of the limb and discovered crepitus; and no intelligent physician
will take hold of a limb to operate on it until they examine it to
see if there is crepitus. It formed an angle of ninety degrees. I
am happy to say that the treatment was successful. She recovered.

The limb was not shortened. There is nothing peculiar in my treatment, sir, from any other. I have stated before, there are two muscles there, which will make the bone come down. When I speak of raising the arm, you may understand that I mean the deltoid muscle. One of these muscles runs down, and is inserted in the fore-arm; but this has nothing to do with the muscles of the fingers. There is no muscle inserted here in the humerus which has anything to do with the motion of the hand. It would be impossible to move the arm without producing muscular contraction. My method of treatment of the fore-arm is, that I would splint the arm properly. I may state I am not fond of these splints. I take a piece of pasteboard cut it into two small pieces, and let it extend from the shoulder to the elbow; I saturate it with starch, and put it on so as to enclose the arm. I satisfy myself of the proper coaptation of the bone. I put this binder's board around. After it becomes hard I remove the splints. I think this splint keeps the surface pleasant and cool. I am not disposed to grumble with my medical friends for using these manufactured splints; I do not use them. But when one of the lower extremities is fractured, I have one prepared by a mechanic under my direction. If the fracture has been reduced, and the parts properly coaptated, the provisional callus will be formed in about a week or ten days, owing to the condition of the patient. When there is callus formed around the bone, as there is a profusion of blood accumulated around the seat of the fracture, if the violence which produced the fracture lacerate the parts, inflammation ensues. It depends entirely upon this muscular action. This muscular action would be more likely to exist to a greater extent in comminuted fracture.

There is an idea which has originated within the last few years, that a union of bone can take place within the soft parts without provisional callus. If that holds true, this bone can unite without it. I did intend to convey the idea that there must always be more or less of provisional callus. After the fracture is produced, nature goes to work and throws around the seat of fracture a provisional callus. If the constitution is susceptible of reproduction of bone, this work cannot be performed without provisional callus. It is the *sine qua non* for a reunion. The surgeon who follows up measurably the dictates of nature is the most successful. If the fracture had been of recent date, I would ascertain from my patient the length of time this superabundance of vascular excitement had existed, and I would pursue an opposite course. It is possible that in this case a violent inflammation might ensue, which if not arrested, the surgeon would have a more difficult case for treatment—if not arrested in season, endangering even life itself. But when nature is a little languid she needs medical aid to stimulate and strengthen her action. You may have destruction of the parts and lose your patient. *Without provisional callus there can be no union of bone.* The necessity of inflammation is imperative. If there be such a case of over inflammation, it is the duty of the surgeon to correct it by antiphlogistic means. But without inflammation there is no such thing as union of bone. If it is a local cause and remains a long time it will become a general cause, and there may be a large amount of provisional callus thrown out. For a while the process of repair may go on. If you have severe inflammation, local or general, it may delay a union for a long time ; there must necessarily be some inflammation to produce union; your patient may go on and live through this, but this over-inflammation will retard the union. If it be below that, it will perform the work ; if it be above, it will not. I do not say that the surgeon can do it; I am perfectly satisfied, from my reading, he cannot do it without this. There will be that long delayed union, provided the patient lives. This excessive inflammation would have its evidences by the *superabundance* of pus. Inflammation, if permitted to go on in this excessive degree, would destroy the parts. It may be, to a certain extent, interfered with. After having gone on in this way for a length of time, the patient may survive. If the inflammation has ceased, or gone by, the surgeon should recall it. I say, that the inflammation may stop short of producing re-union. If there be extensive inflammation it must be a fact that ossific matter is there. If there be excess of inflammation, an abscess must inevitably take place, and this deposit of ossific matter will be thrown off as the result of this inflammatory action. After all this has taken place, the union may be completed and the patient live. I am not prepared to speak of any observation of my own. I gather this from authors —that without inflammation there can be no provisional callus ; without provisional callus no union of bone. I. Bertrand, of Paris, has been investigating this matter, and I take it from him and from a professional gentleman of Baltimore. They take the ground that there cannot be union by first intention, and I give it as my own opinion here. It is at variance with the order of life. This subject has not been long before the medical world. I say, then, there can be no union of bone without provisional callus. I refer you to Sir Astley Cooper and all who have written on the subject from that time down to the present. I have consulted Norris. I regard Sir Astley Cooper as the father of surgery; upon all subjects pertaining to surgery. There has been undoubtedly, some improvements, but there is no proof that provisional callus is not necessary to the union of bone. A compound dislocation of the joint, sometime ago it was thought, must necessarily result in amputation. My impression is, that Sir Astley Cooper advocates such principles. Since then there has been introduced what is called the cutting down of the parts. These are the principal things in Cooper. Surgery is progressive. I say the leading opinions and doctrines laid down by Cooper are not altered materially.

Yes, sir. Flat bones, as a general thing, are less liable to nonunion. Liston claims, I believe, that the humerus posesses less liability to unite than others. Liston, I believe, in speaking of the liability to unite of the long bones, the humerus, he says, has the largest per centum of non-union. That bone is more liable to nonunion than the femur. I cannot say that this is not the opinion of other medical men. I have been more than twenty-two years in the profession; with the exception of two years, I have been engaged in it entirely. I cannot call to mind any cases of Sir Astley Cooper, similar, but I have had some. I have not practiced surgery here much. In the city we have more. I do not know that I have had a case of the femur. I had access to the hospital. I was connected with the Marine hospital. I had the privilege to go into the hospital wards at any time. I never reduced a fracture and carried it through in the hospital. I have in my private practice. I located myself in the city of Baltimore, and practiced about 11 years. I enjoyed an extensive and lucrative practice. I have treated, in private practice, fracture of the humerus, I think. I could not individualize any of these cases. I cannot tell whether they were fractured in the upper, lower end, or middle. (Witness was here shown the canal in the bone of the humerus.) That is what is called the nutritive foramen, where the blood enters. There is a little artery which goes through it. There are little blood vessels which go through the bone, by what may be called little foramina. The surgeon who is deficient of the knowledge of that little foramen, is deficient in his profession. Nature has wisely provided for any miscarriage or interruption of these walls of the arteries by what we call an anastomosing process. Suppose I cut down and tie up the artery of my arm; the parts will die, because I have cut off the blood which nature furnishes to sustain the part. What is called anastomosing. I assisted Dr. Matthew-bury, of Baltimore, to operate on an abscess. We cut down into it, and thought we had lost our patient; after a while he became cold. We thought we had lost our patient, but nature went to work and cured the patient. Let there be a destruction of the nutritive foramen and nature goes to work to supply the loss by other vessels, and it will supply the blood by means of the perios-teum. There are littleb lood-vessels passing through the perios-teum. In case of loss of the artery, these little vessels increase their calibre and they become, or perform what I may call a vicarious office—that is, they supply the deficiency occasioned by the destruction of the nutritive artery. The periosteum is the medi-um through which the blood is carried. The periosteum sur-rounds the bone, and through it the blood-vessels make their entrance into the bone, in the middle, and vicarious action com-mences above and below; each side is furnished by its own peri-usteum. There are said to be absorbents in every structure, and tissue of the animal economy. As to the brain, I am not certain but what absorbents have been discovered even there. There could be no inflammation at the point of fracture until re-action. After a concussion of the brain the vital powers of the brain must re-act. In this boy you might have inflammation in a few hours after the accident. In a case in the navy, where a sailor was blown up some hundred feet in the air, a surgeon was asked what he would do. He said, very coolly, he "should wait until he came down." After the bones were broken I should wait until re-ac-tion commenced, and then reduce the fracture, as he would be already down. After inflammation had commenced, an improper coaptation might hinder the union of bone; nothing else could. It would be impossible to have a compound comminuted fracture without swelling and, threefore, suppuration. There must be inflam-mation, sir. Inflammation and suppuration may occur in the soft parts in a very short time. The time in which you might expect suppuration would be in a few hours. If it were a low type, it would be longer. In an ordinary case it would occur in a few hours. The formation of pus is made very soon after the wound is inflicted. Without inflammation there could be no pus. Pus

may be deposited in the tissue and remain there, and the surgeon
may fail to attend to his duty, and absorption take place. The
pus you find in the lower extremity to-day may be found in the
lungs to-morrow. A nutritious diet would include fried oysters,
meats, highly seasoned roast beef, and capsicum. An abstemious
diet, which'I would prescribe, would be this; I would go down to
the hotel and order a part of the wing of a chicken, and wrap a
cloth around it, put it into a few quarts of water, boil a few minutes, and take that broth and dilute it in a gallon of pure water,
and give the patient a gill of that at proper intervals. This is
what I would prescribe as an abstemious diet.

Question: Do you consider capsicum nutritious, doctor?

Answer: I consider it a local stimulant, rather. This joint
was partially dislocated. There appears to have been some mal-
formation. (Explains to the jury.) (The witness was here shown
the second joint of the thumb of a skeleton hand, and asked to
explain how there could be a partial dislocation of that joint
without a complete one.) Every joint has ligaments thrown around
it to retain it in its location. There may be partial dislocation, that
may depend upon the force brought to bear. There may have
been some displacement and the joint not humanely brought
back, or reduced, and, on account of the condition of the ligaments, might remain for life. There does appear to be some
slight dislocation there of the lower metacarpal joint. It depends
upon the violence brought to bear on the ligaments. The joint
is held and protected by the ligamental structure. The hip is
sometimes thrown out of place. If not reduced, the articulating
surface may be changed. Every joint is retained in position by
the ligaments thrown around it. If not reduced at the proper
time it will form a new articulating surface. The former is fastened into the cup of the thigh for the purpose of retaining it.
When dislocation occurs this joint is thrown forward, and
remains there. The individual may go through life with this
degree of deformity. The larger articulating surface will act the
same as a smaller one. It may be that this is only partially thrown
out. I maintain that a partial dislocation might remain until the
joint became accustomed to it. If that joint was elevated it
would come back; if depressed it could not; that might account
for a partial dislocation. I saw a lady, who, in walking, broke
the neck of the femur. There was no ossific union, and never was,
on account of there being no ossific deposit. Sir Astley Cooper

does say these cases will occur, and he gives the statement I have given you. There may be false joints without any assignable cause. It is the arterial blood which carries the pabulum of the tissues of the human body. It is when the arterial blood has been submitted to the secerning organs of the respective secretions. When we have had the arterial coursings going on, it is thrown back into the veins. We have often ossific deposit in the artery and in the heart, and we have ossific deposit in the whole animal structure. I do not pretend to answer the question, whether it deposits itself in the artery, and not in all other places. Ossific deposits have been found in the heart. The gall duct has been found completely ossified, showing that the ossific matter is flowing through the blood, and is deposited in the soft parts. There is phosphate of lime in the blood. The proportion of phosphate of lime in an infant is forty-eight and some hundredths per cent. It is not the same in all. In some there is more phosphate of lime than in others. I speak of a healthy person. As we grow from infancy to old age, the ossific elements predominate much. The bone of an elderly person will break much sooner than that of a young person. While the bone with fifty per cent. animal matter will not break, with twenty in one and eighty in another, it will easily break. I do not recollect of ever reading an account of a fracture in a person of ninety years of age uniting as soon as in a young person. There is no difference of opinion among surgeons in reference to repair of bones. There may be more phosphate of lime in one person than in another, as different circumstances may exist. There may be some torpidity of the liver, or the secerning of the urine. That bone is the product of blood is certain. I do not know, sir, how much phosphate of lime there may be in the blood in the human system. I do not know exactly, it differs in different persons. There is a difference in the same person at different periods. There may be other secerning organs which take on a vicarious action, and secern to that part. I do not say that a person may have fifty per cent. of phosphate of lime in the blood and in the bone; they must be in similar quantities in each, but they differ in quantity in the same person, at different periods of life, as I have just stated. They are not uniform. Physiology, surgery and anatomy are not susceptible of mathematical demonstration. There is iron in the blood. It is iron that gives to the blood its color, to the check and to the hair. It is the coloring matter of all the body. There is a certain amount of local inflammation produced by fracture. There may be general inflammation of the whole system. The local inflammation does not always produce general inflammation. There may be local inflammation and no fracture at all. If you obstruct the venous circulation by bandaging too tight, this obstruction will engorge the capillaries and produce inflammation in the tissue, and gangrene in the external parts. A slight obstruction of the venous circulation will gorge the soft parts and the general health must participate in this derangement. It will depend entirely upon the arrest of the returning circulation. Under certain circumstances, this inflammation may commence in a week or more after the accident. It may be delayed six months; in this case you will be very likely to have false joint. There are various causes : 1st, Want of proper coaptation. 2nd, Want of proper appliances to preserve proper coaptation. 3d, Too much friction or movement of parts. 4th, Age or constitutional defects. 5th, Some other disease or local inflammation which diverts the inflammation, and prevents a sufficient amount in the fractured part to carry on the process of ossification. 6th, Paralysis occasioned by the injury, sufficient to prevent the action necessary to ossification, also the intervention of some of the soft parts between the broken bones. The treatment is various. If I had examined it and found there was non-union, I would next ascertain the general health of my patient, and this every intelligent physcian will do, and I profess to understand my profession; I would enquire if every organ in the body had performed its proper function. If I should find that to be the case, I would then use friction by taking hold of the ends of the bone and rubbing them firmly together, simply for the purpose of removing the cartillaginous substance, and to bring on an inflammation. Should I fail in that case I next would prepare me an apparatus and adjust it to the ends of the bone. For, after using friction, I should try to produce inflammatory action. I would make a pressure upon these bones and keep up pressure until inflammation ensued. There are other means ; one is a seton, that is, to carry a needle with silk down and in between the broken ends of the bones, and let it remain, for the purpose of producing inflammatory action.

I should probably resort to electricity—galvanic power. I would then try the *dernier* resort, that is re-section; I cannot say much about it, some have tried gold and silver wire. I believe that would not succeed—some have succeeded, some have not.

This re-section would be my last resort. I know something about acupuncturing; I do not use it, and do not believe in it, and know of no surgeon who has succeeded with it; I understand there are some who have. Acupuncturing is carrying down a sharp pointed instrument to the point of fracture, and boring into the bone at different points, to produce inflammation.

Yes, sir; we might have a good limb by these means in from four to six months. I think a case should never be abandoned until all these means are resorted to. Yes, sir; I take it there will always be provisional callus remaining. It does not disappear as true bone forms. The provisional callus is not taken into the new bone. No man would think of an aneurism being absorbed. It is an artery the walls of which have become enlarged and expanded, and forms some peculiar characteristic of fibre. It becomes more and more expansive, until in some physical exertion, these walls give way, and life becomes thereby extinct. Aneurism is simply an enlargement of the walls of the artery, nothing else. There is no branch in aneurism.

It is a proper application of the roller which keeps the muscles quiet.

The Dr. was here shown the splints used in dressing the case, and asked what he thought of them for that purpose?

Answer : I should think them entirely inutile. That material of splint, if long enough, might answer; but of this length, I regard them as entirely inadequate; they are too short. I think the whole arm should be kept in a quiescent state.

The union of bone under such circumstances is the rule ; the failure, the exception. I cannot call up a case where a boy of this age did not have the bone united, when properly treated. I cannot speak positively on the subject of false joint; when it is properly treated it will not occur. Our medical authors do describe certain failures of union of the bone. (Mr. Turner here showed the witness his own thumb.) There is a partial dislocation of the thumb joint here ; I think a partial dislocation could be made of that joint, and remain so through life.

Dr. Buckley's Testimony.

Dr. Buckley, sworn, says : I am a physician and surgeon ; have been in the practice 12 years.

Question : Did you make an examination of this boy's arm— (Frank P. Frisby ?)

Answer : Yes, sir, I have; I made the first examination of that arm, I think, the middle of December, 1863.

Question : What condition did you find it in then?

Answer : Precisely the same as it is now.

Question : Have you made a careful examination of that arm?

Answer : Yes, sir; within a day or two.

Question : From the examination you have made of that arm professionally what was the character of that fracture when it was made?

Answer : I was of the opinion, sir, that it was a simple fracture.

Question : Did you find any evidence of its being a comminuted fracture?

Answer : I did not, sir; I could discover none, sir.

Question : If it had been a comminuted fracture, would any evidences have remained at the time you made the examination?

Answer : There would, sir; there would have been a "provisional callus." Were I treating this arm, I should apply a roller in the first place, from the end of the fingers the whole extent of the limb. Then I should have applied splints, of some preparation of binders' board, or perhaps this form of splint, that would have extended from the elbow to the shoulder, the whole length of the humerus. These splints would not have been long enough. I should say they were not proper splints to use in that case. I think it very essential, sir, to keep the fore-arm in a quiet state, because, if it were not kept in a quiet state, it would destroy coaptation, and secondly, the union. I should think it would not be necessary, if the arm had been properly coaptated, to apply force at each end, equal to one hundred pounds, in order that a surgeon might manipulate the fracture. I should think, if this had been the case, that the extremities had not been properly approximated. I have examined the arm since I came here, and I find it to be a false joint; the muscles are somewhat wasted away. I see nothing in the constitution and age of the boy, indicating any other than a successful result, and union of the bone. I think, if a union had not taken place within four months, the surgeon attending should have known it. I should think it would be four or five weeks, perhaps more, perhaps less, before union in a boy of his age and character would take place. If I found, after six weeks, there was no union of the bone whatever, I think I should extend the time a little longer, say up to ten days or two weeks, and then, if I found no union I should resort to friction, do it up again, and after waiting a suitable length of time, if I found no union, I would resort to some other means. As regards diet, I never made a great deal of difference. If there was not much arterial excitement I should make no change ; if there was, use less. Where there is no swelling of the parts I should not reduce the food, if it was my own case. If there had been union and re-breaking at eight weeks, there would have been some pain. I have examined the plaintiff's right hand and thumb; I find a partial dislocation. I suppose it might have been reduced. If this has ever been in its proper place, it may have been forced out again. I do not think if this bone had been properly reduced, it would be out of place now. From the condition of the thumb now, I think he has not much use of it, although some. I never met a case of false joint of the humerus. The fore-arm should be kept in close confinement from the time the arm was first done up. If this had not been done for three weeks, I should expect to find a false joint, on account of the mobility of the patient.

Cross-Examined.—I did not notice any evidence of a wound in the soft parts. If there had been a severe wound in the soft portions of the hand, it might have had a tendency to draw down the joint. If the bone was broken, also, that would increase the difficulty. If the parents would not submit to having a second reduction, the surgeon, of course, would not be to blame. I do not see why there could not be a partial dislocation of that joint, as well as any other. The ligaments which surround that joint may be so lacerated as to *permit* of a partial dislocation. It might be the integuments on the outside of the thumb would occasion it by laceration. After using friction, I might make another trial in a couple of weeks. If I found the parts tender, I might wait a day or two, or perhaps a week, longer. I should not try friction more than twice. Never having had a case, I cannot tell what I should do next. A seton, I believe, has been used by some surgeons; they take an instrument something like a tape needle and draw a skein of silk through near the ends of the bone. There are ivory pegs used sometimes; that is done by cutting down to the bone, and boring holes in the bone, and riveting them together with the ivory pegs.

Question: Dr., in case the bone was broken directly across its shaft, so as to make the line of fracture at a right angle with the line of the shaft of the bone, how would you use the pins then?

Answer: I would bore into the end of the bone and insert the ivory pins at the ends of the fragments.

Question: Suppose, then, that by some severe blow or force upon the arm or shaft of the bone, the ends of the bone should be pushed by and made to overlap, and you could not bring them back to their proper place; how would you use the ivory pegs in that case?

Answer: I would pin them together on the sides.

Question: Should a surgeon in the treatment of a fracture ever abandon a case until he has tried all the remedies known and used to produce union of bone in the surgical art?

Answer: He should not.

Question: If a surgeon is discharged while using means known to surgery as good surgery, and before he has had a proper time to try all the means recognized as proper in uniting bone in the surgical art, could the surgeon prevent a false joint?

Answer: I do not see any way to avoid a false-joint in such case.

Re-Examined.—Question by Turner: If a surgeon should treat a patient for five months and ten days for a fracture of the humerus and not know whether there was a union of bone, would that be good surgery?

Answer: It would not be skillful surgery. I should expect to be discharged as a surgeon, if at the end of five months no union had taken place, and I had constantly told the family the arm was doing well. It would not be skillful surgery to treat a case like this five months without producing union, and only resort to the first mode of treatment without resorting to the other means I have mentioned.

Dr. B. P. Miller, sworn, says: I have been practicing medicine and surgery in this county and Jo Daviess, twenty years. I have been engaged in practice all the time. I have done the principal part of the surgery in this county; am acquainted with the plaintiff. Saw the arm 6th June last; found the arm to have a false joint. The fracture was on the lower portion of the humerus. There was no union. It was about the same as now. I was sent for, with Dr. McPherson, to see whether there could be an operation performed. I thought it was a simple fracture. From enquiries made of the friends I thought it was a simple fracture, though it may have been a compound fracture- There was a cicatrix, which might indicate a compound fracture. If this was a comminuted fracture, I saw no evidence of it then. The boy appeared to be in good health, except he had been in the house some time and had had a very light diet. The proper surgical treatment would have been, to put the bones in place and confine them. Where there is a simple fracture, I use a roller, commencing at the wrist and roll up to the shoulder. I then put on sufficient splints, coming from the shoulder to the elbow, and from the arm-pit to the elbow, on the inside. I would then put on a supporting splint, and put the arm into a sling. I would then wait a day or two and examine it again; if no inflammation, I would then bind it more tightly. I would then leave it two or three weeks and then see if there was any provisional callus. I consider these splints not sufficient, they are too short. They might do, perhaps, with this outside splint, but I consider them too short. I consider it necessary to put on longer splints to support the fore-arm. The breaking up of the provisional callus would be likely to make a false joint.

Question: Six weeks after the fracture, what would be the necessity of having a person take hold of the arm and pull to the amount of a hundred pounds weight? What would be the object and what the effect of such pulling?

Answer: After six weeks I should expect to have provisional callus, and it would be very likely to break that up. As to dietetic treatment, I make very little difference in food; tell them to keep quiet and not eat quite as much as usual. Toast, crackers and gruel is very good food; I like crackers myself. It is not a proper diet to give such a boy, a little toast and gruel and crackers. It would not be sufficient, in my opinion. I cannot state what the course was in this particular case. I do not know of any cause, except the bone was kept movable, or some improper motion of the limb. I do not know what the cause was. Had I had the case myself I can see no reason why it should not go on and unite if properly attended to. In four months the surgeon ought to have known whether it had not united. He ought to have known it in four or five weeks. If, after six weeks, I found no union or sign of union, I would have used some friction on the bones. If I found the ends of the bones were getting smooth, I might then have put them together somewhat firmer and waited a few weeks longer. It is not proper surgical treatment to permit a fracture to remain from Dec. 20 till the 3d of February following, I think I should have used some means to excite the formation of provisional callus or ossific action. If, at eight weeks, there had been a breaking up of the ossific formation, there would have been some pain. I have had experience in bones partially. I have never failed to have the limb unite. I have had a case of the breaking of the femur; it united at the proper time. Also of the humerus, the second time, and there has always been permanent union. There was a case. I do not recollect of being called to but one case of false joint. I took the case after it had been delayed some time. In six or seven weeks there was union by forcing the bones through the muscles and applying considerable pressure.

Cross-Examined.—This was a case of the humerus. I used considerable pressure to force the bone into place; the fracture was not compound. I do not remember that it had been any thing more than an oblique and a simple fracture. The fact of non-union, and the length of time was the reason why I thought there was danger of false joint. There was muscular substance intervening was another reason. It required extension. If it had been a transverse fracture, I don't know it would be any more difficult. I have always found provisional callus. I think I have read of some cases without it. There may have been cases of union without provisional callus. There would be after a time, a rounding off of the bone. I should feel in my own practice when I found the bone rounding off, that it was a case requiring more stringent measures.

Question: May not provisional callus be carried off by absorption ?

Answer: I have always found provisional callus formed in all my cases. It might be absorbed after a while so that it would not be sensible. I have examined some cases after a year, where I found it. It might be possible that the parts might not have been put in proper apposition. Provisional callus disappears as true bone forms. I have not examined cases to see how long it would take callus to disappear through the circulation. I suppose through the blood there is a set of vessels that deposits the bony substance. I think it is not deposited directly from the arteries, although they contain the bony matter. The vessels through the periosteum furnish the supply of osseous matter. The system is continually throwing off old matter and depositing new matter quicker in the soft than in the harder tissue. I think the lymph furnishes the matter from the blood. The extravasation of the blood first takes place and is carried off in ten or twelve days. In three or four weeks considerable deposit of bony matter is made. I do not think I have seen it take place in ten or twelve days. These splints are too short. That splint might be long enough to clasp the inside portion. I would ordinarily use longer splints than these. I might use them if I had no other. They might answer with this splint on the outside; this is a good splint. I use it myself. The extensor muscles are attached here. These muscles would draw the bone up if not properly confined. I don't know that it makes any difference in the union by breaking this bone at the point of the nutritive foramen. I never heard it would. I don't remember the names of these muscles here. I am the worst hand in the world to remember names; the brachialis and biceps lie along the whole length. The pronator and supinator, flexor and extensor, are all attached to the humerus. In case of refracture the union would be about the same time as the original fracture; it might be longer if the injury was such as to break up the provisional callus entirely. The compound and comminuted fracture are more dangerous than simple fractures. A slight comminuted fracture would be some more dangerous.

Question: May there not be fractures when it is not possible to assign the cause of non-union?

Answer: Most certainly. (Turner resumes.)

Answer: (He was here shown Miller's Surgery.) I consider this a standard author. There are such cases, I rely upon these authors for my opinion that false joint may occur without any assignable cause. The general principles I obtain from these authors, I would make a difference in the diet. In a compound fracture I would order a vegetable diet, if there was evidence of inflammation; if I saw no evidence of inflammation, I would not make much change. Toast, crackers and gruel are very good diet·

Dr. Mason C. McPherson, sworn, says: I am a physician and surgeon; practice at Eagle Point, in Ogle County. I am acquainted with Dr. Pratt and with the plaintiff. I was called to see the plaintiff, 6th June last. I examined his left arm, in the same condition as now. I examined it carefully at that time with Dr. Miller. We concluded it was a simple fracture; no evidence of a comminuted fracture. There would be a provisionary callus detected there. That was the reason we thought it was a simple fracture. I would have applied a roller and two long splints from the shoulder to the elbow. If compound, it is necessary to keep the arm quiet, and if considerable action to keep the bones in place. I would put the bones in a proper coaptation. I use a roller or bandage. I have never treated but one case of this kind. I rolled from the wrist to the shoulder, used long splints, and put the arm in a sling, and kept the fore-arm quiet. If not properly bandaged the use of the forearm might displace the fracture. There are muscles attached all the way down ; the biseps and the " *biseps flexor*" on the forearm might displace the bone. Should have made no change in the diet. There might have been some inflammation, and might make some difference, otherwise I would not. I do not generally make any change. I should have looked for partial union in a boy of this age, under proper treatment, in about three weeks. I should have wanted to know whether the bone had commenced uniting. There would be considerable union in two weeks in such a lad. In case of simple fracture, from six to eight weeks, the splints might be taken off. If compound comminuted fracture, it would be owing to the amount of inflammation, and how bad the fracture was. If properly adjusted, at the end of six weeks, would not have been necessary to make extension by pulling the arm to the amount of a hundred pounds' weight. I have never tried that; I think not. If union of the bone had taken place, it might have broken it up. A skilful surgeon would have known before five months whether it was united. If not united, before two months, I would have used friction. If no union had taken place, the surgeon ought to have known it; if not, some other means ought to have been adopted. I think it would not have been good treatment to wait so long. I have never examined the thumb ; have known the family and boy some four years. I have attended some of the family as physician, not the boy. So far as I know, his health has been good. Don't know his age. In doing up the arm fractured, as that was, these splints were too short. Should have been from the shoulder to the elbow. I do not think they would keep the bone in a proper coaptation. If a compound comminuted fracture, I should think them not proper splints.

Cross-Examined.—I never had but one case of the fracture of the humerus; it was a simple fracture. I cannot say at what point. It was a young man, twenty or twenty-one years of age. I used two long splints from the shoulder to the elbow, bandaged

from the hand to the shoulder; that was the principal thing. I
hung it in a sling, and ordered them to keep it there. I cannot
say how long it took it to heal. Practiced in this county, at Elk
Horn Grove, eight years; practiced some before I attended lectures in Philadelphia Medical College, Pa.

Ques. Where did you graduate, Dr.? (A long pause.)

I have slightly forgotten the place where I graduated. I had no
money to pay for graduating. I never graduated. I attended a
full course of lectures on medical science, anatomy, etc. Attended
six months, or nearly so. Practiced about a year or so with my
preceptor. At the time I examined it I came to the conclusion
as to the nature of the injury as certainly as I could. I answered
that I could not detect provisional callus. I never saw a case of
the kind I could not detect. I would have resorted to friction
before the 13th day of May. It is recommended, I believe, by
Gibson. In case of non-union, I would have tried friction after
two or three months. I would have waited a few days, and then,
if there was tenderness and inflammation, I would have done
it up and waited two or three weeks. If there had been no tenderness I would have repeated the friction, and if that did not
succeed, I would have tried other means. I might have tried the
seton. It is merely done by passing down some silk between the
ends of the bone to produce inflammation. Other operations are
recommended—taking up the ends of the bone and sawing them
off. Different surgeons have different theories. Some practice
other modes. That is about as far as I would recommend. A
case might be treated five months, and treated skilfully, and not
unite. I believe there are such cases.

This (pointing to the foramen in a humerus) point is where
a blood vessel enters. It is diffused to different parts, I suppose. If there was a destruction of that artery there would
be more effusion, I suppose. I don't know that that would make
any difference in the union of the bone; might make some difference.

Question: You spoke of the muscles of the fore-arm that were
attached at this point.

Answer: That muscle has nothing to do with the finger, hand
or wrist. The motion of the flexor muscles has the power of
raising the arm up. There are more muscles here. There is the
biseps and the biseps flexor that are attached to the bone down
there, pretty well in that neighborhood. I cannot tell exactly
where; and one is in the top of the arm. They are attached

within two inches of the place I pointed out. One and a half inches, probability is that it is within two inches ; I do not know exactly where. I understand that they are attached to the lower third of the humerus. The biceps or the biceps flexor is connected back here somewhere, and passes through the occipital groove, which gives it motion. I assisted in dissecting two or three subjects. I do not remember that I ever assisted in dissecting this portion of the arm. I call this formation around the bone "*provisionary*" callus. I cannot say when that begins to form ; it commences in two weeks or so. I can discover it after union commences. There is no material difference between that and definitive callus. There is no difference. I do not know that it could be discovered during life. I have seen it after two years, in the hip, the upper portion. A young man I saw yesterday states it was twenty years since it took place. There is provisional callus there now ; I know it was. It was elevated above ; the surrounding bone not so elevated. I could feel all around it far enough to discover ; the edge of it might be as large as your little finger. I cannot say how large it was. I never saw a case of twenty years standing before my attention was called to it by the man himself. I do not know whether this callus gradually disappears as true bone forms or not. I cannot tell whether a union can be formed without it or not. I have Gross and Miller ; I don't know anything about Hamilton. I never read Sir Astley. I never examined any work but Gibson's and Parri ; that is all I have. It is a good work (Gibson's.) It is about the size of Miller's ; may be a little larger. Well, it is ossiseous matter which it takes to make bone, that is something like *similia similibus non curanter.*

Dr. II. M. Freas, sworn, says : I am a physician and surgeon. Graduated in Philadelphia—practiced since 1854 ; practice now at Milledgeville. Am acquainted with Dr. Pratt and plaintiff. He came to my house two or three years ago to have a finger set. I saw the boy at Dr. Belding's. Dr. Belding, Dr. Pratt and myself were present, 16th May last. Had a consultation ; found the arm in about the same condition as now. I merely examined it. A few days before Dr. Pratt spoke to me about the case. I cannot swear whether these were the splints or not ; similar to these. Dr. Pratt and myself made some friction of the parts and done it up. At the time I saw it was a simple fracture. In the examination I made, I did not see any evidence of its having been a compound comminuted fracture. There would probably have been some ridges left on the bone. My treatment would have been to bandage from the hand, with a splint from the elbow up to the shoulder, and some small splints between. These would do for a child, put on to keep the bone in place, and keep the muscles quiet. I can hardly tell you the result; I never tried them; I don't pretend to know much about surgery. It was necessary to confine the muscles of the forearm. (Here he applied the splints to his own arm.) These splints are shorter than I would use. With such short splints there might be contraction of the muscles, which draw the bone out of place. I *always* consider it about as important to keep the muscles at the forearm as quiet as at the point of fracture. It would not have been necessary to have a man pull a hundred weight at six weeks from the time of the fracture. If there was union, it might tend to break up the bone and cause delay in union. I never give any directions as to diet unless unusual inflammation. They usually will eat enough. Toast and crackers would be enough in a state of high inflammation. I should give nutritive diet; such a light diet might retard a cure if kept up too long. A surgeon ought to know within three weeks. At six weeks at farthest. I should give the arm eight or ten weeks to unite. I would then have tried to get up an inflammation in some way. Not skillful practice to wait five months. If he examined his patients he would know at the end of four months, whether union had taken place, I should think. I never examined that thumb; I don't know that I should know much about it if I did. I cannot decide whether that was a fracture or partial dislocation; it should have been put in place when it was first injured, and kept so. I generally use a bandage and splint to keep the bone in place and the muscles quiet. There was no union when I examined it at Dr. Belding's. I cannot say what Dr. Pratt did say. His opinion about getting up an inflammation was about the same as mine. I believe he claimed at that time, that there had been a fracture above. I did not discover evidences of another fracture. I helped to apply friction, and did up the arm, or assisted.

Cross-Examined.—Dr. Pratt called my attention to there being provisional callus above the fracture, but I could discover none. Nor do I remember of telling Drs. Pratt or Belding since, that I then discovered evidence of provisional callus. The bone was not united. I believe there was an outside splint fastened to the arm above and below the elbow, and a strap of leather or muslin, and several small bandages around the arm. These, or splints similar to these. I cannot tell whether longer or shorter, or whether these are the ones or not. I recollect the Dr. stated there had been a fracture. I do not recollect he stated he had tried friction before. I do not know who suggested friction. I think Dr. Belding asked me what I thought about it. I would have waited two or three weeks after using friction to see if union had commenced. Dr. Pratt and myself did it up. I remember there being other splints. I cannot tell whether they were like these or not. I do not pretend to be a professional surgeon. I spent some time in the East; graduated in 1854, at Pennsylvania College at Philadelphia, as physician and surgeon. Came here six years ago last fall. I don't recollect that Dr. Pratt said, he might have said he had no confidence in friction, and that an operation would have be performed. He might have stated so. I do not recollect; after friction the seton would be used, perhaps, or cutting down and cutting off the ends of the bones. I don't know of any other method. I have heard of the system of Dieffenbach of pegs; heard of one or two successful cases. I believe a case might have been well treated five or six months and not have united. I do not think anybody could have told by examining the arm at that time, whether it had been well treated or not. As a general principle, it is necessary for provisional callus to form, to unite bone. I do not think bone could unite without inflammation. I see no other way but that there should always be provisional callus. It cannot be formed without inflammation. I do not know that there is any other callus but provisional callus. That will disappear ordinarily; that depends how much was there. I cannot state how long it would take. I do not think that provisional callus begins to disappear as true bone begins to form; but not until the bone is fully united. Bone contains phosphate and carbonate of lime; cannot tell how much. I believe there is some difference. Cannot explain the difference between phosphate and carbonate. I guess marble is not carbonate of lime; cannot tell. I understand there is phosphate of lime in bone. Don't think there is much difference in · the provisional callus and bone itself. I cannot tell in healthy bone, what proportion of phosphate there is in healthy bone. Blood contains phosphate of lime. Not much difference in quantity between that and bone. Water is a constituent of blood; cannot tell the per cent. New bone is formed; my idea of this formation of bone, is that the phosphate of lime is carried through the arteries. Probably I got that information from Physiology and Anatomy. Read Carpenter's. Don't recollect any other. Read Dunglison's. My impression is that it is so; cannot tell, certainly. I think I got it from Carpenter's. I believe there are two or three muscles attached to the lower third of the humerus; cannot give their names. In diet, I would, if no unusual inflammation, make no change. For three weeks toast, crackers and gruel are very good diet. Generally have inflammation in compound fracture. That would be good diet if enough of it. Would depend upon the quantity. I do not think it would hinder the union of bone. It would depend upon the inflammation. If high, more sparing. Ordinarily, in compound fracture, where there is inflammation, it might produce suppuration for two or three weeks. I should think a spare diet, in that case, proper. I have not paid much attention to the theories of men who have treated upon this subject.

Harvey Frisby, sworn: I am a brother of the plaintiff. Plaintiff's name is Frank P. Frisby. Has lived at home all his life. He was always healthy. I was with him at the time of the accident. It happened about eight miles from here, near Morris's. He was driving a team with a load of corn. The front end board fell out, and the corn fell on to the horses, and he fell out astride of the tongue. The horses ran and kicked for about twelve rods, and the wagon went into a sort of gully, and he fell down and came out behind. I saw him all the time, and was the first one to him. He appeared to be dead. I took him into Mr. Morris's. Dr. Pratt first saw him about half an hour afterwards. When the arm was undressed, Dr. Pratt and I did it. It was the left arm. Dr. Pratt dressed it in Carroll county. The arm was broke in too. And the arm had been hurt and bled a little. It was not a large wound. It bled some, but not a very great deal. I saw no protrusion of the bone. I did not feel the bone. Dr. Pratt professes to be a physician and surgeon in that neighborhood. Dr. Pratt was sewing up the hand as my father came. He dressed the hand first; it seemed to be torn. He took a needle and thread and and sewed it up. I don't know what bandages he put on; I was not present when the arm was done up. Dr. Pratt treated the arm. (Witness here shown the two shorter splints.) I have seen these splints before. Dr. Pratt brought them to our house the first time I saw them. Don't know how long it was after the injury. He put and kept them on the arm as long as he treated it. I cannot tell when that patent brace was first put on. I went after it. I think is was as much as two weeks after the injury. He used a few other splints which he made out of shingles. My brother was hurt Saturday and was taken home Sunday. Dr. Pratt visited him about once in two weeks. Dr. Pratt treated my brother some five or six months, I should think; I don't know exactly how long. The injury took place in 1862.

Dr. Joseph Haller, sworn, says: I am a physician and surgeon; graduated two years and one month ago, at Chicago Medical College, Lind University. I saw the boy in my office in the month of October last, at Lanark. I examined his left arm, and also right hand and thumb. I found a dislocation of the joint of the thumb. I found the thumb very much atrophied. It is very difficult to tell what was the fracture. I made an examination merely casually; found they terminated without any thickening at the end. If a comminuted fracture, as I have seen these frequently, there would have been considerable thickening. I could not find any. If the case had come before me, as I think it was, I should have treated it as a simple fracture. I should commenced bandaging from the wrist, and bandaged to the shoulder. *I would have used not manufactured splints, but manufactured them myself*, and applied to the whole length of the humerus. These splints are too short. In ordinary cases, it would swell considerably, and too light bandaging might have produced mortification or gangrene. Not proper to apply extension six weeks after the fracture, to the amount of one hundred pounds. If it had been done up properly in the start, would ordinarily been united; if united, have broke the fragments of bone apart. Bone will unite in from four to six weeks. I should resort to friction before ten weeks. Not good practice to allow it to go from Dec. to May following without resorting to friction. If no inflammation, allow regular diet, except stimulating meats; allow plenty of lean meat. Low diet would reduce too much and retard union. It is a reducing process, and of course a low diet would not furnish a sufficient supply of nutriment. If the bone had not united, and eight weeks after the injury was re-fractured by external force, it would hurt the patient.

Cross-Examined.—Would reduce the diet if inflammation was severe, and add to it as it subsided. It would not hurt as much as at first if inflammation had subsided. If out of place at six weeks, I should endeavor to remedy it the best I could. It would be fracturing it over again to attempt to adjust the parts. If it had got out of place, I would reduce the fracture. I would put it in place; it would be necessary to adopt extension and manipulate the parts. If it continued not united for six to eight weeks, I would try friction, and do it up as at first. I should not wait more than seven days after using friction before I would ascertain, in some degree, whether it was uniting. If not by that time, I would call in assistance and try and move it a little more, and I would do it up. If I found no union in two weeks, then I should call another surgeon and perforate the surface, or put in a seton; either is correct practice. I would resort to these expedients, when I found friction did not answer in from four to six weeks; if by attempting slight motion, and it had not united. I think you will find this laid down in Miller's surgery. In Cooper's surgery. Don't state it possitively. I have read several medical pamphlets. Cannot state any thing more. Professor Andrews, Professor of Surgery in the Lind Medical University. I cannot state the authors; think it was Robert Durit. I think this treatment may be found in Miller's. Sir Astley Cooper's Surgical Directory. Don't know whether his name is Astley Cooper, or William. If after trying seton. I would try acupuncturing-seton first. I think, not positive upon the subject. Don't remember which. If I had a case to treat, and got as far as that, I would call for a consultation with some other surgeon. Never got as far as that. I would perforate as often as once in ten days, and keep it in apposition; then let it remain five or six weeks. I have seen that done. I do not know which bone; the tibia, I think, about the middle third of the larger bone of the big lower joint. I had one case of fracture, the middle third, in October, A. D. 1863. I think the humerus is not any more liable to non-union than other bones. I state these opinions from authors and from my teachers. I could find no particular enlargement of the ends of the bone when I examined it. I recollect distinctly of examining both ends of the bone. Discovered a slight scar a little over or above the fracture.

Dr. Beebe being sworn, says: I am a surgeon by occupation, and reside in the city of Chicago—have been engaged in the practice of medicine and surgery for about eight years. I graduated at Philadelphia, in the spring of 1857. I have had a moderately

extensive practice in private life, and a somewhat more extensive
practice in the government service. I was engaged in field and
hospital practice about eighteen months. I estimate the number
of cases which I treated while in the army, or which came under
my personal observation, at 4,000. I had the care of about seventy
regiments. I can safely say that the cases of wounds numbered
4,000. After all battles all severe cases came under my
observation for final decision as to treatment. They might number fifteen hundred more, perhaps. I think that thirty per cent.
of these injuries were of bone. In some of these cases, or rather
taken as a whole, every bone in the body was injured, either by
cannon or musket shot, sabre or bayonet. I have had considerable surgical practice in private life, for one of my years. The
first year of my practice was in Albany, New York, and a little
less than seven years in Chicago, excepting the time I was in the
service. I am now practicing in Chicago; I have had cases of
fracture of the humerus in civil life. I now call to mind two cases.
The whole shaft of the bone is liable to fracture. It is, by all
good surgeons, regarded that a fracture of the humerus or any
other long bone, at or near the nutritive foramen, will unite more
slowly than at other portions of the bone. The humerus is more
liable to non-union than any other bone in the body.

Examination of the boy.—Right hand.—I discover, from an
extensive cicatrix, an evidence that there has been an extensive
lacerated wound through the web of the thumb. It was not a cut
that caused this cicatrix. It draws from various angles, and
seems to be somewhat extensive. In this, the scar is irregular,
and I judge from the integuments forming this scar, that the
wound was lacerated and considerably torn. This first joint of
the thumb is healthy and natural. The second joint I find perfectly in place. I grasp now the point of articulation between
the bone of the thumb—the phalanx—and the metacarpal bone.
Between my finger and thumb I grasp the joint which is not at
all displaced. Behind this joint, a half an inch, I find a project-`
ing point of bone, and tracing along backward I find a projecting
margin of bone, and passing my finger down along the inner side
of the bone I find too great a thickness of the shaft of the bone.
The corresponding bone in the other hand is not as thick as this
one. The shaft of this bone is very much thicker than it should
be in health. The shaft of the bone is also too short, indicating
to me that there has been a fracture of this bone, and I am posi-

tively of the opinion that thus the fracture extends from a point near its articulation with the thumb, nearly the entire length of the shaft of this bone; and the anterior fragment has dropped down somewhat, and is over-lapped by the other fragment. Taking into consideration, then, the fact which I must suppose in this case, that this lacerated wound was produced at the same time that the fracture occurred, and I am led to infer that the injury was quite severe. And if there was a lacerated wound of the soft tissues, and it communicated with the fracture, making it a compound fracture, I consider it exceedingly fortunate, owing to the great laceration of the soft tissues, that the extremity is as good as it is. The thumb appears now to be in a condition of usefulness. So far as the mal-position of this bone is concerned, this thumb would be as useful as it ever was. The surgeon is not responsible for the lacerated wound and the resulting cicatrix or scar. I should say that that case was very successful in its result, sir. I see some slight cicatrices, but no other material injuries in either hand.

Examination of left arm.—I find here an un-united fracture of the humerus, at the junction of the middle and lower thirds of the bone, extending diagonally from below, upward and forward. I notice beveling on the upper fragment, extending downward and backward, and corresponding beveling on the lower fragment, extending upward and forward, which confirms me in this opinion. I examine upon the shaft, somewhat above where the beveling begins, and I find one point which presents tenderness to the touch, as indicated by the boy shrinking away from pressure upon it. There is but a slight tumefaction of the periosteum at this point, and I should be unable to say, from this tumefaction alone, that this was a remnant of provisional callus. But taking the tenderness in connection with this slight tumefaction, I should suspect that there had been fracture of the bone at this point. I find when the arm hangs loosely that the fragments still over-lap, though the bony surfaces are not brought together. I find on the back side of the arm, a patch of skin an inch in extent differing in structure from the surrounding skin, and this is evidence of there having been a wound there sometime. A question as to the depth of this wound presents itself to my mind. If I lift up the surrounding skin, I find that this scar pits in the centre, indicating attachment to the deep tissues. From these deep attachments, it appears that the wound must have extended through the integuments and deep tissues well down to the point of the upper fragment of bone. It does not present the appearance of a clean cut wound. It appears to have been a lacerated wound, torn through by some substance, and the wound immediately overlying the point of this upper fragment. I suspect that this wound was produced by this fragment of bone being thrust through the soft parts. If this supposition be correct, I should then feel safe in saying we have a compound fracture.

A compound fracture is one wherein the bone is fractured, and there is a wound through the soft parts, down to the point of fracture. If the point of tenderness above be an indication of previous fracture, then we have a compound comminuted fracture, or a compound fracture where the bone is broken at more than one point. If, in forming my opinion of the nature of this injury, I should learn that the arm was broken by a loaded wagon passing over it, and especially if the arm rested on frozen earth when the wheel passed over it, I should be strongly of the opinion that the bone was comminuted, or crushed, and we should *then* have a compound comminuted fracture. If the injury to the hand were produced at the same time, giving a fracture of another bone with extensive laceration of tissue, then we should have a compound comminuted complicated fracture—that is, the fracture of the arm is complicated by the injury of the opposite hand, in that, nature, while called upon to repair the fractured arm, is also required to furnish material for the repair of the other injury, and this; by retarding the process of repair, would complicate the fractures and dimish the chances of ultimate union. Especially would this be the case if there were other severe injuries, such as a severe wound on the head, as named by another witness. So that now, sir, if I were called upon to pronounce a professional opinion, as to the nature of the injury received, I should judge, from the evidence before me, that it was a compound comminuted complicated fracture.

I do not find in this arm, a false joint, but simply non-union. In false joint there is not only non-union of fragments, but the fractured ends being brought in contact are tipped with cartilage, so as to glide upon each other, and held in that position by bands of fibrous tissue, extending from one fragment to the other. There is nothing of that kind here ; there is simply non-union. The causes of non-union are various, and are divided by surgeons into two classes. First, local causes, such as the interposition of other tissue between the fractured surfaces, a deficient supply of nervous influence, or the circulation may be cut off or impaired, and its nutrition thus being arrested there might result non-union. A fracture partially united, and then re-fractured, would be less likely to unite a second time. Second, the general causes are such as affect the general health of the patient, and might depend upon the condition of the patient. If the parent had been addicted to a free use of intoxicating liquors, it might so influence the constitution of the son as to retard union. So, also of an hereditary scrofulous tubercular or cancerous tendency. But the local causes are of the first importance, and of these perhaps none more important than the destruction of the nutrition of the bone. If the nutrition of the bone be perfect, then union of the fragments of broken bone follows rapidly; but if this nutrition be arrested, or impaired, or delayed, non-union is the result. When the system is called upon to repair several fractures, requiring large amount of material, some of the fractures may unite and others may not, or may be so delayed that non-union would result by reason of the fractured ends being covered by fibrous or cartilaginous tissue before the system was ready to begin the repair. I may illustrate: It was but a few months since, that a bank of frozen coal, falling upon a man, produced a compound comminuted fracture of the tibia and fibula, at the middle, crushing the tibia for two and a half to three inches. The fragments were united to the upper portion of the shaft some weeks before the lower portion of the shaft was united to them; so that some portions of fractured bones may unite and the union of other fragments be delayed until the repair of the first is secured; and by reason of this delay, it might never unite, although the best surgical treatment has been employed.

The bone receives its nutritious supply from two sources; first, from the periosteum, the membrane which lies upon the surface of the bone, and sends minute vessels into the bony structure from without. Second, The nutritive artery passing in through the nutritive foramen, is distributed to the bone from within, along the canal or cavity which contains the marrow. This canal is lined by an internal periosteum, and from the distribution of blood vessels, as shown in this fresh bone, which I here present, we perceive that the supply of blood to the bone is greater from within than from without. The bone within is seen to be spongy, or less dense than without, and this spongy or cancellated structure is permeated by minute canals, called "Haversian canals," and in these the minute blood-vessels distribute themselves to the bone. The bone, as a whole, is made up of minute cells of an oval form, each of which has the power to re-produce other cells like itself, and it is from the growth and multiplication of these cells that bone is formed, and when fractured repaired. For the development of other tissues different and distinct forms of cells exist; thus, the cell which forms muscular tissue differs from that which forms the mucous membranes, and so there exist in the body distinct sets or types of cells which differ widely one from another. Now, when blood comes in contact with these cells, they have the power to take up that which will promote their own growth and development, and when they have reached a certain stage of development these divide up to form a multiplication of similar cells. The bone cell appropriates to itself only those portions which will develop bone; and so of the other types of cells. As the grain of corn has the power to draw from the soil those elements which favor its growth, and to produce other grains of corn like itself, and as all animals possess the power to re-produce other animals like themselves, so these different types of cells reproduce cells like unto themselves.

Now, if the bone be broken, and a portion of its substance destroyed, nature at once proceeds to repair the loss. The fractured surfaces being brought in apposition, the bone cells are multiplied and thrust out into the gap; but it becomes necessary to steady the fragments, and hence nature throws out around the fragments, what is termed "provisional callus," and within the medullary canal a pin or plug of granular matter extending to either side of the line of fracture. While these provisions of nature aid in maintaining the fragments in position, there is thrown out an exudation of plastic matter which serves as a platform in or upon which the bony cells may be deposited as formed. This exudation of plastic matter between the fractured surfaces is termed the "definitive callus," or in other words, it defines the limit within which bone cells are deposited. As these bone cells are deposited and bony union progresses, the provisional callus is removed by absorption, and so the callus within the canal is gradually excavated into cavities, and these are filled with marrow again, until at length the shell of bone is restored to nearly its former condition and appearance.

We see, from this bone before us, that the nutrition derived from the nutrient artery is greater, by half, than that derived from the periosteum, and if, therefore, a fracture take place at or near the nutrient foramen, so as to cut off the supply of nutrition from this source, then the bone, instead of receiving more than its usual supply of nutrition, as needed, actually receives only about one third the usual amount.

In one of the cases of fracture of the humerus seen by me, the bone had been fractured near the nutrient foramen, and when partially united, was by some accident re-fractured. Instead of uniting a second time, it seemed to have been so far deprived of its nutrition as really to refuse to unite not only, but, by the process of absorption, the bone was gradually carried away, and removed from the system, till nothing remained but the articular ends of this bone.

Bones may be repaired by different methods. In general terms, they may be repaired by two processes, the one without provisional callus, the other with; but, to be definite, there are, as near as I recollect, six distinct modes of union. First, by immediate union, the parts being brought in accurate apposition, they unite at once, as will a clean cut in the soft tissues, and without the formation of any provisional material. Second, the parts being coaptated, the material for repair is thrown out between the fractured surfaces, and the bone unites by means of this without any provisional callus. Third, the bony fragments are surrounded by the provisional callus, the plug or pin is developed within the canal, and then the definitive callus is thrown out between the fractured surfaces, in which the final deposit of bone takes place. Fourth, the provisional and internal callus form, as in the last case; but no definitive callus forms; indeed, the fractured surfaces do not unite, and bony deposit takes place in the structure of the provisional callus, making it a permanent instead of provisional structure. Fifth, when bones overlap, the provisional callus forms between contiguous sides of the bone, and union takes place in that manner. Sixth, the fractured surfaces being more or less widely separated, the provisional callus pushes out to meet the fragments and unites them, and in this provisional structure to deposit bony matter. If there is a covering over the ends of the bone by a fibrous or cartilaginous tissue, and friction is used to remove this from the bone, then, when this is absorbed, the repairative process will go on. It would excite a degree of inflammation, and a more full supply of blood; it would cause a tenderness, and thereby keep the parts partially at rest. The tenderness would prevent the patient from moving the muscles of the part, and thereby favor rapid union. My own opinion would be, that if there was nothing discoverable but non-union, friction should not be resorted to under six months, and I am borne out in this opinion by good authority. Upon fractures and dislocations, Hamilton of New York, is one of the best. Gross is also good authority. Gross, Smith and Hamilton are the most reliable authors. Miller's is a good work. The perforation of the bone in un-united fractures is recommended by Hamilton as good practice. The instrument used is a drill, something like a brad awl, but so pointed as to make no chips. A slit is made through the skin and the drill is passed down to and through the bone. Having drilled once through the bone, the drill is withdrawn from the bone, but not from the soft parts, and by giving the drill a different slant or inclination, other holes are drilled in various directions through the bone at the seat of fracture. Splints are then applied, and the parts kept at rest. The surgeon should wait four or five weeks for a result. If not successful he resorts to other modes of treatment. The seton is one. It does not stand however, very high with the profession. This is done by passing a skein of silk between the ends of the bone by means of a needle. The next one I should resort to, if perforation did not succeed, would be resection. This mode dates as far back as John Hunter. It has been revived lately, especially in army practice. It may be applied to the shafts of long bones or to the removal of joints injured or diseased, and is received by the profession with much favor. In the case before us I think it can yet be used with success. Were I going to operate upon it I should prefer to do so soon, as the boy is growing and in good condition for recovery. The incision should be made from behind to avoid the artery. In oblique fractures, where the fragments overlap and fail to unite, the bones may be brought into apposition and secured by ivory pegs, and some recommend silver wire. Some use blisters over the point of fracture. Electricity is applied by means of wires passed down to the bone at the point of fracture. Cauterization is also used, but this is a somewhat barbarous mode of treatment; and some have applied caustic to the bone itself. It is proper for me to state, that all these varieties of treatment are sanctioned by good authority.

There are several methods of splinting a fractured humerus.

4

One method would be, to put on splints from the shoulder to the elbow, and from the arm-pit to the elbow, with shorter supporting splints between. These splints would answer well enough for that purpose. A roller bandage should be applied from the wrist or hand to the shoulder, and by successive turns be made to envelop the splints and steady the parts. The arm should be brought to the side, and the wrist and fore-arm placed in a sling. The elbow and arm should be allowed to hang unsupported, that by its weight, it may keep the bone extended. This is the treatment given by Gross of Philadelphia. Perhaps no better authority can be found in this country. It is to be regarded as skillful dressing. Hamilton recommends an angular side splint. Smith also approves of these side splints. Another method mentioned is, the application of a hollow splint to the outside of the arm, and a roller outside. (Witness here took up the longer of the short splints.) This splint would be long enough for the inside one at the seat of fracture with the arm resting in the outside splint. This is a good splint. These three methods are the ones generally recommended by surgeons. Some would make splints of sole-leather, some of felt, stiffened with gum shellac, and others of tin or sheet iron. These embrace the range of splints for such fractures, and are sustained by good authority. Either would be called skillful dressing. I should think these splints long enough and proper to be placed on this bone. I think a splint two inches longer than these, with these small ones on the inside, would be amply sufficient, and as well, perhaps as surgeon Gross himself could dress it. If I found the patient restless, I would use the angular splint as an additional protection, otherwise these splints would be sufficient. I should examine it two or three days after the fracture to see if it was in place; it would not be necessary to remove the bandages. Surgeons sometimes apply a roller next to the skin, before applying splints. This practice has been adopted by almost all surgeons, until recently; some have now abandoned this mode. By enveloping the splints with the first roller the arm is saved from being encumbered by too much dressing, and avoids too much heat; still it is good surgery to apply the roller to the skin before any splints are applied. It is only necessary for the surgeon to set the fragments and see that they are in place, to trace the outline of the bone while the dressings are on, and see that the fragments are in line and the dressings secure. It is not necessary to examine them otherwise for eight or ten days. If there is no active inflammation and the swelling had subsided, I would examine and re-adjust the dressings as before, perhaps a little firmer. If the hand should swell some for six or twelve hours, it will do no damage. It will not retard the repair of bone. It is the small vessels that do the work and furnish nutrition. The extremities may be blue from six to twelve, or even twenty-four hours, and still not retard the repair of bone. It is only when the bandage is applied so tightly as to produce inflammation, resulting in gangrene and the death of the part. It is my practice, and the practice of all good surgeons, to apply extension at any time when the case requires it. There is no danger of gangrene from slight swelling of the extremities and blueness of the skin. I should call to see the case once in two or three days at first; after a few days, once in a week or ten days; oftener if there were any untoward symptoms to give me greater anxiety. In the case of fracture of the femur of which I spoke, I go once a week. Pus never forms without inflammation having preceded it. It is the result or product of inflammation. The question would be, has there not been too much inflammation? That, at the seat of fracture, is a frequent cause of non-union, by exciting absorption of the provisional callus or preventing its formation by provoking suppuration. This absorption may go so far as to remove a large portion of the bone itself. I would order a light diet—mostly, if not entirely, a vegetable diet—for the reason that I should expect these grave injuries —severe laceration of the arm, hand and head—would produce a high degree of inflammation, such as would materially interfere (if not timely prevented) with the healing of the wounds. The vegetable diet should be prescribed at first, not wait until inflammation had set in. I have no such objections to vegetable diet as some of the witnesses who preceded me. They did not seem to take into consideration the fact, that the vegetable, the wheat, the corn and the oats take from the ground earthy matter, out of which to make tissue. We derive more earthy matter from vegetable than from animal food. From whence do such animals as the ox and horse derive the earthy matter to make their bone? Is it not from eating these vegetables? And when we, in turn, eat the animal food, as beef, we get the vegetable food, so to speak, second hand, from which the earthy matter has been sifted out to make the bones of the animal. This food furnishes not only material for bone, but fibrin; there is no lack of fibrin in the vegetable. This vegetable food, then, furnishes to the body the earthy matter which the boy wanted in the production of bone. The earthy matter has to be taken out to make bone. We do not eat bone. We do not deprive the system of this earthy matter by eating vegetable food. He had in the vegetable all the necessary elements to produce bone. He was nourished as well, and even better by vegetables, than he would have been by animal food. Had he taken animal food, he must have eaten some fat with every fibre. In this fat is carbon, which, passing into the lungs, is there consumed or burnt, and generates heat. In such an injury you want as little heat as possible, therefore vegetable diet is the best. In continuing vegetable I would be guided by the case. If there was evidence of inflammation, and I still desired an absence of heat in the body, I should continue the vegetable diet. If I found that the vital forces were flagging, or if the patient were becoming emaciated, I would order a mixed diet. I have had experience in cases treated in this manner. I have treated thousands of cases in hospitals, suffering similar wounds. I can speak of the beneficial effects of vegetable diet from much experience. In these remarks, I speak from a knowledge acquired by treatment of thousands of cases for whom I prescribed this kind of diet. I have stated to the jury my views of the diet from the complications of the case and from the evidences now before me. In giving my opinion as to the proper treatment, I assume that the injuries occurred on the 20th Dec., 1862 ; that the period of treatment was five months and ten days, and I say that friction is the severest measure which should have been adopted. My professional opinion is based upon the facts before me, and upon facts assumed, as before stated ; and, based upon these facts, I give it as my professional opinion that this bone might have refused to unite up to the thirtieth day of May next ensuing, under the best of surgical treatment. That it would not have been good surgery to have resorted to any more stringent means than that of friction. To resort to acupuncturing during the period named, would be in direct opposition to the opinion I have just given. It might have been delayed for six or even eight months, and be well endorsed as nothing unusual in good surgery. If the surgeon resort to more stringent measures to obtain union, there must be evidence of something more than non-union. The points of the bone must be rounded off and covered with a cartilaginous tissue. If, when the fragments were

brought in contact, there was grating or crepitus, then there is
the fact only of non-union. The condition of these fragments at
the period of five months, may have been, and probably was, very
different from their appearance now. They are now rounded off
and covered with cartilaginous tissue; this may have been
developing daily since that time. I do not know how the blood
would deposit this ossific matter as it passes through the nutritive
artery, from the fact that the blood does not contain this ossific
matter. There is no bone in blood. In bone there is fifty-one
per cent. of phosphate of lime, and twelve of carbonate of lime.
We are unable to say that any phosphate of lime, as such, is contained in the blood. There is an insoluble salt which chemists
find in the blood, about one part in the hundred; but they are
unable to say how much, if any, is phosphate or carbonate of
lime, or whether it is sulphate or carbonate of soda. There is phosphate and carbonate of lime, as I have stated, in bone; there is
some in the animal tissues, and they enter into the formation of
cartilage. There is a much less quantity of phosphate of lime in
provisional callus than in bone; the plug that extends along the
medullary cavity contains about thirty per cent., and that without
about thirty-three per cent. These are formed by the periosteum
and internal periosteum. The bone cells of which I have spoken
establish bony union within the structure of the definitive callus.
I say union may take place without provisional callus. In fracture of the skull there is no provisional callus. The knee-pan
will not develope provisional callus upon the inner surface, and
but a small amount on the outer surface. Definitive callus forms
in the spongy portions of bone, and fractures through the spongy
portions of the bone are more likely to unite than in the shaft.
The head of the humerus driven into the shaft, constituting
impacted fracture, is united immediately and without provisional
callus. (Witness explains [anastomosing.) I do not, myself,
know how anastomosis can take place in or through bone sufficient to establish collateral circulation. The gentleman to-day
spoke of the ligation of the femoral artery—that when the main
trunk is obliterated the small branches given off above rapidly
enlarge and establish what he termed a "vicarious circulation,"
so as to keep up a supply of blood to the extremity; but if the
trunk of this nutritive artery be destroyed, I do not see what is
to anastomose. Whether the witness meant to say some artery
from within would anastomose, I know of no such artery, and

how an artery which is a soft tissue is to drill a hole through the solid shaft of bone, is beyond my comprehension; or that it will materially enlarge its calibre through the bone, is equally absurd.

This is the difficulty that meets me, sir, at the threshold of this anastomosing theory.

On the first of June, 1863, I could not have told, from the appearance of the boy's arm, what his previous treatment had been, whether skillful or otherwise. The appearance only shows non-union. The failure of the treatment would be no evidence of want of skill. If one of the fragments of bone appeared out of place at any time, it was the duty of the surgeon to put it in place or reduce the fracture and re-apply the pressing more firmly over the point of bone thus elevated. It would be proper to manipulate the arm to see how this should be adjusted, to the end that proper treatment might be applied. If properly coaptated, the wound being healed, I should presume the process of repair would be even more rapid than if there had been an open wound at the point of fracture. The system would have been in a much better condition for carrying on the repair at six weeks after the fracture than previous to that period. If the fragments of bone were then brought in apposition accurately, and there maintained, I see no reason why there might not have been a union of bone in three weeks from that time. I should have expected it (assuming that the nutrient artery was entire) in from three to four weeks, and even at two weeks provisional callus, under the circumstances related by the witness, might have formed. If the bones passed by each other, any course would have been proper which was necessary to reduce the fracture. Extension would, in that case, have been necessary. I do not think it possible for a person standing at the shoulder and another at the elbow, and with it flexed, to pull more than enough to antagonize the contraction of the muscles. It would have been necessary to make this extension to prevent the muscles from drawing the fragments past each other.

Cross-Examination.—I graduated the first of March, 1857. I first practiced in Albany, N. Y. I graduated at the College of Pennsylvania. It had another name. It was known as the Homœopathic Medical College of Pennsylvania. But I had previously taken a full course of study at the Albany Medical College, which *per contra* was known as an Allopathic Medical College, and I had practiced about a year before going to Philadelphia. I came West

in the month of April, 1857, and settled in Chicago. I have practiced surgery and medicine in connection with it, since that time.
I have been connected with the Hahnemann Medical College of
Chicago for two years. I lectured during the last year upon surgery; in the former year upon anatomy. This college advocates
the Homœopathic system.

The term Homœopathy is derived from two Greek words,
" *Omoios*," like or similar, and " *Pathos*," disease. By this we
mean that diseases may be cured by agents capable of producing
similar diseased conditions. That which in a healthy man will
produce a given diseased state, will cure a similar disease existing
from other causes. Not that poisoning by arsenic may be cured
by arsenic, but that an inflammation of the stomach, say, which
is very similar to that which arsenic produces, may be cured by
that drug properly administered. This describes the system of
medicine, so far as medication goes. I practiced in Chicago up
to Dec., 1861, when I entered the service. I was in the field
about eighteen months. I was surgeon-in-chief of Maj. General
Thomas' corps, known as the 14th army corps, which was em-
braced in what was called the "Department of the Cumber-
land." Two cases of this kind have come under my observation
in private practice. In one the fracture was at or near the nutrient foramen. Union took place, but by some accident the bone
was again fractured, when it not only refused to unite, but was
gradually absorbed and carried away, until nothing remained but
the articular extremities. The fact of non-union was established
before it came under my observation. While in the service I was
constantly with the troops in the field. Did not stay in the hospitals all the time. I had charge of about seventy regiments. I could
not estimate now, accurately, the cases I treated personally. In
the course of treatment always after battles, I was constantly
operating. My operations were mostly confined to the more
grave cases. I was not entirely engaged in amputating. I had
a supervision of the whole. After battles I had the care of these
cases for two or three weeks. They did not remain, at longest,
over six or eight weeks under my charge. After the battle of
Stone river, which was fought on the first of January, I remained
with the wounded until the middle of March. That, perhaps,
was the longest period I had personal observation of a given
number of cases.

We sometimes fed them toast, not always, because we could

not get the bread; when we could not, we gave them "hard tack." In the hospitals I kept a supply of farinaceous articles for low diet—corn starch, sago, barley, farina. These articles were always kept on hand along with the army. This food was sufficiently stimulating for severe wounds in the inflammatory stage. I say this system of diet contains all the earthy elements in abundance, which are required in the repair of bone. I did not say that animal matter was only to produce heat. Animal food is not only useful in producing heat by combustion in the lungs, but it contains earthy matter, though in less quantity than vegetables.

I have no notion, of diet *peculiar* to my *system of practice.* What I state is recognized by the medical world as safe treatment. It is very necessary to change the diet if there is much inflammation. I would not wait for it to come on before I changed the diet. I would do it at once, for the purpose of preventing inflammation. I do not think that any surgeon could be held responsible for that injury to the thumb. It would be difficult to have done better. From anatomical knowledge, I may state to the jury, that there are muscles passing through this web, on the inside of the thumb, which enable it to grasp any object. They make their insertion deep in the palm of the hand. From the lacerated appearance of the wound, I infer that these were torn across, and in that case the action of the thumb would be much impaired. The agent that produced this wound may have been a hook. I cannot tell what. If the front-board of the wagon slid out and the boy was precipitated upon the tongue, it may have been the hook of the trace. It certainly was badly torn. I think it was a good job, considering the nature of the injury. I should be proud of it—that is, I should be exceedingly gratified it was no worse. I would not try to repair it in its present condition. He might have got a better union, possibly, at the time the wound was healed, but I should be gratified with the result as it is now. The blood does not always give sustenance alike to all parts of the system, when there are different injuries to be repaired. If the bones were placed in proper position at first, I would not meddle with them. If they were not, or had got out of place, I would then have placed them in proper position. Whether they would have remained in place, and resulted in a better union, I do not know. My object would have been, to get an exact comp. tation of the fragments, but when I go back and imagine the injury, with the integuments torn and lacerated, the bone broken, and the joint dislocated; examining it now, it is better than I could have expected from such an injury. I am supposing the bones of the arm not united in six or eight weeks. It is proper for the surgeon, at all times, in treating a fracture, when he finds the bones out of place, to reduce the fracture. It does not require much knowledge to know that such fragments should be at once replaced. In such a fracture, the surgeon attending would be likely to discover whether the bones were out of place, and it is always his duty to replace and get the fragments in apposition, as perfectly as possible. I could not say that these bones would have been united in six weeks; I should hope they might be. A surgeon should never cease his efforts while there is reasonable hope of cure. If he does not give up and nature seconds his efforts, he should be gratified he has succeeded so well, even though it stop short of absolute perfection. In a compound fracture and dislocation of these bones, most surgeons would have taken off the thumb. I say it was commendable in the surgeon to retain the thumb and try and save it. I do not say I would have taken it off. I would not have taken it off. I feel and know that there are agencies to subdue inflammation in the Homœopathic system, which give us confidence safely to risk and do what, in these cases, the Allopathists can not and dare not do. There is one agent as a substitute for the lancet, which Homœopathy has given to the world, which is invaluable, that is aconite; and there are others. When inflammation is progressing to a destruction of the parts, that agent steps in and arrests it. Allopathy draws from the system the blood which is needed to make repair. Homœopathy comes, with milder means and more sure remedies, to save the blood for the work of repair. Fortunately my researches upon this subject go far enough to ascertain that aconite was not used in place of the lancet until Homœopathy brought it into use. Aconite is now used extensively in place of the lancet. It would control inflammatory action better than the lancet. The lancet, in no case, is necessary. I mean to say to the jury, that I was educated an Allopathist before I studied Homœopathy. I availed myself of all the information I could obtain, and which any student has who passes through the schools of that system. I then availed myself of the superior advantages which may be derived from the Homœopathic schools and practice; and I say to-day, that aconite is an invaluable remedy, and is far better to control inflammation than the lancet. Dr. Pratt mentioned this case to me in May, last year. 'He told me it was a case of non-union. I had a more full description of it in June following. I do not know that he has since spoken to me concerning it; it seems to me he has once. I have not talked with Judge Knowlton since I came here, other than to make a casual remark. We have spoken together but twice, that was yesterday and day before. It was about the medical testimony which has been given here, not particularly relating to the case. I have felt considerable interest in regard to the medical testimony—that is all. I have no idea that the success, or want of success in this case will affect Homœopathy; that is a system of truth which stands upon its own merits. I have no recollection of saying that when I came on to the stand I would make it all right, or any words to that effect. I certainly entertained no such idea, and I say now, I have not said so. I have felt much interest since I heard the medical testimony.

In the case I mentioned there was about two and a half inches of the bone crushed. I said the union occurred in the upper fragments first, and the case is still under treatment. The last examination I made was March 4th. It had been under treatment since sometime in last December, as near as I recollect. There is a nutrient foramen in the tibia; it enters at the middle of the bone, and takes a direction upwards. The nutrient artery sends branches toward the lower extremity of the bone. Fracture of any other bone of the extremities will unite more rapidly than the humerus. There are no other vessels named nutrient arteries, save that which enters at the nutrient foramen. The location is about the same, relatively, in every bone. The hole in this bone points toward the elbow. There is a branch inside pointing upwards. A fracture at or near the entry of this artery will retard union very much. The foramen is this hole in the bone. Some of these smaller holes are for the entrance of small arteries, and some for the exit of small veins which carry the impure blood back to the heart. Sometimes the vein and the artery pass through the same place in the bone. The blood flows so much more rapidly in the artery; a small artery takes in more blood than a vein of larger calibre can carry back. These holes are the places through which the vessels pass in from the periosteum to nourish the bone. This one is known as the nutrient foramen—these small holes are, so far as the outside of the shaft is concerned, nutrient foramen, but a much larger supply of nutriment is from the inner surface of the bone supplied by the nutrient artery.

If above the foramen it would not cut off the supply, but a fracture at or near this point might cause the destruction of this artery. It is the experience of Gross, Smith and Hamilton, who are among the first surgeons in the country, that a fracture above will unite much more readily than one below this foramen. All agree in this—the destruction of this artery causes delay. Suppose it destroyed at the point of entrance, the upper portion receives a much larger supply of nutriment than the portion below. I say many of these small holes are for veins and arteries; in the spongy portions of bone these are more numerous and larger, and the larger portion of spongy bone is at the upper end. There are more above than below the foramen.

Adult bone contains fifty-one to fifty-four per cent. of phosphate of lime, and about eleven per cent. of carbonate. I think there is more than sixty per cent. of lime in adult bone. I think there is some thirty-two per cent. of animal matter. I say the blood contains about one per cent. of insoluble salts. This insoluble salt is not bony matter. These bone cells have the power of drawing from the blood the elements of nutrition, and from these elements developing bony matter. Newly formed bone is not so hard because the bone cells are not so compactly arranged as in the older bone. I cannot go back of the callus and tell what per cent. There is one per cent. in the blood, out of which elements bone is made. I said there is no bony matter in the blood; by bony matter I mean these little cells of which bone is made. I said these are not deposited by the blood; as it courses through the arteries that they are developed and grow within the cylinder of the bone; they derive their nourishment from the blood. The arterial blood brings the nutriment which is needed to develop bone. I do not agree to the proposition that bony matter is deposited from the blood. The blood does not bring along ossific matter and deposit it in its course; but the blood conveys certain elements, through the arteries and distributing vessels; by means of capillaries, these elements come in contact with these bone cells. The artery comes from the outside, pours its blood into the branch inside of the bone and through the capillaries, and by these means these cells are made to grow. This blood, after imparting its nutrient qualities, is returned through the veins to the heart again. These capillaries do not terminate in the bone, but in veins; but they pass through the bone, and these little cells are fed and nourished by this arterial blood. There is quite a difference, sir, whether the Mississippi, coming down from the northern regions, deposits wheat or wheaty matter upon its banks, or whether the kernel of wheat already sown draws from the Mississippi the moisture which it needs to develop it and make it grow. The nutrition is in the arterial blood, which furnishes the elements by which bone cells develop into solid bone. It is, therefore, only in the manner I have described that bone is made from the blood. Bone grows as wheat grows; the rain furnishes moisture, but not wheat nor wheaty matter. Neither does the earth furnish wheat or wheaty matter. There is not in the rain nor in the earth, a particle of starch or pectin, yet the wheat is composed of these substances with others.

We, perhaps, could not say that here was a creation, because Omnipotence created all the matter which exists. The wheat plant, like every other plant, was endowed at its creation with the power to reproduce itself. Comparatively, the more correct term to be used would be pro-creation, by which, as used by physiologists, we mean that faculty in nature by which living objects appropriate from the elements that which causes development and growth, and from these elements construct other objects like themselves. In this confined sense of the term, it is a creation. It draws material from the elements in one shape, and by its own vitality transforms this material into forms and qualities identical with its own. It transmutes one kind of material into another and different kind; but it stamps upon the material thus transmuted its own *identity*.

Withhold from the plant carbonic acid, and it will shrink and die. You can see no resemblance between the starchy matter in corn and wheat, and the surrounding atmosphere which supplies its nourishment. So you cannot say that the plant draws ammonia and carbonic acid from the atmosphere, and holds them there; it does more. It acts from a power, as it were, within itself, which changes the character of these substances. The soil may be never so rich in the quality which the wheat plant requires, yet from dryness the wheat may not be developed; and so of all other vegetables. I said it is the plant which takes up the earthy elements and makes its own particles from these elements. These earthy matters are taken up in solution by the plant. There is an endless variety in these processes. The soil only furnishes elements for the growth, and not the actual material of which the plant is composed in that form. If you plant wheat on a limy soil, the plant readily finds in the solution of that soil, by moisture, the elements to make wheat, because the plant takes its healthy support from the soil. The animal gets his earthy matter second-hand from the ground. If you sow wheat on alluvial soil it will produce straw, not wheat. Lime is necessary to produce wheat. There must be some lime elements in the vessels which feed bone to make bone. There must be lime from some source, but it does not follow that it gets lime from the arterial blood. It does follow that there is some material or quality in blood from which this lime in the bone is fed and nourished. Either the blood must circulate more rapidly or freely to the part, or there will be a slow recovery. Sometimes nature supplies a greater amount of blood to the seat of fracture than to any other portion of the system.

I state to the jury, that I assume that there will be always more or less inflammation at the seat of injury, but it does not from thence follow that inflammation is nature's remedy for the repair of the injury; simply that the violence caused the inflammation. Because it was injured it inflamed. Inflammation is the natural result of injury, not nature's design. I might go farther, and say to the jury, that the repair of bone is not produced by inflammation. Inflammation is a disease ; no matter whether slight or extensive, it is a diseased process, and must necessarily be so; but the repair of bone is always a healthy process. It is a purely physiological process, just as much so as to build up the skin on my hand. It is a healthy process—the method and material are not essentially different in repair from that in the original formation of the bone in the infant. The same general law governs in the formation which becomes operative in repair, but I would not be understood by the jury, that the whole process of repair after injury is the same precisely as in the original growth ; because inflammation is present, although the result of violence solely. The process of circulation is different under the injury and at the point of injury than would be required in the formation or repair of bone. I want to separate, in the minds of the jury, the results of the injury from the process of repair. The process of repair, merely, does not occasion an increased supply of blood. By lymph I mean the same as by fibrous or plastic exudation. I used this term to the jury. It is my own medical parlance. In the first instance, it is a gummy substance, and in wounds of the skin presents itself as soon as the bleeding ceases, where it soon becomes a glossy substance, covering the surface of the wound. The provisional callus depends entirely upon circumstances; the character of the injury, the condition of the patient. Often times this callus is exceedingly small when thrown out; that is, a small amount is required to hold the fragments of bone in position, especially if supported by bandages. I wish to be understood, that by this I do not mean the cells which are thrown out from the fractured surfaces of bone—bone cells. This could be inferred from the very fact that I called it provisional callus. I stated definitive callus is that which intervenes between the bony surfaces and within which are developed these minute cells which grow up to be bone cells, that by multiplication they produce bone. This matter thrown up on the outside cannot form bone. I say nature throws out a sort of platform around the gap and between the extremities. While making these explanations I do not wish the jury to be engaged in looking out of the windows. When there is a gap between the fractured ends of bone, nature throws out a platform which enables her to deposit these bone cells. This plastic exudation forms the bridge within which this bone structure can be built. As in bridging a stream, a platform must be erected upon which to swing the arches across and to sustain the stringers. When the bridge is built the platform is removed. So this plastic matter has little else to do, and is removed by absorption as soon as the work of repair is done. As I have before repeatedly said, these bony cells are pushed out from the points of bone longitudinally, until they fill up this plastic medium—until they fill the entire space, meeting at the centre. *Then*, we say, there is bony union; but the development of bone cells does not stop now, for at this time you will find but a comparatively small per centage of bony matter. These go on multiplying in numbers and increasing in density until it becomes compact bony tissue; only then does this process cease. In a healthy subject; in simple fracture, under favorable circumstances, nature would be employed during the first eight days in clearing away the wreck of the old structure; at the ninth day the plastic exudation begins around the bone, and the provisional callus has commenced forming—this process lasts from twelve to seventeen days, under favorable circumstances—it takes that additional period to build up provisional callus; this extends the time to twenty or twenty-five days in which to clear away the rubbish and put on nature's splint. From the twentieth or twenty-fifth day the real work of repair begins. How long *this* period continues depends upon the extent of the fracture and the amount of space to be filled. There are contingencies which may extend the first operation described from thirty to sixty days. Ordinarily there should be bony union in sixty days, but do not understand me that this new bone will be compact in that period : in a simple fracture it would be strong enough to be used. To complete the work it takes months, sometimes years. When there is a large amount of provisional callus it takes sometimes years. All physiologists agree that it will eventually be removed. There is a difference between the elements and the materials of which bone is made. I understand the material; the bone cells do not and cannot pass through the blood. It is only the fluid which circulates through the artery which goes to make up the bone cells by growth or development. I do not want you should get the idea which is implied in the question, that the blood deposits so much animal and other matter. The blood constantly bears these elements throughout the system. It goes from the heart to the extremities and back again to the heart. In twenty-four hours an immense quantity of blood passes this fractured part, so that it is not necessary the blood should contain fifty per cent. of lime. Its rapid progress would be checked, and even entirely stopped, did it contain any such quantity. I heard the gentleman [Dr. Porter] say that the blood and the bone contain phosphate of lime in about equal proportions. That is clearly impossible.

In a healthy person the amount of provisional callus thrown out depends upon the care with which the points of bone are brought together, the nature of the accident. An oblique fracture would require more than one square across the bone. If comminuted, it would require provisional callus at different points. Surgeons never attempt to estimate this. The plastic exudation takes place from any of the vessels in the human body. The blood is very rich in this fibrin, and what is needed is rapidly supplied. I do not say increased action is necessary to form this. I entirely ignore the idea that inflammatory action is necessary. Inflammation retards all the physiological processes of repair. I say that aconite is a powerful agent in allaying inflammation. It controls the circulation. The heart, the arteries and other blood vessels are all affected by it. It acts upon them to diminish the circulation to the inflamed part. It does not operate like the surgeon's knife, by removing the vital fluid which is so necessary to repair the injury, but it enables us to husband the only source of repair. Nothing is wasted, nothing is lost. With this and similar agents applied, it is unnecessary in any case to take blood. It is always injurious to do so. If that sluggish circulation was attended by a slow, feeble pulse, indicating a want of blood or a feeble circulation, aconite would not be the remedy, unless I found this enfeebled circulation depending upon some distant congestion, as when the brain is overloaded with blood, and when it appears from the injuries, a feeble pulse is the result. There are other remedies which would act upon the impeded circulation and restore it. I think the healthy condition of the blood depends much upon what food we eat. In a sluggish state of the blood and under a low diet, and no inflammation, I would not use aconite, unless the injury was such that inflammation would be likely to ensue ; then I would use aconite.I would put the patient under this remedy to prevent inflammation. A light, healthy diet is necessary. A generous diet is not necessary under all circumstances. It depends upon the time to which you apply the question. If you ask me in reference to an injury just received—a severe compound fracture of the humerus, I must shorten the period of inflammation by a low diet during the early stages.

If, after the inflammatory action had subsided, the soft parts healed, and a healthy action in the injured parts, tending to a repair, I would then give a more generous diet, because there would then be no danger of exciting inflammatory action. The union of bone might be prevented by *starvation*, sir. It might not unite under a diet the next door to starvation. It would not necessarily retard it because the boy complained of being hungry. The bone cells would begin to form about the thirtieth day from the injury. Provisional callus would usually begin to form in ten days, but I did not say that in this case it would. I did not say the inflammatory stage would have passed in that time. Here were complicated injuries of the head, arm and hand; and in that case I could not say the inflammatory period had passed in ten days. I would not have given a generous diet in that period of time. It would have been hazardous to have done so. It would take some eight days for the absorbents to clear away the rubbish in case of simple fracture, and unless there was suppuration the absorbents would do it alone. They are kept at work by the vitality of the system at large, receiving nutrition by the circulation and nerve fibres from the brain. In other words, they depend upon the nutritious and nervous supply. The supply of nutrition is essential; that must be had or the vital powers will give way. It would not necessarily retard the union of bone. There would be a nervous supply though nutrition should be largely diminished. The absorbents might be kept up for eight or ten days upon nervous stimulus alone. The elements of repair come from the stomach and blood. I do not come to the conclusion that it is essential to have a continual supply of nutrition. It is necessary to reduce the accustomed nutrition to maintain an equilibrium. Suppose the usual supply of nutrition to be kept up and the nervous excitement present which the injury would induce—it would terminate in a violent inflammation. The surgeon must adapt his food, in kind and quantity, to the condition of his patient.

Take the laboring man from his active vocation and confine him for some time upon his back, without an injury, giving him his accustomed food, and what is the result? It could be nothing less than disease. The food must be digested. The surgeon presupposes that the injuries of the head, arm and hand, as in this case, will require the patient to be kept quiet. He must not move about and must not be fed like a man in active life. These jurors do not require the same food here that they do on their farms. So the patient must eat less or suffer still more serious consequences. I say that under the allopathic system, if they be intelligent practitioners of that system, they will reduce the diet to the condition of the patient's system. If I should cry for food I should stand in great need of it, I presume. Friction is one of the earliest methods adopted. I said to denude the surface, not to produce inflammation. Fractured ends of the bone may become coated over with cartilage. Friction is partly to remove this and partly to excite the absorbents to take it up and carry it off. The object of puncturing is to give to the fragments points of attachment. When I drill through the bone, instead of inserting ivory pegs, I let nature go on and insert bony pieces. The object is to produce action in the bone, and an increased activity of the parts increases absorption of the portions which are by that means to be removed. There may be a sluggish circulation that needs to be brought up to the natural standard. It is not to excite inflammation, but the production of bone cells. You are begging the question, sir. I speak of fractured bones; you are speaking of the process necessary to remove from the fractured surfaces the unhealthy secretions which prevent union.

You misunderstand me, sir. Your mistake is this: you said the object of drilling was to produce inflammation; I said the object of drilling was to produce activity. I do not seek inflammatory action; that is an incidental accompaniment of what I seek, an active nutrition, an active absorption and repair—the building up of new, healthy material. I do not seek inflammation, but to irritate the bone so as to place it in a condition similar to the first fracture. There is a plug formed in this medullary cavity. It is easily removed. I could not say whether that had been the method adopted. There is no evidence of inside callus, and very little of outside. I could not say there is any positive evidence of provisional callus now. It would, probably, be absorbed now. I do not think the term principally can be attributed to me. (Witness exhibits a beef bone.) If you examine the blood vessels of the spongy portions and compare them with those without, you will perceive there is a much less arterial supply from without than from within. I have stated already, that is called the nutrient foramen. It is not possible, in examining bones of this kind, to say which of these minute canals transmit veins, and which arteries. The bone derives nourishment from other sources than from the nutrient artery, but in much less amount. This artery was cut off in this fracture. Here we approach, in this beef bone, a tuberosity of bone in which the spongy structure of bone comes much nearer to the surface. The minute vessels are seen from within, and these are the minute vessels from the periosteum without. The jury can see the relative calibre of those outside and inside.

Millions are a great many. They are the same as in the shaft of the bone, only a much larger number on the inside. The artery might have been destroyed by the laceration. I said the supply would be diminished. If you cut this off, the supply of nutriment would be much less. I would state that this artery passes along near the bone and near the periosteum, and it branches after it enters the bone; the one supplies the upper, the other the lower part of the shaft. If the bone is fractured as this is, at the point of nutrition, it would cut off all use of the artery to the lower portion of the bone. It would be doubtful whether it would have been introduced afterwards to nourish the bone. It having no

branches without, it could not make new ones through the bone.
I have seen a large number of cases of fracture of the humerus.
I could not call them cases of non-union, though somewhat
delayed. I named a case in which the bone partially united, but
before union was complete, was re-fractured, and although treated
with the same care as at first, the nutrition was so impaired that
the bone itself was absorbed. I saw it at Albany, N. Y. The
non-union had commenced before I saw it. The young man
was about twenty-one years. Saw nothing in his constitution to
have caused it but the destruction of this artery. I think I am
not alone in this. I think Gross and others. (Refers to cases in
Gross and Miller.) There is no constitutional defect, these authors
say. New made provisional callus would be liable to rapid
absorption. Prof. Hamilton's work on the specialty of dislocations and fractures, stands at the head of the list. It has been
published about four years. Hamilton belongs to the Bellevue
Hospital School, New York, Allopathic. This work, which I now
hold in my hand, is the first volume of Smith's Surgery, also Allopathic. Gross is of the Jefferson School, Allopathic. Miller is
of the Allopathic School, University of Edinburgh, Scotland.
These are standard works on Mechanical Surgery. Mechanical
Surgery is the same in all schools—there is no demarcation here,
and cannot be. Their system of surgery is my system; it belongs
to my system as much as to theirs—there is no other to teach.
But so far as treating the patient by medicinal agencies is concerned, the system has been much improved by discoveries made
in Homœopathy. I can stand before this jury and say, in truth,
that the danger from this class of injuries is very much reduced
by the discoveries made by Homœopathists. The treatment has
been much improved through their agency. Surgery, like medicine, will never reach its highest point of success until brought
under the benign influence of Homœopathic medication. And I
predict to-day that the time is not far distant when surgery, like
medicine, must yield the palm of success to Homœopathy. I estimate the number of cases treated by me in this way: At the
battle of Perryville, the casualties in my corps were 2,331. At
Murfreesboro, 2,021. After the battle Gen. Rosecrans ordered
me to take charge of all the hospitals in Murfreesboro, both rebel
and Federal, containing 1,800 rebel wounded, besides some 700 or
800. I think I issued rations to 2,800; making in all, with the
rebel wounded at Perryville, about 8,000. These latter did not

all come under my immediate observation. I said I thought I had examined, and had under my own supervision, about 4,000. It must have been a thousand or fifteen hundred more. I say in that number were fractuers of every bone in the body. I have already stated to the jury, some half a dozen times, that there were no cases which remained in my hands long enough to result in non-union. It would be improper for me to say I had any cases of non-union. Some of these cases were treated Homœopathically —all that I treated myself, and I had one medical man under me, who also used Homœopathic remedies. After all the great battles I was actively engaged, although much of the time was taken up with the more grave injuries or fractures. I decided upon all cases of hazardous operation. I think for fourteen days and nights after the battle of Murfreesboro, I did not take my clothes off day or night. I had entire control of the medical and surgical department of my corps, embracing about 200 Allopathic surgeons, who were subject to my orders. There was one man who out-ranked me, but I had direct authority from Major-General Thomas, to use his name in any order I desired; and to all Brigadiers to carry out the orders so made, I was, therefore, master surgeon, and appointed Surgeon-in-Chief. I am now practicing in Chicago, and am connected with the Homœpathic College in Chicago, where these principles are taught.

Defendant Resumes.—I wish to ask you, Dr., (handing the witness an humerus) to what part of this bone the biceps muscle is attached ?

Answer: It is not attached to that bone at all. One head arises from the margin of the glenoid cavity, on the scapula, and the other from the coranoid process of the scapula. It is inserted into the tubercle on the upper extremity of the radius, one of the bones of the fore-arm, and has no attachment to the humerus.

Question: Dr., will you explain to the jury where the *biceps flexor* is attached ?

Answer: I was ignorant of the existence of any such muscle until yesterday. I am still ignorant. There is no such muscle. I have heard much, however, which is new in regard to the human system since I came here. The brachialis auticus is attached to the shaft of humerus above and to the base of the coranoid process of the ulna, at its lower insertion.

Turner Resumes.—Is it not important to keep all these muscles of the lower portion of the arm quiet ?

Answer: It is. The roller should be applied so as to confine the bellies of the muscles. In the fore-arm you cannot confine them so they cannot move. You may fasten my fingers so I can not shut them, yet the effort, if made, will produce a greater effect at the point of attachment of the muscles above than it would if I were permitted to move the fingers. There should be no splints below the elbow; the patient should be instructed not to use it. If he disobeys, it cannot be prevented by the surgeon. The injury caused would be the patient's.

R. P. Wales, sworn, says : I reside in Lanark, Carroll Co., Illinois. I know the plaintiff and defendant, Dr. Pratt. I first saw the boy on the 20th December, 1862, at John and David Morris's. When I first came there he was on the cot or lounge, his clothes pretty well saturated with blood and a puddle on the floor. There was a wound on the head. The hand was bleeding; on the upper and back part of the head was a wound. I examined it. It was a lacerated wound. It appeared to have been struck on the frozen ground. The skin on the head was torn off some, also, about an inch in diameter, perhaps, and badly bruised. I noticed the thumb had been torn, extending into the palm of the hand and laying some portion of the metacarpal bone, and it was torn in two or three different directions and dislocated downwards, and the bone was fractured obliquely across the metacarpal bone, commencing a little back of the joint and extending nearly back to the next joint. It was dressed that day. The dressing was delayed for some time after the injury, for the reason that the boy was so sensitive he would not let the Dr. touch it until he administered to him some chloroform. John Morris went after it. The wound was drawn together and edges fastened; two or three stitches were taken and tied, and then fastened by adhesive straps. One piece of the bone dropped down, and the Dr. replaced it and secured it by means of adhesive straps. There was one strap put on to hold it up. The dislocated joint and the fracture of the thumb were then properly reduced. It was a question with Dr. Pratt, for some time, how to keep this bone in place ; the muscles on the other side were so badly torn that it was almost impossible to keep it in place. It was, indeed, a question whether it could be done. He finally succeeded by the strap, and by flexible splints extending from the back side of the thumb down to the edge of the wound. The fragments were then put into position and properly secured by a bandage. The arm was still bleeding somewhat profusely. There was a wound on the back of the arm. Dr. Pratt examined it first, and concluded it was made by the bone being pushed through the flesh. I came to the same conclusion. It had that appearance; by drawing the arm sidewise I saw the end of the bone protruded. Dr. Pratt did this to ascertain the precise, condition of the fracture and the injury. It was an oblique fracture. Behind the lower portion of the fragment, and on the upper fragment, the bone was broken directly across it, and making three pieces or fragments. The muscles had the appearance of having been bruised or crushed under the wheel of the wagon, or some body or instrument of great weight. The fracture of the arm was reduced and secured by a dressing or roller, passed from the wrist up to the shoulder, and then there were flexible splints put on like these. There was three of this kind and two other longer ones put between, one on the upper and towards the back side of the arm, and the other on the under side and opposite the upper splint. These splints, made by Morris, extended from the shoulder and arm-pit to the elbow joint. There was a place cut in the roller to dress the wound, and the roller was passed down from the shoulder over these splints to the wrist again, and the bandage secured and the arm placed in a sling. The bones were placed in apposition by Dr. Pratt, by manipulating, and by measurement he ascertained the bones were in place. The arm was of the same length of the other. There were longer splints put on the arm than these, and none as short as these. He was then put upon a sofa. I did not remain until he was moved. I saw him again on Monday or Tuesday, at the residence of his father. Dr. Pratt, Mr. and Mrs. Frisby and myself were present. The arm was undressed far enough to see its condition; it appeared to be doing well. Dr. Pratt thought it not necessary to do anything more to the arm; the thumb was dressed and the wound on the arm and head. There was, at that time, an angular splint on the arm. Dr. Pratt told me he had placed it on to remove the boy and to prevent his getting the arm out of place in moving home. This conversation was had in presence of Mr. Frisby and family, and the boy did not deny it, or say anything to the contrary. There was considerable inflammation in the thumb and back part of the arm. The boy had some fever; the parents stated he had fever the previous night. Dr. Pratt said he would give him aconite. I saw him prepare it, put some eight or ten drops in a half tumbler of water, and gave him two tea-spoonfuls. The head was bathed with arnica, steeped in water, and the arm and thumb were bathed with tincture of calendula or marigold. I have used this remedy and found it useful in preventing suppuration in cases of lacerated wounds. I visited him nearly a week afterwards. Dr. Pratt took off the dressing of the thumb and dressed it with calendula. The thumb had been kept in proper place by the flexible splints. The arm was in its proper position, also. When the shellac splint was taken off, Dr. Pratt remarked that it was a very difficult thing to keep that thumb in place, on account of the ligaments being so badly lacerated, and it would probably be some time before the shellac splint could be removed. Some of the adhesive straps had been loosened by the suppuration, but not sufficient to permit the bone to get out of place. It had to be watched closely. The wound on the head appeared to be doing well. The arm was partly undressed and one of the splints removed; and Dr. Pratt, by feeling carefully, found the bones in place and the inflammation partially subsided. After he had examined it I made an examination of it, and manipulated the arm sufficiently to satisfy myself the bones were in place. The long splint was then replaced and secured by the roller, and the angular splint was then replaced and secured by bands passed through the straps on the splint, and another near the elbow. Dr. Pratt observed, he was surprised to find the arm and the boy in so good a condition. On a former occasion he had doubts whether the arm and thumb might not have to be amputated. He examined it to see if it was uniting; moved it slightly, and found it was uniting. Dr. Pratt thought it not safe to move it much. Some pus had been discharged. He said the boy was better than he expected. He said he thought the boy would not want to eat much; might give some toast or other light food. This was the first directions. At Morris's. At this last time he said the boy could eat any common food in moderate quantities. Something was said by the parents about his having eaten too much, and had brought on some fever, but it had subsided. Dr. Pratt told him not to eat too freely of meat. At the time the bone was set, on making pressure or extension, the wound bled more freely. The roller was placed on the wrist first, and then to the shoulder; the splints were then put on and the roller passed over them twice. The roller was not far from two inches wide, and the edges overlapped as it was rolled along. I saw the boy in from one to two weeks. Dr. Pratt was with me, except once when I visited [the mother. Dr. Pratt and myself carefully examined the arm every time we went to see whether it was uniting, and it was doing well. We also felt provisional callus distinctly at the point of the oblique fracture. On the 20th February he examined the arm and took everything off. Dr. Pratt took hold of the arm and examined it thoroughly, and there was no motion except at the shoulder and elbow. Dr. Pratt told him to raise his hand up to his head, and he did; so Dr. Pratt thought it would do to remove the splints. The mother was present and saw the boy move his arm and raise his hand to his head, and expressed herself satisfied that the bone had united. I suggested to Dr. Pratt, that the boy was very uneasy, and perhaps it would be better to put on the splint to prevent accident; he thought it might be so, and replaced the splints, or some of them, with an angular splint. I saw the boy about three weeks afterwards, and the arm had been refractured. I examined it and saw that the oblique fracture had separated. I could distinctly discover crepitus. This was in March. I was surprised, and enquired of the mother about it. I cannot state whether she said he fell down or hit his arm against the fence. She said he had hit his arm and refractured it; I cannot give the language. The boy did not deny it, or offer any other explanation. I assisted in making extension sufficient to counteract the effects of muscular contraction. There was five splints besides the angular splint. There was some change in the position of the splints. The external wound had healed up. I cannot state when I next saw it. The arm was dressed and placed in proper position. I never saw any blisters on the hand. These splints were made of woolen cloth saturated with shellac; when used, they are placed on a table on a press-board and ironed, heated so as to make them pliable; they are not ironed on the hand. I never discovered the bandages were so tight as to make the arm black and blue; some puffing out of the hand shortly after bandaging, nothing else. I saw the boy last 30th day of May, 1863, at Dr. Pratt's office. There was to have been a consultation there that day. The arm was undone, but the fragments had not united. Some three or four weeks before this Dr. Pratt used friction; I assisted him. It was done by holding the bones and rubbing one against the other. This was about the last of April or first of May.

On the 30th day of May Dr. Pratt mentioned what had been

done, and said he had lost all hopes of effecting anything by friction; that an operation would have to be performed on the arm, and proposed to Mr. Frisby to operate on the arm; said he thought that was the only means which could be adopted to restore it. He explained to Mr. Frisby the different methods which had been used; one was cutting down to the fracture and scraping or sawing off the ends of the bone. Another was by silver wires; ivory pegs were also mentioned. The father asked Dr. Pratt about consulting with Dr. Miller. Dr. Pratt said he would have no objection to any other man, and his only objection to Miller was, that his prejudice against Homœopathy was so great he did not believe he would give an honest opinion. He told him that he thought that an operation would secure a good arm. This was the last of May or first part of June. I cannot state the precise time. I did not examine the splints. Dr. Pratt said he could perform the operation himself, as well as any other surgeon. But if Mr. Frisby wished or prefered it, he would get an experienced surgeon from Chicago, and it should not cost him any more than if performed by a surgeon residing here; or he would go to Chicago, and each should pay his own expenses.

Cross-Examined.—Dr. Pratt is an uncle of my wife. Have been acquainted with him some five or six years; lived in his family some three or four years. Spent part of the time in study and part in practice. I graduated three years ago the first of this month. Commenced reading with Dr. Pratt four years ago, and graduated. I had read some before I attended lectures at the St. Louis Homœopathic Medical College. The course of instruction included Anatomy, Surgery, Surgical Anatomy, Pathology, Physiology and Midwifery. Used Yeoman and Town's Chemistry, &c., principally in that institution. Had studied medicine at my father's. I had practiced some. I had been engaged in practice some six months or more before I graduated. I am at present in partnership with Dr. Pratt, in the practice of medicine. There was medicine given to the boy to prevent inflammation; it was aconite. Aconite grows from the earth as all other plants do. Aconite is a deadly poison. It is made from a plant called Aconitum Napellus, but it is generally known by the name of Aconite. The medicine is prepared by expressing the juice from the plant and root. This juice is mixed with alchohol. Its medical qualities, as used by us, are those controlling the circulation. It has a controlling effect upon the circulation, by its action upon the nervous centres. Its primary effect, when given to persons in health, in large doses, would be depressing. Its secondary effect would be increased sensitiveness of the nervous system and increased circulation. If there is inflammation, with sensitiveness of the nervous system augmented, small doses act specifically upon the inflammation, and allay the nervous irritability. I might use it on saccharum lactus (or sugar of milk), or I might use it in water. It is diluted. The dilution is made by what is called the centesimal scale; ten drops are mixed with ninety-eight drops of alcohol. Medicating by infection was an ancient theory. It is not used now. Years ago, while Homœopathy was in its infancy, this was practiced. It was an ancient theory of some of its advocates. I do not know that it proves Homœopathy to be founded in error. It only shows that some of its advocates made a mistake. Dr. Pratt gave the third attenuation of aconite. The second attenuation is prepared in the same manner as the first, and the third in like manner. He prepared it by putting some eight or ten drops in a half tumbler of water; about a gill, I should think, of water. I forget whether he gave one or two teaspoonfuls, and directed it to be given from half an hour to an hour, according as the fever might be. It would control the circulation; and I think it did do it. Dr. Pratt was surprised to see the boy in as good condition as he was, considering his injury. We did know what effect it would produce on the system. By it, the pulse was reduced to its normal condition, or nearly so. You may shut off the food in disease, and it will not always reduce the circulation. If a man has typhoid fever his circulation is not reduced by fasting. I have not treated any case of fractured humerus. I have had one of the clavicle and fractured ribs, which I treated. I administered the chloroform to the boy, and I examined the fracture myself, and saw Dr. Pratt make an examination. The boy was extremely sensitive when touched or attempted to be touched. The father, John and David Morris were present, and one or two other persons came in afterwards. I think it was on the second or third day, Monday or Tuesday, that I was at his father's, that Dr. Pratt told me he had put on this angular splint to move the boy with; I think this angular splint was on Monday or Tuesday following the injury. It was in the presence of the boy, I am pretty positive; I am positive. I do not think I am mistaken. I did not get there until after Dr. Pratt. The boy was partially undressed; his coat was off. I cannot state positively. The arm may have been undressed; nothing was done to the arm or thumb until after the chloroform had been brought. I cannot state which was dressed first; I think it was the arm. The arm bled profusely. I am positive the arm bled most. Head bled some. I have no recollection as to the time we made examination. I cannot state the time I examined it. Enough to see that the bone was broken into three pieces, that there was an external wound and the bone was broken in an oblique form, and then again across the bone on the upper fragment, and making, as I have said, three pieces of bone. I believe there are cases where bone unites with very little provisional callus. I understand that the surgeon applies his splints to keep the parts in apposition, and that the fractured bone or parts surrounding it, may be kept quiet, and that provisional callus is nature's splint. I believe it has been said that nature is very wise in these matters. I visited this lad during the whole period Dr. Pratt was treating him, at intervals, varying from one to two, and perhaps three weeks. I visited the boy on Monday or Tuesday following the injury. I was there again in about ten days. The first visit I found the boy doing well. Medicine was keeping down inflammation, and the medicine was continued and wounds both dressed, and the arm was in proper position; at the end of a week or ten days from that time the wounds were again dressed as before, and the bones were examined and found in proper position; measured the arm from the coronoid process at the shoulder to the elbow, and found it of proper length and bones in position. I visited the third time between two and three weeks from the first time, and the fractures were again dressed as before. I think the bandages were removed sufficiently every time, or nearly so, to see that the arm was in position, I think I was there some five times in eight or ten weeks. I visited him on the 20th February. I think this was the fifth time. I went there once alone to see Mrs. Frisby. I cannot state when that was. I prescribed for her throat. I had been there five or six times up to the eighth or tenth week. I did nothing for the thumb except to examine it. About the tenth week, I should think, the arm had so far united that he could move it. It was about the 20th February, 1863, I recollect this date from the fact that I remember Dr. Pratt made a passing visit to Seymour Down's on that day. I have a distinct recollection of that fact, and that it was in February. In looking over his accounts one day, I saw that charge was made on the 20th February. In looking over that account, about two months ago, and I remember his making that call. Dr. Pratt did not call my attention to this matter. I know this from recollection, and from other circumstances. I had a patient at Georgetown, and I went to Polo about that time. Mrs. Frisby was present at the time. The boy raised his arm up and the mother saw it. Dr. Pratt placed his hand under his (the boy's) hand to steady it, and the boy raised up his hand above his head, and turned his hand backwards and forwards. Dr. Pratt merely put his hand under the boy's. Dr. Pratt said he did not lift any; merely steadied it. I did not say that after the refracture we moved the bone. I said I assisted in making extension sufficient to keep the muscles from drawing them out of place. I never saw Mr. Yeoman until I saw him here in court. There is always a tendency in the muscles, in case of injury, to contract. All that was needed, was to keep the muscles from getting the fragments out of place. It was after the twentieth of February that this was done, and it was at this time that there was crepitus; it is a distinct grating sound. I distinctly heard that grating sound. It was some eight or ten weeks when we found the bone united; about three weeks after that time it was refractured. Bone will unite in eight or ten weeks; it may unite sooner; it may be longer delayed. A fibrous cartilagnious substance which forms in case of non-union, around the ends of the bone, would destroy crepitus. But it will not form in eight or ten weeks; I give it as my opinion, that it will not. The crepitus would not have been heard if it had. The fragments were put in apposition, and the bandages and splints put on again. I do say, that these are not the same splints, I am positive of that; they were longer and wider. It may be they are the same splints. These splints are not as long as at first, but they are not the same length now. I never made any splints. I saw other splints on, and longer ones. I did not say I visited him at any stated periods. The head may have healed in a week or two; I cannot state. I cannot state when the thumb healed—probably three or four weeks before they all healed. My recollection is, that Dr. Pratt, within ten days or two weeks, directed that the boy might have ordinary food. Dr. Pratt applied friction to the arm three or four weeks before going to Milledgeville. I do not know whether the attention of the family was called to it specially or not. Mr. Frisby was there in the room. I do not know of any thing being said to Mr.

Frisby. It did not appear to hurt him much. At that time I held one bone and Dr. Pratt rubbed the other against it.

Mrs. Hannah Belding, sworn, says: I have no acquaintance with Mrs. Frisby, except I was introduced to her by Dr. Pratt's wife, when the consultation was held at our house. It was the first of May, 1863. I think Dr. Pratt and wife, Dr. Freas, this boy, Frank, Dr. Belding and myself were present. The boy's father came in just after the boy and his mother. I think I was not in the room when the arm was undone. When I came in they were washing the arm. I don't think I noticed any splint except that outside one. I was looking at the arm, and I asked Dr. Pratt how it came that the boy was in that condition, when but a few weeks ago I was at your house, and you were talking of taking off the splints. He raised up this splint and said, " This shows how it was done. The boy was playing ball, and in kicking the ball, he fell against, or hit the fence, and refractured his arm;" and he says to Frank, " That was the way it was done, was it not? If that is not the way, state how it was done." Frank said that was the way it was done. I then spoke to his mother, and said it must have hurt him very much. His mother answered that he didn't complain, but she thought it hurt him more than he was willing to acknowledge, as he went up stairs and seemed to be quite uneasy about it.

Cross-Examined.—They were all present when I asked that question, Dr. Pratt, Dr. Freas and Dr. Belding, Mr. and Mrs. Frisby and Mrs. Pratt. I asked how it happened that this arm was in this condition. He said the boy was playing ball, and went to kick at the ball and hit his arm against the fence. He then appealed to the boy, if that was not so, and the boy said it was. I said to Dr. Pratt, "Did you not state to me that you intended to take off the splints soon ?" I cannot state how long it was before this time, that I had the conversation with Dr. Pratt; it may have been three, four or five weeks; I cannot tell how long it was. Dr. Pratt is a son-in-law by marriage. I am a second wife, married in 1858.

Mahlon Brown, sworn, says: I reside in Rock Creek township, Carroll County, Illinois. I never saw Frank Frisby before his arm was broken. I saw him when he passed with his team; his brother was driving the other team, and trying to run by Frank. I did not see Frank until some two months after it happened. They had got out of sight when it happened, and I did not go down where he was.

Dr. James C. Burbank, sworn. I reside at Polo, Ogle County. I have resided there about eight years ; am a physician and surgeon. Graduated at Philadelphia, in 1856, at the Homœopathic Medical College of Pennsylvania, located at Philadelphia. I saw this boy on one occasion. I cannot state the time precisely ; last of Dec., 1862, after the arm was fractured, at his father's house. His father, and mother and another lady, his mother's sister, and Dr. Pratt and myself were present. I saw the left arm of this boy and examined it; the arm was partly undressed. Dr. Pratt requested me to examine it. Took off some of the splints ; all, I believe, except the narrow ones. I measured the arm carefully, and found it was all right, that it corresponded in length with the other arm. I thought we had not better remove the inner ones. There was something outside, but I cannot state that it was this angular splint. There were two longer splints, and long enough to reach from the shoulder and from the arm-pit to the elbow joint. I examined the thumb ; it was in a very bad condition, much lacerated, and the bone was badly fractured, commencing just behind the joint. The bone was fractured in an oblique direction, nearly back to the next joint. The thumb was out of place as soon as we removed the dressing ; the injury was so great that it was almost impossible to keep it in place. Dr. Pratt dressed it and put it in place. He fitted a splint of gum shellac, and put the thumb in proper place. He cut it so as to have it come down as far as he could, on account of the wound. That splint is a proper one. I think it was as good a splint as could be used for that kind of injury.

Cross-Examined—I graduated at the Homœopathic College, at Philadelphia. There are several other authors on surgery now. When I graduated, we used Druit's Surgery as a text book. I do not know whether that is a foreign author or not. We have better works at present, and I have not consulted it lately. I do not remember of having but one case of the humerus. It was at Polo, a boy of twelve years of age ; it was just above the condyles. It terminated favorably. I think it was the first or second day after Christmas. (Was shown the splints.) I cannot say whether these splints were on the arm or not. I presume they were. I do not know whether there was some of these splints broke. I examined the hand after taking the dressing off. He

put the bones in place. I am not certain that the shellac splint
was cloth. It may be felt; it is a good splint. I helped him put
it in place. He cut the splint out of the piece he had. They have
to be heated pretty hot. It might be hot enough to blister. I
should avoid blistering it if I could. The hand was badly lacerated at that time, and much inflamed on the inside. It would not
be good practice to put it on hot enough to blister much, but it
must be hot enough to put in place.

William Brown, sworn, says : I reside at Rock Creek, in this
county. I do not recollect the name of the boy. I saw him
there on the day the arm was broken. When opposite my
house the horses started to run. I did not see them afterwards.

David Morris, sworn, says : I reside in Rock Creek township,
Carroll county. I have seen this boy, Frank Frisby. I saw him
a few minutes after the accident occurred. My brother went out
to him first, and was fetching him to the house. He looked as
though he was hurt pretty badly. I told him I thought his arm
was broke ; he thought not. He was taken to my brother's, John
Morris. It was torn through the inside of the hand, as near as I
can recollect. Dr. Pratt got there in half an hour. He did not
say anything which I remember. I was present when this arm
was dressed. It was Dec., 1862. I cannot tell the day of the
month. I made two splints of pine out of a shingle. I saw them
put on the arm near the wound, and the other on the inside opposite to the first; there were other splints like these. As near as
I can recollect the splints I made, reached from the elbow to the
shoulder. The arm bled considerably ; it ran on the floor when
we put on the bandage. I do not remember which way he put
on the bandage. I should think he was moved the next day
about ten o'clock. Dr. Pratt was there ; I do not know whether
he examined the arm or not. Mr. Downs and wife were there
and went away with him. His arm was in a sling, and a pillow
placed under it. I saw the boy some time afterwards. It was
after the consultation at Milledgeville. I think I asked him how
he was getting along. I told him I heard he had broken his arm
over again. He said that he fell against a post. That was all
the conversation we had. He said Dr. Miller was going to set it
over again when it was cool weather.

Cross-Examined—Dr. Pratt came there about half an hour

after the accident, but did not set the arm until evening, some hour and a half after the injury. Did up the thumb first. The boy had some pain at times. I do not know whether the thumb was done up before the chloroform came or not. Do not remember what Dr. Pratt did while my brother was after chloroform, except to take the clothing off. Couldn't say what Wales was doing before the chloroform came. Dr. Wales applied the chloroform to the nose. I did not shave all the splints that were put on. I shaved out two shingle splints, the others came from Dr. Pratt's. The shingle splints; I should think, were about one and a half inches in width; might have been narrower, might have been wider.

John Morris, sworn, says : I reside in Rock Creek township. I know Frank Frisby. At the time he had his arm broken I was eating supper. I heard the horses run by and started immediately to go down where the boys were. It was about thirty rods from the house ; before I got there his brother, older, was holding him up, and told me his brother was killed, and wanted I should go and get the Dr., which I did. But before I returned, I went, at Dr. Pratt's request, and got Dr. Wales to assist. I was present when the fractures were dressed. I think the thumb was dressed first. The arm bled considerably. It bled enough to wet the bandages, and then it bled considerably on the blankets were he lay. I saw them while making splints and getting ready to commence operations. These other splints were made out of a shingle, one on the inside and the other on the outside, extending from the elbow nearly to the shoulder. I remember there being other splints. I should judge these were not the same. I did not examine them particularly.

Cross-Examined—I went after chloroform and for Dr. Wales. The bones were not set until I got back.

Dr. Lemuel C. Belding, affirmed, says : I reside in the dense settlement of Milledgeville, in Carroll county, Illinois. I am a physician by profession. I have some acquaintance with Dr. Pratt. I don't know that he is any relation of mine ; he married my daughter, I believe. I have seen this boy, Frank Frisby, once before this term of court. I saw him at my residence in May, 1863. Dr. Pratt, Dr. Freas, myself and family, a woman, said to be his mother, and his father, were there. There was nobody else that I know of. I was invited by Dr. Pratt. I should not have officiated if I had not been invited. I looked to see if there was any provisional callus. We found the arm bandaged and in proper position. But supposing Dr. Pratt to be a graduate, and Dr. Freas also, I do not know but I made my conclusions as much from their examination as my own. I thought I found provisional callus. Dr. Freas said there was, and Dr. Pratt said there was. I got it fixed in my mind, from manipulating the arm, that there was provisional callus. It was a little above the present fracture where the transverse fracture was. The arm was very much in the same condition in appearance then as it is now, except I do not think it was so much elongated. I think the points of fracture were much nearer together than now. (I wish to make an explanation.) It is a long time since I studied surgery, and the first study makes its impress on the mind not easily obliterated; recent things or events do not produce the impression on the mind which past ones do. The old man does not retain these as he does the events of early life. And when Dr. Pratt spoke about using rivets, it seemed to me so absurd. To me it was a funny thing, to pin bones together and think they would unite, and I did not think how it would sound, and I said, "Drive in a couple of shingle nails; they will answer just as well." And derogatory as it was to my professional character, when Mr. Frisby swore to' what I said, I remembered it, and did not wish to have it said that the man lied. For I did say it, but it was a joke brought out by Dr. Pratt's mentioning the ivory pegs. I have practiced Allopathy twenty-five years, and since that I have found something; better and being a progressive man, I have taken hold of Homœopathy, and with my whole soul and strength, am trying to do what I can by way of medicine to save suffering humanity, and let the boys fix up the bones, which is now done so differently from what it used to be. I never studied modern surgery. It was proposed by Dr. Pratt, and assented to by Dr. Freas, that friction should be resorted to. It looked like a very strange proceeding to me. I did not know anything about it, and I thought it would be of no use, and was opposed to it. I was for placing the fragments in juxtaposition, and let nature perform her perfect work, and cure up the arm. I did not advise friction. I had my reasons for it. I have seen bones in that condition before now, and I have known them unite. There was something said about the re-breaking,

8

and it was not denied by the boy. Dr. Pratt said that the bones had been united so strongly that the arm could be moved and lifted by the boy; that it had been tried, and found united. The father and mother and boy were all present, and no one contradicted that statement, or said that it was not so. But I did hear some words confirming it. The mother said it did not hurt so much as she should have thought it would, and the boy said it did not hurt him a great deal. I think the mother said she thought it hurt him more than he was willing to own, that he went up stairs and appeared uneasy. I heard nothing at that time opposing these statements. The splint that was on the outside looked like this, and was split in two places. It seems to me it was not split quite so far as it is now. I do not believe it was. I recollect Dr. Freas making the remark, that it must unavoidably have broken the bone. I do not remember all that was said. My wife was passing in and out, and she had some conversation with the mother about it. This was the substance of what was said about this matter. I saw the arm undone on that occasion; this yellow splint was on the outside, or one like it. There were other splints. I do not know whether these small ones were there or not. There were longer ones, too. I think there were enough to cover the arm, and long enough to extend from the elbow to the shoulder. I do not know about these short ones. I remember there were longer ones than these. I have a very clear recollection of that.

Cross-Examined.—I recollect it was one year ago next May that Dr. Pratt and Dr. Freas and myself held a consultation at my house, over this boy's arm. This old brain gets confused somewhat, and I don't want to say much about my speaking or thinking powers; my friends are better judges than I am. I am somewhat absent-minded; I might recollect your name to-day and forget it to-morrow, and remember it again in half an hour.

Question: How old are you, Dr?

Answer: I don't know when I was born; I was there, I expect, but I do not recollect it. I have the records written by my mother, I guess, which says I was seventy-three years old the 14th day of last August, and my mother said I was born a few minutes past one o'clock in the morning. Whether I shall live to see seventy-four, I know not. I remember she told me I was born in a thunder storm, and got thunder-shocked. Some things I do not remember as well as I did in my youth. I did not expect to have to bring these facts before this jury to-day (not at that time). At that time I was thinking of what could be done to relieve this poor boy from the terrible *calamity* or *misfortune*. I think, sir, what I do give is right, and what I cannot give I will not utter. I think he did say his arm did not hurt him much, or a great deal, when he fell against the fence post.

I now say that the mother did say, that it did not appear to hurt him as much as she should suppose it would, but she thought it hurt worse than he let her know of, as he went up stairs and seemed uneasy. He remained about an hour, I guess. I had over some nonsense of mine about the shingle nails, and I did not want that witness to be accused of lying, because what I said jocosely would injure my professional reputation. I do believe, as I said, that man has an internal memory, in which is stored up all he does, whether good or bad, and under certain favorable cir cumstances, these acts stored in the internal memory, may become reproduced in the external memory, clear and distinct as at first. But I think these facts which I have stated, or a great portion, if not all, have remained in the external memory, and have not passed away. I remember the *terrific* appearance of that boy's arm It is in the external memory, and it will always remain there, per- haps. I can say that we were there met together, as a board, for consultation over the arm of this boy. I suppose, sir, there were no other persons present but Dr. Pratt and wife, and the other persons I have mentioned.

Question: What was said about the right hand?

Answer: I don't know as I heard anything said about it. I don't think I said at that time, I would rather have the arm in its then condition, than the thumb on that right hand; I have not said so, I think. But I have not thought so. If I did say so, I would not be as likely to remember it as I would the remark about the shingle nails. If I had thought the thumb was as bad as the arm, I would have pitied him much more. It is a sad pity for a young lad to get such an injury. I don't think, now, the thumb is very bad.

Isaac II. Hodgeson, sworn says : Isaac H. Hodgeson is my name. I reside in Rock Creek township; have lived there, off and on, for five years. I know Dr. Pratt, and have seen Frank Frisby since this case came up. Saw him at, Dr. Pratt's last of March or first of April, A. D. 1863

Dr. Pratt was not there. Mrs. Pratt, Mr. Frisby, Frank and myself were there. Mrs. Pratt, in the presence of the father and boy, said something about the boy's having re-broken his arm. Mr. Frisby came there with the expectation of meeting the Drs.; they were going to have a consultation, I believe. Dr. Pratt was not present, and the other Drs. were not there, either. Mr. Frisby said it was seed time and he must go home,—that Dr. Pratt agreed to meet him there, and he thought the Dr. ought to have been there. Mrs. Pratt thought the arm would have been well by that time if the boy had not broken it over again. Frisby said he knew that the arm had been broken again, but it seemed to him, it ought to have been well by that time. Mrs. Pratt told him he ought not to have let the boy use his arm, nor play ball out doors. He replied, he would play, he could not prevent it. Mrs. Pratt told him he should not have let the boy attempt to put on his boot, he should have known it would hurt his arm. Frisby said the pulling on his boot did not hurt him as bad as he did playing ball—it was there he broke it over. This was the last of March or first of April, 1863. I was   Dr. Pratt's when Dr. Wales was there. I did not hear anything about the rebreaking the arm, that I remember, but it was about an operation.

Mr. Frisby said he did not feel satisfied about the way the arm was getting along, and they talked about having an operation on the arm. The Dr. said he would do it himself, or he would go to Chicago and have it done. But Mr. Frisby must pay his and the boy's expenses, and Dr. Pratt would pay his own. Dr. Pratt said he would get as good a surgeon as there was in Chicago, and it should cost him no more than it would if done by a surgeon here; that it should be done as reasonably as any man would do it. Frisby said he had not got the means just then, and they concluded to postpone it one week. No day was set, but he was to let the Dr. know the next week. There was something said about having Drs. about here to assist him, or to give counsel. Frisby asked him if he would not have Dr. Miller to assist him. Dr. Pratt replied, he thought Miller would not do justice to the case, he was so prejudiced against Homœopathy; but he would have no objection against any other Allopathic surgeon.

Cross-Examined. I was present on two occasions at Dr. Pratt's, once when he was absent and once when he was present. I heard what Mr. Frisby said. I was living at D. W. Dame's at the time, and was sick. Went to Dr. Pratt's to get some medicine several times; was well enough to get around, and happened there both times the boy was there. The first time was the last of March or first of April. I was present when Dr. Wales was there. I used to go there frequently. I used to go to meetings at the school house near Dr. Pratt's. I heard Dr. Belding preach there. I don't remember the text or anything in particular that he said. But I do remember we used to meet at Dr. Pratt's to sing. We sung some popular songs, sir—as Old Hundred, Lansingburg and others. Do you wish any more? (*Counsel*—Yes, sir.) Well, we sung Dundee a nd "*Why this Look of Sadness.*" George Copp, Henry Worcester and myself sung, sir. Sometimes one requested to sing a particular piece, and sometimes another. Good many things said which I do not remember. Dr. Belding advocated Swedenborgianism, and wanted sinners to repent. I cannot state what he said. When there is anything of importance said I can generally remember it sometime afterwards. I was not very much interested, consequently I do not remember what he preached about. He spoke on different subjects.

Question: Did you go up on the cars Saturday evening, towards Lanark, and can you tell me what you or any one else said to you on the cars?

Answer: I did. Mr. Brown and myself talked about different subjects. We talked about wrestling, sir.

Turner.—Well, you can go now.

Hodgeson.—You might have said so before, sir, I think.

TESTIMONY OF PROF. LUDLAM.

Direct Examination.—My name is Reuben Ludlam. I have resided in Chicago for nearly thirteen years. Am a physician and surgeon, a graduate of the University of Pennsylvania, located in Philadelphia. This is the oldest Medical College in this country, and has no such appellation as Homœopathic. I graduated at the close of the session of 1851 and '52, and began to practice my profession immediately.

[Dr. L. examines the arm and thumb of the boy, Frank Frisby.] There has been an oblique fracture of the metacarpal bone of the right thumb, and perhaps, also, a dislocation of the thumb itself. Such a dislocation is not to be discovered at the present time, the joint being undoubtedly in its proper place. I find a cicatrix in the web of the thumb, which prevents a free motion thereof. This cicatrix is of such a nature as to denote a lacerated or torn wound. A laceration involving this web and the lateral ligaments, as well as the muscles of the ball of the thumb, would interfere with the cure of the fracture and the dislocation.

The left arm presents a case of non-union between two extremities of a fractured humerus, and not a false joint. In a false joint, as I understand it, one bone or extremity is necessarily fixed, while the other plays upon, or in it. If this upper fragment were stationary, and a species of ligament had been improvised, so that the lower one played in or upon it, that would make it a false joint. In false joint, both fragments are held near together. These are widely removed. I find evidence of non-union, but fail to detect any provisional callus. There is a cicatrix on the outer side of the arm, which indicates the original fracture of the humerus may have been a *compound* one. It seems to have communicated with the seat of the fracture. Such a wound may be caused by the fragments protruding through the flesh, or by some external means. In either case a fracture, with an external wound reaching in depth to the bone, is of the compound variety.

In case of *comminuted* fracture, there would necessarily have been three or more fragments. Compound fractures are invariably regarded as more difficult to treat, and more dangerous in their results than simple fractures.

The original wounds upon the head and in the palm of the right hand constituted this a *complicated* fracture also. Such wounds would retard or delay the cure of the fracture proper, and the more complicated, the more time would be required to repair the injury.

If, in the outset, this were a compound comminuted complicated fracture, it might require from six to twelve, or sixteen weeks, in order that union should take place. I cannot be more specific, for a considerable margin should be allowed in such a case. There are many contingencies in the way of a complete cure. In case of a young lad like this one, it might be very difficult, if not impossible, to harness him into the necessary rest and quiet. Unrest would retard the cure. In a fracture of the compound variety, and unless measures are taken to prevent it, inflammation is a certain consequence. In order to its prevention, we must equalize the circulation. For the accomplishment of this object, the great agent in our hands is aconite. With our school of medical practitioners it supersedes the lancet and other antiphlogistics. I speak, from experience, of their relative value, upon which point there can indeed be no adverse opinion.

It would be as absurd always to measure the effects of doses by their size, as to measure the capacity of a physician by his size. In regulating the dose of aconite, as of all other remedies, it is necessary to take into account the condition, susceptibility, and all the peculiarities of the patient. Under the hypothesis that this boy had just suffered a compound comminuted complicated fracture of the humerus, I would have taken the third dilution of aconite, put ten or twelve drops in half a glass of water, and ordered him to take two teaspoonfuls every hour, *in anticipation of the inflammatory process.*

The blood is furnished to all of the bodily tissues through small capillaries, which vessels are supplied by delicate filaments from the spinal and ganglionic systems of nerves. By means of what is called " reflex action," these nerves supply a motor, or moving force to the muscular coats of the vessels, which, by stimulating their contraction, serves to carry on the circulation of the blood through them. Now, aconite, more than any other known agent, holds a specific relation to these nerve filaments, and thus is capable of regulating the circulation of the blood in these little capillary vessels. Its first effect is to stimulate contraction, and consequently an increased rapidity of flow in the current; its second result is to promote relaxation, and thus to retard the flow ; while in the third it may arrest the current and produce what physicians call a *stasis*, or complete stoppage thereof. Aconite benumbs these nerve-filaments, and thus influences the local sensation, circulation and nutrition of a part. My views are based upon personal observation of its effects in the treatment of diseased conditions, and also upon what has taken place under my own eye in field of the microscope.

In case of compound comminuted complicated fracture of the humerus, the surgeon might reasonably wait, for union of the fragments, for the space of two to six months before operating for non-union. In some cases such means should never be resorted to. The proper course would be to keep the limb quiet and wait for re-union. Excepting constitutional means, the first treatment of such a fracture would not differ materially from that which is proper for a simple fracture. Inflammation is not a necessary condition of the reparative process in bone any more than in the healing of wounds of the soft parts. This view of the question I am willing to defend.

I would use two long splints, especially in compound fracture of the humerus. An opening should be left in the dressings, to permit the discharge of pus and other matters, otherwise their retention might serve to poison the wound and, possibly, the general system. The arm should be bound with a roller before the application of the splints, and the whole injury being properly dressed and cared for in the outset, the patient should be visited as often as once in one, two or three weeks, according to circumstances. Too much meddling with the seat of fracture might do harm, as doctors sometimes do mischief by seeing their patients too frequently.

In case of a re-fracture of the humerus, after having once united under the adverse circumstances already specified, the chances for complete re-union would be very much lessened. Indeed, I should not expect a prompt repair of the injury as a result of the very best treatment. The cure would be slow, if it took place at all. Craigie, I think, says that the chances of complete re-union in a compound comminuted fracture are very slight. Perfect union in such a case would be regarded as the exception to the rule ; and the greater the complication, the fewer the chances of union in such cases.

Pus is always to be taken as an evidence of inflammation, and is never found excepting as a result of the inflammatory process.

In such a case as this appears to have been, I would have prescribed a mild vegetable diet for the first eight or ten days, at least. I certainly should have denied the boy both fat and lean meats. Circumstances should govern as to the length of time in which this diet should be employed. If necessary, I might continue it for a month or two. The diet I am speaking of might be composed of farinaceous articles, such as farina, rice, toast and crackers, or might include mealy potatoes, corn starch, etc. If the wound discharged profusely and for a long time, the excess of flow might constitute a drain upon the system against which I should fortify by means of a more liberal diet.

It is difficult to determine the exact proportion of phosphate of lime in the blood. The earthy salts are found in about eight per centum, or eighty parts in one hundred of blood. In bone there are said to be fifty-one parts of phosphate of lime, and eleven parts of carbonate of lime in one hundred. The blood does not make

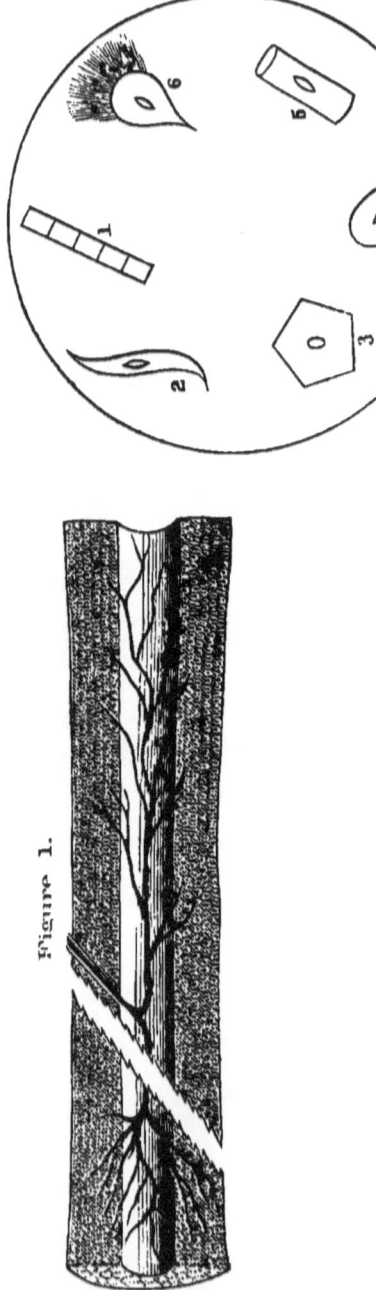

Figure 1.

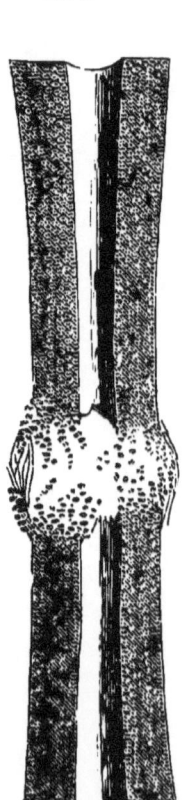

Figure 2.

Figure 3.

EXPLANATION:

Figure 1. Fracture of Shaft of bone, and of the Nutritious Artery.

Figure 2. Cell Development in process of Repair.

Figure 3. Cell-Types of Principal Tissues.

   1. Striped Muscular Fiber.

   2. Non-Striped Muscular Fiber.

   3. Squamous Epithelium.

   4. Osseous Cell.

   5. Cylindrical Epithelium.

   6. Cilitated Epithelium.

bone, but *bone is made of blood.* With your permission I will explain to the jury.

Here is a diagram which I have drawn, in order that I may be understood.

(See Fig. 3.)

All the tissues in the body are made of cells. These cells have each their own proper form and size and function, or duty assigned them. The history of the nerve-cell is the history of the nerve; of a muscle-cell, the history of a muscle; of a bone-cell, the history of the bone. Tissues are composed of cells, as communities are composed of individuals. What concerns one concerns all; the history of one is the history of all. I have labeled each of these type-cells in the diagram, in order that you may know where they belong.

Now these cells are the agents or architects, which, out of the blood that is brought to them by the small capillaries, build up and repair all the tissues, just as the carpenter and mason are the agents or builders of timber and brick and mortar into a dwelling or edifice. The muscle-cell, out of the blood, constructs a muscle-cell having the same form and properties with itself. The bone-cell develops bone; the cartilage-cell, cartilage, and so on. In health, each reproduces its own kind. The law of types is as marked in tissues as it is in species among animals.

What is true of the healthy development and growth of the tissues is equally true of their repair after injuries. Life itself is chiefly manifested in this double process of waste and repair. Again and again the textures are broken down and built up. Repair is a healthy physiological function, although it may be accompanied by the diseased or morbid consequences of injury to the solids, or bad quality of the blood from which they are all to be nourished.

There is nothing in our bodies which is fixed and unchangeable. The blood itself is made chiefly from substances taken in at the mouth. The chyle is not the blood, neither is blood tissue. The elements of the blood may and do exist, in chief part, in the chyle, but, in all animals that have red blood, the chyle is one thing and the blood another. So with the tissues and their relation to the blood. These are composed of, or made from elements which pre-exist in the blood, but the blood is not muscle or bone, or nerve, or ligament, any more than the chyle is blood. The chyle is made of food which has been digested and is ready to be absorbed. It is poured into the circulation by means of the lacteal system. Another portion of the blood-making product finds its way into that fluid through what is called the portal system, or, in plain English, by way of the liver.

The bone-cells and the blood are, therefore, chiefly concerned in the repair of injuries to the osseous textures. The first of these are the *agents*, the latter supplies a *condition* of reparation. This diagram will give you an idea of the manner in which the blood is furnished to bones.

(See Fig. 1.)

The fibrous membrane around the bone, constituting its outer envelop, is the periosteum. The inner membrane is of similar texture and function, and lines the medullary canal in the long bones,—that canal which contains the marrow. Flat bones do not have any well defined medullary canals. The external membrane, the periosteum, is supplied with innumerable small vessels carrying arterial blood, which are twigs set down from the capillaries of the soft textures overlying the bone. The inner periosteum derives its nourishment chiefly from a nutrient artery which penetrates the shaft of the bone at its nutrient foramen, and, running down to the medullary canal, passes along its course. When this artery has passed through the compact tissue of the bone, and reached the medullary cavity, it divides, as you see represented in the diagram, into two branches, each of which travels towards its respective extremity of the bone. This artery supplies the internal periosteum with blood, and from it the long bones derive a very considerable share of their nourishment. There may be one or more of these arteries running along together through the marrow.

In case of oblique fracture of the lower third of the humerus, with rupture of this nutrient artery, as shown in the drawing, you will readily perceive that re-union would be retarded, if indeed it took place at all. When the artery is fractured in this manner, nature plugs up its open extremity with fibrin ; but you will readily see that the nutrition of this inferior extremity of the bone could not go on through its internal periosteum, until its circulation was restored. In such case, the means or elements of repair must be furnished to the osseous cells by the little twigs from the periosteum. As these latter could not enlarge or multiply very considerably, since they pass into little holes in the bone, and cannot,

therefore, dilate, neither be pierced by new vessels from the outside, a compensatory circulation through the outer envelop would be
impossible. The flat bones may be nourished exclusively through
their external periosteum, but as a rule, the long bones cannot.
It is a property of cells, wherever we find them, to multiply
themselves by segmentation, or division. This process takes
place in the reparation of bone. For some days after the fracture
the time is occupied in removing the *debris*. At about the eighth
or ninth day the provisional callus is thrown out. This callus or
sheath, thrown around the seat of the fracture, the extremities
being placed in apposition and kept there, is formed chiefly by
the exudation of plasma from the periosteum and other neighboring tissues that have been wounded. Its hardness, as well as the
readiness of its absorption, will depend upon the amount of bony
or earthy matter deposited within it. This drawing illus-
trates the site of the provisional callus, and the organization of
the plasma into a fibrous structure in which are interspersed a
few osseous or bony cells.

(See Fig. 2.)

In October 1841, more than twenty years ago, M. Flourens presented to the French Academy of Sciences a paper upon the Repair
of Bones after Fractures, in which he said : "The so-called provisional callus is a fact altogether apart from the proper formation of bone ; it results from the rupture of the vessels of the
periosteum and the surrounding parts."

Inflammation is a diseased and not a healthy or physiological
process, and is therefore not essential to the production of bony
or other tissue. Union of bone may take place, as in case of the
flat bones, the neck of the thigh bone, and the olecranon and
coracoid processes of the ulna, when fractured, *without the formation of provisional callus*. In case of transverse fractures of
the long bones directly across their shaft, providing the extremities are kept in direct apposition, there may be no provisional
callus thrown out. Fractures, like wounds, may sometimes heal
by what is called the "first intention," that is, without inflammation or suppuration.

The bone-cells do not receive the earthy matters as though they
were dumped into them by the blood. The blood is not to be
regarded as a peddle distributing his wares. The cells select from
this common reservoir what they need. They are real agents,
bona fide organs, as may be seen in the field of the microscope.

I have made this study a kind of specialty, having had the honor of holding the chair of Physiology and Pathology in the *Hahnemann Medical College*, Chicago, during the past four years.

There is no fixed and positive period for the complete re-union of broken bones. Within the space of four months, in an extreme case, I might be able to determine whether the fragments would or would not unite.

I would not resort to friction or other means to induce re-union, other than the dressings and rest aforesaid, within four to six months after the fracture. The best evidence of non-union would consist in the mobility of the fragments without crepitus, which condition would indicate that the ends of the bone were rounded off, become smooth or ivory-like, or their surfaces covered with a fibro-cartilaginous envelop.

In case of a re-fracture, after ten weeks had elapsed, from six weeks to three months might be required before it would unite again. In case of non-union after a second fracture, we should at least wait as long as that before resorting to surgical or operative means for its cure. Friction should first be tried, after which it would be best to wait from four to six weeks. If this means is successful, it may unite in three to four weeks, or thereabouts.

Among the means for the cure of non-united fractures there is one which has not been mentioned by former medical witnesses. This is an old expedient which consisted in enclosing the limb in a cast of Plaster of Paris, and permitting it to remain quiet, in order that Nature may have the best possible chance to re-unite the fractured bone. When I had resorted to friction, I would treat as in case of an original fracture. Resection, in my opinion, promises the best results. This operation is more frequently performed than either Brainard's or that of Dieffenbach. Either of these operations would occasion an increased afflux or determination of blood to the parts, and thus, by stimulating their cell activities, minister to the production of definitive callus.

There is no question but this lad's arm might be cured by re-section, although the chances of complete recovery are somewhat lessened by the delay already experienced.

It would be impossible for any physician or surgeon, by an examination of this arm, at this remote period, one and a half years after the accident, to decide as to the nature of the original fracture, or what was the method of treatment, or the degree of skill practiced in the outset.

The humerus, when fractured, is more liable to non-union than is any other of the long bones; and in case of fracture into or across this nutritient artery, the danger of such a sequel would be very greatly increased.

For the reproduction of bone, merely, I would regard vegetable food as relatively more nutritious and appropriate than animal food. Taking all the tissues into account, this would not hold true. The vegetable cell is the laboratory in which the earthy matters are elaborated for the use of animals. It prepares the earthy salts in the grass and grain which the animal eats, and which ultimately find their way into our own blood. Vegetables live upon the earth, and animals upon vegetables. We do not eat these substances directly, but indirectly. This is the plain Saxon of it.

This boy might have been treated with the best possible skill, and yet be found in the condition in which he now is. As I understand it, when a surgeon consents to take professional charge of a fractured or dislocated limb, he by no means guarantees a good recovery independent of contingencies. The amount of force required to re-fracture a broken humerus might be very slight. I have known a preacher to fracture his arm by moderate gesticulation, and a boy to fracture his leg by a mis-step upon the carpet. A fall against the fence, or a blow against a post when kicking a ball, might be sufficient to produce a re-fracture of the arm.

These splints would answer to dress that arm with. A year and a half ago, in so young a subject, they might have been quite long enough. Before the invention of Day's elbow splint, cures of a fractured humerus, and with just such splints as these, were by no means uncommon.

In dressing a fractured arm, the bandage should begin at the wrist and extend upwards, and so compress the belly of the muscles of the fore-arm as to render the hand and fingers immovable, or nearly so. If the arm were bandaged too tightly, the first effect thereof would be manifest in the soft parts. Sloughing and ulceration of the skin and adjacent tissues would ensue before the circulation and nutrition of the bone could be impaired. Any discoloration of the surface which could be readily removed by friction, could not possibly do harm. A slight ecchymosis, or discoloration of the skin, is a frequent and almost an invariable result in case the proper and appropriate bandaging and dressing are applied. The more compound and oblique the fracture, the greater the necessity for a snug and secure application of the dressings.

Cross-Examination.—I graduated in the Medical Department of the University of Pennsylvania, in which school Homœopathy has never, to my knowledge, been taught. A change in my medical sentiments is the result of a promise to investigate the subject experimentally. I entered upon the practice of medicine as I had been taught it, immediately after graduation. Have formerly occupied the chair of Clinical Medicine, in addition to that of Physiology and Pathology, in the *Hahnemann Medical College*.

My interest in this trial is not founded upon a fear lest a verdict against the defendant should injure Homœopathy. Truth is not especially influenced by such local causes. My physiological and pathological investigations were made before the commencement of this trial; indeed, I may say, long before the fracture itself occurred. My diagrams are roughly drawn, but they represent the idea which I wish to convey to the jury. My desire is to be plain and specific, in order that the jury may comprehend my meaning. Surgery, as taught and practiced in the Homœopathic school of medicine, is the same as in other schools, with the single exception of the medical means which are sometimes used as adjuvants to the mechanical treatment.

My prejudices in this case are not strong. I am, and have always been an advocate of the largest liberality and toleration in medical, as in political or religious preferences. My interest and confidence in the success and triumph of Homœopathy is based upon the belief that it is a form of truth. I have been much interested in this trial since its commencement, in hearing the medical and other testimony. I have felt as one would in rummaging through an old garret or museum which he had not visited in a long time. Besides, I have learned some new things in anatomy and physiology, as for example, we have been told of a new muscle on the arm (McPherson's muscle), of the termination of the osseous capillaries within the bone cells, etc., etc.

The text books upon surgery, in use in the Hahnemann Medical College are the works of Gross, Smith, Hamilton and Helmuth, or Hill and Hunt. Miller is and has long been a standard author upon surgery. Norris is certainly regarded as a very good authority, and I am happy to have heard him lecture, during at least two winters, in the Pennsylvania Hospital. His edition of Liston was published some twenty-two years ago. It would now be regarded as belonging to the old style.

The manner of dressing a fracture of the humerus would be to apply a bandage from the hand or wrist to the elbow, and perhaps also to the shoulder, before adjusting the splints ; then bring the roller down over the splints in order to secure them firmly. This is the method which I learned from the teaching of Prof. Gibson in the University of Pennsylvania. It was also practiced by Dr. Norris when I was a student in the Pennsylvania Hospital. I am not positive if Hamilton, Miller and others insist that, in all cases of fractured humerus, the bandage must first begin at the fingers and not at the wrist. The object of this bandage is, so to secure the muscles of the fore-arm as to prevent motion. As far as possible, this object is attained by binding securely the belly of these muscles at the middle of the fore-arm. Authors have their own peculiar views about this matter of bandaging the hand and fingers.

The muscles of the fore-arm are chiefly attached, at their upper extremity, to the external and internal condyles of the humerus. Any considerable motion of the fingers and hand would necessarily involve motion of the inferior fragment, in case of fracture of the lower third of the humerus.

Aconite controls and regulates the capillary circulation by means of its action upon the nerve filaments of these little vessels. It appears to be the only known agent that, in any very marked degree, acts thus. I have already described what are [called its primary and secondary effects. Belladonna operates by first unpressing the nerve centre and afterward the part to which those nerves are distributed. Aconite is the analogue of the first or congestive stage of the inflammatory process. In order that it shall be Homœopathic it is only necessary that it be capable of producing a like set of symptoms with those which it is expected to remove. The question is one, not of *identity*, but of *similarity* of action. In collapse of cholera I have given larger doses than those already specified. Here it would be better to employ the strong tincture, diluted with water and given every half hour.

Digitalis acts upon the heart, controlling its movements and modifying the pulse through its specific effect upon what is called the " cardiac plexus"—a knot of nervous matter belonging to the ganglionic system. It never can be properly used as a substitute for aconite. Both these remedies control the pulse, but in a very different manner.

Prior to the time in which Hahnemann lived, and excepting only by a few eccentric physicians, aconite was not used as a febrifuge. It is only a few years since the distribution of nervous filaments upon the smaller blood-vessels has been demonstrated. The dose and strength of preparation of aconite should be regulated to suit different cases and conditions of the system. It might be indicated in congestion of the brain, of the liver, or of any other organ or tissue. Starvation itself might be accompanied by a frequent pulse.

Vegetable food contains relatively more of the earthy salts than animal food. Milk is the only exception to this rule. The milk of young mothers is especially rich in matters which are designed for the growth of the child's skeleton. The bone is made of blood constituents, but the blood alone cannot create bone. The cell is the agent in the manufacture of bone, as it is of every other tissue, animal and vegetable. The elements of the tissues, as of the various secretions, pre-exist in the blood, and yet neither the tissues nor the secretions are to be found in that fluid. The saliva does not exist in the blood, yet no one will doubt that all of its elements are derived by a particular set of glands from the blood. A condition of the secretion or manufacture of sugar by the liver is an active flow of blood to that organ. The elements of this liver-sugar are found in the blood of the portal vein before it reaches the liver, but the sugar itself is manufactured by the cells of which that largest of all the glands is really an aggregation. The elements of a bone may be found in the blood, but those elements can only be constructed into true osseous tissue by the direct agency of the bone-cell itself.

An active circulation is a most important condition of the growth and repair of tissue. It is also a condition of a healthy performance of the glandular functions. The gastric juice, which is the solvent for the food, is secreted most actively when the mucous membrane has become reddened by an increased flow of blood, to the organ; an injected condition of its capillaries. The same is true of every gland in the body. Increased flow of blood toward, and in them implies increased glandular activity. There is this difference, however, between an *injection* and a *congestion* of a tissue. One is a healthy, the other a diseased process. The former passes away as soon as the secretion has been thrown out by the glandular cells of the organ; the latter is not so speedily renewed. The former passes away without troublesome sequela, while the latter does not. In the repair of injuries to any tissue, a mere temporary injection of its capillaries may supply the necessary condition for the reparative process to be carried on by the cells of the part. A congestion thereof could do no more, and might possibly do harm by establishing a diseased condition where a healthy one would have been equally satisfactory and salutary. This distinction is therefore a practical one.

When organized into tissue, the elements are changed in character. Thus, the farmer is aware that bone-earth, which has once been an element in the animal skeleton, is richer in nutritious material for the soil than the phosphate of lime which is obtained from the laboratory. The fibrin of the blood and the fibrin of muscle are quite different in character. Organization works specific changes in these elements, so that they are not the same within the animal organism as we find them in the inorganic universe.

Cross-Examined.—Carniverous animals, like the dog and lion, have no need of a vegetable diet to supply them with earthy matters. They get their supply of these saline principles by eating bones and cartilages with their food,—both kinds of nutriment at once, and in the most available form. I never feed my patients upon bones, for the simple reason that I can safely trust to the proper cells the work of elaborating the elements which the osseous structures need. A tub-full of blood could not, of itself, create a man. We must have a type-cell in bony tissue, just as in the grain of wheat or corn, the acorn and the full-grown tree. The blood contains the elements from which all the tissues are formed. The plant finds its blood in the soil. The rootlets of the man are the lacteals in his intestinal tract. In both cases the nutritious elements are held in solution in water, while the solids are developed from them by, and in conformity with a specific type-force.

Inflammation is not necessary to produce union in a fractured bone. Pus is not formed, save as a result of inflammation. In case of non-union of a broken bone, I would stimulate or covet an increased activity of the local circulation of the part as a condition of re-union. Provisional callus is usually, and sometimes speedily absorbed. The absorbents, technically the organi co-

7

molecular absorbents, take it up again, and it is finally thrown out by the skin or kidneys as excrementitious matter. The hardness and permanency of the provisional callus depends upon its ossification. Provisional callus is not formed to the same extent in flat as in the long bones.

I am not at present in active surgical practice, it not being the custom in cities for all of our physicians to practice surgery. We usually refer our surgical business to a competent person who makes a specialty of surgery. I have not assumed that there has been any especial or general reform in this branch of medicine since my graduation, neither to be an authority for myself in surgical matters. My remarks have been chiefly confined to the subject of physiology, or healthy action, and of pathology, or diseased action, as bearing upon the question of the growth and reproduction of bone and of other animal tissue. In my own practice, I have never had a case of non-union of the humerus after fracture.

Resection of the extremities of a fractured bone, which has failed of union, in my opinion, promises a better result than either of the various operations proposed. Different authorities differ upon this subject. Authors have their peculiar preferences. · In case of non-union in a transverse fracture, Dieffenbach's method might succeed better than any other.

In case the nutrient artery is broken across at the point of fracture, I do not see any means by which a collateral circulation into the medullary canal of the separated extremity could be carried on, unless its branches should anastomose through the definitive callus while it is being formed. The office of the internal periosteum is certainly very analogous to that of the external one. The veins in the long bones are very numerous, and find their exit through small foramina, or holes, about the heads of the bones.

A complete cure in case of fracture depends very much upon constitutional conditions and other contingencies. I would not be too anxious if union were delayed, nor resort to friction until after waiting a long time,—say from four to six months. In young, or in very aged persons more especially, bones are refractured by the most trivial causes. After such an accident the cure would progress more slowly. The careful examination or manipulation of a bone by a surgeon, while it is knitting together, and the repair progressing, would not necessarily be injurious, while if the limb were handled as roughly as just indicated by gestures of the counsel, harm would be very likely to result.

From a careful examination of this boy's arm, I am not able to say whether there hsa ever been any provisional callus formed since the original fracture occurred.

And the defendant here closed his testimony, and the Plaintiff further to maintain the said issue on his part, then and there gave in evidence, the following testimony, to wit :

Charles Frisby, sworn, says : I have heard the testimony of this man, Mr. Hodgeson. I could not say that I had ever seen the man before. I never said anything about the boy's putting on his boots. I am positive, sir, that I never said anything about it.

I never knew, or suspected that the arm was broken, only at the time they stated it had been loosened a little. I said to Mrs. Pratt, about the boy's playing on that occasion. There was nothing said by me about the boy's not hurting the arm so much in pulling on his boot. I don't see how he could do it with both hands tied. I know he never did to my knowledge. I deny ever telling Mrs. Pratt anything of the kind.

Mrs. Frisby recalled.—(Here shown the splints). These splints have not been shortened since. Dr. Pratt brought a splint of the length of this longer one. My husband took his knife and cut it off by Dr. Pratt's orders, and these are the splints that were on the first time the arm was dressed, and one short one which got broke. The pine splints were about as long as the longest splint here before me. The two short ones and the long one were on together. I was present at every visit Dr. Pratt made. Dr. Pratt didn't reset that arm any time I was not present. Dr. Pratt did not tell Dr. Wales he had set the arm over. Dr. Wales was not at my house only three times with Dr. Pratt, besides he came once without Dr. Pratt. Dr. Wales did not examine or manipulate that arm in my presence. I was present when Mr. Yeoman and my mother extended the arm. Dr. Pratt did not say, the first time he came after the boy was brought home, in presence of Dr. Wales, that he had put on this brace to keep the boy's arm in place while riding home.

Mrs. Moscript recalled.—I was present at the time those splints were taken off, about two weeks after I went there, and they have not been shortened since. They are the same splints Dr. Miller and Dr. McPherson took off his arm on the 6th day of June, 1863. They have not been shortened since, sir.

Dr. Freas recalled.— Question: I ask you if at the time of the consultation at Dr. Belding's, whether you stated to Dr. Belding, as your opinion, that the arm had been once united and refractured?

Answer: I did not state that, sir.

Question: Sir, if on that occasion you heard the remark from Dr. Pratt, that the arm had been united once and refractured?

Answer: Dr. Pratt remarked that the arm had been broken, but did not state that it had been united and rebroken; my attention was not called to a former union. I believe Mrs. Frisby was present *during* that time. I did not, to my recollection, hear the conversation between her and Mrs. Belding. I might, and I might not have heard the conversation between her and Mrs. Belding. I was busily engaged in tending to the fracture, and not to what the ladies had to say. Mrs. Belding might have been there, and I not have noticed her. Dr. Belding paid particular attention to the arm, as we were manipulating it considerably. If anything had been said about the arm being broken over at that time, I could not tell what Mrs. Frisby said, if she said anything.

(*The argument of Counsels are inserted at the end of the volume.*)

Which was all the evidence offered and introduced by either of said parties, upon the trial of said cause. Whereupon the said plaintiff then and there moved the said court, upon the evidence aforesaid, to instruct the jury as follows, to wit:

PLAINTIFF'S INSTRUCTIONS.

1st. If the jury believe, from the evidence, that Dr. Pratt, the defendant, held himself out in the neighborhood, as a physician and surgeon, competent to dress and attend upon the plaintiff's wound in question, and that as such physician and surgeon, he undertook, for fee or reward, to properly set and arrange the plaintiff's said bones, and that he failed to use ordinary skill and diligence in setting, arranging, and putting in proper position, said bone, whereby the plaintiff's arm and hand were never cured, the jury must find the defendant guilty.

2nd. A physician or surgeon, as well as a mechanic, is liable to respond in damages for the ill consequences resulting from want of due skill in the management of a case, or the treatment of a patient, which he has undertaken to manage or treat, for fee or reward, or the hope of fee or reward.

3rd. False in one thing, false in everything, is a maxim of the law, and means that if the jury are satisfied, from the evidence, that any witness in the case has testified wilfully false in any material point, the jury are at liberty to disregard the entire testimony of that witness.

4th. If the jury believe, from the evidence, that the defendant did not use due skill and diligence, as a physician and surgeon, in the treatment of the plaintiff's wounds in question, as alleged in the declaration of this case, and having undertaken so to do, while professing to possess the requisite skill for that purpose, and that as a consequence the plaintiff's wounds were not cured, they must find the defendant guilty, and in that case, the jury may assess the damages in any amount not exceeding ten thousand dollars ($10,000).

5th. In case the jury find the defendant guilty, they are at liberty to assess the damages of the plaintiff at any amount not exceeding ten thousand dollars.

6th. The court instructs the jury, that when a person undertakes to perform the duties of a physician and surgeon, the law will hold him responsible for the consequences of a want of due ordinary skill, even if there is no express pretense of sufficient skill as physician and surgeon.

7th. The court instructs the jury, that the mere discharge of the defendant from the treatment of plaintiff's arm, before all the means known to surgery had been by him employed, to bring about a union of the broken bones, is no bar to the recovery on the part of plaintiff; if the jury believe, from the evidence, that previous to such discharge, the defendant had failed to use due medical and surgical skill and care in the said treatment, that is ordinary skill and care as a surgeon.

8th. If the jury find that during the time the defendant treated the plaintiff, he did not treat him properly, and with ordinary skill and care, then the plaintiff had a right to discharge the defendant, and recover in this action his damages for the injuries he sustained for the want of ordinary skill and care on the part of the defendant in treating the plaintiff, as laid in the declaration.

And the said defendant then and there moved the court, upon the evidence aforesaid, to instruct the jury that,

I. If you believe, from the evidence, that without any agreement as to compensation, the defendant was employed, and that, as a surgeon, undertook the treatment of fractures, dislocations and wounds under which the plaintiff was suffering, then the following relations arose between the plaintiff and defendant:

1st. That the defendant should be paid a reasonable compensation for the services rendered, if bestowed with ordinary care and skill.

2nd. That the defendant should, with ordinary skill and care, treat the plaintiff's injuries, and if necessary, resort to all the modes of treatment, and in the order recognized as proper and generally or usually employed by gentlemen of the surgical pro- fession ; and to such treatment the plaintiff was bound to submit, and himself do no act that would materially interfere with such treatment.

3rd. If, then, from the evidence you further believe that the defendant did treat the plaintiff in the manner just above stated— that is, with ordinary skill as a surgeon, and that the *plaintiff*, or his *father*, would not allow the defendant to go any farther in attempting to cure the plaintiff, and that all the well recognized modes had not been resorted to, and that at the time it was still possible, by further and different treatment, (but well recognized as proper) to have cured the plaintiff, then this action cannot be maintained, and your verdict must be for the defendant.

II. If you believe, from the evidence, that the *non-cure* or non-union of the plaintiff's left arm was, in some considerable degree, caused by the fault of the plaintiff in not keeping out of danger, or in other words, by refracturing his arm, or loosening the parts by a fall,—in consequence of kicking at a ball, or in some other way,—after union had once fully, or to a considerable degree taken place, then this action cannot be maintained so far as the arm is concerned, and as to so much, your verdict must be for the defendant; even if he was also guilty of some previous failure to use ordinary skill, care and judgment in treating the plaintiff. The law will not permit a person to maintain an action for an injury of which he was himself the cause, or to which he, in some considerable degree contributed. If you are satisfied, from the evidence, that there are different modes of treating such injuries as the plaintiff was laboring under when the defendant commenced to treat him, all of which are approved by good surgery, then the defendant had a right to select and pursue any one of these remedies, including the diet of the plaintiff; and if you also believe that the defendant did so, and *therein* and *thereabout* exercised ordinary skill, care and judgment, this action cannot be *maintained*, although you should also believe, from the evidence, that the plaintiff was wholly incurable when the treatment of the defendant closed ; and accordingly your verdict should be for the defendant.

III. The *gravamen* of the charge in this case is, that the plaintiff has not been cured of a fracture of his left arm, above the elbow, and of a displacement of the joint of his right thumb, *but that* he has been greatly *delayed* therein by the defendant's never properly setting and arranging the broken bone of that arm, and by not properly setting, arranging and restoring to proper position the displaced joint of the right thumb. No *other* lack or *want* of skill, care or diligence, either as to splints, bandaging or anything else, is complained of, or alleged in the declaration, and none other can be considered by you. Unless, then, the evidence establishes the fact, that the plaintiff's left arm was *never* properly set or arranged, or that the displaced joint of the right thumb was *never* properly set, arranged or restored to its proper position by the defendant, *no right* of recovery has been made out ; and your verdict must be for the defendant.

IV. If you believe, from the evidence, that on the third day of February, 1863, the defendant discovered some displacement of the bone of the plaintiff's arm, and that it was proper to reduce the bone to its natural position, and that defendant did so replace the bone, then instead of this act of the defendant being wrong or actionable, it was commendable and right, and for that act this action cannot be maintained.

V. In this case, as to the thumb of the plaintiff, if you believe from the evidence, that sometime after it was first injured, the defendant wished to adjust it and put it in its natural position, and that he could have done so, but was prevented, or not allowed to do so by the plaintiff or his father, then, as to the thumb, this action cannot be maintained, unless the defendant, up to that time, had failed to properly set, arrange and put in its place the dislocated thumb joint of the said plaintiff, with an ordinary degree of surgical skill and care.

The fact that the plaintiff was not cured of his injuries, is not sufficient to maintain this action, but it must be established by the evidence, that he was incurable at the time the defendant ceased to treat him, and that he was rendered thus incurable by the failure of the defendant to use, with ordinary skill and care, the means which, by the surgical art, were proper and necessary to effect a cure. If the plaintiff was curable at the time the treatment of the defendant ceased, and he was willing (and you so believe from the evidence) to go on, and try to effect a cure; and that he was not permitted to do so, but was prevented by the plaintiff or by his father, then this action cannot be maintained, and your verdict must be for the defendant, unless the evidence shows that the defendant had, up to such a time, failed to arrange, set and put in their proper place the said broken and dislocated bones of the said plaintiff, with the ordinary skill and care of a surgeon.

VI. When a surgeon undertakes to cure a person of a wound, fracture or dislocation, he does not become a guarantor or insurer that a cure shall be effected; nor does he undertake that in case of cure, or in a curable case, that such cures shall be effected within any particular time. He simply undertakes to treat the case with ordinary skill, care and diligence, and, if necessary, to resort to all the modes of treatment recognized as necessary or proper, and employed generally or usually by good surgeons. If he does this, although he does not exercise or use the *highest* skill possessed by some in the surgical art, *he is not* liable in law to answer in damages for not curing the patient. In such a case the patient must submit to the consequences of *non-cure*, however serious, without right of action against the surgeon.

VII. If you believe, from the evidence, that the cause of the plaintiff's not being cured of the fracture of his left arm, was a re-fracture of, or loosening of the parts after union had once fully or to some considerable degree taken place, or that such injury or re-fracture was occasioned by a fall of the plaintiff, or by the hitting of the arm against a fence post, or anything else, without the consent or fault of the defendant, then this action cannot be maintained, as to the arm; and as to so much, your verdict must be for the defendant.

And upon the evidence *and instructions* aforesaid, said cause was submitted to the jury, who returned a verdict for the plaintiff, of which mention is within made.

Whereupon the counsel for the defendant filed the following motion for a new trial, to wit.

The defendant, by Lyman E. D. Wolf, his counsel, appears, and moves a new trial in this case, for the following reasons, to wit :

First—The verdict of the jury in this case is plainly against the instructions given to them by the court.

Secondly—It is clearly against the evidence given in this case.

Thirdly—It is directly against the law governing the case.

But the court overruled the said motion and gave judgment upon the said verdict of the said jury, against the said defendant, to which said verdict of the said jury against said defendant, and to the said ruling of said court, upon said motion, the said defendant then and there excepted, and inasmuch as the matters aforesaid do not appear of record, the counsel for the defendant presents this bill of exceptions, and prays that the same may be signed and sealed by the court, and made part of the record in said cause, and it is done accordingly.

(SEAL)   W. H. HEATON, *Judge.*

ARGUMENTS OF COUNSEL.

GENTLEMEN OF THE JURY :—We have got along to this point, that it devolves upon me to open this case to the jury, and in doing so I do not intend, and do not suppose it to be necessary to go over this long detail of testimony, and occupy your time with it. It will not be proper for me to do so. You have sat here with a great deal of patience, every one of you, and I have noticed you have paid particular attention to this case, showing that you appreciate its importance. So, going outside of this matter, as we thought it to be right, you have been selected here as jurors. I know most all of you, and it is not flattering you when I tell you that I believe that you are honest and candid men. And you have no prejudices in this case one way or the other, and you have stated that you did not know anything of Dr. Pratt. You had no feeling one way or the other about these *pathys and isms.* We come here presenting this case before you. A poor boy has had his arm badly treated. You have seen it, and I think the proper word was used when Dr. Belding said it had a very *"terrific" look.* We claim it was for want of skill in Dr. Pratt, for he had it, and has failed to exercise it. If he had skill he did not exercise it. He professes surgical skill, and expects to make his living from the community by rendering assistance when called upon. If he had it in his power to exercise skill he did not do so, and the present condition of the boy's arm is the con-sequence. We have charged here a large amount of damages. It is hard to tell what disadvantages this boy may have to over-come if he goes out into the world maimed—if he lives to the age of forty or fifty years. It is not proper that we should come up here, lawyers and doctors, firing and cross-firing about Allopathy and Homœopathy, Hydropathy, or any other pathy, and get up a fuss, and this boy goes out of here without a fair trial. If this should enter into the minds of this jury it is not doing the boy justice. The boy does not care anything about these pathy's. We have the facts that when Dr. Pratt was called there he was called as a physician and surgeon, and they supposed, one that under-stood his business. The father did not care anything about his being Allopathy, or Homœopathy or any other pathy, but asked Dr. Pratt if he was capable to take charge of the case. Dr. Pratt says "I can do it," and went on from the father's orders to treat the case. We have nothing to do with this doctrine of Homœopathy or Allopathy, but are trying the case of this boy. I do not find fault with other men for practicing any system because I do not have faith in that particular system. I must have faith to accompany pills, but I have not got it, so the pills would do me no good. If they have faith that it acts all right, it makes no difference about that. I asked them not to let any of this pathy kind enter into the case. It is not right that it should. We do not have any feeling on that subject. I do not know why it was that Judge Knowlton, when he opened this case, said to the jury, that this man wanted to send for [Dr. Miller] and that he was a brother of the counsel, and that I, as an attorney, had taken up this case because my brother was an Allopathist. The idea was, that he connected it with bringing this suit on account of Dr. Pratt's being a Homœopathist. I do not know why it was important to mention here that I was a brother of Dr. Miller, and that I had a feeling between these two systems of medicine. Gentlemen, I want you and all the people to understand that so far as there is any personal feeling, I have just as good feelings towards Dr. Pratt, as a man, as any other man, and he knows it. If he had come to us with his case to be tried, we would have done it with much pleasure. We hold ourselves out here as attorneys. When a man comes to us to have a suit attended to, if we think it can be sustained, we bring that suit. If my friend, Dr. Pratt, had applied to us we would have done the same. I would not neglect that boy's rights because I have good feelings towards Dr. Pratt, nor because Dr. Miller is my brother. I have no such feeling. When I have any doctoring done it is upon the other principle. I say this much for myself. My friend Smith is a Homœopathist and employs a physician of that school. I do not know how it is with friend Turner. It makes no difference. I would not have said anything about this if Judge Knowlton had not mentioned it. I will leave this to you. I do not care how these lawyers, or Judge Knowlton, or witnesses feel about this matter. This has nothing to do with it. I claim here that they brought this boy and showed him to you. They have shown that the boy was entirely healthy, of about fourteen years of age, his mother and father appear to be healthy. If there has been any hereditary disease in the family they have failed to show it. He shows to you a healthy boy, full of vigor, who, by an accident, has had his arm broken, and Dr. Pratt has failed to make it a good arm. If you have heard all these celebrated doctors from Chicago have said, every one of you are entitled to a diploma from the Hahnemann Medical College. That gentleman [Dr. Ludlam] has been a farmer, and has now the credit of holding a high position, and has shown to you that he is a very extraordinary man. I claim to have only common sense, just like you. You claim to know something. Some of you are mechanics. Some of you may have children who have had limbs broken, and you know when broken bones are put together they unite, except in extraordinary cases. If a person is healthy there is no reason why they should not unite. I never heard of any such thing as we have upon that point here, as to whether there was anything in the constitution of the person to prevent the union of this bone. The witnesses detailed how it was broke, that there was a small wound. It does not make any difference whether something made it by going down to the bone, or whether it was made by the bone running out. It was reduced, and went to work and healed up, going to show that everything was right. If so, they all agree that it would have knit and worked right. And when they go to work to show how it was done, they show that *they have got wise above what is written.* They have not got anything of the kind. They have theories and speculations. They agree and disagree. My Chicago friend said that which I understand to be true, that any old woman knows, that too tight bandaging would destroy the soft parts of a limb, before it would effect the repair of bone. It only proves this fact, that doctors disagree, when you get them spun up in this mighty science. Dr. Ludlam says, "I wish you to understand that the bony matter is *not* carried to the part by the blood and dumped down where it is needed. It comes down." *How* does it come *down?* It is a speculation, and you and I have as much right to speculate as he has. I take the privilege to do it, anyhow. We have a right to believe that things are so or not so. It is a free country. And when they tell us they know these little vessels do not dump this matter, they don't know. It is a system of nature. Man is an enigma. You cannot understand anything about man. You cannot tell how it is done, and they can just as well tell how this repairing of bone and muscle is effected as well as they can tell how grass grows. The good book tells us this, and man has never found out how it was done. Now here, Dr. Porter says ossific matter is deposited by the blood. Now, if Dr. Porter was from Chicago, it would add a great deal to the force of what he says. Here I must be allowed to assume a little. I am proud that we have got a man settled among us here who can tell us something new. Dr. Beebe, the seven years' wonder, says he came from a college a graduate of seven years. He goes on to tell all. I will tell you as it comes along; you will get my ideas, anyway. Now, they went out on the presumption that these gentlemen in the country don't know anything. We have the two Dr. McAffees, Dr. Belding and another doctor, and Dr. Kennedy, all are in court. They did not want their opinions. We went upon the principle that these men out here knew as much as any of them. We have called Dr. McPherson and Dr. Miller, Dr. Porter and all these other doctors, and we have called some from another adjoining town, Drs. Buckley and Hantz. Can you tell where this honor comes from? They came from where these men did, and how did they get ahead? They learned it from the same books. They are not old enough to-day. My friend (Dr. Ludlam), he had naught to do with this matter. It is not a specialty with him. He has not had any cases. Dr. Beebe has treated only one case. He was called to see another where there was a stump left, the balance had become absorbed; and one case he treated came out all right. Dr. Haller has treated one case of this kind, and that turned out favorably. Dr. Miller said he had a number of cases, and they turned out favorably. Dr. Miller has been in a situation to have more cases and perform more operations than the others, and he has witnessed but two cases which resulted unfavorably. He was near the mines, where the breaking of bones was very frequent. He has treated several cases of this kind, and none of them turned out unfavorably. We judge from this, that if bones are only put together properly, that nature will go on and make that thing right. Nature has a system of its own, and it struck me as being in accordance with the operations of nature when Dr. Porter says, if you take an artery that becomes enlarged. [My friend the judge knows more about that than many others.] He spoke of its being very large where it swells out. What is to be done there? Tie the artery above the swelling, and nature goes to work and makes a way around. The doctor said it had been done recently, and the limb below that point dwindled away.

Nature goes to work and throws out all this and carries on the circulation. *First*, Dr. Beebe goes on and tells you; and he made it as clear as mud to me, and no doubt to you. I know something, too. We thought so before Chicago enlightened us, and we know it yet. Dr. Beebe went to work and tells about throwing out pegs. The pegs reached out from that side and this side, and met together. The other gentleman—I don't recollect his name—[Dr. Ludlam], he has fixed up here that it is thrown out in this way by cells; that these cells run out in this kind of shape, as you see on his diagram. We don't know how, and I don't know that it makes any difference to us. When we come to inquire how it is done, we are lost in the fog. We don't know anything about it. They have made it as clear as mud to me, and I don't think you got any light from it at all. I was troubled somewhat about this provisional callus and did not know what they were driving at. They all agree that this provisional callus was thrown off around the bone. Why? We take it that as soon as there has been fracture of the bone, nature goes to work to do the work right. We find it is all right when we have examined it. They all agree that this provisional callus is a sort of a band around it, as a hoop around a barrel, *as they conclude to hold it there*, but we don't know whether that was it or not. We may judge that in science, which they say is improving all the time, that this provisional callus may be something else, or it might make some other use of it.

No doctor ever knew what was going on under that bone. We have no information that *that* went to work at that time. We have to speculate and judge about that. At any rate there is a band thrown around there—that is, a provisional callus, as they call it. There was a good deal of difficulty about whether the callus went away or not. Why does he want us to state that? I thought, after a while, that their theory was, that it was a compound comminuted fracture. They wanted to establish that there was three bones broken, and therefore it was harder to form a union. Afterwards they only established the fact that there was one bone broken. They must get rid of this matter by absorption. It might be there was a little bone broken off above this, and there united. Wales may tell the truth about it, but you cannot see any remains of the provisional callus. The doctors on our side say that there is now no provisional callus. There has been but two others examined with reference to provisional callus, and

they are the two learned professors. They introduced here Dr.
Belding and Dr. Wales, who graduated at St. Louis, and they
did not ask his opinion. They did not care anything about it.
Dr. Burbank was introduced, and his opinion was not asked for.
But Dr. Porter (and as to his science and intelligence in books
and practice, I leave with you,) and Dr. Miller, they all agree
here, has had considerable practice. Dr. Freas, Dr. Buckley,
Dr. McPherson and others have been examined in reference to
this same question. They have been asked their opinions, and
they all agree on this point. We have the opinion of those other
two gentlemen, and they do not materially disagree. None of
these men tell you, who have examined it, why this bone did not
unite. There is only one proposition that they tell about, and
that is, these bones were not properly put together. These men
have had practice, and have the same books, and have grown up
upon the same milk, if I may be allowed the expression, that the
professors have fed upon. These gentlemen do not know the
reason that these bones do not unite. Can you tell me, from any
thing that these gentlemen told you, that there is any constitutional derangement. What says these gentlemen? They started
off here, on the high horse, on a perfect trot. We have heard a
great deal about cohabitation. That is pretty good. [Laughter.]
I called it cohabitation. They had to explain it to you. It was
putting together two things and making them fit. But when I
heard Wales I thought he was trying to make everything fit.
[Here told to go slow.] I don't care how my speech may read
in print, I cannot go slow. I claim here, as I started out, to be
a common sense man, nothing more. When they tell you these
things in technical terms, there is nothing so dangerous after all.
It means putting the bones together. When we come down to
the common sense of the thing we know it. They call a plant
by names which would break any common man's jaw. When it
means nothing but cabbage, then we understand it. We always
transverse arrangements, in making these figures. I don't know
that there is any testimony that this bone was broken that way.
They call it breaking straight across. They can put them
together just as well. But I was astonished, of course. I am astonished at everything, and every other man would be. When the
judge discovered a little hole in the bone, there was something
there wrong. Dr. Beebe found out something about that little
thing there. Before this he says, the doctor, and I understand

it perfectly. The doctor says this is the nutritient foramen. I always get it wrong. It is a little hole here, any way. It is no matter about the name, because it is said that the "rose will smell as sweet by any other name." There is a number of little holes here, and these little blood-vessels go in there. The proof of these doctors is, that the vessel goes in there and is broke short off, and that is going to delay this. The doctor says : "Well, now, that is not giving nature sufficient credit, because in every wound there is power in nature to go to work and repair it." Would it not be the same on that bone, if brought together ? Bring these bones together and here comes this little vein to nourish the bone, and all these veins that lie down below there are arteries. I would like to know, myself, the judge's idea of things. There is a canal or artery. It is an opening through which blood flows any way. There is two kinds of blood ; one is that which goes from the heart ; it is passed through the lungs, and is laden with chyle, what we eat ; and it comes from that, that all these things are made up, and afterwards being unburdened of these things, it goes back to the heart. It is all called blood ; one arterial, the other venous blood. Dr. Porter gave us an illustration that has not been controverted at all. Nature clears off the rubbish, as he says, and goes to work and repairs it. Then, why not put *this* together, and let nature do its work ? If she could not operate to carry this blood with the arteries, as this was intended to do, how does it get its sustenance. They showed you here a beef bone, with these veins, and this is a little branch that runs off. It is the little artery that runs down the arm here, as a vein. Here are more. There is a little thin membrane, and it is ramified by millions of veins that fill up with blood. The blood goes in and the most of it went up them. He has got it, not so extensively. Nature always goes to work and does things right. But they do not say so. Well, now, we would ask, for we asked them the question : Is not this sufficient to furnish this bone with nutriment ? and they say it will not do it. This surgery is measured by success. A man is a horse doctor, and goes to work to fix up a horse's leg, and does it up right ; he is successful, and he gets practice. If a boy gets his arm broke, call a physician ; he wants to put these bones together. It does not make any difference how the work is done. If there was a fracture above that acute small piece of bone broken off, and it went to work a knitting, why should not the other ? If the cut on the

head, this compound comminuted complicated fracture had made
any difference, I understand that this cut on the hand and on
the head complicate it. Did not they feel it, that is the common
sense of the thing? They went to work and done the thing up
all right. It healed. Is it not reasonable? It proved that the health
and constitution of that boy is all right. If it is not, why do we
not find some difficulty with the head and hand. It went to work
and in ordinary time, all healed up. Oh but, say, the nature
was attending to that. She had to let something else go. So
they are putting nature to fault again. I claim that, if this thing
was going on here, and nature, as they undersand it, had to
expend a great deal of her help to this wound and hand, they
ought to make more blood. They ought to have given him something more to eat which makes blood. With the aconite in their
hands, that wonderful remedy, could not they have done anything? Has inflammation anything to do with it? With such
a thing as aconite, having two times the success with it as other
doctors had with their lancet and other means. They wouldn't
let him eat a bit of food. It was to reduce the circulation, therefore they kept him from food. Why do that, with that wonderful agent, aconite? That would do it up so nice, and supersedes the
the lancet and everything else. The most wonderful thing ever
heard of. They had to adopt this old way of practice for inflammation. Was there a necessity of starving him down? I should
think, according to the testimony of those two physicians, that
Dr. Pratt should be held to a more strict accountabilitiy, because
he had this wonderful agent, aconite, and by putting a half tea-
spoonful into the Mississippi, and taking out two, they put it
down to the thousandth part of nothing, and by giving two teaspoonfuls, they go to work and make it all right. If this aconite
would perform such wonderful cures, they would have had no
difficulty with this inflammation. That could not have been the
cause of it. Why do they say this complication had anything to
do with it? This one piece of bone seemed to have cut off, and
shut off this nutrient foramen. When they admit the fact that
blood makes the bone, why was it necessary to put him upon this
diet? They would not give him food, although he cried for it.
With their wonderful aconite in their hands to prevent this inflammation, yet they would not give him any food. Because they
said this application would not do the work, under these circumstances it would not heal at all. And nature commenced her

8

work and went on with it. I do not think there is a Dr. here who spoke of a case of this kind. All of them agree that if they ever had a case of that kind, they have proved successful. They say, if there was anything to hinder it, or to retard it, it would stop its growth. There is nothing of the kind here. Now, what was the testimony here, as to the manner in which this arm was done up? This boy's arm was broken; Dr. Wales says the arm was fixed up first. I think you will come to the conclusion that the hand should have been fixed up first, I know enough for that myself,—for the reason that they all agree that it is necessary to wrap the whole hand here, and to keep it quiet. You know that we must keep the hand and the muscles here all quiet, in order to keep the bone in place. The common sense of this thing is, if this arm had not been kept quiet, that it was not properly treated, The wrapping of this around did not keep the belly of the muscles quiet. Their own physicians claim that this ought to have been done, and it accounts for this being out of place. For the proof is, that it was not fixed right in the first place, it was just as hard to keep that bone in place as it was to keep this one on the thumb in place. If these wounds healed up, then nature was not in fault, and it went to work and did everything right. Now, when that boy's arm was done up, there was, at that time, these splints, or similar ones put upon it. Mrs. Frisby says these splints were taken off there at the same time they fixed them on Monday. After that time these were the articles upon that hand. Now these Drs. here, Miller, Porter, Freas and the gentlemen from Freeport say they do not think that they were sufficient. They say the bones is broken off here; they want something here to hold them. As we understood them, the muscles working here extend to the fore-arm, and would cause motion. When you draw up your arm the muscles here contract. When I raise the weight of fifty pounds there is just so much strain on the arm, and these two ends must be properly confined; they must be kept quiet. The testimony is that he went there and examined it in about two weeks, and went to feeling it, and fussing around it; that he never discovered anything out of place, but he told them the arm was doing well all the time, till the 3d of February, when Dr. Pratt took off the bandage and it was not united. It was after this that this boy knocked it against the fence, about the 20th February. It was after the time that the old man was there, and Dr. Pratt said the arm was not united, and went to work and put it together. Now, then, if that was the fact, and this thing took place afterwards, it did not put it out of place. He did not say there was any signs of refracture. If there was, he ought to have set it over. Dr. Miller had such a case, and he set it over again, and it came out all right. It was knitted on the 20th February. This pulling on the 3d of February would have put it out of place, if it had been knit. If on the 3d of February it was in place, why did he go to work and pull it, can you tell that? It was not at that time in its place. He said it was loosened a little. There had been no union at that time. Now, that was after the time it should have united; was it not? What does this thing of his having knocked it against the fence have to do with it? Now, the Drs. all agree upon this, that if it had been united at this time it would put it out of place. Why was it that he went to work and pulled? Here common sense would teach us that if a fracture of this kind had been rebroken about that time, it would have hurt him; the boy did not complain. That little boy that was with him, and tells the truth about it, says he was out some time after that playing ball. After he hit his arm against the fence, he went into the house and went up stairs; there was no complaint of its hurting him. Now do you suppose that, if that bone had been broken up and torn loose, that that boy would not have made some complaint about it?

The Drs. say it would have produced pain, more or less. The boy said it did not hurt him. Now, these people had every confidence in Dr. Pratt, and did what he told them to. Do you suppose they would not have had it done up, if it was broken again? They are no such fools, not to do so. These circumstances show it was not broken, and Dr. Pratt examined it. They did not keep anything from Dr. Pratt. This splint was broken a little. He went to kick a ball, and caught it slightly against the corner of the fence and broke it a little; it could have been displaced a little, and nothing wrong about it. They take him to Dr. Belding's to see Dr. Freas. Dr. Belding said he had nothing to do with surgery, had quit practice, said he did not examine it, or in other words, he had nothing to do in the matter. He said, Drive a couple of shingle nails in it. Dr. Freas says there was nothing said then by Dr. Pratt about there having been a refracture. There was non-union. I suppose, the judge will insist, as long as there was anything left to try, that surgical science had discovered, they might go to work and pursue it. Nature does the work in this way,—it forms gristle around it, and they could not get this off, and he has got to have his arm cut up which is a dangerous operation. The bones have got to be pulled out and sawed off and fixed together. They have got to rivet it; and if that won't do, they have got to go to work and stick down an awl, and do all this before he can say he has done his duty. If I take my watch to a man, I do not know anything about watches, he has got to go to work and fix it; if he does not fix it rightly, he has got to pay me for it. He assumes to do what I cannot. Therefore, he is held responsible to do it well. Now, this boy has got to have his arm cut open; he has got to have these gentlemen from Chicago cutting and slashing. I would not have these gentlemen of Chicago cutting and slashing my bones in this way, before I could get a chance to recover damages. And whether a man should have to give up his boy into the Dr.'s hands until this could all be done before he can get damages, is what I don't believe. The law does not claim that he should do it. The law would be against the common sense of the thing. The boy goes down there and submits to the arm operation, which they do not call hazardous. The rubbing of the bones is not called a hazardous operation. We admit, we must have the jury decide these damages. The Drs. were at him rubbing these bones some two weeks before he went to have these bones rubbed together at Dr. Belding's, about the last of April or first of May, and the examination of that arm took place. Dr. Freas came to the conclusion that there had been no union. Dr. Pratt did not claim that there had been any refracture; he said the bones was rubbed together. He said there was some of this gristle matter around the ends of the bone. It is told here by all, that if you break a bone, it must be put together or nature can't do anything. After a while, nature says, it is no use for me to go any further, and I will coat them over so that they cannot hurt the rest of the body. She goes to work and throws this gristle around it, so that these bones can play and not hurt the integuments. If nature did otherwise than that, this grating would be heard all the time. It does not when it is coated over. But it goes to work and knits it together in some way. We claim to say, that it does it because the blood sets the lime in it to work,—I forget what they call it,—to make a bone. We can speculate just how she does it as well as they can. We do know that this was at that time the situation; so says Dr. Freas. He examined at that time, for nothing else. Dr. Pratt said, at that time there was another fracture there. What were the evidences that it had been refractured? Provisional callus —it is certain that provisional callus should have been seen there then. They ask the Dr. if there had been a callus where the bone had been broken—that is, the band thrown round there, they call provisional callus. We can detect it a long time afterwards. After a while it is taken away. My friend, *the Chicago Dr.*, says he could see no evidences of provisional callus. He says it was too long, a year and half ago, to be now discovered. It was not too long on the tenth of May. There was no evidences at that time that this provisional callus had ever been thrown out. It was not there so it could be detected. Then we say that it was not a comminuted fracture—there was no other bone broken. Now, then, we are answered by the Dr. from Lanark—[the Dr. will pardon me for not using any other term]—but saying he would not have known there was a comminuted fracture, if there was any—that is my honest conviction. From the evidence here of Mrs. Frisby, the boy's mother, that all Dr. Wales did was to hold the chloroform. When he came there he did not make any examination. That is reasonable. Now, Dr. Wales was a partner and student of Dr. Pratt. Dr. Wales had lived with him in his family. He had no experience at this time in matters of bones at all ; had only two cases of fracture of bones, but none of these long bones· That was all he knew about the business. Said Dr. Pratt did all this business. What did Dr. Pratt want of Dr. Wales? In this testimony we find he only went with him. And he comes, and then and there listens to all this testimony, and makes a coaptation of this whole thing. If he wanted him for anything, why did he not ask him down to Dr. Belding's. He had no confidence in Wales for he was a student. He swears there was another piece of bone which was broken. Now, the fact is, there was no evidence of that on the 10th of May ; none say there were any traces of it afterwards. Well, it is true Dr. Beebe said right here, that I pinched his arm a little and he flinched, and that that was evidence of this callus, and this is the only evidence there is of this fact. He saw all the time what was going on here, and has has fixed it to suit Dr. Wales' statements. I don't know but Mr. Turner will present this case in a different way. We asked Mr. Beebe if he did not tell Mr. Orcut that when he came on to the stand he would make it all right. Mr. Orcut said afterwards that it was not Dr. Beebe, but Dr. Ludlam, who said he would make it all right. I forgot to call Mr. Orcut. You saw the interest that those men felt, and how they gave their testimony as to their knowledge, and you may take it from the manner in which they went at it. I have not had the idea all along that the jury would take into consideration these free lectures. They got it all from books. They have nothing of their own at all about it. They disagree; and what can you make of it when Drs. disagree? And I say Dr. Porter gave his illustration about it and it was right, and these gentlemen's object seems to be to knock over Dr. Porter's testimony. But when they come down to a cross-examination, the bony matter which comes from the circulation was not sufficient to carry on this repair, that it did.in reference to the hand and everything went on well and right. Now, you must come to the conclusion that it all comes from the blood after all. It was in a healthy condition; it healed over. If it was broken at all, it must have been broken on the 3rd Feb'y. If it was set then, there was not time for it to have been united. Now, this angular splint was not put upon that arm at all; it was bandaged from the elbow up. These short splints were put upon it and these were not sufficient by the testimony of all the Drs. Dr. Wales says, this splint was sent for at Dr. Pratt's, and was put on for the purpose of taking the boy home. The mother knows and understands the ways of the boy, and it is likely that she should know and recollect all these things. She set up and watched with him for weeks, and everything was done the Dr. said should be done, and that splint was not put on there for three weeks after the fracture. By that time it would have commenced uniting. In four weeks it would have been in a very good condition; in six weeks the splints could have been taken off. Before this time the old man helped pull it into position. This makes it about the 20th of Feb'y that they said he was there, and it would do to take off the splints. Now then, there was nothing of any complaint heard from it at all until Dr. Pratt went there and undertook to fix it—few days before that, Dr. goes to work and puts on that splint, it is true, and they cannot get around it. Then it can be settled that nature was attending to those other wounds—the hand and head—herself. The head had healed up and there was no difficulty about the circulation.

There was at this time of the rubbing of the bones no inclination in the bones on the 10th May, 1863, to unite did not produce

any inflammation ; but my learned friend, Dr. L., says they did
not want inflammation. Dr. Porter says there must be inflammation ; the object of this is to carry the blood to the point of fracture. If there is too much inflammation it would result in mortification. What was the object of putting down this awl ? To produce inflammation ? What was the object ? We want a sort o
disease to set together the bones. If you cure another disease
you must get up another just like it. If that is the object, Dr.
Porter is right. If there is too much inflammation, give aconite
or use the lancet ; go to work and complete the thing. Give
moderate food, and in ordinary cases this makes no difference.
There must be a certain amount of inflammation. It must be the
injection of blood into that part. They give aconite to create a
gradual flow of blood. What is the difference ? The inflammation is the same. If you get up a certain amount of circulation
there is blood goes there—that is the object of pegging, to get up
inflammation. It is a distinction without a difference. The object
in cutting down is, to excite the parts to produce inflammation.
There is some blood goes there, and the part is disturbed, and
nature puts her forces to work in this way. Well now, gentlemen, these are the main points in this case, as I told you in the
opening. I am to be followed by Mr. De Wolf. He will shield
me a little, and make the blow come easy. Chicago has come
out here to crush us, and I want it to come easy. I suppose the judge will give me the big maul as I have been furnishing him a text. It is throwing all this thing of science away, and
they do not know anything more about it than you or I. It is
evident that there has been an arm broken and the boy has been
wronged. We know if this arm was set right, all would be right.
Now, in reference to the thumb, as far as I can see, I believe the
thumb is a bad job, and I must say it is curious, and it is carrying
out the coaptation system that Dr. Beebe thought it was an admirable job. All done up right. It did not look as though the hand had
been torn out. Beebe thought a hook might have caught in there
and cut it. That thumb was out of joint, and there was a fracture, and it might have been fixed then as well as any time. It
was fixed all right at the second dressing. When they took off
the bandages it would fly out. It is all speculation. He said
it was a horrible state of affairs. Dr. Pratt said after it was fixed
he was ashamed of it. He knew he ought to have done that
thing better. The difficulty was, he knew he ought to have put

it up right. He wanted to crucify this boy by cutting it up and cutting it down, because he did not fix it right the first time. They do not say he could not do it. He said it was not right, and might be fixed right yet. In the start he told you that it was admirable. He says now he should be proud of such a job. When the man himself said he was ashamed of it, look at the absurdity of it. Well, gentlemen, I believe I have said all that strikes me is necessary. All in the opening that is proper for me to say. If I was closing the case I would examine it more thoroughly. It is probable that the other two gentlemen will do it. But the conclusion I have come to is to say whatever struck me. I have been much interested in this case; these things have made deep impressions on my mind. In the short speech I have made to you I have given my views of the testimony, which will bear me out without going into it in this particular way. And now I must sit down and wait quietly until the sledge hammer comes, which will use up everything I have said, because they have all the wisdom concentrated in Chicago—they have not asked anybody but the profession, as they knew all about it. They have brought my learned friend the judge here, and I must *sit* still until he hits me.

Remember the poor boy and decide his case instead of mine.

ARGUMENT OF L. E. DEWOLF, FOR DEFENDANT.

MAY IT PLEASE THE COURT—*Gentlemen of the Jury:* I do not know but I shall interrupt, too suddenly, the pleasing vein of humor with which my friend, Miller, was exercising his unusually good powers for your entertainment this morning.

I had supposed you were sworn to try the issue between the parties according to the law and the evidence. Mr. Miller thinks otherwise. If he is right, I am clearly wrong.

The defendant, in view of the scientific aspects of the case, has obtained the testimony of two medical gentlemen of the city of Chicago, of well established reputation, and of minute ability in their respective department of science.

In Mr. Miller's eye, this was a most grievous offence, and he now asks you to turn away from these important questions of right, to vindicate the very *equivocal* position of certain medical gentlemen, *merely* because they reside in the country; but I apprehend, gentlemen, you occupy your places for no such purpose, and that you will do no such vile act.

The counsel says he has known you for many years and paid you the compliment, to say he *knew* you to be plain, common sense, honest men.

But the attempt to make this a mere question of country physicians against city physicians, and the call upon you to vindicate the former, because they reside *among you* is a very equivocal compliment, both to your judgment and to your sense of justice. I should be very unwilling to believe that you will permit yourselves to be actuated by any such motive. The defendant, in his defence, relies upon facts clearly proven, and the law fairly applied. He has not and will not raise any other issue. There ought not to be any other on the part of the plaintiff. There is no other issue which you can properly try.

The facts which we have proven, not only exonorate the defendant from all blame, but they also show that he exercised more than ordinary skill, and the most unremitting care in the treatment of this difficult case. These facts ought, and will, we trust, exercise a controlling influence in your decision.

But Mr. Miller claims that this important testimony should be discarded, because the witnesses were from Chicago, and because scientific knowledge is the mere *will 'o wisp* of a fanciful brain, of all things real, the most unreal.

Thus, in his estimation, ignorance is the height of bliss.

But gentlemen, let me say to you, that Messrs. Beebe and Ludlam are scientific men ; the testimony they have given is founded on no visionary theories, but well established, scientific truth, and belongs to that department of knowledge which may be denominated actual knowledge.

If, then, you have any impression that this testimony is of the character represented by Mr. Miller, it is certainly a *great* error, and I trust we shall be able to show you, before we get through, that these opinions are based upon grounds which are admitted to be correct by scientific men of all the different schools of medicine. If there are any visionary or false theories, or any empiricism here, you will find it all on the other side.

I do not blame the gentleman for his antipathy against scientific knowledge. He has, undoubtedly, good reasons for it ; but that is a matter relating personally to himself. He need not have published it here. It could all be gathered from the tenor of his argument.

Yet, when he undertakes to make you believe that, at this day, scientific knowledge is all a delusion, he is imposing on you a most extraordinary delusion, indeed. I do not intend to enter into a full discussion of the many questions of a purely scientific character which ¡have [been presented. I shall leave this field entirely for Judge Knowlton, who is better prepared and better qualified to do the subject justice than I claim to be.

Yet, I will say, Mr. Miller is the last one who should talk of "*visionary theories*," or "*being wise above what is written.*" I think his friend, Dr. Porter, and those who followed in his wake, would make a sorry figure when tried by the practical test which he proposes. The counsel, in opening, told you that his client, or those who represented him, had no predilections for, nor prejudices against any particular system of medical practice. That this action was purely to recover damages for injuries actually sustained. This declaration was significant. What was said did not convey an idea of what was meant. But broad as was the allegation, it could not cover up and hide the real cause of this legal controversy. It was not that a boy had been injured either by the neglect or want of skill on the part of Dr. Pratt. He had exerted all his energies and more than ordinary skill to save him from the effects of his own indiscretion and folly; but his imprudence and restlessness added to the severe character of the injuries, delayed the recovery. Broken limbs, at any time, are not desirable. The boy was uneasy under his long restraint, and the parents, from the same causes, became dissatisfied. They fell into Dr. Porter's hands. Now the doctor hates Homœopathy, and here was a rare chance.

By his manipulation the mole hill became a mountain; every variance, real or supposed, between the two systems was unduly magnified. All of the boy's misfortunes, in short originated out of a failure to observe the wise axioms of Allopathy. The animus of this whole case is the deadly hate of *Allopathy* against *Homœopathy*. Dr. Porter told you that he was *educated* in the Medical University of the city of Baltimore—that he enjoyed an *extensive* and lucrative practice. Having exhibited to you his rare opportunities for acquiring medical knowledge. He commenced his testimony by a dissertation on the uses of the arm, and he dangled the arm of the plaintiff before you, not in a manner calculated to manifest his surgical skill, but as a means of exciting sympathy. Every important question which he has asked is made the occasion of a stump speech; and no opportunity is lost in making a malignant fling at Homœopathy. He told you this is a false joint. He then, descanted upon the causes which would be likely to produce such a result. In these opinions he was followed by every medical witness on that side. This was the programme, and the family of the plaintiff are gifted with a wonderful recollection of such facts, as will be likely to tally with these medical opinions. The boy wants a generous diet, said the doctors. He was half starved, the family replied. The arm wants rest; tight bandaging and long splints are necessary, said the doctors. Short splints and insufficient bandaging are on hand. The bandaging only reached to the elbow, and the splints are not half the length required. The two long splints escaped alike their hands and their memories. They have not brought the long splints here; no one recollects them, and the angular splint, which they attempted to withhold, and which we have brought here, has a very uncertain history in their minds. The time it was put on is a question of argument. Had we not secured it and brought it here, there would probably have been no question on their side that it was not put on, and the splint itself would have been a myth. The doctors for the plaintiff all said that to treat the arm five months and ten days without knowing whether it was united or not, manifested gross inattention, or ignorance on the part of the surgeon. The family at once remember, unanimously, that Dr. Pratt never told them it was not united, nor did he tell them it had been refractured. They merely saw the bone bend every time the injury was dressed, and Dr. Pratt, after the boy hit the arm against the fence, only told them that the arm was loosened. They did not know bones would not bend, nor that loosening them was not union. All these important revelations was left for Dr. Freas to make, at Milledgeville. But, gentlemen, I tell you that these bones never bent for five months and ten days. If they did this family knew the fracture had not become united. Nor did that boy plunge against the fence post with force sufficient to break loose the brace fastened together with two screws and glued, and split the splint, as you have seen, without both parents and child being aware that the arm was refractured thereby. How came this family to bring these short splints here, and not the long ones? How came them to remember that the arm bent every time it was dressed, and not know the bone was not united? How came them to remember what Dr. Pratt said about diet, or about the loosening of the bone? If they remembered all these things so accurately, why did not they remember how this arm was situated on the night it was dressed? Why not remember the conversation at Dr. Pratt's in the presence of Mr. Hodgeson? Dr. Pratt and wife, Dr. Belding and wife was present, and heard the parents admit the refracture and describe the manner it was done. Mr. Morris, too, had a conversation with the boy, and he told him about the refracture. There was no concealment or denial about this question previous to this trial. There is no probability that the boy was injured by the spare diet; it only lasted ten days, while inflammation lasted; and the father tells you that after that he was fed on farmer's diet, pork and potatoes.

How, then, came all this strange testimony to be given on the part of the family? All of it is to be accounted for, not upon the original facts, there is no base here for it to rest upon; but it is the medical opinions which required it. In short it is the medical opinions which was made the facts, and not the facts the Medical opinions and these will explain it. Dr. Porter told you that the repair of bone is effected by " *the deposit of ossific matter,*" which is contained in the blood, and which, by means of the arteries, is deposited as the various tissues require; that a generous diet is needed to supply ossific matter; that animal food contains this in much larger quantities than vegetable food; that tight bandaging would check the free flow of the blood, and thus the deposit of ossific matter. Here, then, is a solution of the family testimony respecting diet, and so of all the important statements made by them, wherein they differed materially from the many creditable witnesses examined on the part of the defendant. Dr. Porter has gorged this family with his medical opinions as he would have gorged his patient with roast beef, and with a like deleterious effect.

But how stands this *ossific depository* theory as a matter of science? Has it any better foundation in science than the flimsy facts relied on for its support?

Drs. Beebe and Ludlam tell you that there is no ossific deposit; that the blood contains no such material; that the bone itself and all the tissues of the human body are but an aggregation of different kinds of cells; that, in case of fracture, these little cells, called bone cells, are thrown out from the end of the bone, and deposited in a plastic substance, which is gathered around the seat of fracture, and which answers as a platform or scaffolding in or upon which to repair the injury. They further tell you, this is no mere theory, but well established scientific truth, acknowledged and taught by every physiologist of note, and not disputed by any. Here, then, is a world-wide difference between them and Dr. Porter. Mr. Miller tells you this is all guess work—that any one can guess as well as Messrs. Beebe and Ludlam, and that, for one, he is determined to exercise that right, and he calls upon you to do the same. Now, the practical question is, who is right, and who is wrong? And I propose to examine these opinions and to compare them with the doctrines laid down by standard authors, and see how they agree therewith. I hold in my hand Miller's Physiology and Anatomy. It is a standard work, and so recog-nized by the different medical schools. You see these plates; they are to illustrate cells. Dr. Ludlam made a rude sketch or chart, to illustrate his views upon that subject; and these cells, you see, are similar. I will read you a description from this author —page 47 : title, *Development of bone* : " To explain the develop-ment of bone it is necessary to inform the student, that all organ-ized bodies, whether belonging to the vegetable or the animal kingdom, are developed primordially from minute vesicles. These vesicles, or, as they are commonly termed, *cells*, are composed of a thin membrane containing a fluid or granular matter, and a small rounded mass, the *nucleus*, around which the cell was origin-ally formed. Moreover, the nucleus generally contains one or more small granules, the *nucleolus* or nucleoli. From cells having this structure all the tissues of the body are elaborated ; the ovum itself originally presented this simple form, and the embryo at an early period is wholly composed of such nucleated cells. In their relation to each other, cells may be isolated and independent, as is exemplified in the corpuscles of the blood—chyle and lymph ; *secondly*—they may cohere by their surfaces and borders, as in the epiderma and epithileum ; *thirdly*, they may be connected by an intermediate substance, which is thin, termed intercellular, as in cartilage and bone ; and *fourthly*, they may unite with each other in rows, and on the removal, by liquefaction, of the adherent surfaces be converted into hollow tubuli. In the latter mode capillary vessels are formed, as also are the tubuli of nerve and muscular fibre. One of the properties of cells may also be adverted to in this place ; it is that of reproducing similar cells in their interior. In this case the nucleoli become the nuclei of the secondary cells, and as the latter increase in size, the membrane of the primary parent cell is lost.

"Bone, in its earliest step, is composed of an assemblage of these minute cells, which are soft and transparent, and are disposed within the embryo in the site of the future skeleton. From the resemblance which the soft tissues bear to jelly, this has been termed the gelatinous stage of osteo-genesis. As development advances, the cells, heretofore loosely collected together, become separated by the interposition of a transparent intercellular substance, which is at first fluid, but gradually becomes hard and condensed. The cartilaginous stage of osteo-genesis is now established, and cartilage is shown to exist, of a transparent matrix, having minute cells *disseminated* at pretty equal distance, and without order, through its structure. Coincident with the formation of cartilage is the development of vascular canals in its substance, the canals being formed by the formation of the cells in rows, and the subsequent liquefaction of the adhering surfaces. The change which next ensues is the concentration of the vascular canals toward some one point, for example, the centre of the shaft of a long, or the mid-point of a flat bone, and here the punctum ossificationis, or centre of ossification, is established. What determines the vascular concentration now alluded to, is a question not easily solved, but that it takes place is certain, and the vascular punctum is the most easily demonstrable of all the phenomena of ossification.

"During the formation of the punctum ossificationis, changes begin to be apparent in the cartilage cells. Originally, they are simply nucleated cells ($\frac{1}{5000}$ to $\frac{1}{7000}$ of an inch in diameter), having a rounded form. As growth proceeds, they become elongated in their figure, and it is then perceived that each cell contains two, and often three nucleoli, around which smaller cells are in progress of formation. If we examine them nearer to the punctum ossificationis, we find that the young or secondary cells have each attained the size of the parent cell ($\frac{1}{3000}$ of an inch), the membrane of the parent cell has disappeared, and the young cells are separated to a short distance by freshly effused intercellular substance. Nearer still to the punctum ossificationis a more remarkable change has ensued, the energy of cellule reproduction has augmented with proximity to the ossifying point, and each cell, in place of producing two, gives birth to four, five or six young cells which rapidly destroy the parent membrane and attain a greater size ($\frac{1}{1500}$ of an inch) than the parent cell. Each cell being, as in the previous case, separated to a slight extent from its neighbor by intercellular substance. By one other repetition of the same process, each cell producing four, five or six young cells, a cluster is formed, containing from thirty to fifty cells. These clusters lie in immediate relation with the punctum ossificationis; they are oval in figure (about $\frac{1}{2000}$ in length, by $\frac{1}{5000}$ in breadth), and placed in the direction of the longitudinal axis of the bone. The cells composing the cluster lie transversely with regard to its axis. In the first instance they are closely compressed, but by degrees are parted by a thin layer of intercellular substance, and each cluster is separated from neighboring clusters by a border layer [$\frac{1}{2350}$ of an inch] of intercellular substance. Such are the changes which occur in cartilage preparatory to the formation of bone."

From what I have read it will readily be perceived, that the formation of bone, as here described, agrees with the testimony given by Messrs. Beebe and Ludlam. This author says that these contain, within their inner surfaces, smaller cells, which are pushed out from the parent cell. They spoke of it as a creation, or more properly, a pro-creation, and said this prolific principle is contained in the cell itself,—that its production and growth was similar to that of the wheat, corn, and other vegetables. There is no conflict there between the testimony of the defendant's witnesses and the works of standard authors, they agree precisely. If bone is formed in this manner, it would be reasonable to conclude, without other evidence, that it would be likely to be repaired in a manner somewhat analogous—otherwise there would be a gross defect in dame nature's perfect, handiwork. You will perceive, too, that the standard authors, those authors who furnish the milk which, Mr. Miller says, supports the plaintiff's witnesses, as well as ours, pretend to know at least, what is going on under the surface and within the precincts of that gorgeous temple, the human body. If Mr. Miller was better acquainted with science and with scientific men, he would be guilty of making no such argument as he made here to-day. It is not our witnesses who are "*wise above what is written.*" But how stand *theirs* when tried by this test? What becomes of Dr. Porter's ossific depositing theory? What of his anastomosing theory? Where is the author that the gentleman have or will read, who will sustain Dr. Porter in these theories? You will bear in mind that he said the bone is *wisely* provided by nature with a thin substance, called the periosteum—that this ossific deposit is effected by the blood through the periosteum, by means of inflammation—that without inflammation there is no such thing as repair of bone. He further said that bone contained some fifty per cent. of phosphate of lime, and the blood a similar quantity. But Drs. Beebe and Ludlam told you that there is no such ossific deposit, and that the blood only contains about one per cent. of an insoluble salt—that it does not contain phosphate of lime. Dr. Ludlam said that the bone cells do not receive their earthy matter as though they were dumped into them. That the blood was not to be regarded as a peddler distributing his wares—and that the order of nature was an orderly development. That bone is made of blood constituents, but the blood alone cannot create bone. The cell is the agent in the manufacture of bone, as it is of any other tissue, animal and vegetable. The elements of the tissues, as of the various secretions, pre-exist in the blood and yet neither the tissues nor the secretons are to be found in that fluid, that the soliver does not exist in the blood. Yet no one will doubt that all of its elements are derived by a particular set of glands from the blood. A condition of the secretion or manufacture of sugar by the liver, is an active flow of the blood to that organ. The elements of this liver-sugar are found in the blood of the portal vein before it reaches the liver, but the sugar itself is manufactured by these cells, of which that largest of all the glands is really an aggregation. The elements of a bone may be found in the blood, but these elements can only be constructed into true osseous tissue by the direct agency of the bone-cell itself. That a tub-full of blood could not, of itself, create a man. We must have the type-cell in bony tissue, just as in the grain of wheat or corn, the acorn and the full-grown tree. That the blood contains the elements from which all the tissues are formed. The plant finds its blood in the soil. The rootlets of the man are the lacteals in his intestinal tract. In both cases the nutritious elements are held in solution in water, while the solids are developed from them by, and in conformity with a specific type force. Now, after what I have read from Wilson's Physiology and Anatomy, I need not attempt to convince you, gentlemen, that this testimony explains fully the true process of forming, and the repair of bone; and that it is much more reliable, as a matter of science, than Dr. Porter's ossific depositing and amostomosing theories.

Only think, for a moment, of the blood carrying fifty per cent. of the phosphate of lime. It would soon cease to flow, and the man would become, not a statue of salt, but of solid bone. As to inflammation being necessary to the repair of bone, both Drs. Beebe and Ludlam agreed it was not necessary. Dr. Ludlam said inflammation is not necessary to produce union in a fractured bone. The repair of bone is a healthy physiological process. Inflammation is a diseased condition—the effect of injury. Pus is not found save as a result of inflammation.

Here, too, I need not refer to authors to show which of these witnesses are correct. The testimony I have referred to carries with itself, an evidence of its correctness, too plain to need any other support. We all know that inflammation is the result of injury. Pound your finger, and inflammation is the result; yet who supposes that inflammation is the necessary condition to repair the injury? Dr. Porter is the first one sworn who has made that discovery. The other side will bring no scientific writer o modern date for his support.

From these premises then, I infer : *First.* That the testimony of the plaintiff's family cannot be relied upon, on account of its inconsistency with itself; and besides, it is contradicted by too many credible witnesses for it to be true.

Second. There is that kind of harmony between this testimony and the medical opinions which have been promulgated here, which shows that the memory of this family has been too much stimulated or excited by these medical opinions to be relied upon ; and,

Thirdly. That the plaintiff has a very questionable state of facts, and a still more questionable state of medical opinions. If the facts are *questionable,* the medical opinions are worse. I ask you, gentlemen, what reliance can be placed upon the opinions of men who will make a false joint where there is none, and who testify that there is a dislocation of one joint and a partial one of another, when the former has no existence and the latter does not and cannot exist, on account of the peculiar formation of the joint. Messrs. Beebe and Ludlam showed you what constituted a false joint, and you saw there was no such joint here. The fragments of bone were loose ; there was no ligamentous substance fastening them together, as with a hinge.

I ask you, too, to scan well that testimony which would supply the loss of the nutrient artery by anastomosing through the solid

9

bone. If that artery was destroyed, how could the blood-vessels, through the bone, be enlarged to supply its place. You have competent testimony that it could not be done. The loss of this artery, as the cases in the books show, reduces the chances of a union of bone nearly one third. Yet Dr. Porter and all the witnesses on that side did not know that THAT would make any difference.

I say, then, such testimony is a very unsafe guide by which to judge of human rights in a court of justice. These matters of opinion, to have any force as testimony, should be grounded in an accurate knowledge of science. The witnesses to be entitled to pronounce an opinion, should have such a knowledge of the subject, and of science, to enable them not to pronounce an injury of one *character* when it is of another and entirely different, especially when such opinions are made upon an actual examination of the case itself. If, then, these witnesses have made such gross blunders upon matters which they have seen, and examined for themselves, what blunders may not be expected in their opinions, based upon the uncertain testimony of non-professional witnesses, and upon a state of facts occurring months before. If these witnesses do not know a false joint or the dislocation of a joint, how can it be expected that they can give testimony which is to be relied upon, as to the effect of treatment of injuries in a given case, which they have not seen; and especially when the opinion thus given does not agree with standard authors upon that subject.

I tell you, gentlemen, plainly, such opinions are not to be relied upon in determining rights of the importance of those involved in this case, and I caution you how you receive such testimony, and not to place too much reliance upon it. It is not entitled to credit. For it is not sustained by facts, nor by good surgical authority, and is at variance with the just dictates of reason and common sense.

But having exposed some of the deep malignity and gross ignorance of this medical testimony, I want you to divest your minds, as much as possible, of the extraneous matter thrown around the case by the ingenuity of the counsel, and go back and see how it stood on that memorable night, the 20th of Dec., 1862.

The boy was riding upon a load of corn. Mr. Brown says he and the brother were running horses. The brother testifies that the horses ran until they struck a *gully*, when the end board was burst out and this boy thrown astride of the wagon tongue. His right hand was lacerated, head bruised, and his arm was broken. Mr. Miller says it makes no difference how this was done. But I think it does. The mode and manner and character of the injury has everything to do with a proper decision of the case. Dr. Wales, who was present at the time, says that, in moving the arm to ascertain the character of the injury, the bone protruded through the flesh,—that the bone was fractured, or crushed into three pieces—the thumb of the right hand was fractured in the lower or metacarpal bone, the first and second joint of the thumb dislocated, and the head badly bruised and lacerated. Now, place yourselves in the position which Dr. Pratt occupied on that eventful night, and, under the testimony, tell me how you or any one else could have done better. The plaintiff's family did not observe much, either as to the character of the injury or its treatment. But Dr. Wales, who was present, has given a full and accurate account of it. He testifies that Dr. Pratt reduced the fracture of the thumb and arm, and dressed the wounds, while he assisted. A word in passing, as to the intelligent manner in which Dr. Wales testifies. He may not have answered the scientific questions proposed as fully as older men, but his answers were correct.

He says, Dr. Pratt reduced the fracture and applied a roller to the arm, between two and three inches in width, commencing at the wrist and overlapping it about one half at each roll. This was extended to the shoulder; the splints were then applied to the arm—two long ones and three shorter ones,—that these long splints extended from the shoulder to the elbow, one upon the upper and back portion; the other on the under and for eside of the arm, opposite. That the small splints were placed between and the roller was then wound from the shoulder to the wrist and back again, enveloping the splints with the bandages twice. The arm was then placed in a sling. Dr. Burbank testifies that when he examined the arm, some six or eight days after, he found the bandaging applied from the wrist to the shoulder; that he saw these long splints extending from the shoulder to the elbow; and David and John Morris both testify to these long splints. David Morris states he made these splints, at Dr. Pratt's request. Dr. Belding, who saw this arm four or five months afterwards, found bandaging of a similar character upon it, and these long splints. Dr. Freas is very indefinite in his recollection about the splints, but mentions there was two or three bandages on the arm. Mr. Frisby did not pay much attention to this matter, and does not recollect anything about it. I claim, then, that there was put on to this arm, on the night of the 20th Dec., '62, five splints, two long ones and three short ones; that two of these extended from the shoulder to the elbow; that the bandage or roller was applied from the wrist to the shoulder once, and then twice over the splints in the manner I have before described. Now, gentlemen, where is the testimony by which this position can be successfully controverted? and where is the medical witness who has given his opinion upon this state of facts, that these bandages and splints were not amply sufficient. If there has been any such testimony, I have not heard it. I ask you, looking at the object to be attained by this process. Wherein could Dr. Pratt have done better? Taking the authors which have been referred to here, and the medical testimony upon this subject, as your guide. I ask you if he did not do all that could be reasonably asked of him?

But here comes up the question of the angular splint, or brace, as it has been called. Dr. Wales testifies that on Monday or Tuesday he was at Mr. Frisby's, and saw this splint on the arm, that Dr. Pratt, in presence of the boy and family, remarked he had put it on to move the boy. Mr. Frisby does not remember when it was put on; thinks it was the next morning. Cannot state certainly. But Mrs. Frisby and Mrs. Moscript fix it on the second week, some ten days after the injury. I am of the opinion that Dr. Wales is right. He was a young man just commencing practice, and from that fact he would be likely to observe and remember the mode in which the work was done. But admitting he is mistaken, the splinting was sufficient without it. The putting it on was only a matter of extra caution. Even Dr. Miller admitted that with this splint the short splints would have answered, though he said he should have used some longer ones.

That is precisely what Dr. Pratt did, he put on longer splints. Taking Dr. Miller, then, as authority, and Dr. Pratt so far was right. As to this angular splint, admitting it was not put on until the time Mrs. Frisby and Mrs. Moscript claim it was, still Dr. Pratt is fully up to the requirements of the medical testimony upon both sides as to bandages and splints, excepting, perhaps, Dr. Buckley, the man who pins or dowels bones together—he would bandage from the tip of the fingers. With that single exception Dr. Pratt is all right upon that question.

Now, I will take up the treatment of the hand. Dr. Wales tells you that the hand was very badly lacerated—that the metacarpal bone was fractured obliquely, extending from near the second joint of the thumb back almost to the next joint; that one piece of the bone would drop down, and that the only way it could be held in place was by means of adhesive straps and by a splint made of woolen cloth saturated with shellac gum. By heating or pressing this with a hot flat iron, the splint was pliable, and Dr. Pratt, with Dr. Wales' assistance, reduced this fracture, but with much difficulty. From time to time these adhesive straps would get loose by the discharge of pus. Dr. Pratt watched it closely, and put on new strips and new splints as often as required. Dr. Burbank also testifies that he examined the hand and arm; found the hand much lacerated, and it was difficult to keep it in place, but by means of the adhesive straps and the flexible splint it was kept in place; that he helped Dr. Pratt dress it on that occasion; that the fracture was properly reduced and bandaged. He mentions the fact, too, referred to by Dr. Wales, that the bone would drop down and it had to be held up by adhesive straps. He said these flexible splints were good splints—the very best that could have been used for that purpose. Mr. Frisby told you that Dr. Pratt wanted to reset the thumb and he would not permit him to do it, and that ne never blamed Dr. Pratt for the thumb. Yet, after all this, the plaintiff comes in here and claims damages on the thumb. Mrs. Moscript testifies that the Dr. blistered the thumb, and all these learned doctors come in and testify that there is a partial dislocation of the thumb. Dr. Porter testified that there was a dislocation of one joint, and a partial dislocation of the other. Yet, when Drs. Beebe and Ludlam come to testify, they show that there is no partial or any other dislocation whatever, that both joints are in proper position, that there has been a fracture of the bone as testified by Drs. Wales and Burbank; that the joints are both in place; that the use of the thumb is somewhat impaired by the severe injury to the integuments which surround it and the resulting cicatrix, but there is no other deformity. Dr. Beebe tells you he should be proud of that surgery, and considering the character of the injury, exceedingly gratified that the thumb is no worse. Now, this disposes of the question respecting the injury to the thumb, and I could not, if I desired, place the subject in a more favorable position than it is placed by the testimony.

The subject of diet next claims our attention. Mrs. Frisby stated that Dr. Pratt said the boy might have toast, crackers and gruel. Mrs. Moscript said she should call it no diet at all. The father, the mother and Mrs. Moscript claim that the boy was clamorous for food. Now, taking their testimony together, this order of Dr. Pratt's about food only lasted some ten days. He merely prescribed his articles of diet, and cautioned them about over-feeding while the inflammatory stage lasted. If the boy was starved under this regime, who is to blame but the parents? Besides this, Dr. Wales told you that the boy had considerable inflammation; that the parents told Dr. Pratt of the boy having eaten too much, and brought on some fever, but it had subsided then, and Dr. Pratt told them they might let him eat any ordinary food. Why, then, this clamor about food? There is no foundation laid in the facts to show to the mind of any sensible man that there is even a probability that the boy was injured in the matter of diet.

What nonsense it is to suppose that the limiting this boy to toast, crackers and gruel for ten days might produce a *false joint*, as testified to by Dr. Porter. But listen for a moment to the oracular responses of this learned gentleman. Was it a proper dietetic treatment to keep this young lad upon a small supply of toast, crackers and gruel in the absence of inflammation?

Answer: By no means, sir. The dietetic treatment would be aggravating instead of furnishing the organizing stimuli which nature requires.

Question: What is that, Dr., which forms bone?

Answer: Permit me, sir, to state to the jury that the bone is wisely provided with ossific matter to keep it up. *The false joint, the simple fracture and dietetic* answers are about the only direct answers which Dr. Porter gave, and in neither is he correct. There is no false joint. It was not a *simple fracture,* and his *system of dietetics* shows he does not digest science well if he does roast beef. We have seen by the testimony that the injuries received by this boy were severe. The fractures and dislocations were properly reduced; the bandaging and splinting was done in the manner pointed out by the best surgical authority, and the diet is such as is recommended by good medical authority, and such as a *prudent* physician would be very likely to adopt. The next question is, the degree of attention which the defendant paid to this case. Mr. Frisby seemed to think that the Dr. did not call as often as he ought, but Mrs. Frisby tells you that Dr. Pratt was there several times in the absence of Mr. Frisby; that accounts for Mr. Frisby's lack of information upon that point. But Drs. Wales, Burbank, Belding, Freas and Hodgeson's statements of what took place shows that there is no ground for any complaint on this score, and Mrs. Moscript and Mrs. Frisby also testify as to the care used in dressing the arm ; that the doctor held the arm himself and had some one to assist him. He was present on Sunday, on Tuesday and Thursday following the injury, and examined the arm. It appears he did not remove the inside bandages, and that this was proper is shown by the medical testimony, too much intermeddling being injurious.

A few words here as to the medical treatment. Dr. Wales testifies that he saw Dr. Pratt prepare some aconite of the third attenuation, by putting some eight or ten drops in half a tumbler of water, and ordering two teaspoonfuls every half hour ; that he saw him administer one dose of this. He farther states that some arnica blows were furnished, and some calendula to prevent suppuration, and the proper directions given as to their use. Drs. Beebe and Ludlam, Burbank and Wales, all testify that this was proper treatment.

Drs. Ludlam and Beebe, and all others who testified upon this point, all agree that the giving of aconite was not only the proper remedy, but the best one to control the circulation and prevent or subdue inflammation, and that this treatment is to be preferred to that of the lancet or any other mode yet known. Dr. Beebe, who has had much experience in the army surgery, tells you that aconite is the best remedy for this purpose, and that surgery will never attain its highest perfection until this Homœopathic treatment is generally resorted to. There is no medical witness on the other side who has contradicted this testimony. They attempt to meet this by merely ridiculing the small doses. I shall only say that if any of you have tried the small doses of aconite in cases of fever or inflammation, and I believe some of you have, you very well know its effect, and I am willing to risk that question with you under the medical testimony, adding thereto your own experience, if you have used this remedy in such cases. The next question which I shall discuss is that relating to the length of time it will take fractured bone to unite, and at what period of time friction should be used. The time generally fixed upon by the plaintiff's witnesses for bones to unite seems to be from four to eight weeks. In case of non-union, that friction should be resorted to in from six to ten weeks. But Drs. Beebe and Ludlam show that there is no fixed and definite period in which nature will perform her work. But each case must depend upon the character of the injury, the age and condition of the patient, and especially the condition of the fracture, how far it had progressed, either in uniting or in refusing to unite. If there was simply non-union, it should remain under the ordinary modes of treatment from six to eight months before resorting to friction. If, however, there appeared to be a ligamentous substance forming, evidenced by the fragments of bone becoming rounded off, then friction should be resorted to sooner, but in no case which they could imagine should it be used in less than from four to six months from the date of the injury. From the testimony, and from the current of the medical authorities, I think, in this case, that from four to six months may be assumed as the correct period in which friction should have been employed. But it will also be borne in mind that this was not only a severe injury, but it had been aggravated by repeated injuries. Let the plaintiff cover up the case as much as he will, yet he cannot hide from your view the fact that after the boy had fractured his arm, and after the bone had been knitted together, it was re-fractured. I know a strenuous effort has been made to hide this from your sight; that the family of the plaintiff are now entirely oblivious to any re-fracture of the arm. But take the facts which they relate, and which stand out in bold relief against their verbal statements, and it shows that when they would make you believe that the boy's arm was not re-fractured, in plain, blunt Saxon, it is a lie. The arm was re-fractured, and their own stories show it. Their testimony is, that this boy and a neighbor's boy were playing ball; that the boy went to kick the ball and fell or hit his arm against the fence; that he stopped playing, came into the house and went up stairs. When he came down he said to his mother he did not know but he had injured his arm; that he had hit it and split the splint a *little*. The father and mother interrogated the boy about it. He said it didn't hurt him *any*, and therefore, they would have you conclude the *hitting* the fence was a very small *matter*, merely splitting the angular splint, could not have done any damage. But, gentlemen, some of you are mechanics, and all of you must have some knowledge of the laws of physical *force*. Now, I ask you as reasonable men, taking that angular splint, or brace, as the plaintiff chooses to call it. If that brace was split at the elbow by a blow at the wrist, how could it split it at that point on one side ? Judging from its appearance, and from the manner it is split, how could it help being split on both sides at once ? I judge it could not, for the obvious reason that the splint being hollow, with a screw on each side, and a brace screwed on the outsides of each piece of which the splints was composed. The splint, you perceive, is much narrower on the inside than upon the outside. If the elbow was struck with such force as to split the splint on the inside, and thrust the bones of the arm outwards, it would have certainly split both sides, and it would as certainly have refractured the arm. If, on the other hand, the splint being fastened at the wrist, at the elbow, and just below the arm-pit. If it was hit at the wrist so as to split it, the same result would follow—it would have split the splint on both sides and re-fractured the arm. The elbow, in that case, would have acted as fulcrum for the lever, and the split on the outside exactly agrees with this view, showing that the whole was done at one blow, and upon the lower end. It is idle, therefore—not to say ridiculous—to suppose for a moment that anything else could result from such a blow, but a refracture of the arm.

Now, this conclusion is based solely upon the facts detailed by the family of the plaintiff, and from the condition of the splints, but when to this is added the direct testimony of Dr. Wales, that such was the case; that the arm was refractured, Dr. Belding, Mrs. Belding, Mr. Hodgeson and David Morris, show that previous to this trial, neither the family nor the boy himself ever denied that the arm had been refractured, and they themselves testify here, that Dr. Pratt, when they spoke to him about the arm, said it had *been loosened a little*. These facts establish the refracture beyond a doubt. Now, then, gentlemen, with these accumulated injuries, it seems to me that, under the testimony, and under the medical authorities which have been referred to, from four to six months was a proper period in which to resort to friction ; and friction was resorted to in between four and five months. Dr. Wales testifies to the fact, that he assisted Dr. Pratt in applying friction about two weeks before the meeting at Milledgeville. At a consultation with Dr. Freas and Dr. Belding at Milledgeville, friction was again resorted to. When this failed, Dr. Pratt

desired to operate upon the arm, and described the different
modes which had been used. After the meeting at Milledgeville,
which was on or about the 6th of May, 1863, Mr. Frisby and Dr.
Pratt had agreed to have an operation performed on the arm, at
Chicago, and Mr. Frisby was to let the Dr. know the next week
when he would go down for that purpose. He said he had not
the money then. This was the only excuse. So that during this
whole period we find Dr. Pratt ever in his line of duty, treating
the fracture in the manner pointed out by the works on surgery, and ever willing and anxious to ameliorate the condition
of the boy, and to save him from the effects of his terrible injury.

AFTERNOON SESSION.

When the court adjourned, I had reviewed this case at some
length, and was endeavoring to show that everything recognized
as good surgery had been done by Dr. Pratt during the time he
treated the plaintiff's injury. If the injury was not repaired, it
was not his fault. All that he contracted to do was, to use such
skill and care as is recognized as correct practice by men
skilled in the surgical art. By undertaking to treat this case he
did not guarantee a cure; all he did contract to do was, that he
would use due skill and care in the case. *This he has done.* I
ask you, gentlemen, to look these facts squarely in the face and
judge it, under the whole testimony, by what the Dr. has done, or
omitted to do, and not by the mere present condition of the boy.

On the other side, they have spent two or three days in supposing a certain state of facts entirely at variance with the real
facts, and then getting the opinion of diverse professional men,
not overlearned in their profession, as to this supposed case.
What part this will be made to play in this case I know not; its
design is apparent; it is to lay a foundation for a decision adverse
to the rights of the defendant, by the medical opinions, based on
this false foundation. Indeed, the effort on their part seems to
be to carry this case by influences entirely outside of its merits.
Their whole stock in trade being on the hypothesis that you
will be more likely to be prejudiced against Homœopathy than
against Allopathy. Hence they say it is visionary and absurd,
and this speech-making gentlemen, Dr. Porter tells you that Allopathy is venerable for its age, and is entitled to your respect on
that account. I am willing to admit its claims to antiquity; that
it is ancient, I acknowledge. That it is deeply imbedded in the

memories of the present generation, I also admit; but that it is entitled to our grateful remembrance I can only admit upon the principle that its strongest claims are founded upon the maxim that "Dead men tell no tales;" that the grave hides alike from our view, the injury and the injured.

But our learned friend, Dr. Porter, has further claim. When upon the stand he went back to the old fathers and patriarchs of the system.

Oh! his system was no new-fangled theory. It was as old as science—handed down from the fathers, age after age. This new system was all heterodox. Not so, his. It stands upon its old base. The fathers had discovered all in the system which was essential, and made a record of it. As the fathers left it, so it stands now. In short, it is a system or school which rests upon antiquity, and its watchword is *orthodoxy*.

But, gentlemen, I have ever found that, in science, as in theology, when a man can present no better claim for his system than orthodoxy or antiquity, his claims simply means a false system, fossilized, incapable of progress or improvement. His statements and his judgment should alike be distrusted. His blind veneration of the past makes him overlook the important truths of the *ever moving, ever living present.* Advancement is stamped upon every thing by which we are surrounded. The stand-still policy means death. So with his system, life has departed from it, but its dead carcass is among us, and among us to hinder the advance of true philosophy and true science in the case of disease. But we are told that these questions of system have nothing to do with this case; yet, at every turn we are met with a thrust at our system. The counsel will not pretend to discuss its merits; his weapon is ridicule, and Dr. Porter, when upon the stand, under the solemnity of an oath, attempted to get off a very stale Allopathic anecdote upon Homœpathy, and under this oath he told you, gentlemen, that a *spare* diet consisted in taking a part of the wing of a chicken, wrapping it in a cloth, and boiling it a few minutes in a gallon of water, and then giving the patient half a gill at proper intervals. I wonder he had not given it in the old style he so much admires, and that was, that Homœopathic broth was made by hanging a chicken on a limb and let the shadow strike the water, then take that water and boil it ten minutes, then take three drops and mix it well in Lake Superior, then give half a gill every two hours. That was said to be Homœopathic

broth for sick people. Yet the counsel has no intention of raising any question about systems.

But, aside from this question of systems, gentlemen, the counsel of the plaintiff would not dare present his case before you.
He relies upon these vulgar prejudices, and not upon the merits
of his case.

Dr. Pratt comes before you asking justice at your hands.
He took this boy all mutilated, torn and bleeding, and he acted
the part of a good samaritan towards him—he bound up his
wounds in an intelligent and skillful manner; and he has placed
before you, the way and manner in which this work was done,
and he asks at your hands a judgment upon the facts here presented. He asks that you take the facts and the whole facts in
making that decision. And he justly claims he is fully entitled
to an acquittal at your hands. Col. Turner will close this case
on the part of the plaintiff. I cannot anticipate the course he
will pursue. Judging from what he has already done, I anticipate he will rely upon your sympathies, and upon the prejudices
created, or attempted to be created, by the Allopathic school
against the Homœopathic. I know he is a man of decided ability in this line of practice. He is well skilled in the art of making
the worse appear the better reason. I have no disposition or
wish not to have you listen to what he says; on the contrary, I
say, listen to it all, but when you have done so, under the instructions which the court will give you, take up the case and examine
it carefully and critically, and where the current of testimony
leads, follow, and you cannot well go astray. But as you examine this case, bear in mind that in such a mass of testimony, there
may be conflicting statements of witnesses. You are to reconcile
these statements, if you can, if not, you are to look at the testimony as it is, see who are entitled to credit and who are not so
entitled; compare one portion of a witnesses testimony with
another portion, and see how they agree. Then look at the means
of information possessed by the witnesses, the mode and manner
of testifying, and when you have done this, draw such conclusions as to the facts detailed, as you think just. But, especially
let it be remembered, that much of this testimony is of a professional character, where opinions are to be received. While due
weight should be given to this testimony where it come
recommended with a proper knowledge of authors and of the
principles of science, upon which such evidence is based. Yet,

without such knowledge, opinions thus given are of no account, for this reason, you should carefully examine every opinion, and see what foundations have been established, in fact, for the giving of such an opinion, and as far as you can, compare these opinions with the standard authors, whose works, so far as they are applicable to this case, will be read before you. In this connection, however, permit me to say, that Dr. Pratt is the only medical man who has ever attempted to save this boy from the fruits of his own folly, or from the misfortune which has befallen him, and while a most labored effort has been make on the part of the professional gentlemen, who have taken the lead against him in this prosecution. Yet that boy has been permitted to remain without treatment for nine months, without any attempt on their part to cure him. Physicians and surgeons whose opinions are entitled to respect, testify that this boy can be cured, and that delay renders the chances of recovery less certain. There is a neglect here, both on the part of the parents and on the part of their medical advisers, which should be duly weighed in determining this case. The man who has faithfully discharged his duty should not be held accountable for this negligence of the boy or parents, and especially when, without any reasonable excuse, he is denied the privilege of effecting the cure.

From all these considerations, then, I conclude that the defendant ought to be acquitted from any costs or damages on account of the plaintiff's misfortunes, and my conclusion is based upon the following facts :

First.—The plaintiff has not shown that the defendant has been guilty either of negligence or want of skill.

Second.—The defendant shows that, for the cure of the boy, he exercised all the skill and diligence that was required for his recovery; that in reducing the fracture, bandaging, splinting, and in prescriptions of medicine, he was scientifically correct.

Third.—It has been shown that the plaintiff was guilty of gross negligence and inattention to the directions which were given for his recovery; besides this, that he was injured by his own voluntary act, without the agency of the defendant, in a manner which would be likely to retard, if not entirely prevent his recovery.

For these reasons, then, I conclude your verdict should be for the defendant.

But I have already taken up more of your time than I intended, and perhaps more than I ought to have done, yet the importance of the case, if I have done so, is my apology, and so far as I am concerned, I will conclude by saying, take up this case and judge of it in the manner you would be willing to be judged by, under the facts detailed before you. Dr. Pratt has performed his duties faithfully and with more than ordinary skill. He has done this without fee or reward. After having for months attended to the plaintiff's injuries thus faithfully, to be now subjected to the expense and trouble of a long trial, is a poor return for the services thus rendered. Yet, to all this he cheerfully submits, conscious that he has performed his duty; and having by the testimony, placed a full knowledge of these facts before you, he trusts that in accordance with these facts, you will render your verdict. and with this, and this alone, he will be fully satisfied.

ARGUMENT OF J. H. KNOWLTON FOR DEFENDANT.

MAY IT PLEASE THE COURT—*Gentlemen of the Jury.*—I propose to discuss the facts in this case in as brief space as I well can, and to draw such conclusions as I think warranted by the testimony, and in so doing I shall, probably, occasionally allude to what I understand to be the law applicable to the facts.

In the outset, in opening this case to your consideration, I stated to you the primary principles of the law which should govern your action.

Now, I crave your most careful attention, not that I shall be interesting, or that I shall amuse, or occasion merriment, as did the gentleman who opened the argument on behalf of the plaintiff. I possess very little, if any, of this kind of capacity.

I ought, perhaps, before I go further, confess that I was, probably, guilty of an indiscretion, for which I ought to ask your pardon, by indulging in more than a smile, and coming to an audible laugh when the gentleman (Brother Miller) was talking about the blood vessel that enters the "*nutritious foramen.*" He said, "*these arteries are all veins.*" I laughed; I could not well avoid it. You as farmers, would be very likely to laugh should I say, "these horses are cows."

I understand the difference between *arteries* and *veins*, and this is all the apology I have for this little indiscretion. This is not a case for merriment in any point of view.

When we consider the condition of the boy's arm, the fact is lamentable. What is the cause of this condition? This question involves enquiry of a highly scientific character. We ought to seek and explore this scientific field. You, twelve men of this county, have been called from your ordinary avocations and placed upon this pannel. It is fortunate that you have heard something, and so much of the structure of your own bodies. We are all too ignorant upon that subject; all men, even the most learned, are too ignorant in this behalf. We can no more than say, all knowledge is a grade of ignorance.

I say, you have been more than ordinarily fortunate upon this subject. This fortune is one of the results of the breaking of the boy's arm. I trust that, upon this trial you have learned something, and that you will treasure it up and make it useful to yourselves and fellow men in after life. Something, perhaps, is due to myself, gentlemen, after the many assaults made by brother Miller, not only upon the professional gentlemen from Chicago, but upon myself. In plain English he assures you that I am to annihilate him by my argument. I shall submit to your learned judgment whether I have evinced any such disposition. Yes, when my duty shall end and yours shall begin, in the quiet of the jury room, you will, I trust, bear witness that I have not during this trial, attempted by word, or deed, to injure that gentleman or any one else. I have had, and now have no such intention. I shall also submit to your judgment whether I have made any attempts at display upon any point under consideration. If I have, it was unintentional; of its existence I am wholly unconscious. I despise all attempts at display.

The position I occupy in this case gives me the right to animadvert upon such conduct, whether the actor be witness, or other person. In practice, I have often had occasion to do so. The counsel seems to think it very strange that I should have been called so great a distance for no other purpose than to attend to this case for Dr. Pratt. I suppose the Dr. employed me because he wished my assistance, and I can only say that I hope my connection with the case, will not prejudice your minds, so that you cannot properly decide the case upon the evidence.

I shall be gratified if I can in a plain manner perform the duties which devolve upon me in this truly important case. And now, gentlemen, it is proper that I should say to you that we stand here simply *denying* what the plaintiff has alleged, and what he is bound to prove, or establish by evidence. It was not necessary that we should go into the proof of facts which would amount to a justification. All that was essential for us to do, was to see that the plaintiff made, or *failed* to make a case, which, in law, is *prima facie*, or at first blush, or first view ; and we claim, and I trust that I shall demonstrate, that they have entirely failed to establish such a case. In their attempts to do this we had a right to a full and complete investigation of the whole case and its surroundings. We had the right to introduce witnesses, in order to unfold to you our views of this case, as to the non-union of the fractured bone, and account for it upon physiological principles. In this case we claim to have succeeded. We also had a right to show what, in point of fact, was the treatment of this case by Dr. Pratt, and thus establish the negative, or disprove the facts alleged by the plaintiff. To do this, the consumption of considerable time was indispensable.

We wished to lay all the facts before you—not only as to the actual practice—but everything connected therewith, and having a probable bearing upon the case. There is in this case, nothing which even borders upon truth, that Dr. Pratt had, or has any reason to fear, or to shrink from.

Therefore, we had no hesitation in presenting to your consideration, every question in the fullest form, which can with any propriety, be said to throw light upon the case. Men differ very widely upon subjects of this kind. But in these cases there are certain phenomena, common to them all, of which a man should have an opinion of his own, founded, to a great extent, upon his experience—broader or narrower, as his observations may have been limited or extended. The mind may be capacious. It may be attentive and discriminating, or it may not.

There is a greater variety of opinion in the medical world than in any other branch of science. It is natural that this should be so. There is no mechanism so wonderful and so nicely adjusted in every part as the human body. There is here a wide latitude for difference of opinion.

I think that this complexity of mechanism, in a somewhat satisfactory manner, accounts for this great diversity of opinion. I mean upon the hypothesis that men who have investigated this subject, have endeavored to do so without prejudice, and for the purpose of ascertaining the truth. There is another theory which will aid us in accounting for this diversity of opinion. Men sometimes make up their minds, or adopt some theory at the commencement of their investigations, and never probe the matter any farther, or if they do, they make every new fact bend to the

the support of preconceived opinions. Previous opinions control them, perhaps, unconsciously. Others investigate with no predilections for opinions once formed, but disarmed thereof; and the consequence is a change of opinion—mayhap very suddenly. Hence, it is said that wise men sometimes change their opinions, but that fools never do.

Now, gentlemen, the question of different theories of medical practice, known as Homœpathy and Allopathy having elicited considerable discussion, and some examination of medical gentlemen, I doubt not you will be told that I believe in Homœopathy. I do not want this matter left to conjecture, nor do I wish the counsel on the other side to get the start of me upon this matter. I assure you, gentlemen, that I do firmly believe in the Homœopathic theory of practice. It is based upon experimental knowledge, and I have often demonstrated the efficiency of this theory.

My brother, Miller, talks very flippantly about the ten thousandth part of nothing as a Homœopathic dose of medicine ; and that common sense will tell any man that these small doses can produce no effect upon a human being. He also assures you that he is a common sense man. I do not know whether I am or not. I am a poor judge of myself. I shall pretend nothing of the sort. I shall leave this matter of common sense to you, so far as I am concerned.

Mr. Miller further says that there is nothing in the Homœopathic theory that he can understand or comprehend. If we were to ignore every thing which he does not comprehend or understand, our stock of knowledge might not be very extensive.

But, gentlemen, I trust that I shall be able to illustrate to you, in some degree, how it is that these infinitossimal doses may produce great effect upon the human organism. I propose to do this, so that it shall be obvious to your mental vision.

It is said that these doses are too small to produce *any effect.* This is mere assertion. How gentlemen can, with propriety, make that assertion who have never tried the experiment, is more than I know. It is mere speculation.

Have you ever heard, or known of a person having a disease called the small pox ? If you have, you have heard of, or known one of the most loathsome diseases to which the human body is subject. Take a subject with confluent small pox in its worst form,—and what an object for the human eye to rest upon ! His whole visage black and bloated to the full,—his body not dotted with sores, but the whole frame one grand mass of corruption. Can you tell me how much of the *small pox virus* entered the system by olfaction, or otherwise, in order to produce this awful disease—to produce this great effect upon the body? I apprehend not. Yet, the quantity must be greatly less than a Homœopathic dose of medicine, which is sufficiently large to be seen. Not so with this small pox *virus.* This illustration proves the fact, that these small quantities will produce an effect upon the human organism, although the quantity is so small that the gentleman, by way of derision, says that it is the ten-thousandth part of nothing.

Gentlemen, neither you nor I know how small must be the quantity of a virulent poison, administered to a person so that it shall produce no effect upon the system. I mention this because you must understand that all the remedies given by physicians, whether mineral or vegetable, are poisons. It matters not whether they are Allopaths, Homœopaths, Eclectics, Thomsonians, or what not. Disease is a morbid or poisoned condition of the system. It would, therefore, it seems to me, require a poison, or antidote to the disease, in order to remove it.

Now, upon this subject, gentlemen, you may remember that Mr. Turner told you, in opening this case, that his client had no prejudices upon this subject, nor antipathies to any system of practice, and that upon their side they should not raise any question about different systems. I made no promises, not knowing what might occur. We did not open this question. But the other side did, notwithstanding their engagement not to do so.

We have been favored with quite a number of thrusts from counsel, as well as from the professional witnesses upon the part of the plaintiff. They were, however, quite modest until they came to cross-examine Dr. Beebe. Then the door was thrown so wide open that Mr. Turner will not be able to shut it. That this field is open to inspection is not our fault.

When I come to this point of the testimony as applied to the subject matter of this case, I shall present my views, as well as upon all the other points involved, and I hope to so conduct this discussion that you will have a clear understanding of the facts developed by the testimony and the law appliable thereto, as given in charge by the court. I must also inform you that, as I go along I shall read from books upon surgery, which are looked upon and conceded by the other side to be, good authority. Yes,

I shall read from the works which their medical witnesses testify
are the sources from whence they derive their knowledge, so far as
the principles of surgery are concerned. I shall read from these
books for the purpose of showing the relative value of the testimony of the professional witnesses. And if it shall appear that
our professional witnesses have testified in line with these authorities—the common source from which they all get their knowledge;
—then we shall properly claim that the testimony of our witnesses is entitled to credit, and that that of theirs is not, if
opposed to these authorities. The opinions of professional witnesses are valuable in the proportion that they coincide with
those authorities which contain a collection of the experience of
those who have given attention to, and have had great experience
in, the matters treated of.

I propose to discuss this case in a somewhat connected and
logical manner—going through with one point at a time. In this
way, I think you will much better understand me than you would
were I to run from one point to another, and discuss them piece-
meal, as my brother Miller did. He ranged the field with much
rapidity, and threw out, what seems to me, many curious notions.
I shall endeavor to present the case in its true light and compare one part with another, so that we may have the value of
the whole and of the various parts.

You are to judge of the credibility of the witnesses. In determining what weight should be given to the statements of a witness, which are mere opinions, you must take into consideration
the amount of information which he possesses upon the subject
matter whereof he ventures an opinion. A witness of unques-
tionable integrity must have the opportunity, as well as the ability
to see and learn; and after having had the opportunity, it must
have been improved and something learned. Rare opportunities,
even without being improved, will not do. That opportunity
has been presented and improved, must be gathered from the
opinion expressed, as coincident with human experience. I had
designed briefly to have reviewed some of the positions assumed
by Mr. Miller; at least those of most interest, but I shall content
myself, by giving them attention as I proceed with the discussion of the case—having regard to the testimony, and particularly as to the different modes of treatment of injuries of the
character now in question. Mr. Miller said, with great emphasis,
that Dr. Pratt told the father of the plaintiff that he was compe-

tent to treat this case, and that they had nothing to do with any particular *"pathy."*

It is well that you understand, that we do not deny that Dr. Pratt did so say. On the contrary, we concede it, and now say that he was competent. And not only competent, but that he, as established by the testimony, did treat the case in all its phases, in the most approved manner known to modern surgery, and as much as was practicable for any surgeon in this country, or in any other. This is precisely what we *do claim.* Another thing that Dr. Miller complains of, and for which I may owe him an apology, is, that in my opening remarks I said that the case was taken out of the hands of the defendant and placed in charge of Dr. Miller, a brother of one of the attorneys of the plaintiff; so that Dr. Pratt was not permitted to resort to all the modes known to the surgical art which promised success. Mr. Miller seems to think disrespect was intended by this remark. Certainly, I had no such intention. I made the reference as one of *identity* of *the* Dr. Miller to whom the case was entrusted, not knowing but there might be more than one Dr. Miller in this region of country. Again, Mr. Miller says that he cannot see any reason why the bone of the arm did not unite, as the boy was perfectly healthy all the while. I may not see, you may not; yet this does not help the case of the plaintiff. He is not to maintain an action upon the ground that all the world cannot see why the bone did not unite. But he must show, by competent, testimony that it failed to unite because Dr. Pratt did not properly set this bone, or, in surgical parlance, properly reduce the fracture. If, during all the time that Dr. Pratt was attending the plaintiff, he was in good condition and healthy, so that his general condition cannot be assigned as the cause of the non-union of the bone, then another theory of the other side—namely, that the boy was so reduced by a low, stingy diet as to essentially prevent re-union—must fall to the ground.

This cannot be true, if, as the father and mother and a sister of the mother all testify, the boy was in good condition and perfectly healthy during all the time that Dr. Pratt treated him. This testimony coming from the side of the plaintiff, annihilates the theory of improper treatment by Homœopathic medication and diet, and speaks highly in favor of both the medication and diet. Think of the boy with his right hand torn to pieces, the thumb dislocated, and bone fractured, a considerable wound upon the head, the arm broken in two places, and one of the fragments protruding through the skin, thrown from the wagon and taken up for dead, recovering, save one fracture of the arm, without any serious inflammation, or other difficulty. If this does not disprove the idea and assertion that Dr. Pratt was guilty of unskillful treatment, it will be difficult to divine what will. But not only do these witnesses testify to these facts; they go further, and say that the boy never complained of any pain from the time he was injured until he passed from under the charge of the defendant. This is certainly extraordinary, and contrary to the general rule. I hardly think one of you could be subjected to the infliction of such severe injuries with so favorable a result. The plaintiff has utterly failed to show any reason why this arm bone was not repaired long ago. If the low diet so much dwelt upon was kept up a sufficient length of time to injure the patient, by impairing the health so as to prevent the reproduction of bone, then different results would have followed than those which have been detailed by the witnesses. They have taken much pains to elicit testimony upon the dietetic part of the treatment. I may as well discuss this part of the testimony right here.

You will recollect that I was particular in asking the sister of the mother to give the language used by Dr. Pratt when he designated the kind of food the plaintiff might eat, or, in other words, how he might be fed. Her words were, "*that the boy might have some toast, crackers and gruel.*" You will remember, gentlemen, that this is precisely what she said in answer to my question as to what Dr. Pratt did, in fact, say. These are the *articles* or *kind* of food prescribed by the Dr. But what has this to do with the quantity of food to be taken? The *article* and *quantity* of food are very different things.

Dr. Pratt said nothing about *quantity*. That was left to the parents, or those who attended the boy. Is there any evidence that the Dr. evinced a disposition to starve the plaintiff? None whatever. They would have you believe that the defendant had been trying to starve his patient.

Is it reasonable, or do you suppose that the Dr., who gets his living and acquires his wealth by the practice of his profession, would adopt the mode of starving his patients, or that he would prescribe so small a quantity as to materially interfere with the process of re-union of the bone—that he would be guilty of an act that would be suicidal to success? Why, his own selfishness would prompt him to an opposite course. He would naturally allow him food in sufficient quantity to facilitate, and not prevent a cure. Is it reasonable to ask you to believe that Dr. Pratt gave any such orders about quantity of food as is contended for here? If so, where is the evidence of the fact, or where is the evidence that the boy was so reduced by lack of food that union of this bone would not take place?

The young woman and the mother testify that the boy cried for food. Was it strange that he should? It requires no evidence to establish the fact that an active boy driving about the country, chopping, plowing and hoeing, in the constant habit of eating much hearty food, would cry for food when not allowed his accustomed meals. Even the taking a considerable less quantity of the same kind of food would leave a craving appetite for more. These two ladies also testify that when the Dr. was informed that the boy wanted, or cried for more food, that he asked the boy whether he would not rather have a good arm and eat less, or eat more and have a bad arm? To this, the boy and the parents yielded. If they did not, they should.

The Dr. seems to have been very attentive to this case. According to the testimony of the mother and sister, he was there on Tuesday, the third day after the accident, then on Tuesday, and again the next week.

This was the time when the boy cried for food. The very time when there was the greatest danger to be apprehended from inflammation. However, some of the professional gentlemen who have testified for the plaintiff, seem to think that the usual diet should be allowed, and that, *too*, however severe the injury. Such would be their practice, unless they found inflammation pressing upon the patient with much violence—*then* they would order a *low* diet.

Does it require any greater means to prevent inflammation by commencing early, than it does to remove, or cure it, after it has fairly laid hold? When inflammation is upon the patient, the physician must resort to more stringent measures to arrest it than would be requisite to prevent it.

It is much better to prevent an injury or disease than to cure it after it has become seated. *Then*, I say it was highly proper for Dr. Pratt to order this kind of diet in the outset, with a view to prevent inflammation to as great an extent as possible. No person could reasonably expect repair when the injury was so severe as was this case, without some inflammation. The precaution taken was highly commendable. In such injuries, means to prevent inflammation, should always be instituted at the earliest practical moment.

In this case this was promptly done. But independently of reasoning, I assert that they have totally failed to show anything more upon this subject, than that Dr. Pratt prescribed the *kind* of food to be used by the boy for two or three weeks, without saying one word about the quantity to be given. That was determined by his parents. But take their theory—that it was the diet that prevented the restoration of the arm—and in this connection, let us admit that the boy was fed as their witnesses testify; and that the defendant ordered them to do precisely as they did. Yet, this does not show that this *was, or is* the cause why the bone did not unite. Even Mr. Miller cannot account for the thumb and all the other wounds healing kindly in the usual time, if the diet caused non-union of the arm bone.

How is it possible that the kind of food furnished, was given in sufficient quantity to supply the tissues and cause the other wounds to heal so rapidly? or, *how* could this diet supply one tissue, or one part of the body and not all be supplied? The external wound at this point of non-union, however, must have been supplied, because their testimony is, that this was healed in about three weeks, which was quite as soon as the wound of and around the thumb was healed.

No particular part of the system is therefore shown to have been better supplied than the other. But next comes their theory, that to have, or to reproduce bone, the patient must have animal food. Dr. Porter seems to be of this opinion, and for the reason that animal food contains (as he thinks) more phosphate of lime than vegitable food. Is this a fact?

Look at the testimony and illustrations of Dr. Beebe. He says that the blood contains the *material* out of which the bone-cells, or bone are formed, or manufactured out of the food taken into the stomach; and that by this process bone tissue and every other tissue is kept up and nourished from day to day; and that this condition is well maintained by vegetable diet alone. How much more vegetable food does a person eat than an ox? Does an ox eat animal food, such as meats? You know that he does not. And has the ox bones of less size and strength than man? The reverse is the fact. Here, then, is a demonstration that vegetable diet alone is adequate to the formation of bone. Not only the bone, but the muscle and flesh of the ox, the horse and the sheep are formed from vegetables. When we eat the meat of the ox for bone material, we eat vegetables, as it were, second-hand.

But Mr. Turner seemed to think, when cross-examining our medical witnesses, that he would *non-plus* the doctor upon the theory that a purely vegetable diet was all sufficient for the production of bone tissue, or reproduction of bone. So the counsel confidently says : "A dog eats meat or animal food, how can this food keep up the bone tissue if it does not contain the bone material ?"

The doctor replies : "The dog eats bone with the flesh sufficient, perhaps, to give him all the phosphate of lime and other bone material that his system needs. But not only this, the animal whose flesh the dog eats is sustained by vegetable food." The doctor also said that all carniverous animals consumed bone with the flesh eaten. That what was true of the dog, in this respect, was also true of the lion and tiger. Is there any doubt whatever upon this subject? The dog swallows the bird, bone and all. Take the hen. She does not ordinarily, eat a large amount of meat. Her food is mainly vegetable, yet she has bone.

Another theory (Dr. Porter's) is, that you can tell that man is an animal that requires *beef and vegetables;* that he is omniverous. That the kind of food that animals should eat is ascertainabe from the form of their teeth. When I asked the doctor what conclusion should be drawn as to the food of a man who should be born without, and remain without teeth, his reply was, that he should consider him *lusus naturæ*—a monster—something out of the ordinary course of nature. That was an extremely clear elucidation. When I carried the doctor's theory a little farther, and asked him how we could determine the proper food for the crow, or the hen, who have no teeth, his best answer was his silence. The crow can and does eat animal food, and that, too, after decomposition has been carried to very considerable extent. This saves him in the operation of digestion. Mainly the food of the crow is meat ; that of the hen is vegetable. Now, if you can tell, on Dr. Porter's theory, what is the proper food for the crow and the hen, by the different formation of *their teeth*, you can do more than I can comprehend.

I think, gentlemen, that whoever started this *"teeth theory"* had very little base to stand upon. Animals which eat vegetables and meats simply use their teeth to masticate—and this as well with one kind of food as of the other. And such animals have teeth as well adapted to the eating of vegetables as of meats. Take the dog—his teeth have a somewhat different form from those of man ; yet he will eat meat or bread as readily as man. I remember that my father once had a dog that hardly ever ate anything but bread and milk. Bread is vegetable diet, most certainly.

I do not, upon the whole, see how you can tell, from the formation of man's teeth, what kind of food he should eat. I take it that the reason why the lion and tiger do not eat bread is, that they cannot get it. Man will eat meat as exclusively as the lion when he can get nothing else, and in time would be quite as averes to vegetable food.

The climate has, I think, more to do with what a man's diet should be than the formation of his teeth. Under a vertical sun he should eat no meat, or very little, for the reason that there is too much carbon in it, which would of necessity produce sickness. In the cold region of the north, the inhabitants must use highly carbonaceous food to keep up the equilibrium of the body with the surrounding atmosphere. Hence, they make food of tallow and the oils of the whale and seal. Their teeth are good, but they have little use for them. In the temperate zones, a mixture of animal and vegetable food, if not the best, is certainly less objectionable than in the frigid, or torrid zones.

But the theory that you can tell by the formation of the teeth of men, even in this temperate climate, that he must have animal food in order to maintain or reproduce bone, has been absolutely proved unfounded as a fact, by great numbers of vegetarians, who will eat nothing but vegetable diet. They discard all animal food, and yet have good bone and less disease, generally, than their neighbors, whose diet is partly animal and partly vegetable. This proves that there is sufficient phosphate of lime in vegetable diet for the maintenance and reproduction of bone, or bone tissue in man, which must end the theory of the counsel and witnesses of the plaintiff, that the non-union of the bone of the plaintiff's arm is attributable to his vegetable diet for three weeks after the accident.

It is, perhaps, sufficient for me to say, that this young lad, as shown by the testimony, had food enough, and of the requisite kind, to supply the tissues of his body, so that the serious wounds upon his head and hand were healed in the usual time. From the testimony it is evident, that the external wound on the arm at the seat of fracture, healed in a remarkably short time.

It is next to impossible that all these extensive injuries could have gone on in the work of repair in the orderly and timely manner shown by the proofs, if the boy had been starved, or not allowed the proper kind or quantity of food.

The recuperative forces worked well, which shows proper diet. The results entirely disprove the starving or dietetic theory of this case. Upon the hypothesis that this part of the treatment was kept up three or four weeks, (and there is no pretence of any longer period,) and that these torn wounds all healed in this time, it is quite evident that no injury resulted from the diet allowed.

The cicatrix at the point of the external wound on the arm shows that it was not made with a sharp instrument. You saw Dr. Beebe take up the flesh at this point, and thereby exhibited the fact by a sort of string or pipe, that the wound extended to the bone, and that it must have been of the same severe character as that of the thumb. No more is necessary to show the incorrectness of this theory of the professional gentlemen who say they never change the diet, unless there is a high state of inflammation.

However, none of them have come up to the point of denying that diet has a very decided effect, or is important in case of inflammation. When that exists to any considerable extent they would *all* change the diet and order a " *low diet.*" They would, therefore, *not take* precaution to prevent inflammation, but would wait until the disease was, at *least,* quite firmly seated, and *then,* to aid removal, would put the patient on *low diet.* I apprehend it requires but little common sense, to determine which mode is preferable, and that their own testimony sufficiently disposes of this question in our favor.

But when you take the testimony of Dr. Wales upon that subject, who says that Dr. Pratt told them they could let the boy have any ordinary kind of food on the 10th day (as I remember his testimony) from the Tuesday next after the accident, which would make thirteen days in all, then it was the fault (if fault there be) of the parents, that the boy was kept on the diet ordered in the first instance, for three weeks, or for any time beyond thirteen days.

This was not, and by no possibility could be, the fault of Dr.

Pratt—that is, if you believe Dr. Wales. This you should do unless you believe that he has committed perjury, or that he, at least, is wholly mistaken. But, however you may think about this testimony, they prove the fact that all these severe wounds healed, as already remarked, at farthest in four weeks. To do this, general good health was absolutely necessary ; which could not well be the case with a person who was (to use their own language) " *starved.*"

Another thing they complain of, and about which their witnesses testify, is that Dr. Pratt gave the boy *aconite.* Now, gentlemen, as all the professional witnesses on our side testify that the giving of *aconite* was *proper,* and not one of theirs testifies that it was *improper,* I would like to know how they can, with any propriety, claim, or how you can believe, that this part of the treatment was improper.

Have they brought a single witness to, or who does, testify that aconite will not have the effect to prevent, or *remove* inflammation, as testified by Drs. Beebe and Ludlam? No, gentlemen, there is no such testimony. They have not even attempted to prove any such fact, which is evidence most convincing, that they could not. Drs. Beebe and Ludlam testify before you that they know that aconite will produce the effects they detail in reference thereto, and that they know this from actual personal experiments. One well attested fact by experiment is worth more than a thousand untried theories. I would rather have one grain of experiment than all the theories in the world. Dr. Ludlam informs you, in answer to their cross-interrogation, that aconite acts directly upon the nervous centers, controls capillary action and moderates the motion of the blood as it circulates through the body, thus preventing or removing inflammation or congestion.

But here Dr. Porter comes to their aid, and prompts the counsel to ask Dr. Ludlam how digitalis acts, or upon what it acts if aconite acts thus upon the nervous centres, and controls capillary action, &c., and whether digitalis does not act in a similar manner upon the nervous centres, &c. Dr. Ludlam readily answers that it does not; that there is around the heart a set of nerves called the ganglionic, and that digitalis acts peculiarly on this bundle, or set of nerves. This explains why digitalis is so fine a remedy, and so very useful in diseases of the heart—for instance, in palpitation of the heart. Now, the testimony of Drs. Ludlam and Beebe upon this subject stands before you wholly uncontradicted. No one has attempted to contradict them; no one has even dared to insinuate that their testimony is not true. They have, in their testimony, established the important fact, that they are highly educated in their profession. They talk about things they know. They can give you, on all occasions, a good reason for any fact to which they depose, or for any opinion they give. I am sorry that I cannot truthfully say this of the professional witnesses brought forward by the counsel for the plaintiff.

There not having been even an attempt made to contradict, or in any way to discredit, Drs. Beebe and Ludlam, we are bound to take their testimony as facts. Mr. Turner asked Dr. Ludlam if aconite had not been used by physicians before the system of Homœopathy existed.

The answer was, that it had been; but not for the purposes or with the view for which Homœopathic physicians use it. That its great specific virtues were unknown to the medical world before the days of Homœopathy.

They got this answer, and do not attempt to contradict it. This, too, stands before you with the force of a conceded fact. Could they have contradicted this statement, they most assuredly would. No, gentleman, until the days of Samuel Hahnneman, (who was the founder of Homœopathy),the great virtue of aconite was unknown. Its virtues, or the effects which it would produce, were ascertained by experiment—by taking large doses at intervals. This was done by Hahnneman, when in a healthy condition, and the effects were noted. Any other vegetable may be proved in the same way. It makes no difference whether it is aconite, belladonna, hyosciamus, digitalis, or anything else.

When it is ascertained what effect any particular medicinal agent will produce upon a person in health, then we know whether it will do to administer it to a person laboring under disease. By this mode we learn not to administer as a remedy, something that can do no good, but may do harm in a given case.

Now we have *proved* that it was proper to give aconite in this case, to prevent undue inflammation. They have *not proved* that it was improper. Yet, this is what they *must* prove before they can claim damages at your hands, on the score that the giving of aconite was unskillful or improper treatment. We say that the propriety of giving this remedy was demonstrated by the results.

Their witnesses swear that the boy was in good health all the while. Inflammation is not a state of health, but of disease.

Severe inflammation is likely to follow such injuries as the plaintiff had inflicted upon him. As this did not follow in this case, and as we have proved that the effect of giving aconite would be to prevent this inflammation, which is wholly uncontradicted, it is but a rational inference that aconite prevented the suffering of the plaintiff from severe inflammation. To prevent such suffering would certainly be proper treatment.

It is true that Dr. Porter contends, or rather testifies, that there can be no reproduction of bone so as to obtain reunion, in case of a fracture, without inflammation. How much there must be, he does not tell us. But, upon this theory, he does not testify, nor does any other witness, *that there was not sufficient inflammation* to induce union of the fracture by the production of *new bone.* This proof must be made in order to make this theory available to the plaintiff; and they would have to go farther, and prove that *this lack of inflammation* was produced by the giving of aconite, or by some other act or order of Dr. Pratt; and that such action by Dr. Pratt was not skillful surgical or medical treatment. In these things they have failed *in toto.* But Dr. Porter goes farther; he swears, positively, that there can be no formation of *provisional callus without inflammation,* and that *without provisional callus* there can be no *re-union of bone* ; and that this is so, as to *every* bone in the human body. You will remember that I pressed this subject particularly upon the attention of Dr. Porter; and that in his answer he was *very* positive that, in case of the fracture of *any bone,* there *must* be provisional callus, or that there could be no re-union of bone ; and that there could be *no* provisional callus without inflammation. He testifies, also, that there could be no *re-union* by definitive callus. In fact, he did not seem to know much about definitive callus, which, as I shall show by authors on surgery, that he concedes are good authority—particularly Miller,—*is the material,* he great and absolute *necessary* thing. And by the same author I shall show, as testified by Drs. Beebe and Ludlam, that *neither* inflammation nor provisional callus are *necessary* to the re-union of bone in case of fracture. And I shall go further and show that, in case of a fracture of the *femur* or thigh bone at the point called the capsular ligaments, there can be no re-union, except by definitive callus alone. That at that point there *can be no* provisional callus. This provisional callus is a sort of cartilaginous, or (if I may be allowed the expression) semi-cartilaginous substance, that clasps the bone at the point of fracture, in similitude, as the hoop clasps the barrel. This may well be in the long or round bones; but you will readily perceive the danger to the brain by pressure of provisional callus in any considerable quantity in case of a fracture of the flat bones of the head, and the entire impossibility of this *formation* in the thigh joint.

But no *more* at present, of this theory of Dr. Porter's as to the *reproduction* of bone.

Their theory of diet, in this case, and the giving of aconite is not maintained by evidence, or otherwise; but the propriety of both stands forth with all the boldness of truth. The counsel for the plaintiff sneeringly talks about the wash for the head and hand. The sister of the mother of the plaintiff says that it was arnica. Dr. Wales, who was present when it was ordered and dealt out by Dr. Pratt, testifies that it was what is called calendula, or marigold. It matters not which it was, as both have been proved, again and again, to be very efficient in the healing of wounds of the kind inflicted upon the plaintiff. Their virtues, and particularly arnica, in such cases, stand conceded by all intelligent physicians, no matter to what school they belong. The effect of arnica is no matter of doubt. It stands as a fact, as much as does the curative power of belladonna in scarlet fever. Allopaths have been compelled to yield both, and to use them in their practice.

However, there is no proof, nor is there even a surmise, that any injury resulted from the use of the wash ordered.

From the speedy healing of these terrible wounds, we have the right to infer that good came by the use of the ordered wash, whatever it was. Then, on this part of the treatment, we have *nothing* to *sustain*, but *something* to *defeat* the plaintiff.

On the part of the plaintiff, they have not dared to ask a single witness whether washing these wounds with arnica or calendula was proper or improper treatment. Nor have they asked any witness whether it was improper to give aconite to a patient in the condition the plaintiff was, or in any condition. Upon these points they have no evidence whatever. But we have proved the propriety of Dr. Pratt's treatment in all these particulars. Nor have they proved by, or asked a single witness, whether the non-union of the arm bone is to be, or can be, attributed to the whole or any of this treatment. That this can not be the case, is established by the fact, so far as material for the defendant, by our proof that this part of the treatment was proper. This is further demonstrated by the favorable results, as to all the injuries except this of the arm.

Next in order, let us consider the question whether the dislocation of the thumb and the *fractures* were properly reduced, or set and dressed.

To the end that there may be no confusion, and that you may clearly understand how the matter stands, I will consider one at a time, fully, before touching the other. And first, as to the thumb. What is the testimony?

Dr. Wales says he thinks the arm was first dressed, but he is not positive. It is quite immaterial whether the hand or arm was first dressed. Two witnesses who were present, the Morrises, say that the thumb was first dressed. We find, however, whichever was first dressed, that the whole was well done. Neither of the Morrises, nor the father or mother of the plaintiff, say that the dislocation, or fracture of the thumb was not properly set, reduced, or dressed. Nor do they state any fact from which it can be inferred that the thumb was not properly arranged and dressed in all its parts. Dr. Wales testifies that he assisted Dr. Pratt, and that the fracture and dislocation were properly reduced and then dressed. That flexible splints were applied so as to keep the fragments in proper place. That these splints were made of strong cloth, saturated with gum-shellac. That they were warmed with a flat iron, on a table, or board, so that they would readily conform to and fit the parts. That they would soon cool and become stiff, and were eligible splints, to be used upon this thumb. He also testifies that this lacerated wound of the ball of the hand, was well arranged and dressed.

This fractured thumb bone is called the metacarpal bone. You do not need the superior skill of a surgeon to know that it must have been very difficult to keep the joint and broken bone of the thumb in proper place. The ball of the hand, including the web, or skin between the thumb and fore finger completely torn to pieces. Here was a very bad wound; and when the bandages were removed, muscular action alone would be sufficient to displace the fragments and permit dislocation of the joint. And this would very likely be the case with the bandages on as tight as the patient could bear. There is a great difference between a simple fracture, or dislocation and *there* combined with such a severe lacerated wound as the plaintiff had. I must think as Dr. Beebe testifies,—that he should be gratified to have so good a thumb when the injuries were so severe as those of the plaintiff. Not as Mr. Miller says, that "He would be proud of such a job," *but* that he would be proud that it was in no worse condition.

There has been no evidence,—not one word, that any part of the treatment of the hand and thumb was unskillful, or evidence which establishes the fact that the treatment was not proper and highly skilled. Yet the law only required the evidence of ordinary care and skill. The results demonstrate the exercise of skill much above the ordinary grade.

Upon the opposite side, none of the witnesses have said anything about a fracture of the thumb bone. Their medical witnesses have not discovered that there had been a fracture; but they say there is a *partial dislocation* of the joint. Dr. Porter tells you, upon the stand, that he has examined the thumb before, and that there is partial dislocation. Drs. Beebe and Ludlam both testify that the joint is in proper place and *no* dislocation.

Now, gentlemen, I want you to exercise your common sense on this occasion. Here is this part of the human skeleton, (holding the same before the jury). Now look at the articulating surface, and see if you can tell how there can be partial dislocation of this joint. How this joint can be partially out, and yet the boy be able (as he can and has, in your presence) to move this joint at pleasure ; I confess I cannot imagine how this can be. If you can discover this, you will exceed in discrimination the professional gentlemen who have been before you. It is true, some of those called by the plaintiff have asserted that it was so, but have given no clue to means whereby it can be done. Dr. Porter tells you he finds partial dislocation, but discovers no other injury. But when Dr. Beebe came to examine the thumb, he said that the joints were all in correct position,—so said Dr. Ludlam. Moreover, Dr. Beebe said that there had been a fracture of the bone from the joint obliquely, and that one portion of the bone had slipped down from the other portion. You could see how that was, from the articulating surface, as he exhibited to you. Now, Dr. Porter, with all his surgical skill or knowledge, never discovered this fact. Dr. Beebe, with the skill of the practical surgeon, detected the injury at a glance. Dr. Pratt had the skill to detect this,—because, when he went and examined the thumb after the lacerated wound was healed, or nearly so, he asked the privilege to properly fix it, and the parents would not permit him to do so. The testimony of Frisby is, that he never attached any blame to Dr. Pratt on this account, or for the thumb being in its present condition.

They dare not attempt to show you from their examination of the thumb, that Dr. Pratt did not properly treat it. It makes no difference how much knowledge of surgery a man has—he may be as skillful as Sir Astley Cooper, who is the father of surgery, as Dr. Porter tells you—if he is not allowed to exercise that knowledge.

The parents of this boy would not allow Dr. Pratt to exercise his skill, or any skill, in order to make this thumb better than it is. How could Dr. Pratt cure, when prevented by his parents? You have got to conclude that he could, in order to convict Dr. Pratt, so far as the thumb is concerned. Gentlemen, you will do no such silly thing, if you are the men of common sense, which Mr. Miller says you are. You have only to exercise a small portion of this common sense to determine this question.

This application will be sufficient, without referring to the testimony of Drs. Beebe and Ludlam. This is a matter so simple and plain that you can all readily understand it. Dr. Beebe was the only man who, before you, gave the thumb a critical examination, and he has the requisite knowledge to give an opinion upon which reliance can be placed.

And here, I must do Drs. Beebe and Ludlam the justice to say, that of all the professional gentlemen I have examined as witnesses, (and I have had the pleasure of examining a good many,) they are the best posted in all the details and minutiæ of their profession I have ever seen upon the witness stand. They are perfectly at home upon every question and subject, and can give a good reason, and explain the philosophy of everything upon which they venture an opinion.

I think I ought to know something of surgeons, as I have, among others, had the honor frequently to examine Dr. George W. Lee, of Wisconsin—who was formerly Demonstrator of Anatomy in the La Porte Medical College—and who is one of the best and most successful surgeons in the Northwest. Drs. Beebe and Ludlam came here at our request, without previous expectation that they would be called upon so to do, and knew

11

nothing of the case until so requested. You could see, gentlemen, that they are thoroughly acquainted with their profession, and I ask you to bear in mind that they both testified that the joints of this boy's thumb were in proper position. But independently of their testimony, the action of the joints, if, indeed, anything more were needed, is conclusive evidence that the joint is in proper position, and *not* partially dislocated. If it was partially dislocated, the motion of the joint which you have seen would be impossible.

This fact, with the testimony, shows that, instead of there being any lack of skill, that the treatment of Dr. Pratt may be considered a very rare exercise of great surgical skill.

We do not need to say much about splints. As already remarked, they were made of heavy cloth, saturated with gum shellac. They were warmed to pliancy before they were applied, and when cold they were excellent splints. We claim that these were proper splints to have used, and there is no testimony that *they were not*.

There is another matter I will notice here, and that is, that the sister of the mother says that Dr. Pratt used the hot flat iron on the thumb in putting the splints on, and that it was so hot that the thumb was blistered. But from other testimony we find that this splint-cloth was put on a press-board, or table, and prepared before attempting to put it on the thumb; and that the Dr. had to handle it before, and when putting it on. How much more heat could Dr. Pratt stand, whose hands are tender, than the boy, whose hands are tough? Dr. Wales saw nothing, nor did he hear of any blistering or burning of the boy. There was no heating, except to make the splints pliable, before being applied. Is it reasonable to suppose that Dr. Pratt's hands are harder than the boy's, who had been inured to chopping and plowing? If the Dr.'s hands were not burned, it is not likely that the boy's thumb was blistered.

It violates human probability to suppose that the boy was injured by being blistered. Why was there no evidence of such burning when Drs. Wales and Burbank examined the thumb. Upon this subject we do not understand that the testimony makes against the defendant. This statement of this lady witness is purely imaginary. There is no pretence that the boy suffered any inconvenience from this alleged burning. It is possible that the splints were warm enough to make the skin of the thumb red.

If so, this may have been sufficient for the woman to believe that the thumb was blistered.

I think this will sufficiently account for her statement without impugning her motives for the strange testimony which she gave upon this subject. I think I possess a reasonable degree of charity, and would rather explain her testimony in this way than charge her with a wilful intention to falsify. When she was testifying I understood that Dr. Pratt laid the cloth on the thumb, and then applied the hot flat iron, and thus produced pliancy of the splints.

But subsequent testimony shows that this was done, as before remarked, on a board or table. But so far as the thumb is concerned, it was, perhaps, not necessary for me to have said any-thing, but to call your attention to the testimony of Drs. Wales, Burbank, Beebe and Ludlam, and that of the father, that they would not let Dr. Pratt do anything more with the thumb, and that he never attached any blame to the Dr. as to that thumb.

All the witnesses agree as to the kind of splint applied to the thumb. Upon this subject there can be no doubt, and there can be no doubt that there is no testimony showing, or tending to show, that they were not proper. If improper, it was incum-bent upon the plaintiff to prove the fact. That this has not been attempted, is tacitly admitting that they were proper, as we have *proved.*

Now, having disposed of this part of the case, we come next to the wound of the head. We say the treatment was proper. The wound was healed in a short time. In fact, there is no particular complaint that the head was not properly treated ; and it is not necessary to spend any time upon this matter.

We will next take up the question of the arm, and as to this, as well as the thumb, let me say, that I shall contend that the plain tiff is confined to the allegations of his declaration ; that beyond these he cannot be permitted to go. In the declaration there is no allegation that there was any unskillfulness, want of care, or improper splinting, bandaging, dieting or medication. These, I say I shall contend, are wholly out of the case. The gravamen of the charge in the declaration is, that the defendant did not adjust and set the broken bone properly, and that in consequence thereof, the bone did not, and would not unite ; and thereby, and by reason thereof, the plaintiff has lost the use of his arm, or that, to speak more closely to the averment, he has been greatly delayed in the cure and useful restoration of the arm. The only point, therefore, is, whether the usefulness of the arm has been lost, or the cure delayed in consequence of the broken bone not being properly adjusted or set, or whether there was not a proper adjustment of the fragments.

The plaintiff alleges that there was not. He is bound to establish by testimony this negative, and we are not bound to prove that there *was a* proper adjustment. But not knowing what may be the charge of the Court upon this subject, I shall discuss the case upon this theory, and also upon the theory that the whole field is open to the plaintiff, and that he may ask at your hands, a verdict on the ground that the arm was not properly bandaged, or splinted, or in any other respect improperly, or unskillfully treated. And I shall claim, and have no doubt I shall show, that upon no hypothesis can this action be maintained.

First, then, *the fact* that they have got to maintain by proof is, that Dr. Pratt *did not properly* set, or adjust, the fragments of this arm bone, or in other words, that he *did not properly* reduce the fracture. No other want of care, or skill is alleged. There is no pretence in the declaration that it was not properly bandaged, or that the quantity of bandage was not sufficient, or that it was not applied low enough upon the *arm*, or that the arm was bandaged too loosely, or too tightly, or that there was not put upon the arm a sufficient number of splints, or splints of the proper kind or length. No witness has testified that Dr. Pratt *did not properly adjust or set the broken bone*. This, it seems to me, ought to forever end this case, so far as the arm is concerned. But we have proved by Dr. Wales, who was present, and assisted Dr. Pratt, that this bone was properly adjusted by bringing the fragments in correct apposition, and that the arm was well splinted and bandaged from the hand to the shoulder. That besides short splints, there were two long splints made by one of the Morrises, one of which was applied to the back of the arm, which extended from the point of the elbow to the shoulder; and the other on the inside, which extended from the bend of the elbow to the arm-pit; on the top and bottom of the arm, between these long splints, were placed these shorter ones, which have been paraded before you on the part of the plaintiff.

Dr. Burbank testifies that when he examined the arm, some two weeks after the accident, he found the arm thus bandaged and splinted. He further testifies that on that occasion he examined the arm and found the fragments in proper apposition;

and that they were particular, and went so far as to measure the boy's arms, and found that the fractured arm was of the same length as the other.

We have, then, established the fact affirmatively, that this arm was properly set, or the fracture properly reduced or adjusted. And this is all that you have to enquire about, unless you can be permitted to go beyond the allegations of the plaintiff. This, I contend, you cannot be allowed to do. The proof upon this point annihilates the entire *substratum* of their case. Without foundation, they can have no superstructure, and the defence is completely established.

However, I will discuss this case as though the declaration was broad enough to permit enquiry to the extent as now claimed for the plaintiff, and then we shall find that Dr. Pratt has been right in his treatment. Take it for granted that he possessed the requisite amount of skill, and that he did put in proper apposition the fragments of the broken bone; and that there is mere non-union; then you have nothing upon which to found a verdict for a false joint. There is no evidence that the result is the effect of improper treatment. And we have seen that there might be union of fractured bone where the parts were not placed in proper apposition.

So that the fact of this non-union is not established to have been caused by the parts not having been properly put in apposition. Again, there may be non-union of the bone, or false joint, where the parts have been put in the most complete apposition, and kept in this position long enough to have had a most perfect re-union of the fragments, as a general rule, or even much beyond this time, and yet union may not take place. So that we cannot predicate non-union of bone, or false joint, upon either placing the fragments, or not placing the fragments in correct apposition.

When done, there may be no union, and there may be false joint. When not done, there may be union of the fragments, although in this case there would be more or less deformity. That these results might not follow is not the subject of doubt. They have not had a single medical witness who has even attempted to swear that such results might not take place.

If mere non-union or false joint was sufficient to establish the fact, that the surgeon was unskillful in his treatment, then he would be liable, although he treated the case throughout with the highest skill known to the art. We have proved by our medical witnesses, and by some of theirs on cross-examination, that there may be false joint, or non-union of bone, when the fragments have been put in proper apposition, and retained in this position so long that it is certain that union will not take place by the ordinary mode of treatment; and when the treatment and all its parts has been the highest and most approved known to the surgical art. Something more than mere non-union of bone, or false joint must, therefore, be shown by testimony in order to maintain an action against a surgeon. The *great fact must be proved*, that the treatment *was not* what it should have been; and that such improper, or unskillful treatment might culminate in non-union or in false joint. In all this proof, the plaintiff has most signally failed. On the other hand, we have proved that we properly set, bandaged and splinted the arm, and pursued the ordinary course of treatment until the case was taken from us; and this proof of ours is in no particular done away with, or contradicted.

The plaintiff's case rests solely on the fact of non-union of bone. But why this non-union exists is not made to appear. The fact that no one can tell why this is so, is not sufficient. There are a great many facts that we cannot, nor can any man give a satisfactory reason why they do exist. But this inability does not prove the non-existence of the fact, nor does it authorize us to assign any particular reason for the facts, or fact. There is a class of animals called the *polypus*, which (it is said) if cut into a thousand pieces, each part is replete with life, and becomes a new animal, like the whole of which it was once a part. The fact that I do not see, or that you do not see, how this can be, does not disprove this strange fact. We should endeavor to understand what we know to exist; and we are not authorized to ignore or dispute the existence of facts which we do not understand. We know that there is non-union of the bone of this boy's arm. We are not to dispute this fact, because we do not understand, or cannot tell why it is so. While, however, we know the fact of non-union, we do not know the cause or reason *of the fact*. No witness has attempted the task of telling *the cause*.

When no witness, professional or non-professional, has told you what the reason or cause of non-union is, can you say that you know the cause? If you know, you have a knowledge not based upon the evidence, and upon evidence *alone* you are to determine facts. But let me ask you how you know, or can know,

that there is *non-union* of this bone, because Dr. Pratt *did not*
properly adjust it; or because he *did not* properly splint or bandage it; or because anything else which he did, or omitted to do,
was improper or unskillful? I assure you, gentlemen, you do
not and cannot know this fact because of all or any of these
things.

As you do not and cannot know the cause of this non-union,
let me ask you whether you *believe* that it exists because the
bone *was not* properly set by Dr. Pratt? If you answer yes, I
ask you how comes this belief, when Drs. Wales and Burbank
both testify that it was properly adjusted, and no one swears to
the reverse of this. You must, as reasonable men, say that you
do not believe that this fact exists from that cause. If I ask
whether you believe the cause of this non-union was not properly
bandaging or splinting, still your answer must be, that you do
not. Upon this subject I shall speak more at large hereafter. I
here say, that the extent of their medical testimony is, that they
do *not know what was or is the cause of this non-union.* And I
do not see why this should not be a sufficient answer to their
whole case, without any other being given. But I shall not stop
here. I shall be able to give you satisfactory reasons, before I
get through, why this bone did not unite, or rather, why it is not
now united. These reasons will be founded on the testimony of
the witnesses—both professional and non-professional. They
show that there was a refracture of this bone at the point of non-
union, after it was once well united, so that the boy could move
the arm in any direction.

The professional witnesses on our side who have spoken upon
the subject, say that this would materially interfere with, or lessen
the chances of *re-union.* Now, this, of itself, is a complete explanation of this whole difficulty. Dr. Ludlam tells you that if there
was a refracture of this bone shortly after it was once united,
it might not unite under the treatment of the most skillful
surgeons.

I put the question to the surgeons on the other side, whether it
would not make a difference with the proper union in case of
refracture, or whether at this time they could tell that the non-
union of this bone was occasioned by unskillful or improper treatment, or whether they could tell whether the treatment had, or
had not been proper. They answered, that they did not think
that refracture would make *much* difference. What we are to

understand by this *much* difference, I do not know, but I apprehend that it is admitting that a difference might result, but that they did not know. This is not equal to testimony that *it would* make a material difference; nor does it in any way contradict this testimony; but gives force to it, if it has any effect whatever. The plaintiff's professional witnesses all testify that they cannot tell, by an examination of the arm, what the treatment has been, or that the present condition of the arm is attributable to unskillful treatment or want of proper care. This is simply saying that they do not know what is the cause of the arm being in its present condition; but this is far from establishing the fact that this *non-union* is the result of lack of skill or want of care in Dr. Pratt.

Here, again, their case obtains no strength, but remains unproved. Their witnesses do not pretend that they can tell whether the arm had been refractured. I assure you, gentlemen, that there is no man on earth who, in his normal condition, can, by an examination of that arm (such as their witnesses have made), tell whether there had been a refracture at the point of *non-union*, nor can he tell by any such examination, what the treatment of Dr. Pratt was,—whether proper or improper—nor what was the condition of the arm during the period of Dr. Pratt's treatment; nor whether the *non-union* was the result of want of skill and care upon the part of the defendant, or what is the cause of this *nno-union*.

Ask any man to look at that arm, now—no matter how skillful he may be, and he cannot tell, from the mere fact of non-union, whether the treatment has been skillful or not. Most, if not all the professional witnesses on the other side admit this. Had this case been placed in the hands of the most skillful surgeon, this non-union might have occurred; so that it does not follow that the treatment has not been proper or skillful, from the fact of non-union. You are not to convict Dr. Pratt for what their medical men cannot see, or do not know. He is in no wise liable for what they do not know. When the attending surgeon or physician has not been actually guilty of not exercising ordinary skill and care, he cannot be liable, even on their theory of the case. Nor can he be convicted of want of proper skill and care when it is not shown in what that lack of skill and care consisted. We apprehend that when we show the surrounding circumstances, we show a reason over and above, and better than their want of knowledge, why this bone should not have united. But when we get at, and consider the fact, that when re-union had once taken place, there was a refracture, or loosening of the parts,—(it makes no difference whether you say there was a refracture, or that the union was *loosened*,—either shows a rupture of the newly formed bone,) then the cause of the present non-union of the bone is still more apparent.

It is also proper that we should understand what amount of force would be required to thus loosen the recently united bone. With this view, I interrogated Dr. Ludlam. He testified that sometimes it would occur without any apparent cause ; that sometimes a bone may be fractured that was never before fractured, by mere muscular action. And he mentioned the fact, that he once knew a clergyman, while preaching, to fracture the *humerus* by the motion of his arm in gesticulation.

Medical books abound in still more extraordinary cases. If bone can thus be broken without being previously injured, we can readily conceive how easy it would be to re-break, or loosen a bone recently united, as in this case. It is but reasonable to suppose that it would require but little to produce refracture. But we have shown that there was something beyond muscular action to produce the refracture of this boy's arm. But the ques- tion may be asked, Was there a refracture ? Mr. Miller could not deny this, but he says that he thinks there was *only a little loosen- ing* of the *parts*, but *no* refracture. This concession is the same as admitting a refracture. When the parts are loosened all the troubles of fracture must be expected.

This admission answers the question whether there was a refracture, and shows a reason why the bone is not now united.

The gentleman says that I stated, in my opening, that this exter- nal splint was *split*, as would be shown to you, but that the proof shows that it had been split farther up since. I may have said this, and the testimony may be taken as true. Yet the fact stands before you, that the *splint was split* by a fall or blow when the boy played ball, some nine or ten weeks after he was first injured.

This splitting is proved by their own witnesses. When the boy came in from out doors, *where* he had been playing, as he went up stairs, his mother (as she says) noticed the splint being split, being on the outside of the bandages, and fastened at each end with straps to keep the arm in place.

This splint, as shown by the testimony, was not necessary, but was put on by Dr. Pratt, out of abundant caution. It was so fastened that it would break before it would let the arm give way. A fall upon the ground or against a fence post, with this splint at the angle which was braced across *must*, almost of necessity, refracture the arm or loosen the newly formed bone. The young lad that was playing ball with him says that he threw the ball to him, and as young Frisby kicked at the ball and bent forward, he lost his balance and *he was thrown against a fence post and hurt his arm.* Of necessity, he must have went against the fence post with a good deal of force. This must have been the result from his attitude and motion.

There it was that this arm was hurt and this splint was broken. The breaking of the splint he admitted to his parents,—at least to his mother. After this injury he went directly into the house, and as he went in, went up stairs immediately. His mother noticing that the splint was broken, was led to inquire of the boy what he had done,—but she says that it was not broken, or split as much then as it is at present; that there was only one crack instead of the two. But, gentlemen, some of you must have some mechanical knowledge, and hence, must know that, if that was broken by a blow at the lower end, screwed and glued together as it is at the elbow, or angle, it would be impossible to split it by one crack and not make both. But take one of these splits and then it must have yielded so much that the arm must have been refractured. The end is where it received the blow, or where it came in contact with the fence post, as demonstrated by the splint.

There would have been no tendency to break on one side and not on the other by a blow at the elbow. Had the blow been there, *then* the lower, instead of the upper piece, would have been split *inwards*, instead of outwards, as we find it. The blow being at the end of the splint, became a lever with the elbow for a fulcrum, and was amply sufficient to *separate* the bone of the arm again. And such must have been the result, had the boy put forth the arm to prevent himself from falling. You readily perceive, gentlemen, that if this splint was split no more than they now claim, the arm must have been re-broken, or the newly formed bone must have been separated by the accident in falling against the fence post. But I do not see how this splint could be split on one side, by a blow or fall, and not on the other. If you are mechanics, and by natural philosophy can do this, you are ahead of my capacity.

You can readily perceive that the injury of refracture must have occurred whether the splint was split as much as now, or only so much as they claim. If the arm was not injured in the way we claim, and to the extent, can you, upon any rational hypo. thesis, explain why the parents wished to withhold this splint from Dr. Pratt? The reasonable explanation of their attempt to keep the splint is, that they wanted to keep from the Dr. one of the instruments of evidence that would injure their chances of maintaining an action. They must have felt that the injury of the boy was so great that it was material to keep the evidence of that injury out of the way. Why was it that the father directed his wife to keep this splint and not let the doctor have it if called for? He knew that this would be tangible evidence of the refracture which he knew had taken place. Do you suppose that he, or any of his family had the idea of keeping this splint so that they would have it to use, should any of them break their arm? You can not believe that this was the object. There was no thought of a general system of breaking arms in the family. Refusing to let the Dr. have his own splint, upon any other hypothesis than that he wished to retain the instrument, which would be evidence of a refracture, would be palpable folly. I must confess that I can see no other good reason.

But I readily perceive that the counsel, in the exercise of his ingenuity, may say that, if this was the object, why did the father not burn the splint, and thus absolutely destroy this instrument of evidence, so that it would never appear in court? I will tell you why. He was fearful that should it turn out in evidence, that they had burned the splint, when we could prove the injury and fall by the boy who was at play with the plaintiff,—he was fearful, I say, that a jury would conclude that the fact of burning was conclusive evidence of their being wholly in the wrong, and that an action might more certainly be defeated thereby than by an exhibition of the splint, with the family to swear that it was not as badly split by the fall as it now is. In other words, he concluded that the presence of the splint would not operate as badly as its destruction by willful burning.

It was matter of sagacity in the father to preserve the splint from destruction. But the attempt to withhold it is very conclutive evidence that he was fearful of it as an instrument of evidence on the question of *refracture* of the arm bone.

It seems to me that their own witnesses conclusively show that the bone was re-broken; that their testimony is sufficient to satisfy any reasonable mind of that fact. But we do not stop here, or at the point of the evidence by young Shaffer.

You will recollect that the testimony unfolds different conversations about the arm being re-broken It was talked of by the father and mother in the presence of Dr. Belding and Mrs. Belding. Dr. Pratt and the plaintiff were also present. On this occasion Dr. Pratt, in alluding to it, said that he had broken the arm a second time, playing ball; and told him if that was not the way, to tell how it was; and the boy said, "That was the way it was done." Remember, this was stated in the presence of the father and mother, and of Dr. Belding and his wife. The two last named, both testify that this conversation occurred. And Mrs. Belding testifies, also, that when she was talking with the mother, remarked that she should think that it must have hurt him very bad; and the mother replied that he did not complain much, but she thought that it hurt him more than he pretended, or would admit. The mother, in this, was undoubtedly right. It was very natural for the boy not to disclose his feelings after what he had done, as he undoubtedly thought that he had done wrong, and that he would get scolded if he owned up fully. We were all boys once, and then we were shy about disclosing what we had done. I know that was the case with me when the results were bad. You are all aware of this disposition in boys. Some boys would have dreaded a talking to more than others would a whipping. I do not know how this was with this boy. It is enough for me to know that it would be natural for him to keep a knowledge of the worst facts from his parents. If neither the boy nor the parents anticipated a second breaking of the bone, why was he so silent, and they so particular to interrogate him respecting the matter?

I think the statement of the mother to Mrs. Belding was very natural; and it was not singular that she should make that remark on that occasion. Yet she says that she did not make this remark, nor anything like it, on that occasion, either to Mrs. Belding or to any one else. She goes further and says that she did not talk with Mrs. Belding, nor even see her that day. I mean the day of the consultation over the arm at Dr. Belding's.

Dr. Freas does not recollect anything but the bare fact that she was there on that occasion. But Mrs. Belding recognizes the mother here in court, as the lady who was introduced to her, at her house, the day of the consultation, as Mrs. Frisby. She swears positively to the fact of this conversation. The mother either has forgotten, or she does not, on this trial wish to remember.

The fact that Dr. Freas does not recollect hearing anything about the arm having been refractured, in no sense impugns or weakens the testimony of Mrs. and Mr. Belding, who testify that they did hear it. But Dr. Belding and his wife are not the only persons who have been present when the fact of the re-breaking of this bone has been talked of in the presence of the boy, or of the father, or both.

The young man, Hodgeson, swears that in the conversation about the boy injuring his arm, at Dr. Pratt's office, the father made the remark that he did not think the boy had hurt his arm as bad by putting on his boots as he did when he fell against the fence, in playing ball. And here, *too*, the father says, that he never made any such statement. Do you suppose that this young man made up this story ?

How unnatural. Why should we believe these denials of the father and mother, to the exclusion of the testimony of these disinterested witnesses. The more charitable view is, that the father and mother have forgotten. But we *cannot*, to accommodate them, believe that young Hodgeson, Dr. Belding and his wife have all sworn falsely about these conversations. I take it, that Hodgeson is a young man of fair mind, although he could not tell much about the sermon, or discourse he listened to some time ago. But this proves nothing against his capacity to comprehend, nor against his character for truth. I have known many good and intelligent people, who, upon returning from church, could not even tell what or where the text was, much less what the sermon was.

Is it remarkable that this young man, who hears two or three sermons of a Sunday, should not be able to state much or anything that was said in a particular sermon, and should yet remember what he testifies Mr. Frisby said at Dr. Pratt's about his boy hurting himself? Not at all. It is all very probable. Is it not more probable that he would remember what was said about such an arm as this, than what was said in a sermon ? It would be very singular if he did not. He remembered that at church they sung "Dundee," and also "Old Hundred," which was such a favorite of Elder Brewster that he expected to hear it sung by the angels when he got to heaven.

The counsel was so particular in his enquiries about what occurred at the meeting alluded to by young Hodgeson, that I expected to hear him ask the witness to sing one of the Psalms. That would have tested the accuracy of his statement that he helped sing, especially, had it turned out that he could not sing. Like some persons who claim to have signed documents, as witnesses: we sometimes test them by having them try to write their names, and find that they cannot do it. But, I ask, do you anticipate that this young man made up this story? Is the story not probable? It is more likely that he should be right in his recollection of what the father said, than that the father should be right when he says he did not make the statement. This is a mere want of recollection, if the father, in this particular is truthful. Want of recollection is not equal, as evidence, to recollection. The young man recollects the fact and testifies to it.

The boy was present when this conversation occurred, about his falling against the fence post and hurting his arm, and he does not deny the fact. Mr. Morris, who was at the neighbor's, also heard that the boy had fell and hurt his arm. But independently of these conversations, the refracture is clearly proven. We prove by Dr. Wales, that at the end of eight weeks from the time the boy was first injured the arm was examined in his presence, and with his assistance, by Dr. Pratt. All the dressing was removed from the arm. On this occasion the boy could raise his arm and move it about, Dr. Pratt simply steadying it by taking hold at the hand to prevent any injury in case the union should not be so firm as it appeared. There was no action, or motion at the seat of fracture, but it was *intact* and *firm*, with no deformity,—but natural.

But the counsel asked Dr. Wales how he knew that Dr. Pratt did not lift when he had hold of the boy's hand? Do you suppose it reasonable that Dr. Pratt would have done this when the object was to see whether this boy could move the arm by his own muscular power? We should form the reasonable conclusions from acts when there is nothing to warrant a conclusion the reverse of ordinary conclusions. But if Dr. Pratt had raised the arm by taking hold of the hand, then motion would have been

discovered at the point of fracture, if the fragments of bone were
not united. If the Dr. thus raised the arm and no motion was
perceivable at the fracture point, then it is clear that union had
taken place.

If the boy could and did raise the arm himself, without Dr.
Pratt lifting, then it was also clear that there was union of the
bone. As there was no motion at the seat of fracture on this
occasion, it makes no difference whether Dr. Pratt did or did not
raise the arm, or *lift*. The lack of motion in either case proves
the union of *the bone*. It would, however, be passing strange,
that a surgeon should do more than steady the arm when the
object was to test the fact, whether the bone was united. How
are you to account for such an act upon ordinary principles of
human action? Certainly the boy would know if the Dr. raised
or moved the arm. Yet he says nothing of the kind, which he
should, had such been the fact. I assert that no surgeon would
have done any such thing. Had the doctor done this, is it not
very singular that he should have called the mother to see that
the boy could move his arm?

He did this, according to the testimony of Dr. Wales; and
when she looked at the arm, it was exposed to the skin, and she
could readily have detected the fact of non-union, had such been
the fact, whether Dr. Pratt raised the arm or not.

Upon any reasonable hypothesis you will have no difficulty in
appreciating the fact that Dr. Pratt did not lift the arm on that
occasion. He must have felt proud of the success of his treatment, and wanted to test the accuracy of his opinion that the arm
was united, by an examination and exhibition of it. He found
the arm in such good condition that he talked of leaving the
splints off; but finally, out of excess of caution, he replaced the
bandage and splints. Even this outer splint was again put upon
the arm, and the boy was permitted to go out of doors. This
was well enough, if the body was properly protected from the
cold, and he was careful not to injure the arm,—the fresh air
would be beneficial. How many times he was out of doors
besides the occasion when young Shaffer played ball with him,
we do not know. He may have been out many times before and
after this. The boy was not in our custody, and the evidence of
such facts are, of course, beyond our reach. And we have to protect ourselves against this false accusation by such incidents as
have come to our knowledge.

One thing, however, is very certain, and that is, that the boy played with young Shaffer after the examination of the arm, in the presence of Dr. Wales, when the union of the bone was demonstrated. It may have been less or more than two weeks after that time. We do not know the time exactly. But it could not have been far from that time. This examination took place about the twentieth of February, about two months after the fracture. You will remember that on cross-examination, Dr. Wales says that he knows the time, from the fact that it was the day he made a passing visit to Seymour Downs', and that his books show that that visit was on the 20th of February. And his recollection is, that it was about that time.

To contradict Dr. Wales, they call the mother, who says he never did anything with the arm. Just contrast that statement with her testimony in chief. She then said that he only occasionally came there and dressed the arm. I asked her if she recollected that he ever came there and dressed the arm, and took the bandages all off. She said she did not pay any particular attention; and did not remember that the dressing was all taken off on any occasion,—sometimes she did not look. How is it possible to reconcile her own testimony with itself, or with that of Dr. Wales? She says he did not take any part, or do anything in dressing the arm. He says he did. Do you not suppose that he knows what he did in that behalf? They wish to contradict everything testified to by Dr. Wales. And in a number of particulars which the court ruled out. They attempt to carry the joke too far when they put the question to her so as to have her answer as echo to the question.

It is probable that she would answer any question put by Mr. Turner to suit him, when, from the question, she could see what answer they desired. But is it probable that Dr. Wales would go upon the stand and commit perjury, by swearing positively to certain facts if they had not taken place?

I am glad to see that the father and mother prove that they have an interest in the boy. Still, I think it improper for his counsel to so interrogate them as that the answer is plainly indicated. Nor do I think such evidence worth much. Such has been the case, however, of the other side. And they have sought mere supposition for facts.

With what charity I possess I cannot reconcile such statements as have been made by these witnesses with the ordinary occurrences of human life. I do not attribute this disposition to a bad, or depraved nature. It is not necessary that I should. I attribute it to an undue desire to have the boy gain this case at all events. In this attempt they have sworn to a little too much for ordinary credulity; and that, too, in reference to matters which could not have much, if any thing to do with the case.

I cannot be made to believe that Dr. Wales would swear that he made the visits and did what he says, unless such were the facts. He says he was present and assisted Dr. Pratt on the first occasion. Then in about two weeks from that time.

On one occasion when Dr. Pratt was not there, when he gave the mother some medicine for a sore throat. That he was there and assisted Dr. Pratt in examining the arm, on or about the twentieth of February. He made no memorandum of these visits, but remembers the number. He also says that he saw the arm after it was *refractured.*

You will remember that Dr. Wales testified that he took hold of the arm and examined it himself at the visit of February twentieth, and found the bone in proper place and united ; and that after he had done so, the arm was re-dressed and the splints replaced. We then have his statement of union of this bone, and of the fact of refracture.

They wish you to disbelieve Dr. Wales upon this subject, and believe the mother, who stands contradicted relative to the matter of refracture, by two other witnesses, namely, Dr. Belding and his wife. They also want you to disbelieve the witnesses, Hodgeson and Morris, upon this point. Do you believe that these five witnesses have all sworn falsely ? To ask you to believe this, is asking a great deal, and more, I apprehend, than you will do. But their anxiety upon this subject shows that they consider the fact of refracture a circumstance that must weigh heavily against the plaintiff and strongly in favor of the defendant.

This anxiety is well founded. But Dr. Wales' statement that he found the arm in proper position on the twentieth of February, is sustained by the testimony of Dr. Burbank, who had previously examined the arm. He says that enough of the dressing was removedd, so that he could feel an discover that the fracture was properly reduced. He did this, and lest there might be a possible doubt from feeling, he measured both of the boy's arms from the shoulder to the point of the elbow, and found them both of the same length. They must ask you to believe, and you must believe, that Dr. Burbank and the other five witnesses all swear falsely to make the shadow of a case for the plaintiff, even if we were obliged to show affirmatively, that we had properly reduced this fracture, and had in no respect been guilty of want of proper care, or skill. I can see no reason or motive for their testifying falsely. But I say, gentlemen, that, taking the testimony of the father and mother, about the splitting of this external splint, and then not more than one case in a thousand could result in any other way than refracture, or rupture of the newly formed bone. As I have already remarked, Dr. Pratt seemed to desire that the boy should correct his statement as to how the arm was re-broken, when he was playing ball; and told him that if that was not the way it was done, to state how it was done. And the boy promptly replied, that was the way. Do you suppose the boy then told a falsehood, or that he did not know the fact that his arm had been broken a second time? Now let me repeat, this conversation occurred at Dr. Belding's, in the presence of the father and mother, and of Mrs. and Mr. Belding and Dr. Freas, who says he does not recollect this conversation, nor has he much recollection of what was said on that occasion. I do not now recollect that I questioned the father about this conversation. But I do recollect interrogating the mother about it; and also whether she did not, on that occasion, converse with Mrs. Belding about the boy breaking his arm a second time; and she swore positively that she did not, and further, that she had no conversation at all with Mrs. Belding, and did not even see her while she was at Dr. Belding's. Is this woman to be believed when contradicted by so many credible witnesses, in preference to them; when no one contradicts their statements but her alone? It cannot be. Upon all the evidence there can be no doubt that this arm was broken a second time.

Again, the father and mother testify that the few short splints which they have paraded in court, are the identical splints that Dr. Pratt put on the boy's arm, and *their* medical witnesses all testify that they alone would not be sufficient to keep the fragments in place, excepting Dr. Miller—he thought that they might be sufficient with the external splint. But look at the disposition of the parents, testifying that these are the identical splints used on the boy's arm, without disclosing the fact, that there were also two other long splints made by the witness Morris—one of which was put upon the outside of the arm, which reached from the elbow to the shoulder; and the other on the inside, which reached from the arm-pit to the bend of the elbow.

The making and putting on these long splints we have proved by too many witnesses to have the fact doubted. It is true, the mother and the father do not swear that these short splints were all that were enclosed within the bandage.

Yet, the only inference that could have been drawn from their testimony was, that these short splints were all that were put on, besides the external one. It was a clear attempt to color the testimony and suppress a fact that would be material to the plaintiff if, in the hurry of the trial, we should forget to prove the fact that other splints were put upon the arm.

Dr. Pratt has never pretended to think that these short splints alone were sufficient to properly protect the arm, although, as I have already intimated, Dr. Miller thought one long enough for the outside of the arm, and the other for the inside, and sufficient, with some of the others, for intermediate splints.

If there was no intention to deceive, why were they so particular to parade and prove the use of these splints, and not bring in the others, nor say anything about them?

That is a question, gentlemen, for you to solve. But the young lady (she will pardon me for calling her young, as ladies seldom object to being called young,) testifies, that these short splints were *all* that were put upon the arm, except the external one. She is for closing up every avenue. However, I have come to the conclusion that she was greatly mistaken, although she testifies to the fact with much emphasis. Dr. Wales and the two Morrises testify to the fact of these long splints (which were made by one of the Morrises) being put upon the arm, one upon the outside and the other on the inside, and of their reaching from the elbow to the shoulder. This lady is too flatly contradicted by too many witnesses to be believed.

But again, Dr. Burbank found these long splints upon the arm at the time he examined and measured it. He tells you that one was on the back side, and the other on the inside of the arm, and he agrees with our other witnesses about their length. Dr. Belding also testifies that these long splints were upon the arm at the time of the consultation at his house.

Here are five witnesses, all swearing positively and affirmatively to the fact that these long splints were upon the arm. Yet, this lady testifies that there was another splint on the arm, and it got broke, and Dr. Pratt brought another, and that the father cut it off by the Dr.'s directions.

We have proved to you how these splints were put on, and that they were entirely sufficient to keep the parts in apposition without this external splint. Dr. Ludlam tells you that this splint is of modern invention.

That these other splints which we have proved to have been put on the arm, were entirely sufficient without this newly invented splint. The putting on of this angular splint was merely a matter of extra caution.

Dr. Beebe says the same thing; you cannot believe that all of our witnesses have sworn falsely about these splints. The entire medical fraternity testify that splints of the length, kind and number which we have proved were put on, are proper and sufficient. Do not do yourselves and Dr. Pratt the injustice to decide otherwise.

[Here the court took a recess, and upon again meeting Mr. Knowlton continued his argument.]

Gentlemen of the Jury—At the adjournment of the court, I was about to approach the subject of bandaging. Upon this subject, the witnesses on the part of the plaintiff, all agree that the bandage commenced in the first instance, at the wrist, and was carried, or continued from there to the shoulder. This is all for the purpose of keeping the bone in place, and the muscles at rest. When the muscles of the fore-arm, which are connected with this, the lower portion of the *humerus*, which was fractured, are sufficiently bandaged to prevent motion, and so as not to disturb the bone in the fractured portion, it is sufficient.

Some of the time they seem to want to insist, or contend that there was too much bandaging, and that it was so tight as to turn the hand black. It seems that Dr. Pratt's attention was called to that fact, and that he ordered the hand to be rubbed.

The medical witnesses testify that this is not unusual, and that it sometimes becomes necessary to loosen the bandage on account of swelling, and that as the swelling diminishes, it can then be readily tightened. As I understand the point about the bandaging, they do not expect to make anything out of it specially, except its necessity to keep the parts in apposition. They have attempted to prove that the bandaging should commence at the point of the fingers, and carried from there to the shoulder. I do not know but they will contend that the arm should have had,

like the ancient Egyptian mummies, an envelop of seventy wind-
ings, in order to prevent muscular action. We have proved that
it is not necessary to bandage lower down than the wrist, in order
to prevent undue muscular action. Some authors direct the bandaging to commence at the wrist, and others at the fingers.

There is a difference of practice upon this subject among eminent surgeons. The point is not at all settled, so that either mode
cannot be improper or unskillful practice. The point made by
good surgeons is, that the bandaging should be sufficient to keep
the fractured parts in apposition, so that the process of re-union
may go on. On the part of the plaintiff, it is contended that the
bandage should go lower down than the wrist, so as to prevent all
muscular action. Mr. Turner interrogated Dr. Ludlam very particularly upon this subject, and his answers negatived their whole
theory of bandaging.

Upon its tightness he said, that this could do no harm unless it
materially impeded circulation. That this had not been the case
is proved by the fact, that the external wound at the seat of fracture healed in the usual time. This could not have occurred, had
the circulation been materially impeded. Healing progressed,
and the fragments were found in apposition, or in proper place
when Dr. Burbank examined and measured the boy's arms some
three or four weeks after the injury. Again, at the end of about eight
weeks after the arm was first set, Dr. Wales testifies that the bone
was properly united. The evidence abundantly shows that the
bandaging was such as to secure all the important objects enumerated as essential.

It is nonsense, then, to contend that there was not a sufficient
amount of bandage, that it was too tight, or too loose, or that it
was not put on low enough down. What more do they want, or
could they have from bandages than to keep the bones in proper
place and the process of repair to go on?

When these are the facts, where is the propriety of contending
that the bandaging should have commenced at the ends of the
fingers? But they say that the old man, Yeoman, testifies, that
on the third of February, the bone was not *united;* that he then
assisted in holding the arm of the boy. He says that he was behind
the chair in which the boy was sitting, and with his arms around
the body of the boy, he held him to the back of the chair, while
his wife had hold of the boy's elbow with one hand, and of his
hand with her other hand. That that arm of the boy was bent

to the extent he shows us, which would be an angle of about *forty-five degrees*, and that his wife pulled about *one hundred pounds*. This he judges from the amount of strength he exerted to keep the boy up against the back of the chair.

Now, it is obvious that he might have exerted strength enough to have raised two hundred pounds, or even more, and yet he could not tell from that whether his wife pulled even one pound—for the reason that the back of the chair was between him and the boy, and he may have held him very snugly against this chair back, when not an ounce was pulled on the arm.

But, further, he shows you that one of the hands of his wife was under the elbow, as if to hold it up, and the other hold of the hand of the boy, and that the boy's arm all this time was at this angle. Now, gentlemen, if you or any other human being can tell how it was possible for this woman to have pulled enough to raise one hundred pounds, with her hands in the position described, and that, too, without straightening the arm from the angle it was in, you can do more than I think is within the power of mortal man. The thing is a physical impossibility, and that the old man could tell how much his wife was pulling is a flat absurdity.

He says that he and his wife performed this service to aid Dr. Pratt in setting the arm—as the bone was then not in the right place, and that the bone was then set. Now, as to all the other facts testified to by this witness, and which bear upon this case, I have, as I think, shown that his statements are flatly absurd. This being so, I do not see how any confidence can be placed in his other statements.

But the other side think his testimony very important and reliable. Upon the hypothesis that the witness tells the truth, when he says Dr. Pratt set this arm bone on that occasion, does it establish anything in their favor, or in ours? Let us consider this. First, then, he swears that Dr. Pratt set the arm. It is not impossible that the small pieces of bone may not have been in exact apposition, and needed adjustment. It is this *possibility* that renders the statement of the witness *probable*. If such were the fact, then the evidence also shows that the surgical eye of Dr. Pratt readily detected the displacement; and that he immediately set it, or put the fragments in place, shows his good *attention, care and skill*. This witness does not pretend that the bone was not properly set on this occasion.

No want of skill, no want of care, no want of attention is here shown, but the very reverse of all of these. We prove, by Drs. Beebe and Ludlam, that this bone might have been set at this time, and have become well united by the twentieth of the same month—that is, in from fifteen days to three weeks. As late as the third of February the formation of new bone must have been well under way, and fifteen or eighteen days more might well make the work of repair complete. It was on the twentieth day of February that Dr. Wales testifies that he, in company with Dr. Pratt, examined the boy's arm, and found it *well* and *properly* united. So that this testimony of the old man Yeoman, if true, is in our favor, and in no particular against us. This testimony of our professional witnesses, namely, that this bone may have been set on the third of February, and firmly and well united on the twentieth, is not contradicted, nor attempted to be contradicted by any witness.

It must therefore be taken as true, as much so as though the fact had been admitted by the other side. I care not how you measure this testimony, whether by the Ell-Flemish, or the Winchester Bushel. It all ends in the same thing, when contrasted with the other testimony.

You may take all the theories and all the testimony about bandages, splints and everything else, and yet you must conclude that the bone was united on the twentieth of February, as stated by Dr. Wales. No one has testified that union was not complete then, nor that the boy could not then move his arm in any direction, as Dr. Wales has testified, so that it makes no difference whether you believe, or do not believe the statements of the old man Yeoman. If the bone was out of place, it was proper to put it in place whenever that fact was discovered. From the testimony I have no doubt that the bone was united on the twentieth of February, and the attention of the mother called to the fact, and that she expressed herself gratified. She says she does not recollect anything about it. Very well, suppose she does not recollect; Dr. Wales does recollect and swears to it, so that the fact is established and in no way contradicted.

She says that she never, at any time, saw the arm undone to the skin, but that she was always present when anything was done to the arm. They do not interrogate her as to the facts sworn to by her father—the old man Yeoman, who saw the arm naked, and could see that one piece of the bone was higher up than the other; and he also saw Dr. Pratt manipulate the arm so as to get the fragments in proper place. They bring the old man upon the stand, who swears to a set of facts not maintained by any other witness—not even by his wife, who tugged at the arm and pulled a hundred pounds, as the old man says. The mother always present, and yet not one word from her about this matter sworn to by her father. There is something singular about this matter, to say the least.

The fact that Dr. Pratt manipulated the arm, as stated by this old man, might well have been done for the purpose of seeing whether the fragments were in proper place, for it is next to impossible to get them in exact place.

I now wish to read from page 240 of Hamilton on Surgery. The reading is:

"At a very early day, so early, indeed, as the seventh or eighth day the splints should be removed, and, while the fragments are steadied, gentle, passive motion should be inflicted upon the joint. This practice should be repeated as often as every second or third day, in order to prevent, as far as possible, anchylosis. If much swelling follows the injury, it is my custom to open the dressings without removing the splints—on the second or third day after the accident, or at any time when the symptoms admonish of its necessity."

I also call your attention to the book alluded to by Mr. Turner last night called Homœopathic Surgery, 2nd part, page 105:

"The treatment, when the shaft of the bone is broken is simple. The proper extension has first to be made by drawing up the wrist or elbow, the fore-arm being about half bent, and the adjustment then accomplished by comparing the length and appearance of the limb with its fellow. If it be an oblique fracture, great care must be taken not to let the ends of the bone slip by each other, and thus render the arm permanently shorter. The muscles materially tend to bring about this result. Have the parts held, when once in proper juxtaposition, by an assistant, while a roller is applied, rather loosely from the shoulder. Then place one splint about a quarter of an inch thick and of convenient width, so as to cover nearly the whole surface of the arm. Let them be nearly as long as the humerus itself, the inner one being a little the shortest, so as to allow the elbow to be bent. Then continue your roller, bringing it down again over the splints from one end to the other a sufficient number of times to fix them firmly to the arm, and prevent any motion or contraction of the muscles."

I do not know why this author is not entitled to as much credit as other authors. There appears to be a considerable variety of splints, as well as diversity of opinion, as to which is best; as well as considerable diversity of opinion upon the subject of bandaging. The latest, and perhaps the best author we have is Hamilton.

From all we have been enabled to learn, there does not appear to be the least want of skill, care, or attention in Dr. Pratt, as to setting the limb, in splinting, bandaging, or in any other particular. The fact deposed to by Dr. Wales, that Dr. Pratt made slight motion of the elbow so that it should not become stiff by continuing in one position, was certainly commendable practice. This elbow joint is, to all appearance as good as it ever was. Its motion is free and perfect. This, with the fact that the arm has not wasted away, proves that it was properly cared for by Dr. Pratt while he had it in charge. True, Dr. Porter says the muscles have become relaxed. But Dr. Belding tells you that such was not the case when he saw the arm in May, on the occasion of the consultation. This relaxation of muscles is the effect of abandoning the care of the arm, which was bestowed upon it by Dr. Pratt. They have left the arm to dangle about without any splint, bandage or other support of the muscles. Remember that the longer the arm is left in this situation the more the muscles become relaxed. Measures should be taken at once to make it a good arm.

Had the arm been treated as recommended by Dr. Pratt, the arm would undoubtedly have been a good one long ago. We have proved that this can yet be made a good arm, and that the operation is a simple one, and not very painful.

As to when this angular external splint was put upon the arm, for the first time, is not positively and definitely settled by the testimony. The father says it was put on the day after the injury was inflicted. The mother says she sent the boy after it, and she thinks it was not put on until the second week. The sister of the mother puts it at a different time from that stated by either the father or mother. Here are three persons in the same family and no two hit upon the same time as to *when* this splint was put on. This conflict shows that their statements are not to be relied upon,—because, if so, which is right? We have shown that this angular splint was put on, on account of the restlessness of the boy, and that it would not have been necessary in an aged person. All the surroundlings show that it must have been put on at an early period; and such is the testimony of Dr. Wales; and such, too, is the testimony of Frisby—the father. He says that he thinks it was put on to take the boy home, but he will not be positive about it. But Dr. Wales says that it was on when he saw the boy, on the Tuesday following the Saturday when the injury occurred.

Some of the witnesses say that there was other protection put upon the arm when he was taken home. So that there is nothing to be made out of the pretence that the arm was not properly protected at the time the boy was removed home. They have struggled hard to make something out of this point; their load, however, is greater than Samson's when he shouldered the gates of Gaza.

Now, gentlemen, there is another important matter to which I wish, right here, to call your attention, and that is, the last started *pretence* that the boy's arm and thumb are incurable, and that they were rendered so by Dr. Pratt. Now, it so happens that there is no such testimony. There is not a single witness who swears to the incurability of either the thumb or the arm. But it is a waste of time to talk about this thumb, when their own witnesses swear that, at an early day, the parents would not allow the defendant to reduce the thumb to better position. And, as to the arm, we have proved by skilled surgeons, that, even at this late day, there is no difficulty in making this broken arm a good one. They were evidently aware that this could be done, when the declaration was drawn,—and hence, the cautious language used in the pleading. In *this*, they simply aver that the plaintiff has been "*delayed*" in the *cure* of the said arm and thumb. This averment of *delay* is tacitly an admission that the arm and thumb *are* curable. To contend that the arm is incurable, and to recover damages for such incurability, they must aver the fact in the declaration. This they have not done; and they cannot go beyond the scope of their own declaration. However, we have proved that this arm *is curable*, and no one has sworn that it *is not*. The curability of this arm, therefore, stands forth with the force of an admitted fact. They wish you to give them damages for incurability, but only allege in the declaration that a cure has been *delayed*.

This is the only actionable averment. All the balance is mere inducement, or mere form. As to the anguish, it is not possible that there was much. All the witnesses who speak upon the subject, say that the boy has never complained of any pain from the outset. Without pain from these wounds, there could have been no *pain and anguish, or anguish* alone.

Here we have a case of delayed union of the arm bone. In this state of the case the arm should not be abandoned, but other, means should be resorted to, for the purpose of effecting a cure. There are a number of methods which surgeons adopt as promising success. Among these we have proved that of the seton; that of silver, or ivory pegs; that of *resection* of the bone; that of acapuncturation. That the three last named at least promise great success. The mode of acapuncturation is now more generally called Brainard's plan. Our professional witnesses have explained to you, the manner of operating in each plan. We have also proved that none of these operations are difficult to perform, nor are they very painful.

We have also proved by the medical witnesses, that no case of non-union like that of the plaintiff's should be considered or given up as incurable, until all these means have been tried and have failed. No witness testifies to the reverse of this. None of these last enumerated modes have been resorted to. Yet Dr. Pratt wished to do so. From the very nature of his employment, and undertaking, he had a right to resort to any, or to all of these modes of treatment. They are all recognized by eminent surgeons as proper; while some prefer one mode, and others give the preference to a different one. There is a diversity of opinion which of all the different plans is best. But Dr. Pratt was not allowed to resort to any of these plans. Nor would the parents of this boy allow Dr. Pratt to bring a surgeon from Chicago to perform any of these operations. This he offered to do, and upon the basis, too, that it should not cost them any more than as though he performed the operation himself. Dr. Pratt, however, did not stop here, but he offered to go with them and the boy to Chicago, and have any good surgeon perform any operation which might be considered preferable, and that he would defray his own expenses without charge to them. There was Dr. Brainard, Dr. Smith, Dr. Beebe, Dr. Ludlam, and Dr. Boardman,—any one of whom, under this offer of Dr. Pratt's, they might have had to perform this operation, with no extra costs except their own traveling expenses.

It is not to be doubted, that among the Chicago surgeons named by me, there are those of skill quite equal to any on this continent. It is certain that Dr. Brainard has a world-wide reputation as a surgeon. But none of these would do ; none of these received favor. On the contrary, all were rejected, and the case was entrusted to Dr. Miller—who, to this time does not appear to have taken any measures to effect a re-union of this *un-united* fracture. At all events, no progress has been made in that direction.

Gentlemen, what more could be asked of a poor human being than was done by Dr. Pratt? He offered to perform the operation himself. This was not allowed. Then he offered to have the operation performed by as good a surgeon as there was in Chicago, with no additional costs if the operation was performed here. And if performed in Chicago their own expenses was all the excess.

Now, gentlemen, I wish to ask you this pertinent question : If you had a nice surgical operation to be performed, at the same cost, would you have it done by one of your home surgeons, or by Drs. Beebe or Ludlam ? They have all appeared before you, and you have had an opportunity of forming an opinion of their capacities respectively. In this list of home surgeons, I do not intend to exclude Dr. Porter, who, with all his stump speeches on the witness stand, is chiefest among them all, as Paul said he was among the sinners. I do not know what you would do, but٠ if I had such a case I would sooner trust the operation to Dr. Ludlam or Dr. Beebe than to all the doctors examined on the other side combined.

But perhaps some of you would be extreme in your notions. If so, you might prefer Dr. McPherson, who set there fully five minutes under the solemnity of an oath, and could not tell where he graduated. He finally testifies that he never graduated at all. Did you ever before hear of a person forgetting a fact that never existed ?

He is the surgeon who would resort to friction in four weeks after fracture, if at that time union had not taken place. Then, in two weeks more he would try friction again, if he found the bone had not united. What a surgeon, and what a man ! ! Their other surgeons, who have spoken upon the point (except Dr. Miller, who may be a good practical surgeon), all testify that there can be no union of fracture without provisional callus. I will venture the assertion that these other surgeons took their clue about provisional callus from Dr. Porter. He leads off, and testifies so positively, and with such emphasis, that there can be no union of fracture without provisional callus—that the thing was impossible as to any bone. And he was just as positive that there could be no provisional callus without inflammation. Inflammation was necessary to produce provisional callus, and provisional callus was necessary to produce union of fracture.

This positive and emphatic manner of Dr. Porter might well produce the like opinion with these young men who were not thoroughly posted, and, if possessed of but little firmness, might be easily led astray. This is rendered probable, as Dr. Porter ranged out in the most glowing terms about beneficent Nature and her unlimited wisdom. With such a fulmination they must have seen and felt that his knowledge was most extensive and accurate, and that they were ignorant. I venture to assert, that from his frequent reference to authors, they would take what fell from his lips as true, instead of consulting those authors. Oh, they are a hopeful family, as Paine said of the Royal family of England.

Professional gentlemen, who claim to be surgeons, should be tolerably well acquainted with what is contained in works treating upon that subject. Here, they all concede, they have to go to determine the modes of treatment.

Some of these young men, under Dr. Porter's training, would wait six or seven days after trying friction, and then they would try it again.

They speak of the seton as one of the plans to be adopted when the ordinary means have failed, and friction has also proved abortive. Beyond this they seem to know but little, if anything. Yet, first class surgeons have other and better modes than the seton, which has nearly disappeared from practice. Upon this subject you have the testimony of Dr. Ludlam. He mentions resection of bone, ivory pegs, and puncturation. He says that all these modes have merits, and so does Dr. Beebe; and no witness denies the fact. Which should be resorted to would depend upon the particular case and its surroundings? In the case of this boy, Dr. Ludlam says that, in his opinion, the mode of resection would be the most promising of success of any of the whole catalogue. And he further says that he has no doubt that the plaintiff's arm can be made a good one.

The professional witness from Freeport did not seem able to go beyond the seton and ivory pegs. He seemed to know nothing about resection or the system of Brainard. I think there is some opportunity for him to read yet.

Why, gentlemen, you can hardly open a book on modern surgery which does not treat of these different modes of treating non-union of bone.

That gentleman would try friction, although not so soon as some of the other of these *learned* gentlemen. Dr. Miller would wait eight weeks and then try friction. If no union then followed, I do not know how soon he would resort to friction again. Very few of these gentlemen have stated what they would do before resorting to friction. They thought it a very long period to wait from the twentieth of December to the last of February, or the first of March, before resorting to friction. But Drs. Beebe and Ludlam think from five to eight months not too long. Dr. Ludlam tells you that he thinks that a cure is or may be retarded by this much haste in hurrying the treatment from one mode to another. He says the test as to when friction or other stronger modes should be resorted to, is the smoothness of the ends of the fractured bone, by the growth of a sort of cartilaginous substance over them; that, rubbing the fragments against each other, non-union may be detected when no crepitus is discovered, and that, when this is found to be the condition, it would not be improper practice to keep the fragments for a time in close contact. So that in no way that we look at the testimony, can any other conclusion be arrived at than that they have utterly failed to show that this arm is incurable, or that it was not properly treated by Dr. Pratt.

You will find that after this case is over they will go to work and have this arm made a good one.

This they have delayed for the purpose of getting a verdict of heavy damages in this action. I insist that on the facts developed, this action cannot be maintained, inasmuch as that the case was taken from Dr. Pratt, and he not allowed to do what he wished to do, namely, try other modes of treatment which promised success, and which are regarded as proper by skillful surgeons.

Upon the subject of difference between a simple and a compound fracture, the medical gentlemen on the other side who speak upon the subject, think there is not much difference as to the probabilities of union taking place, that is, that union is nearly as likely to occur in compound as in simple fracture; and some of them think there would not be any difference. They do, however, all admit that a compound comminuted fracture is more dangerous, and less likely to unite than a simple fracture; and that when it is complicated with other wounds, the chances of recovery are rendered still less certain. While upon this subject, I again call your attention to the testimony, that the humerus was fractured transversely above the *nutritive foramen*, and obliquely below the *foramen*, severing one branch of the nutrient artery; that there was an external wound leading to, or communicating with the fracture; then there were the wounds of the head, the thumb and hand. This testimony shows beyond doubt, that this was a compound comminuted complicated fracture.

Even upon this trial Dr. Beebe exhibited the evidence of the character of the fracture; and herein are presented the difficulties besetting, if they should not prevent union.

But under the judicious medication and care of Dr. Pratt, we find, that after the lapse of eight weeks from the time the injury was inflicted, all these wounds were healed, and the fracture completely united. What better results could have been anticipated? Obviously, no better could have been hoped for. Subsequent to this time it was again fractured, or the fresh union ruptured. This second separation of the parts greatly reduced the chances of re-union by the ordinary modes of treatment. If the result was favorable it would be an exception and not the rule.

The probabilities were, that it would not again soon or readily unite. Dr. Beebe mentioned a case within his knowledge of a re-fracture of a compound comminuted fracture, where it again united at the upper fracture, but refused to unite at the lower point of fracture, within the same time, but was greatly delayed; and whether it would finally unite was not yet known.

He mentioned another case, which was a fracture of the humerus. In this case there was a re-fracture, and it not only refused to unite but the whole bone was removed by absorption. A similar case is mentioned in the books, which has also been alluded to, but which I will not now take the time to read. These facts are not denied, and there is no doubt of their truth. There is no chance for caviling.

It is to my mind a very grave question, whether, under the law, the plaintiff can recover damages for being merely delayed in the restoration or cure of the arm, which is the only injury complained of. The father has planted himself on the ramparts of the law, and claims to recover damages for this delay in an action now pending, undetermined in this court.

If the father is right in his action, then it is impossible for this plaintiff, who is a minor, to maintain this action. However, it is quite immaterial what they contend for, as upon no hypothesis are they sustained by the evidence.

There is another important feature in the testimony of their professional witnesses. They all know, or have heard something of provisional callus, or *provisionary* callus, as Dr. McPherson calls it. But they appear to be wholly ignorant of any other callus.

They know nothing of the humerus being less likely to unite in case of fracture than any other bone in the human body. Yet, authors of the greatest merit, say that this is so, and they give statistics to prove the fact.

Again, these authors say that definitive callus must invariably form in order to complete a permanent union of the parts; of this, these gentlemen appear to be ignorant. That provisional callus is passing away, while definitive callus is forming, is another thing that these learned gentlemen are ignorant of. They go so far as to deny that provisional callus ever disappears, and say that it lasts through life, and that, should a man live to the age of Methuselah, traces of this provisional callus could be detected. The books teach the very reverse of their doctrine, and Drs. Ludlam and Beebe both tell you that this is not the case. Dr. Ludlam tells you most distinctly that provisional callus is being removed while the definitive is forming; that when provisional callus is slight it soon disappears; and when there is much of it, it may last a long time.

Dr. Freas does not recollect whether, as Dr. Belding testifies, that they found provisional callus or not, on the occasion of the consultation in May. This consultation was held a long time after the re-fracture.

Dr. Freas says that Dr. Pratt spoke about the provisional callus being there at that time, but he does not remember that he mentioned it himself, but thinks he did not. Dr. Belding says that Dr. Freas did mention it, and that it was then perceptible to the touch. Dr. Miller did not find any when he examined the arm, which was some time after. I do not remember any other professional testimony upon this point. The sum total as to Dr. Freas is, that he does not remember what he did say, or how the fact was; while Dr. Belding does remember what the fact was, and what Dr. Freas said about that fact.

Dr. Freas does not remember whether there were other splints on the arm than those produced here in court. But he recollects that there was conversation about splints, and about resorting to friction; and that Dr. Pratt had previously tried friction, and was willing to try it again. Dr. Belding *does* remember that there were two other long splints on the arm. This occurred about the tenth or thirteenth of May, 1863; and the case was taken from Dr. Pratt on the thirtieth day of the same month.

At this time Dr. Pratt thought a further operation than friction should be performed, but yielded to the suggestions of others, and consented to again try friction. Dr. Miller thought an operation ought to be performed, but advised waiting until cold weather before proceeding to operate.

They do not deny that an operation should have been performed, as suggested by Dr. Pratt, but they propose to defer this until this experiment of damages is through with. Then, I have no doubt, the operation will be performed.

So far as the professional testimony goes to the matter of treatment, I think I have touched upon all that is material, as well as all that relates to general subjects which are incidentally connected therewith, or at least, that I have done so so far as is necessary to a correct understanding of the case; and so far as is necessary to test the amount of knowledge possessed by the professional gentlemen whose opinions have been given in this case. And for the purpose of contrast, and of fortifying the views which I have expressed, I shall hereafter read from standard authors on Surgery.

I now propose to consider the testimony of their professional witnesses, as to the mode by which the reparatory process is carried on so as to produce union of fracture. And propose to see how far they are sustained by the authors who are conceded to be standard authority, in all medical schools of whatever practice. First, upon the subject of provisional callus. This, gentlemen, is a book that Mr. Turner seemed to be anxious to show was orthodox. That it was, we admitted. It is Miller's Principles of Surgery, and I read now from page 624:

"In some cases, no splints are required; coaptation being both effected and maintained by mere relaxation of muscles, and attention to position; as in fractures of the clavicle and patella.

"*Prevention* is best achieved by duly carrying out the just principles of reparation; keeping the fragments rightly adjusted,
18

preventing motion, and taking care that bandaging is never too tight at any part of the limb. The limb, it has been stated, is to be kept in a posture favorable to muscular relaxation, and consequently conducive to the feeling of comfort. Besides, it should be placed so as to favor venous return, while an opposite influence is exercised towards arterial influx; the fore-arm, for example, is slung, with the hand raised; and the lower limb is kept on the same level as the rest of the body, with the foot elevated.

"Undue motion and over *excitement* are the *opponents of union*, and *either is quite sufficient to prevent it wholly.* Inflammation having occurred, exudation is aplastic, the pouch becomes that of an abscess, an opening is necessary, the case becomes compound, and cure may be indefinitely delayed. During the first few days, it is consequently our object to watch the indications of local excitement; and to take every precautionary means in our power to prevent its excessive advancement. At the first, we have contributed much towards the object in view, by gently, yet at once, effecting reduction and maintaining it undisturbed; the main cause of inflammation has thus been taken away—and that timously. Diet is low, yet not strictly antiphlogistic; *unless* suspicious symptoms arise. The bowels are regulated; but purgatives are never expedient, the manifold motion which they necessarily occasion tending to much injury. In hospitals, the fracture bed is useful, by preventing evacuation of the rout bowels without movement of the limb. If sensations of heart, pain and throbbing occur in the part, restlessness (this boy was restless), flushing of the face, and acceleration of the pulse, blood may be taken from the arm in the *robust* and healthy; antimony, or *aconite* is administered, (you see this author recommends *aconite*,) and *diet* is brought down to the strictly antiphlogistic scale. And antiphlogistics will be especially *active, and early* in *those cases* in which fracture is in the near vicinity of important parts; as in the case of the ribs and calvarium. If there be much involuntary spasm of the implicated muscles, jarring the fragments, opiates may be useful.

"If the signs of inflammation are distinct and advancing, notwithstanding the ordinary *precautions,* the retentive apparatus must be undone, and *discontinued* at the part; to admit of leeches and fomentation. But this casualty is of rare occurrence, in the *simple* fracture, when ordinary treatment is duly conducted. Should abcess form, it must receive the common treatment; an early and dependent opening. After the first eight or ten days, the risk of the inflammation *may*, under ordinary circumstances, be said to be past.

"Diet, accordingly, is gradually improved; for it is essential to maintain considerable vigor in the frame, in order to obtain a due and early completion of the process of union. And this ulterior necessity should never be lost sight of, in the *earlier part* of the case; more especially when antiphlogistics have unfortunately become expedient.

" The retentive apparatus is undone and re-applied, as seldom as possible.

" At each change, the condition of the fracture should be carefully observed; more especially as regards accuracy of adjustment. If the survey prove satisfactory, the apparatus is simply re-applied as at first.

" If distortion exists, the splints and bandaging are to be so arranged as to obviate this; gradually restoring the normal position. At the end of the fourth or fifth week—sooner in a young and healthy, later in those in advanced years and debilitated frame—union, to a certain extent, by soft and new formed bone has occurred; and our substitutes may be discontinued. If a y oedema exist in the distal extremity of the limb—as sometimes happens, notwithstanding all our care to the contrary—friction is to be employed, with continuance of the bandage, uniformly applied. But so soon as oedema has gone, let *all bandaging be thrown aside;* otherwise atrophy and permanent debility of the limb may ensue. The joints, by friction and passive motion, are then gradually brought to their accustomed freedom of play; and *when* a joint is in the near vicinity of a fracture, it is well to practice passive motion of it very carefully, at an earlier period, at each undoing of the retentive apparatus, that stiffness may be avoided.

" Use of the part must be resumed very gradually; more especially in the lower limbs. Many a fractured leg has been set free, at the ordinary time, of proper length, and void of all deformity; which, nevertheless, soon becomes both shortened and bent, to an extent which impaired both its symmetry and function. The callus is soft and pliable at first, as has been already observed; and the motto of the convalescent should be '*Festina lente.*' "

Again, this author, speaking of compound fracture, on page 627, says :

" And the splints and bandage should be so arranged as to leave the wound capable of being readily exposed, for the purpose of inspection and dressing, without any undoing of the general apparatus. At first, antiphlogistic regimen is more especially necessary than in simple fracture; both the likelihood and the hazard of inflammation being greater."

On page 616 this author says :

" *The mode of union*, or preparative progress, is a subject of much importance; on the right understanding of which the indications of treatment depend. It may be conveniently divided into the following stages; understanding that the fragments have been duly readjusted and are so retained :

" 1. Blood is extravasated at the site of fracture; and, accumulating, distends the surrounding parts into a kind of pouch, in which the fractured ends are laid; and the cavity of this pouch, is occupied by the extravasated blood, partly fluid, partly coagulated. The surrounding parts are condensed; and, obeying the stimulus of the injury and displacement, become more energetic in their circulation—prepared for the usual effort in nutrition which is about to be demanded of them.

"2. The extravasated blood is absorbed; and the ends of the fractured bone also undergo alterations, being deprived of their earthy matter to a great extent, and so prepared for higher efforts as a vascular tissue. Liquor sanguinis is exuded from the parietes of the pouch, from the ends of the bones, and from the periosteum which invests them; and this plasma assumes the position which the blood occupied. The pouch, however, has somewhat contracted from its first dimensions, by tumescence of the parietes—favored, or at least permitted, by gradually decreasing extravasation. It has been a source of hot dispute, to determine from from what tissue this plasma proceeds. Probably it is the offspring of every tissue implicated; exuded from bone and from periosteum, and also from the texture constituting the parietes of the containing pouch, whether these be muscular, fibrous, fatty, or areolar. Perhaps it may be held enough for the practical inquirer, that there is the plasma, come whence it may. The plasma, having been exuded, consolidates; its serous portion is absorbed; the fibrin remains, and becomes organized. And this organizing plasma not only occupies the pouch, but is also situate between the fractured ends of the bone, and in their interior. At the same time, fibrinous exudation is taking place in the soft tissues exterior to the pouch, whereby they are still further condensed. A portion of this is imperfectly organized; and remains for a time—sometimes of considerable duration. The rest is absorbed previous to organization, on subsidence of the vascular excitement by which it was exuded. This is a part of the inflammatory process; but only a part. It never raises higher than *active* congestion; *otherwise the process of repair would be arrested and undone*." (This is the very reverse of Dr. Porter's theory, that inflammation is necessary to the repair of broken bone).

"3. The period of plastic exudation may be said to have passed, after eight or ten days.

"Then the process of organization advances. The plasma sometimes passes into the transition state of fibrous tissue; at others into fibro-cartilage, or even true cartilage. The first of these is most common in the human subject; the last rare, but on the other hand, common in the lower animals.

"4. The organized and transetional mass contracts, by interstitial absorption; increases in density; and *gradually* passes into the condition of bone. At the same time, the surrounding parts, where immediately in contact with the ossifying mass, are more and more condensed; they become continuous with the ruptured and engorged periosteum, and assume the general characters of that tissue, as well as its function of investing and administering to bone.

" 5. Ossification advances from the periphery. The most exterior part of the plasma is that first ossified; and thence ossification gradually approach·s the interior. In obedience to the law formerly noticed, (p. 175), the first act in the process would seem to be that of the parent bone. Nodules of new osseous matter form on it where, in contact with the ruptured periosteum, the rough extremities at the same time undergoing an opposite change; parting with a large share of their original earthy matter, as already stated. These nodules would seem to constitute the nucleus or base of the new bony structure; and are found on each fragment, and on its every aspect.

From these nuclei the ossification advances, and a case of bone forms on the exterior of the plasma; advancing *from each fragment*, and meeting near the centre of the space; the ossification *begun by the original bone*, continued and maintained by the soft parts, first, by the original periosteum, and then by the ordinary tissues, which by condensation and other change of structure, have come to assume not only the appearance, but the function of the investing membrane of bone. Where the original *periosteum is deficient, there is no corresp nding hiatus in the new bone*, as in the case of necrosis (p. 396); f.r the ordinary soft tissues *are not in a state* of true inflammation, and a'l their exudation is plastic. As ossification advances, the mass contracts more and more; ultimately forming a firm *osseous* ferrule, by which the fractured ends are clasped; and the continuity of bone is apparently restored. This ossified mass is termed *provisional callus*, and the period of its formation averages from four to six weeks. At the end of this time, the bone fe·ls firm, for the fractured ends are tightly held together by the ferrule. It is probable, however, th it between the fractured ends ossification may not yet be completely accomplished.

6. *Definitive callus* is that which is formed between the ends of the bone, and which *constitu'es* the *final medium of incorporation of the ends* Its organization and ossific ition are accomplished by a more slow and gradual process than that of the provisional callus; apparently in obedience to the general law, that whatsoever is destined for an en·luring existence, is constructe·l leisurely and well. *By the definitive callus, the ends are firmly glued together; and the fracture is truly* united. In proportion as construction of *definitive callus advances, the provisional callus gradually diminishes by absorption;* the latter being merely subservient to the former. The provisional callus, indeed, may be termed nature's splint, whereby the parts are kept in close and undisturbed contact, until their real consolidation shall have been completed.

" When this has been achieved by definitive callus, all necessity for the presence of provisional callus has gone by; *and consequently it is soon thereafter removed by absorption.*

Practically, *it is important* to remember that provisional callus remains to a certain extent soft and pliable, during the first few weeks of its existence; not so yielding as to admit of motion between the fractured ends, under ordinary circumstances; yet, pliable enough to admit of mal-adjustment being gradually rectified by pressure duly applied; also pliable enough to permit serious and untoward binding, if the functions of the part be too soon and too freely resumed. A broken leg must be warily used, for some considerable time after apparent consolidation; and a broken bone anywhere may have its *contour remedied,* if need be, by suitable pressure, applied even after the process of reparation seems to have been completed.

In some fractures, as in that affecting the neck of the femur, within the capsule *there is no opportunity for the formation of provisional callus.* The recipient pouch cannot be made; and there are no surrounding textures to supply the required plasma. And this is the main reason why union at that part is so difficult and rare; the latter and more tedious half of the process only being obtained. In like manner, the flat bones, more especially the cranium, have a deficiency of provisional callus.

"And it is well that such is the all wise-arrangement. For were a cranial fracture to unite through the aid of a bulging hard matter on each aspect, the functions of the brain would assuredly be interfered with to a dangerous extent. *In these bones, re-union is by definitive callus alone;* and this, if the intervening space be not great, very efficiently repairs the breach; usually at no distant period.

Should, however, the hiatus between the fragments be at all considerable, osseous reproduction is incomplete; it advances only a certain way; and the remainder of the plasma is converted into a dense fibrous substance.

Sometimes this fibrous re-union is desirable rather than otherwise, as in the case of the patilla."

On page 663, on the subject of displacements, this author says:

" *Occasionally* it is found very difficult, *notwithstanding every care to keep the bone in apposition;* muscular action being *constantly* at fault.

"Under such circumstances, it has been proposed, and not unreasonably, to have recourse to tenotomy. For example, in fractures of the leg, which may not otherwise be kept duly arranged, subcutaneous division of the tendo Achillis may be practiced; with immediate and decided advantage, as regards the fracture, and with impunity as regards any ulterior result."

Upon the subject of false joints, *ununited* fracture, and *disunited* fracture, Miller, page 629, says:

"A fracture may fail to unite from various causes.

"1. If motion be permitted, and still more if it be made daily, or even occasionally, the formation of provisional callus will be disturbed, and the *definitive* is likely to be altogether frustrated; the part will probably remain pliable.

"2. *Or the parts may be duly adjusted and retained, and re-union may fail* by excess of the inflammatory process, in any way induced; *true inflammation being quite as adverse to the process of healing in bone, as* it is in a wound or ulcer of soft parts.

"3 From constitutional defect, or *atmospheric* accident, there may be a want of effort in the part; *plasma* is deficient; and what is produced is but imperfectly organized; just as indolent ulcer of the leg refuses to heal."

Next of disunited fracture.

"A fracture, having been consolidated in the ordinary way, may again become loose and movable. This may be the result of fresh mechanical violence, occasioning immediate disruption of the connecting medium.

"Or it may be a more tardy but equally certain process, the result of inflammation; induced by a less degree of external violence, *or by any other cause;* as a wound, recently united by adhesion may be made to gape wider than before, by accession of inflammation, suppuration or ulceration.

"The *false joint* which results either from *disunited,* or from *un-united* fracture, bears no true resemblance to normal articulation. There is neither articular cartilage, nor synovial apparatus.

"The ends of the bone taper somewhat, and are rounded off; they are invested by a dense fibrous expansion; and by a similar texture of less density, they are *joined together.*

"To undo the apparatus of a fractured limb, at the end of four, five, six, seven or eight weeks, is no demonstration of the expected union having altogether failed. It may be that the formation of *definitive* callus is yet in progress; and, if undisturbed by movement of the limb, this may be completed in no unreasonable time. The provisional callus has, doubtless, failed; but in *truth, this is not essential to osseous re-union.* When it does exist, it is but a ferrule or clasp, tightly embracing the broken part, rendering it immovable, and seeming to restore its actual continuity, as a like binding agent may give continuity to two pieces of wood and make them one. But, so far as the binding agent is itself concerned, there is as little actual restoration of continuity of texture in the bone as in the birch.

"Provisional callus only enacts the part of a steady splint, until the process of true consolidation has been completed by elaboration of the definitive callus, whereby there is, as it were, an interweaving of texture between the broken ends. It takes some time to construct this splint, and to apply it with due tightness; four, six or eight weeks, as may be. During its construction it is necessary to steady the parts by external means; and that is the province of the surgeon.

"After it has become firm in itself, and tightly applied to the bone, then it is capable alone of restraining motion, so as to permit of true consolidation of the broken ends; and the surgeon's splints may be now taken away. In short, under such circumstances, there are three distinct means towards the final cure: 1. Surgical splints to steady the parts until provisional callus is formed and completed. 2. Provisional callus, or nature's splint, to secure perfect immunity from motion, until the definitive callus has been constructed. 3. This definitive callus, by whose gradual elaboration and modification, true continuity in every part of the texture is ultimately restored. When No. 2 is furnished, No. 1 is useless, and is taken away by the surgeon's hands; when No. 3 is complete, No. 2 is *removed* by the busy labor of absorption; No. 3 remains, but is ultimately much modified also by absorption. Neither No. 1 nor No. 2, however, *are absolutely essential* in themselves to the formation of No. 3 (p. 619); and if No. 1 be present. No. 2 may all the more be dispensed with.

" *Of the series*, the *only one* which is truly essential is the last. Bones may knit by provisional callus, though no surgeon is by, and no splint is applied—though not so well; and *they may also unite—perhaps not much after the ordinary period—though provisional callus may have proved either faulty or altogether defective.*

"That is, *union may* take place, independently of the splints, both of the surgeon and of nature. Flat bones, such as the cranium, *unite mainly*, if not *solely* by definitive callus; and fractures of the neck of the femur, within the capsule, if it unite at all, *can do so in no other way*. The process of union, no doubt, is favored by the presence of both splints in due succession, first the surgeon's and then that of nature; but still it *may* be completed, independently of one or other of them, or of both.

" Supposing then, that on removal of our splints, at the end of the accustomed period of probation, we find the broken ends still movable on each other, it is *manifestly* our duty to *re-apply the retentive* apparatus with still greater care than formerly, and *to keep it so applied* for a considerably *greater period* than was at first contemplated, it having now a new duty to perform; not to keep the parts steady till provisional callus clasps them tight; but to take the place of this callus and to keep the parts steady for a longer period than before, so that the *definitive callus now* supposed to be in progress, may duly advance to completion.

"And not until a reasonable period of probation—say four, five, or six months—for the construction of this, the essential part of the uniting process, shall have passed away does the surgeon abandon *either the careful use of his simple retentive apparatus*, or the hope of cure.

" In regard to this form of ' un-united fracture,' there need be no two opinions as to the right mode of treatment; namely, to put up the limb afresh, to keep the parts immovable, and to maintain the general health and powers of system, in as vigorous a condition as possible. Starch splints are here extremely suitable. At the same time, the general health is attended to; diet is generous and stimuli may also be necessary—to maintain energy of system for duly sustaining local repair.

"But when, at the end of *four, five, six months, or more,* we find the limb still loose and movable at the site of fracture, it is *a sign that* the ordinary process of re-union has failed in all its parts. And the same conclusion is forced upon us in cases of an earlier date—six or eight weeks only, it may be, after the accident—in which mobility is great, in which a space, *defective in everything* like restorative means, can be felt between the ends of the bones, and in which these can be plainly felt blunt, tapering, and rounded. In such cases it is that difference of opinion prevails as to the best modes of treatment, and *latitude exists as to their selection.*"

Speaking of the different modes of strong treatment, on page 632—first of " *subcutaneous incision,*" he says :

"My experience, as far as it goes, speaks in favor of the practice. Lately, this method succeeded, quite beyond my expectation, in consolidating an un-united fracture of the humerus, which had sustained compound injury, about ten months before. The bones over-lapped, and could not be adjusted. Altogether the case was so very unpromising as led me to remark, while performing the subcutaneous puncture, that it was an unfair test of the practice ; and that, under such circumstances, a successful issue could hardly be expected. Yet, on the first undoing of the splints, five weeks after the fracture, the parts were found quite firm. (Note 2.)

" It is surely better than—though somewhat like—the practice of John Hunter, whose treatment of an un-united fracture of the humerus, Mr. Samuel Cooper tells us, was as follows :—' There was an artificial joint, and he made an incision into it ; and then having introduced a *spatula,* he irritated the whole surface of the artificial joint. This brought on considerable inflammation, which ended in anchylosis, and the patient was cured.'

" White's severe operation of cutting down and sawing off the ends of the bones, was not only hazardous to life, but not unfrequently failed to accomplish the end in view; in some cases it proved fatal. Dr. Physick's seton is less formidable than the saw ; but chance of failure with it is not slight, and in fractures of the *lower extremity,* indeed, its success may be regarded as only the exception to the rule.

Dieffenbach exposed the bone by incision, drove a peg of ivory into each extremity about half an inch from the line of fracture, and then by wire firmly and closely connecting the two ; expecting that the foreign body would rouse a plastic exudation which would abundantly suffice for consolidation of the fracture now so accurately retained. Experience has spoken favorably of this practice ; an ossific process being established similar to what takes place in necrosis. Should the method by seton be preferred a caoutchouc tape, or skein of silk or cotton, is inserted between the ends of the bone, and permitted to remain there for some days, until sufficiency of plasma has been exuded around in the shape of the organizable fibrin which always attends more or less on the lodgment of such a suppurative agent.

"On the whole, perhaps the following statement will express the right sequence of practice. In recent and favorable cases, place the limb in strong bandages with or without subcutaneous puncture.

"In more advanced and determined, but yet favorable cases, employ subcutaneous puncture, freely, and perhaps with repetition. In the least favorable cases—more especially if these other means have failed—employ either the seton or the ivory pegs." Page 634, Miller.

You will observe that this author does not speak favorably of re-section of bone, while Gross does. I shall hereafter read to you from this author upon the subject.

Eminent practioners and authors differ very much as to which is the best mode of treatment when the ordinary means fail. And even in some matters of ordinary treatment they differ somewhat —particularly upon the subject of bandaging,—the most eligible kind of splints, and the effect of motion, as conducing to, or interfering with the re-union of bone. As you have already seen, this author, Miller, is against permitting any motion of the fractured limb. He makes no distinction upon this subject between different bones, while Hamilton (who is, I believe, the latest writer of any note that we have, and very eminent in his profession) does.

And upon this subject and other matters I now read from Hamilton, commencing on page 64. He says:

"In order to hasten the consolidation when it is simply delayed, we resort to all of those expedients which are calculated to invigorate the general system; and for this purpose the employment of a nutritious diet and the use of mineral or vegetable tonics may not be properly omitted; that in our experience nothing has proved so efficient as encouraging the patient to leave his bed and get out into the open air; for which purpose, if the fracture is on the lower extremities, crutches will be necessary.

"As local means we may enumerate, first, the removal of these local causes which seem to have interfered with the consolidation or with the union. If the fragments have been officiously disturbed, it may be sufficient to impose upon the limb absolute rest for a certain length of time; and the fragments may be more closely pressed against each other; in other cases it will be found necessary to expose the limb freely to the light and air at least once or twice daily, and to rub it gently with the dry hand, or with some moderately stimulating oil, so as to induce a more healthy condition of the soft parts, and encourage the natural circulation.

"Moving the fragments freely upon each other, sufficient to determine a degree of excitement in the adjacent tissues, and upon the opposing surfaces of the bones, and then confining them during one or two weeks in firm and well fitting splints, will often succeed when other means have failed.

"Indeed, I may say that by one or another of the simple methods now enumerated, I have never failed, sooner or later, to effect consolidation in recent fractures; and it has only been in fractures of at least four, six or eight months' standing, that I have been compelled to resort to more extreme measures.

"As a means of combining immobility with compression and healthful exercise, the "apparatus immobile," in many of its forms, is peculiarly adopted. White, of Manchester, employed a firm leather sheath for the thigh. H. H. Smith, of Philadelphia, recommends a more complex artificial support, upon which the limb may be allowed to rest while in the act of progression. With some surgeons the object of allowing the patient to walk in fractures of the thigh or legs is chiefly to excite, in the tissues adjacent to the seat of fracture, some degree of inflammatory action, but which, as the result in one of White's patients was sufficiently shown, may be carried too far, and even determine a suppuration. Blisters, mustard cataplasms, the tincture of iodine, caustics, &c., applied externally over the seat of the fracture, can have no other effect than to increase moderately the congestion of the tissues, and in so far this may aid in the accomplishment of the bony union; but in this respect they are inferior to the violent twistings, or flexions and rubbings of the broken ends of which we have already spoken.

"Electricity was first employed by Mr. Birch, of London, but Dr. Mott obtained no effect from it in two cases where he seems to have given it a fair trial. Lente, of the New York Hospital, has more recently furnished an account of three cases treated in that institution by electricity in connection with acapuncturation; the mode of using which was to pass a needle down to the periosteum on each side of the bone, and to attach the poles of the battery to these opposite points. Lente thinks that electricity, employed in this way, is much more efficient than when the poles are merely applied to the surface. He informs us also that other cases than these now reported, have been treated successfully in this hospital by means of electricity.

"Mercury, urged to ptyalism, will no doubt, prove serviceable occasionally by virtue of its powers as an anti-syphilitic, but its beneficial influence in other cases is far from having been established.

"The seton is said to have been first suggested by Winslow, in

1787; but what is of much more consequence, the credit of its first successful application, and its general introduction into practice, is due to Dr. Philip Syng Physick, of Philadelphia, by whom it was employed in 1802.

"Physick used for his seton, generally, silk ribbon, or French tape; and this he introduced by means of a long seton needle between the ends of the fragments. He recommended that the seton should remain in place four or five months, and longer if necessary, and it was his opinion that the failures were generally due to its being removed too early. At the present day, however, surgeons who employ the seton think it serves its purpose better where it remains in place but a few days, not longer, perhaps, than ten or fifteen, always taking care that it is removed before excessive suppuration is induced. It has been found especially valuable in fractures of the inferior maxilla clavicle, and upper extremities generally; but in case of the femur, it has so frequently failed, that Dr. Physick himself did not recommend its use. In case the seton cannot be passed directly between the opposing fragments, as recommended by Physick, we may adopt the practice suggested by Oppenheim, and carry the setons, one on each side, close to the bone.

"Somme, of Antwerp, preferred a loop of wire to the silk seton employed by Physick. Sarig passed a ligature around the ligamentous mass connecting the two fragments, and then proceeded to tighten the ligature until it fell off. Dr. Hulse, of the U. S. Navy, employed stimulating injections with success in a case of non-union, accompanied with an external and fistulous opening. In 1848, Dieffenbach recommended that ivory pegs be introduced into holes previously made in the bone by means of a gimlet or drill; and Mr. Stanby has succeeded once by this method. Malgaigne, in 1837, tried to introduce acupuncture needles between the ends of an un-united fracture, but although he thrust the needle down to the bone thirty-six times, he was unable to make it pass once between the ends of the fragments. Niesel succeeded better. In a case of un-united fracture of the ulna of nine weeks' standing; having passed two needles between the fragments at the end of six days the needles being removed, consolidation rapidly ensued. This practice does not differ essentially from the metallic loop of Somme. It is only a modification of the seton.

"Brainard, of Chicago, has attempted to show that setons of any kind, whether of wood, ivory or metal, placed in contact with the bone, occasion absorption, caries and necrosis, but that they never directly give rise to bony callus; and that the occasional success of the seton, which success he believes to have been greatly exaggerated, has not resulted from any tendency to favor the formation of callus, but from the induration and tenderness of the soft parts, produced by it; circumstances which, by conducing to rest, indirectly favor the consolidation.

"•In May, 1848, Miller of Edinburgh, reported five cases treated successfully by subcutaneous puncture. The operation consisted in passing the point of a needle or small tenotomy bistoury down upon the ends of the bone and freely irritating the surfaces at several points. George F. Sandford, of Davenport, Iowa, has successfully imitated this practice in two cases.

" Brainard employs for this purpose a strong metallic perforator, consisting of a handle, into which points of different sizes may be inserted, and which have been hardened so as to penetrate the hardest bone, or even ivory, in every direction easily. The points are " somewhat awl shaped, but more pointed in the middle rather than like a drill, which leaves chips." His manner of using this instrument is as follows : In case of an oblique fracture, or one with overlapping, the skin is perforated with the instrument at such a point as to enable it to be carried through the ends of the fragments to surround their surfaces and to transfix whatever tissue may be placed between them. After having transfixed them in one direction, it is withdrawn from the bone, but not from the skin, its direction is changed, and another perforation made, and this operation is repeated as often as may be desired. Dr. Brainard, who has already succeeded by this procedure in a number of cases of un-united fracture, thinks it is better to commence in most cases with not more than two or three perforations, in order that the effect produced shall not be too severe. It is scarcely necessary to add that, after the punctures have been made, the limb should be put completely at rest in appropriate splints or in apparatus of some kind.

" Scraping or rasping the ends of the bones is a practice which dates from a very early period. Mr. Brodie scraped the ends of the bones, and then interposed a bit of lint; Mayor, in 1828, contrived to introduce an iron, previously heated in boiling water, through a canula, and thus brought heat to bear directly upon the ends of the fragments, and by repeating the application several times a cure was effected.

" Re-section of the ends of the bones first brought into notice by White, of Manchester, in 1760, and opposed by Brodie as dangerous, and by Malgaigne regarded as generally useless or unnecessary, has still been practiced a great number of times with more or less success. It is especially applicable to superficial bones, and in cases where the bones overlap.

" Roux practiced resection in one instance and then managed to engage the point of one of the fragments in the medullary canal of the other.

" White, of Manchester, Henry Cline, of London, Hewson, of Boston, and Norris, of Philadelphia have applied caustics directly to the ends of the fragments, after having exposed them by a free incision. Pelit applied the actual cautery.

" Tying the fragments together by means of metallic ligatures, is as old as the days of Hippocrates; but in 1805 Honore adopted the same procedure in a case of un-united fracture. J. Kearney, Rodgers, Mott and Cheeseman, of New York, Flautert, of Rouen, and N. R. Smith, of Baltimore have repeated the operations with complete success. The operation is not, however, without its hazards. Norris has seen one case in which a broken patella was wired together and a fatal result followed on the fourth day.

"Finally, having thus brought rapidly before us all of the various modes of treatment which have been suggested and practiced for the non-union of broken bones, we are prepared to affirm the following conclusions or summary of what we believe ought to be the general course of procedure in these cases.

"First, Improve the general condition of the system.

"Second, Remove, as far as possible, the local impediments, such as a separation of the fragments, local paralysis, local scurvy resulting from long exclusion from light and air, congestions, &c.

"Third, Increase the action of the tissues immediately adjacent to the fracture, upon which tissues rather than upon the bone, as Malgaigne thinks, the formation of callus depends. A theory which, as applied to old and un-united fractures, we are not prepared to deny. This may be accomplished by friction, and violent flexions of the limb at the seat of the fractures; possibly in some measure by the application of vesicants or of other stimulants to the skin itself.

"Fourth, Employ again compression, and rest from a period of from two to four or eight weeks.

"Fifth, Resort to the practice recommended by Brainard, namely, perforation of the soft parts and bone with an awl.

"Sixth, If in the lower extremity, allow the patient to walk about after the plan of White or Smith.

"Seventh, If the fracture is not in the femur, and as an extreme measure, employ theseton.

"Eighth, Re-section is applicable only to superficial bones, and in cases of overlapping.

"When these measures have failed, after a fair trial, we should either abandon the case as hopeless, only supporting the limb by such apparatus as may be found most serviceable, or we should recommend amputation."

You see that this author is very critical upon this subject generally. And upon the subject of treating the fractured humerus, he is probably the most accurate of any author. Upon this subject I read from his work commencing on page 224. He says:

Fractures of the humerus—causes.—In a record of eighteen cases in which the cause of the fracture is stated, I find this portion of the shaft broken, from direct violence eleven times; from indirect blows,—the concussion being received upon the elbow, twice; once it was a consequence of tertiary lues, once it occured during birth, and three times in the same patient it has been broken from muscular action alone, each consecutive fracture occuring at a different point. The records of surgery furnish many examples of fractures of the shaft of the humerus from muscular action, as in throwing a stone, or a snow ball; but the most singular examples are those in which the bone has been broken in a trial of strength between two persons, by grasping the hands, palm to palm, with the elbows resting upon a table, and twisting, when the humerus has suddenly given way a little above the condyles. I have seen one case of this kind, which was under the care of Dr. Winne; and Malgvogne has collected five other similar cases, two of which were reported by Lonsdale.

"The example of fracture during birth, to which I have referred, occurred in a healthy female child, whose parents were also healthy. The mother was in labor six or eight hours, but the labor was not severe. She was attended by a midwife, and does not know whether violence was employed or not. Dr. Lockwood, of Buffalo, was called on the third day, and found the arm broken a little below its middle, and moving as freely as it did at the elbow joint. He applied lateral splints, with bandages, &c. I saw the child, on the seventeenth day after its birth, with Dr. Lockwood. There was then a perfect ferrule of ensheathing callus surrounding the fragments, and which, owing to the softness of the flesh, could be easily detected and defined. The fragments were firm, and had been at least three or four days. Nearly a year after, I again examined the arm, and could not discern any traces of the accident.

"Dr. Lowenhoutt has also reported a case in which the evidence was conclusive that the fracture was caused solely by the contractions of the Luterus, which forced the arm against the pubes, the arm being heard distinctly to snap when it was passing this point, and while the hands of the accoucher were not aiding in the delivery. In that case the humerus was broken in its upper third.

"*Seat and direction of the fracture.*—The seat of the fracture is more often below than above the middle of the bone; thus, I have found the fracture eight times near the middle, and the same number of times below the middle third, but only seven times above the middle third. The observations of Norris, who found four fractures of the shaft above the middle and nine below, correspond with my own; but M. Guercten, in the same number of fractures, found nine above the middle and four below. The line of the fracture is generally oblique, but more often transverse than in the fractures of the clavicle, femur or tibia.

"*Displacement.*—The direction of the displacement depends, no doubt, sometimes upon the precise point of the fracture and upon action of the muscles operating upon the two fragments; thus, if the fracture takes place just above the inser ion of the deltorid, the lower fragment is liable to be drawn upwards and outwards, in the direction of its fibers, while the upper fragment is carried toward the origin of the pectoratis major, &c.; but, in a great majority of cases, the influence of these muscles is more than counter-balanced by the direction of the force and by the direction of the fracture. Practically, therefore, it is seldom of much importance to determine the exact point of fracture, as to whether it is just above or below the insertion of a particular muscle; nor indeed is it generally very easy to ascertain this point with much precision. The amount of displacement varies considerably in different persons, and in fractures at different points, but it will average about three quarters of an inch. When the fracture is produced by muscular action alone, it is generally transverse, and displacement seldom occurs. Such was the fact in every instance when my own patient broke the arm three times consecutively at different points, and union was speedily accomplished, and with no deformity. Dupaytren, however, saw a case which constituted an exception to this general rule. The fragments became completely separated, and were so movable that union could not be effected, and he was compelled, after three months, to resort to resection.

"_Results._—In twenty-three examples, the average shortening is about one quarter of an inch, but of these, thirteen are not shortened at all, so that the average of shortening in the remaining ten is three quarters of an inch, the amount of overlapping varying from one quarter of an inch to one inch and a quarter.

"In thirty-one examples, I have twice seen the humerus refuse to unite, once when the fracture was in the lower third of the shaft. This was an oblique compound fracture, and no union had taken place at the end of five months. The man was intemperate, but in pretty good health. In the second case the fracture had occurred a little below the middle of the bone, and it was simple. Five months after the accident this patient consulted me, when I found the elbow enchylosed, the fore-arm being fixed at right angles with the arm. Neither of these patients had been under my care previously, but I learned that an intelligent Canadian surgeon had treated one of them, and the other had been seen and treated by several surgeons.

"In two other cases the elbow remained somewhat stiff a long time after the splints were removed; in one case, complete freedom of motion was not restored at the end of fifteen years.

"Generally, however, the motions of the elbow joint have been very soon restored after the removal of the splints and sling.

"I ought to mention that not unfrequently, fractures of the shaft of the humerus, and especially when they are occasioned by dead blows, are followed by great swelling, and sometimes by abscesses. In one instance, the fracture having taken place within the insertion of the deltoid muscle, the sharp extremities of the lower fragment was made to penetrate the flesh, causing an abscess and finally titanus, of which my patient soon died.

"The following remarks of Malgaigne are too pertinent to be omitted in this connection. When there is obliquity with overlapping, or a fracture with splintering, or a multiple fracture, a certain amount of deformity is inevitable, and the formation of callus demands one or two weeks more. With the inflammation comes also the danger of suppuration, and, later, a rigidity of the articulations difficult to dissipate. *In short, we must not forget that of all fractures, those of the humerus are most liable to fail of consolidation.*

" On the other hand, we shall find in the case of this bone, as in all others, some remarkable exceptions when, although the fracture may be compound and badly comminuted, yet the limb has been saved and made useful. Ayres, of New York, reports a case of this kind, in which he removed a portion of shaft; and although the brechial artery was probably obliterated, a good union took place; and Walker, of Boston, has noticed two or three similar examples. For an account of the remarkable cases of compound fracture of the shaft of the humerus, illustrating the powers of nature in childhood, in the restoration of broken and comminuted bones, the reader may consult, in the New York Journal of Medicine for November, 1864, a paper entitled, "Amputations and Compound Fractures," by John O. Stone, Surgeon to Bellevue Hospital. The accidents occurred in children, one of whom was four, and the other six years of age, both of whom recovered with useful arms.

" *Treatment.*—(Shows the jury a plate.)—' You see, gentlemen, by the plate that the bandaging commences at the hand, and not at the ends of the fingers. This is the mode which Dr. Pratt adopted.' [*Reads.*] In the treatment of fractures of that portion of the shaft of the humerus under consideration, I have preferred, generally, a broad, thick splint of gutta percha—felt or sole leather may answer nearly as well—sufficiently long to extend from the neck to the wrist, moulded accurately, and applied to the outside of the shoulder and arm, while the limb is flexed to a right angle, and while the extension is being made upon the humerus. This being properly padded, and secured in place by rollers, I place the arm in a sling beside the body. The sling must, however, be so arranged, by being looped under the wrist, and not under the elbow, as that the weight of the elbow and lower part of the arm may aid in making extension. Welch's splint will answer the same purpose ; or these splints of different lengths may be used, but I do not find them so convenient as Welch's, or gutta percha, applied as I have directed done.

Other surgeons have sought to make permanent extensions in certain other fractures of the humerus, by various contrivances. Mr. Lonsdale constructed an instrument which might be lengthened or shortened to suit the case ; it was made of steel, and was worked with a screw operating upon cogs in a sliding bar, resembling in some respects the arm portion of Jarvis's adjuster. In the second London edition of a series of plates illustrating the action of the muscle in producing displacement in fractures, by

14

S. W. Wind, is a drawing of an apparatus invented by the author for the same purpose, which is very simple, and in some respects more complete than Lonsdale's, and which may be easily adapted to almost any form of arm-splint. Indeed, nothing more is necessary than to attach to the ordinary long splint a moveable crutch.

"I believe that all these contrivances may prove occasionally useful, but the common experience of surgeons has shown how difficult it is to accomplish much extension by means of pressure in the axilla; a mode, too, which I think must tend to d splace the fragments upon which they act inwardly, and which seldom can be applied with much force to fractures near the condyles, on account of the probable existence of inflammation and swelling about the joint.

"Malgaigne, when speaking of the apparatus of Lonsdale, remarks : 'But the surgeon should never lose sight of the fact that permanent extension is a resource always dangerous, often useless, and which demands in its application much caution and watchfulness.'"

The following example will illustrate the practical difficulties of employing permanent extension in fractures of the humerus :

"A laborer, aged thirty, was admitted into the Buffalo Hospital of the Sisters of Charity, on the second day of October, 1853, with a simple oblique fracture of the humerus, which had occurred three days before. The fracture was situated within the insertion of the deltoid, and having been caused by the rolling of a log upon the arm, the whole limb was much swollen. The night following his admission, in a fit of delirium tremens, he removed all the dressings. When I visited the wards in the morning, I found the fragments displaced and the muscles contracting violently. The ordinary dressings were applied, and continued until the fifth day, when, as the delirium had not ceased, and the muscles continued to contract with great violence, it was determined to attempt permanent extension. For this purpose we lifted the elbow upwards and outwards, to relax the deltoid, and then, having made extension with the fore-arm, we fitted carefully a large gutta percha splint to the fore-arm, arm, axilla and side, in such a manner that when the splint was secured to these several parts, the arm could not fall to the side of the body completely, and in proportion as it did fall downward, it would make extension upon the arm. This splint was well padded, and secured in place by rollers.

"On the sixth day the delirium had ceased, and never returned. The dressings were all in place, and seemed to accomplish the indication we had in view ; but, on the seventh day, although he had kept very quiet, everything was disarranged, and the whole had to be re-adjusted. On the eighth and ninth, the same thing occurred. During this time we had varied the dressings, position, &c., each day, to meet, if possible, the difficulties, but it was at length deemed unwise to pursue the attempt any further, and we returned to the use of the ordinary splints, laying the arm against the side of the body. The union was finally completed without either overlapping or angular displacement.

"Something may always be accomplished when the patient is walking about, by allowing the elbow to escape from the sling, so that its weight shall make constant traction on the lower fragments, and the plan I suggested some years since of treating certain cases of delayed union of the humerus, namely, extending the arm at full length by the side of the body, so that the lower fragment shall receive the whole weight of the fore-arm and hand, might occasionally prove reliable in recent fractures, where the tendency to override was very great. In two instances I have already put this plan sufficiently to the test to determine its safety and ability.

"The precise plan, and my reasons for its adoption in certain cases of delayed union, were set forth in the following paper, read before the Buffalo City Medical Association, and published in the Buffalo *Medical Journal* for August, 1854 :

"'I have observed that non-union results more frequently after fractures of the shaft of the humerus, than after fractures of the shaft of any other bone. Comparing the humerus with the femur, between which, above all others, the circumstances of form, situation, &c., are most nearly parallel, and in both of which non-union is said to be relatively frequent. I find that of forty-nine fractures of the humerus, four occurred through the surgical neck, twelve through the condyles, and twenty-nine through the shaft. In one of the twenty-nine the patient survived the accident only a few days. In four of the remaining twenty-eight, union had not occurred after the lapse of six months, and in many more it was delayed beyond the usual time. Two of the four were simple fractures, and occurred near the middle of the humerus. The third was compound, and occurred near the middle also ; the fourth was compound, and occurred near the condyles.'

"'This analysis supplies us, therefore, with four cases of non-union, with a table of twenty-eight cases of fractures through the shaft. Of eighty-seven fractures of the femur, twenty occurred through the neck, one through the trochanter major, and one through the condyles. The remaining sixty-five occurred through the shaft, and generally near the middle, and not in one case was the union delayed beyond six months.

"'To make the comparison more complete, I must add, that of the twenty-eight fractures of the shaft of the humerus, six were compound, and of the sixty-five fractures of the shaft of the femur, six were either compound comminuted, or both comminuted ; the six compound fractures of the shaft of the humerus, two cases of non-union ; the six cases of either compound or comminuted, or compound and comminuted fractures of the femur, furnished no case of non-union. I beg to suggest to the society what seems to me to be the true explanation of these facts.

" ' It is the universal practice, so far as I know, in dressing fractures of the humerus, to place the fore-arm at a right angle with the arm. Within a few days, and generally, I think, within a few hours, after the arm and fore-arm are placed in this position, a rigidity of the muscles and other structures has ensued, and to such a degree that if the splints and sling are completely removed, the elbow will remain flexed and firm ; nor will it be easy to straighten it. A temporary false anchylosis has occurred, and instead of the elbow joint, when the fore-arm is attempted to be straightened upon the arm, there is only motion at the seat of the fracture. It will thus happen that every upward and downward movement of the fore arm will inflict motion upon the fracture ; and inasmuch as the elbow may become the pivot, the motion at the upper end of the lower fragment will be the greater in proportion to the distance of the fracture from the elbow joint.

" ' No doubt it is intended that the dressings shall prevent all motion of the fore-arm upon the arm ; but I fear that they cannot always be made to do this. I believe it is never done when the dressing is made without angular splints, nor is it by any means certain that it will be accomplished when such splints are used. The weight of the fore-arm is such, when placed at a right angle with the arm, and encumbered with splints and bandages, that even when supported by a sling it settles heavily forward, and compels the arm-dressings to loosen themselves from the arm in front of the point of the fracture, and to indent themselves in the skin and flesh behind. By these means the upper end of the lower fragment is tilted forwards. If the fore-arm should continue to drop upon the sling, nothing but a permanent forward displacement would probably result ; the bones might unite, yet with a deformity.

" 'But the weight of the fore-arm, under these circumstances, is not uniform, nor do I see how it can be made so. It is to the sling that we trust mainly to accomplish this important indication. But you have all noticed that the tension or relaxation of the sling depends upon the attitude of the body, whether standing or sitting, upon the erection or inclination of the head, upon the motion of the shoulders, and in no inconsiderable degree upon the actions of respiration. Nor does the patient himself cease to add to these conditions by lifting the fore-arm with his opposite hand whenever provoked to it by a sense of fatigue.

" 'This difficulty of maintaining quiet apposition to the fragments, while the arm is in this position, at whatever point it may be broken, becomes more and more serious as we depart from the elbow joint, and would be at its maximum at the upper end of the humerus, were it not that here a mass of muscles, investing and adhering to the bone, in some measure obviates the difficulty. Its true non-union is, therefore, near the middle, when there is less muscular investments, and when, on the one hand, the fracture is sufficiently remote from the pivot or fulcrum to have the motion of the upper end of the lower fragment multiplied through a long arm, while, on the other hand, it is sufficiently near the arm-pit and shoulder to prevent the upper portion of the splint and arm-dressings from obtaining a secure grasp upon the lower end of the upper fragment.

" ' It must not be overlooked that the motion of which we speak belongs exclusively to the lower fragment, and that it is always in the same plane forwards and backwards, but especially that it is not a motion upon the fracture as upon a pivot, but a motion of one fragment to and from its fellow. This circumstance I regard as important to a right appreciation of the difficulty. Motion alone, I am fully convinced, does not often prevent union, as surgeons have generally believed. It is exceedingly rare to see a case of non-union of the clavicle. Of forty-seven cases of fracture of the clavicle which have come under my observation, and in by far the greater proportion of which considerable overlapping and consequent deformities ensued, only one has resulted in non-union, and in this instance no treatment whatever was practised; but from the time of the accident the patient continued to labor in the fields and hold the plough, as if nothing had occurred. I have, therefore, seen no case of non-union of the clavicle where a surgeon has treated the accident.

" ' Indeed, what is most pertinent and remarkable, its union is more speedy, usually, than that of any other bone in the body of the same size ; yet to prevent motion of the fragments in a case of fractured clavicle with complete separation and displacement, except where the fracture is near one of the extremities of the bone, I have always found wholly impracticable. Whenever bandages or apparatus has been applied, I have still seen always that the fragments would move freely upon each other at each act of inspiration and expiration, and at almost every motion of the head, body or other extremities. It is probable, gentlemen, that you have made the same observation.

" ' From this and many similar facts I have been led to suspect, for a long time, *that motion has had less to do with non-union than was generally believed.*

" ' I find, however, no difficulty in reconciling this suspicion with my doctrine in reference to the case in question ; and it is precisely because, as I have already explained, the motion, in case of a fractured humerus, dressed in the usual manner, is peculiar.

" ' In a fracture of the clavicle through its middle third (its usual situation), the motion is upon the point of the fracture as upon a pivot ; although, therefore, the motion is almost incessant, it does not essentially, if at all, disturb the adhesive process. The same is true in nearly all other fractures. The fragments move only upon themselves, and not to and from each other. I know of no complete exception but in the case now under consideration.

" ' Aside from any speculation, the facts are easily verified by a personal examination of the patients during the first or second week of treatment, or at any time before union has occurred both in fractures of the humerus and clavicle. The latter is always sufficiently exposed to permit you to see what occurrs, and as soon as the swelling has a little subsided in the former case you will have no difficulty in feeling the motion outside of the dressings, or, perhaps, in introducing the finger under the dressings sufficiently far to reach the point of fracture. I believe you will not fail to recognize the difference in the motion between the two cases. Such, gentlemen, is the explanation which I wish to offer for the relative frequency of this very serious accident, non-union of the humerus.

" ' I know of no other circumstances or condition in which this bone is peculiar, and which, therefore, might be invoked as an explanation. Overlapping of the bones, the cause assigned by some writers, is not sufficient, since it is not peculiar. The same occurs much oftener, and to a greater extent, in fractures of the femur, and equally as often in fractures of the clavicle ; yet in neither case are these results so frequent. Nor can it be due to the action of the deltoid muscle, or of any other particular muscles about the arm, whether the fracture be below or above these insertions, since similar muscles, with similar attachments, on the femur and on the clavicle, tending always powerfully to the separation of the fragments occasion deformity, but they seldom prevent union.

" ' If I am correct in my views, we shall be able sometimes to consummate union of a fractured humerus when it is delayed, by straightening the fore-arm upon the arm, and confining them to this position. A straight splint, extending from the top of the shoulder to the hand, constructed from some firm material, and made fast with rollers, will secure the requisite immobility to the fracture. The weight of the fore-arm and hand will only tend to keep the fragments in place, and if the splint and bandage are sufficiently tight, the motion occasioned by swinging the hand and fore-arm will be conveyed almost entirely to the shoulder joint. Very little motion, indeed, can in this feature be communicated to the fragments, and what little is thus communicated is a motion which experience has elsewhere shown not disturbing or pernicious, but a motion only upon the ends of the fragments, as upon a pivot.

" ' I do not fail to notice that this position has serious objections, and that it is liable to inconveniences which must always, probably, prevent its being adopted as the usual plan of treatment for fractured arms. It is more difficult to get up and lie down, or to sit down, in this position of the arm, and the hand is liable to swell. But I shall not be surprised to learn that experience will prove these objections to have less weight than we are disposed to give them. Remember, the practice is yet untried—if I except the case which I am about to relate, and in which case, I am free to say, these objections scarcely existed. The swelling of the hand was trivial, and only continued through the first fortnight, and the patient never spoke of the inconvenience of getting up or s t ing down, or even of lying down.

" ' The following is the case to which I have just referred: ' Michael Mehar, laborer, æt 35, broke his left humerus just below its middle, Dec. 14th, 1853. The arm was dressed by a surgeon in Canada West, and who is known to me as exceedingly ' clever.' After a few days from the time of the accident, the starch bandage was put on as light as it could be borne, and brought down on the fore-arm, so as to confine the motions of the elbow joint. Six weeks after the injury, Jan'y 29th, 1854, Maher applied to me at the Hospital; no union had occurred. The motion between the fragments was very free, so that they passed each other with an audible click. There was little or no swelling or soreness. In short, everything indicated that union was not likely to occur without operative interference. The elbow was completely enchylosed. I explained to my students what seemed to me to be the cause of the delayed union, and declared to them that I did not intend to attempt to establish adhesive action until I had straightened the arm. They had just witnessed the failure of a precisely similar case, in which I had made the attempt to bring about union without previously straightening the arm.

" ' On the 2d of February, 1854, we had succeeded in making the arm nearly straight. I now punctured the upper end of the lower fragment with a small steel instrument, and, as well as I was able, brought it between the fragments. Assisted by Dr. Boardman, I then applied a gutta percha splint from the top of the shoulder to the fingers, moulding it carefully to the whole of the back and sides of the limb, and securing it firmly with a paste roller. March 4th, (not quite four weeks after the application of the splint,) we opened the dressings for the second time and carefully renewed them. March 18th, we opened the dressing for the third time, and found the union complete. This was within less than forty days. The patent was now dismissed. On the 29th of April following, the bone was re-fractured. Maher had been assisting to load the ' tender' to a locomotive. As the train was just getting in motion he was hanging to the tender by his sound arm, while another laborer seized upon his broken arm to keep him on the car, and with a violent and sudden pull wrenched him from the tender and reproduced the fracture. The next morning I applied the dressings as before, and did not remove them during three weeks; at the end of which time the union was again complete. The splint was, however, re-applied, and has been continued to this time, a period of about six weeks.'

" ' Since the date of the above paper, I have twice had opportunities to test the value of this mode of treatment in cases of somewhat delayed union of the humerus, and in each case with the same favorable result.' "

By the authority I have read, you perceive that inflammation is *not* the condition desired for repair of bone.

And not only this, but that true inflammation will prevent the cure. That when it exists it must be allayed and removed, or restoration is impossible. This is in accordance with the testimony of Drs. Beebe and Ludlam. They testify that inflammation is a diseased, and not a healthy condition; that this is not the desired condition, but it is rather the almost inevitable consequence of the fracture.§

Dr. Porter, and those who follow in his wake, contend for the very reverse of this. Every person's common sense ought to teach him that the more perfect the patient's health, the more rapid will be the cure.

By this authority we also show that, when there is an external wound of the soft parts, as in the case of this boy, an opening should be left in the bandaging, so that the wound may be dressed without removing the bandage. We have proved that Dr. Pratt dressed this arm in that way.

In case of a compound comminuted fracture, as was that of this arm, this author (Miller) recommends the anti-phlogistic diet as an essential from the very outset. So testify Drs. Beebe and Ludlam, and such was the practice of Dr. Pratt.

In no particular has it been shown that Dr. Pratt did not treat this case as laid down by the standard authors from whose works I have read, but, in every particular, in accordance therewith.

Now, gentlemen, let us more closely approach the subject of false joints and un-united fractures. Dr. Porter and the other witnesses of the plaintiff tell you that the case in hand is one of false joint. Drs. Beebe and Ludlam tell you that this is *not* a false joint, but is merely a'case of non-union of the bone not being false joint.

Mr. De Wolf has, perhaps, sufficiently read from the authors, and explained to you the difference between false joint and non-union of bone.

I may, however, remark that, in false joint the fragments, or ends of the bone, are connected or tied together in sort, by a species of cartilaginous substance without union of bone, and the fragments do not play upon each other, as you have seen is the case with this arm.

This latter fact shows that their professional witnesses are wrong in saying that here is false joint, and that ours are right when they say there is not. But I care not whether it be called a false joint, or merely non-union of bone, as Dr. Pratt is not to blame for that condition. The fragments are not united by the interweaving of bone, one fragment with the other.

Another thing that we have shown by this surgical author, (and coinciding with the testimony of our professional witnesses,) is, that (among other causes) undue excitement of the patient and deficiency of plasma, will either of them prevent union of bone. For aught we know either or both of these causes may have existed and prevented the cure. We find that the boy was restless, uneasy. This could hardly be without undue excitement. Either of these causes were more likely to exist after the re-fracture or rupture of the newly formed bone than before. In these, or in either of them, we have a probable theory for the failure of union of this fracture. On the other side they have failed to show any cause, whether constituting a probable theory or otherwise, why this bone is not united.

A probable theory is to be adopted rather than follow the wild speculations of imagination, or rather than form opinions without any defined basis. But to maintain this action the probability or possibility that Dr. Pratt is to blame for the condition of this boy's arm will not do ; they have got to go farther, and prove the fact that this condition is the consequence of Dr. Pratt's want of ordinary skill and care. This is not shown by not showing any cause at all.

Again, we find by the authority before referred to, that to undo the limb at the end of five or six weeks from the time of the accident, and finding that union has not taken place, or that the work of repair is not then going on, is not conclusive that union will not take place. In such a case (reads the book) the retentive apparatus should again be applied as in the first instance, only with more care, and then allowed to remain in this condition for a much longer period than that previously indulged. That when this is done, union may take place in no unreasonable time. Not only this, but we find that union may be delayed from six to eight months, and not until the lapse of this time is hope to be lost that cure is out of the question through the intervention of ordinary means. Now, this applies when there has been no re-fracture or rupture of the newly formed bone.

When such an unfortunate occurrence is presented, I take it that a longer, rather than a shorter period is to be allotted counting from the date of re-fracture. This case was taken wholly out of Dr. Pratt's hands at the end of five months and ten days from the time of the firstinjury, and with in twenty days after consultation had, when other surgeons recommended friction, which was applied. Time was not allowed even to test the efficacy of that friction. How stands Dr. Porter, when contrasted with this authority, upon the question of the time beyond which union should not be delayed?

He would have union in six or eight weeks at the outside.

But further, this author says, that when at the end of six or eight weeks, union is found not to have taken place, provisional callus, doubtless, has failed, but that this is not always essential to re-union, and that union may yet take place by the formation of the definitive callus, which is presumed to have commenced forming.

Dr. Porter asserts, *positively*, that there can be no such thing as union of fracture *without provisional callus*. This author also says, that provisional callus is no part of bony or true union, and that this callus is eliminated by absorption as definitive callus forms. Dr. Porter says that provisional callus never wholly disappears.

Dr. Porter also will have it that provisional callus is formed much earlier than as stated by this author, who says that it takes from four to eight weeks for it to form and become firm; and that it is useless when the definitive callus is formed, and when no longer necessary it disappears in accordance with well known laws of nature, that whatever is produced for a temporary purpose, is taken away or removed when that purpose has been subserved. That the definitive callus is formed more leisurely and well, being intended for a more permanent purpose than provisional callus.

That the latter is a mere splint to hold the ends of the bone tightly in apposition, so that the definitive callus may form and complete true union of bone. And that the surgeon's splints may be removed when provisional callus is complete, which is nature's splint; and that this splint of nature may be, *nay*, actually is removed by absorption, thus giving normal symmetry to the limb when definitive callus is formed. That this definitive callus is the *only essential* thing in the repair of bone, and without which there can never be true or bony union; and that even this definitive or permanent callus is much modified by absorption.

We show, by our professional witnesses and by standard authors, that Dr. Porter is wholly wrong in every material point as to non-union of bone.

1st. He says that there must be inflammation, or there can be no provisional callus.

2d. That there can be no union without provisional callus—that it is *the* essential thing—that it is the only callus that he knows of that is material.

3d. That provisional callus forms within four weeks from the accident.

4th. That provisional callus never disappears.

5th. That there is not less probability of union in the humerus than in any other bone; or, in other words, that this bone is as likely to unite in case of fracture as any other bone.

6th. That provisional callus contains about the same quantity of phosphate of lime as human bone, which he thinks is about fifty parts in the hundred.

7th. That human blood also contains about the same quantity of phosphate of lime as bone.

8th. That in case of fracture the ossific particles are deposited (which form the new bone) at the site of fracture from the blood as it passes from the heart through the arteries.

9th. That fracture of the humerus at or below the *nutritious foramen* and a rupture of the nutrient artery, or one of its branches, would not cause any delay in the union of the bone.

10th. That bone and every other tissue is in the blood; in fact, that the whole is blood.

11th. That the flat bones of the *cranium*, and the femur or thigh bone at the point of the capsular ligament, must unite by provisional callus.

It is proper that I here concede that Dr. Miller does not speak with any such assurance as Dr. Porter upon these points, and upon some of them does not agree with him. But Brother Miller asks why we did not interrogate all these other Physicians, Drs. Belding, Wales, Burbank and McAffee, about this provisional callus and reproduction of bone.

I ask why we should have called or interrogated any more than we have? Those we have questioned are quite sufficient without consuming any more time, when all the standard authors agree with them, and are against their professional gentlemen.

Two well-posted surgeons like Drs. Beebe and Ludlam are all that we desired. The books I have read from give the general mode of treatment. But each surgeon and author has some particular mode of treatment which he considers best in a given case, when the ordinary mode of treatment has proved abortive. All the modes are open, and any may be selected without the hazard of action in case it fails.

Hamilton mentions three cases of re-section, all of which resulted favorably. We find a like favorable result noted by Gross in a case where Brainard's plan of puncturation had been tried and failed; and cure has been effected by re-section after the lapse of twenty-seven months.

I take it that much depends upon the bone and the totality of condition, which of these extreme modes is the one promising most success?

Hamilton and other good authors, I believe, all agree that the destruction or rupture of a main artery, whose office is to supply a bone with blood, greatly lessens the chances of re-union of the fracture.

So testify Drs. Beebe and Ludlam:—And that a rupture or division of the lower branch of the nutrient artery, as is the apparent fact in this case, would materially interfere with the chances of curing the arm. They also agree (particularly Gross and Hamilton), that in the upper extremities, and when there is anchylosis or injury of an important artery, that re-section may be resorted to with reasonable prospect of favorable results.

Hamilton considers this mode dangerous when applied to the lower extremities, but not so when applied to the upper extremities.

Here is what Gross says upon this mode of treatment. I read from page 955, vol. 1:

"Finally, excision of the ends of the fragments, an operation devised, and first performed in 1760, by Mr. White, of England, is occasionally employed. Such an operation, however, should never be resorted to without due deliberation, and until after the failure of the more ordinary and simple means. To say nothing of the difficulty of its execution, it is by no means devoid of danger; indeed it has not unfrequently proved fatal. A very free incision is made through the soft parts down to the ends of the broken bone, which are then brought out at the wound and retrenched, either with a stout knife, a saw, or a pair of pliers. Sometimes the mere removal of the cartilaginous crust is sufficient for the purpose, an object which may be easily accomplished by scraping.

"To maintain the freshened ends in accurate and steady apposition, it was proposed by Horeau, in 1805, to connect them together by means of a wire, and to retain them in this position until the completion of the cure. The procedure, which has, I believe, been generally condemned by European practitioners, has been frequently employed in this country, in consequence, apparently, of the high authority of Dr. J. Kearny Rodgers, who was the first to perform it on this side of the Atlantic. It consists, first, in cutting off the rounded ends of the fragments; secondly, in drilling a hole through each; and lastly, in tying them firmly together with a silver wire, so as to keep them closely and evenly in contact during the consolidating process.

"It is generally imagined that this procedure is necessarily followed by violent inflammation, jeoparding both limb and life; but this is an error. If the operation be carefully performed and the after treatment conducted upon proper principles, I believe that it will commonly be found to be *entirely free from danger, while the utmost confidence may be placed in its efficacy.*

"In the only case in which I have had an opportunity of employing this method—in a case of *un-united* fracture of the *humerus* of eleven months' standing, in a young man of twenty-two years of age,—the patient experienced very little pain, inflammation, or fever, during the stage of the treatment, and the result was, in every respect, most satisfactory."

The following is an outline of this case, as drawn up by Dr. S. W. Gross, for the *Louisville Medical Review*, July, 1856. It may be *premised* that the fracture was situated about three inches above the condyles, and that various remedies, *among others Dr. Brainard's, had been faithfully but fruitlessly employed for its relief :*

"The patient being placed under the influence of chloroform, a longitudinal incision, about three inches in length, was made on the posterior aspect of the arm, through the triceps muscle, over the site of the fracture. The lower fragment was found to overlap the upper about an inch and a half. The ends of the bone were surrounded by a strong fibrous membrane, which was firmly adherent to the neighboring parts, and formed a sort of shut sac, in which the bone was imbedded. About an inch of the lower portion of the upper fragment, and half an inch of the upper portion of the lower fragment, were removed with a delicate saw; but on account of their firm adhesions, and especially the shortness of the inferior piece, some difficulty was experienced in bringing them entirely into view.

"The fragments were conical, rounded, smooth, and invested with a thick, fibrous periosteum: no synovial membrane or fluid existed. The next step of the operation consisted in drilling the extremities of the bone, which having been done with a common gimlet, a piece of wire was introduced, to maintain them in apposition. The ends of the wire were twisted together, and allowed to protrude from the wound, the edges of which were brought together by three sutures and adhesive strips.

"Two splints and a roller being applied, the arm was firmly supported in a sling.

"There was very little hemorrhage, and no vessel required ligation. As the patient suffered a great deal of pain, a grain of morphia was given immediately after the operation. Very little constitutional disturbance followed. Nearly all the wound healed by the first intention, and at no time was there much swelling, discoloration or suppuration.

"At the end of the eighth week, the process of re-union had advanced so far that there was scarcely any perceptible motion.

"In a fortnight after this, the wire being removed, the patient went home perfectly restored, the arm being about an inch and a half shorter than the sound one. It is proper to add, that, by frequent passive motion, the elbow joint was gradually regaining its original function.

"In another case, that of a man, aged thirty-two, I treated with equal success, by an operation of this kind, an *un-united fracture of the humerus of twenty-seven months' standing.* The ends of the fragments were connected by two silver wires, which were permanently retained. The case is reported at length in the *North American Medico-Chirurgical Review* for July, 1861.

"The results of some of the above operations have been placed in a striking and interesting light by the statistics of Dr. Morris. Thus, in forty-six cases in which the seton was used, thirty-six were cured, three died, three were partially relieved, and five received no benefit.

"Of thirty-eight cases of re-section, twenty-four were cured, six died, one was partially cured, and seven received no benefit.

"Of eight treated by cauterization of the ends of the fragments, six were cured. It is worthy to remark that the treatment by the seton is less successful in fracture of the *femur* and *humerus*, than in that of any other bones. The danger of the more severe operations, especially the seton and re-section, follows the same laws as in amputation, increasing with the *size* of the limb and *its proximity* to the trunk. When all the known remedies, after a thorough trial, fail, and the limb is utterly useless, the only resource is amputation. *Few cases,* however, demanding such terrible alternative, will be likely to arise in the *present state of the science.*"

It is to be regretted, that in the statistics given by this author from Norris, no mention is made of what bones were treated by the different modes named.

However, this author very closely agrees with Hamilton. Both sustain Dr. Ludlam in his opinion, that in this case re-section would be most promising of success. The statistics given by Hamilton show that,

"While the *femur* and *humerus* are most nearly parallel, and in both of which non-union is said to be relatively frequent, he found that of forty-nine fractures of the humerus, four occurred through the surgical neck, twelve through the condyles and twenty-nine through the shaft. In one of the twenty-nine, the patient only survived the accident a few days. In four of the remaining twenty-eight, union had not occurred after the *lapse of six months* and in *many* more it was *delayed beyond* the usual time.

"Two of the four were simple fractures, and occurred near the middle of the humerus; the third was compound, and occurred near the middle also; the fourth was compound, and occurred near the condyles. This analysis supplies us, therefore, with four cases of non-union from a table of twenty-eight cases of fractures through the shaft. Of eighty-seven fractures of the femur, twenty occurred through the neck, one through the trochanter major, and one through the condyles. The remaining sixty-five occurred through the shaft, and generally near the middle, and not in *one case* was the union delayed beyond six months. To make the comparison more complete, I must add that of the twenty-eight fractures of the shaft of the humerus, *six were* compound; and of the sixty-five fractures of the shaft of the femur, six were either compound, comminuted, or both compound and comminuted. The six compound fractures of the shaft of the humerus furnished two cases of non-union (one more would have been just half). The six cases of either compound or comminuted, or compound and comminuted fractures of the femur, furnished *no case of non-union.*"

I now read from Gross, vol. 1, page 925, upon the subject of fractures near the nutrient arteries. He says:

"Fractures situated at or near the entrance of nutrient arteries unite less rapidly than those situated further off, owing to the fact that they interfere more or less with the circulation and nourishment of the osseous tissue.

"It is easy to suppose that a laceration of these vessels, as occasionally happens both in simple and compound fractures, might be a cause of non-consolidation, especially when conjoined with other unpropitious circumstances. Statistics show that, when the supply of blood is cut off, to any considerable extent, so as to impose upon the periosteum the exclusive duty of nourishing the fragments, either one or both pieces will become atrophied, their walls being visibly thinned, and their areolar structure rarified.

"Want of union is sometimes dependent upon the *absorption* of the ends of the fragments, or even of the greater portion of the fragments themselves."

On page 953 this writer says that, want of *nutritive* action and loss of *nervous influence*, however induced, are constitutional causes which interfere with the process of repair. And on page 951, he says that,

"It is practically important that a distinction should be drawn between a fracture that unites tardily and one that does not unite at all, or only through the medium of a fibrous, ligamentous, or fibro-cartilaginous tissue. Slow consolidation is by no means uncommon; the parts may be both to take on the requisite degree of ossific action, and the result may be that a fracture that is ordinarily repaired in four or five weeks, may, perhaps, be still *imperfectly* united at the end of twice that period.

"The process of restoration is only held in abeyance, neither advancing nor receding ; by and by it begins again, and then often proceeds with its wonted rapidity. Such cases are frequently very trying to the surgeon's patience, but they generally turn out well in the end, provided sufficient care has been taken to preserve the parts in their proper relations."

This doctrine completely sustains Drs. Beebe and Ludlam in their statements as to the length of time that should be allowed to elapse before resorting to more than the ordinary treatment. That you should be conservative—that you should wait, and not go from one mode to another too rapidly.

I will now call your attention to some more statistics given by this author, on page 947, from which you will see the great number of failures in compound fractures of the lower extremities, and which are more likely to result favorably than fractures of the humerus. He says :

"The following account, for which I am indebted to Dr. Frederick D. Lente, relates to cases of compound fractures of the lower extremities, treated in the New York Hospital from January, 1848, to July, 1847, the whole number being 392 fractures of the tarsus and metatarsus not being included.

"Of these, 68 occurred in the thigh and 324 in the leg. Of the former, 3 involved both thighs, and of the latter, 16 both legs. Of the entire number, 190 were cured, 182 died, and 20 were relieved. In 39, or 20.5 per cent., amputation was performed.

"Of the 68 fractures of the thigh, 18, or 26.5 per cent. were cured, and 2 relieved ; amputation having been performed in 7. Of the 324 fractures of the leg, 175, or 54.0 per cent. were cured, and 14 relieved. In 35, or 20.0 per cent. of these, the limb was removed. Of the whole number of cases of fracture, amputation was employed in 91, or 23.3 per cent., and of these, 49, or 53.8 per cent. died. Of 301 cases treated without amputation, 140 or 46.5 per cent. died, 3 having refused to submit to amputation. Of the whole number of fatal cases in which amputation was not performed, 74, or more than one-half, died within the first week; in many of these there was no re-action, and death ensued in from twenty-four to forty-eight hours. Of 45 fractures of the thigh which occurred at or below the middle, 14 recovered, or 31.1 per cent. ; while of eleven that occurred further down, 4, or 36.3 per cent. recovered.

" Of 227 fractures of the leg, occurring at or below the middle, 130, or 58.1 per cent. recovered ; of 30 above the middle, 17, or over one-half, got well. Of 334 compound fractures of the thigh and leg, 164 occurred on the right side, and 170 on the left."

From this showing, this boy, with a compound comminuted fracture of the arm with the other serious complications, ought to be thankful that his life was saved. Here we have another evidence of Dr. Pratt's correct dietetic, medical and surgical treatment. And the same thing is also shown from the statistics given by Hamilton.

I also wish to read from this author a short paragraph about union without provisional callus, on page 932. He says :

" There are certain pieces of the skeleton in which in fractures *no provisional callus ever forms.* Such are the obcranon, acromion, patella, and neck of the femur."

While I have the book in hand, I wish to show you this bit of bandaging from the wrist upwards which I exhibited last night, but which you could not well see by candle-light. And this was the case of fracture of bone in the fore-arm, which certainly would require bandaging as near the point of the fingers as in case of fracture of the arm above the elbow.

Another thing I ought to notice in the argument of Brother Miller : He says that Dr. Ludlam has had but one case of fracture of the humerus, and Dr. Beebe but two, one of which resulted in non-union; and he seems to think their practice very limited.

I might answer this by saying that all of their surgeons have only one case each of fractured humerus, except Dr. Miller. It is certainly a little remarkable that these doctors have each had such a case in the short time they have been practicing in these parts. One would suppose that this was a dangerous region for that bone.

As to Dr. Ludlam ; he tells you that he does not now make surgery a specialty in practice ; but that he turns over his surgical cases to those who make surgery a special business.

Such is the general course in large cities like Chicago. But Dr. Ludlam fully understands the science of surgery.

As to Dr. Beebe ; he has had in private practice (now remembered by him) of fractured humerus two cases. He has, however, had great numbers in his military practice—none of which were wholly restored when they passed from under his care.

They were, however, all doing well the last he saw of them, which was, say from four to six weeks after the fracture. Then, these patients were removed to other quarters. He does not, therefore, know how many cases resulted in non-union. He tells you that he has treated fracture of every bone in the body, caused by ball or shell. That he has had (without stopping to consider) at least four thousand cases. But in the way he gives you the number in detail at the different battles, there must have been nearly eight thousand.

Why, gentlemen, he has already had more experience in fractures than generally falls to the lot of a surgeon in a long life.

From the authors I have read, as well as from our professional witnesses, you have heard a summary of the different modes of practice, and the manner of operating in each. Of these modes, in the main, Dr. Porter and these other *surgical* witnesses seem to be wholly ignorant. Still, Dr. Porter tells you that Sir Astley Cooper was the father of surgery. For aught that I know, he might as well have been the father of surgery as any man, but we find that surgery was practiced in the days of Hippocrates, who lived long before Astley Cooper saw the light of day.

Dr. McPherson says there are two muscles which are inserted into the fore-arm and attached to the lower third of the humerus, the action of which would have a tendency to create motion at the point of fracture. He says that one of these is the " *biceps flexor*," and that its upper insertion is in, or that it passes through, the occipital groove. I should be pleased to have you tell me how this can can be when the occipital bone is at the back part of the head. Drs. Ludlam and Beebe tell you that they do not know, and never before heard of a muscle by this name in the arm.

The arm has no such muscle, yet this Dr. is one of those who ventures to give his *opinion* as evidence.

This testimony *tests* his anatomical knowledge. Gentlemen, Dr. Pratt has better sense and more knowledge of the human organism, and of fractures and the mode of repair than their professional witnesses; who all, save Dr. Miller, think there is as much phosphate of lime in human blood as in human bone, and many other equally strange things. But these young men merely followed Dr. Porter, this modern Hippocrates, and most certainly his opinions in point of error have seldom been equalled, and never surpassed. Now, I happened to bring with me Gardner's Medical Dictionary, not knowing whether I should have occasion to use it or not. And I propose to read, under the words *bone* and *blood*, as to their constituents as discovered by chemical analysis, and see how the proportion of phosphate of lime stands.

This author says, that "Bone consists of gelatine, &c., 33. 3; phosphate of lime and magnesia, 54. 2; carbonate of lime and other salts of soda, &c., 12, 5.—*Berzelius.*

"But the composition of different bones and those of various animals, differ.

"The animal matter may be dissolved out by hot water in a digester; it yields a soup containing gelatine and fat. On the other hand, the phosphates and earthy matter may be dissolved by strong acids, the gelatine remaining in the shape of bone."

Of blood he says, "Much attention has been paid of late to the normal composition of healthy blood for the purpose of obtaining a standard of comparison to judge of the effects of disease on this important fluid. The mean of Simon represents healthy blood as consisting of 80 per cent. water, and 20 of solid residue; with 2 per cent. of fibrin, and the same amount of fats; 10 to 12 per cent. of globules; 6 to 7 per cent. of albumen; and 1 per cent. of extractive matters and salts.

"The salts consist of chloride of sodium and potassium, carbonate of soda; phosphate of soda, lime and magnesia; peroxide of iron and sulphate of soda."

So you see, as we have proved by our professional witnesses, that there is not even *one part* in the hundred of phosphate of lime in blood, while there is in bone from fifty-one to over fifty-three parts in the hundred of phosphate of lime. Dr. Ludlam gave you the relative quantity of phosphate of lime in bone upon a scale of one thousand as well as upon a scale of one hundred.

What a fund of ignorance their professional witnesses possess upon the scientific questions whereon they have given opinions!!

In discoursing upon these matters brother Miller says, that he thinks I know more than is written in the good book. I do not know what he means by the term "good book." The Mohamedans call the Koran the good book ; most people in Christian countries by this expression, mean the Bible.

But, gentlemen, that book does not profess to teach surgery, anatomy, pathology, nor physiology. However, I have been sustained in every position which I have assumed by standard medical and surgical authors. It fortunately or unfortunately happens that Dr. Porter and those youngsters who followed him, did not only not know what was written, but they only knew a few who had written upon the science of surgery. They were ignorant of the contents and of the authors of these books. Not one of them had ever heard of Hamilton, and they seemed to be equally ignorant of Gross. They come here with a copy of an old edition of Miller's Principles of Surgery, containing many errors which are corrected in the late edition of which we present a copy. You see, gentlemen, that if blood contained fifty parts of phosphate of lime in the hundred, that it would cease to flow with much rapidity; yet, we know that it flows with great rapidity throughout the system. Fill it with fifty per cent. of phosphate of lime, and man would immediately become a living monument of bone. You now see the difference between this opinion of Dr. Porter and his lesser lights, and of scientific men who know what they are talking about. You will recollect that I asked, in different forms, the question as to the quantity of phospate of lime in the human bone and in the blood ; and he testified, as his deliberate opinion, that the quantity was about the same in each ; and the quantity was about forty-eight to fifty-one per cent. We have proved that blood does not contain even one per cent. of phosphate of lime, and not more than one per cent. of the insoluble salts combined, and that bone contains at least fifty per cent. of phosphate of lime, and of the insoluble salts combined, from sixty-one to sixty-six per cent. Gentlemen, do you think it possible for a professional man to have committed more egregious blunders than has Dr. Porter? He certainly could not unless he was more voluble, and I think that would be useless.

When I questioned him about the repair of bone by the aid of the nutrient arteries, instead of answering my question he branched out into a regular lecture upon the anastamosing process, and the beneficent operations of nature.

He would have it that the delicately thin membrane, called the periosteum, which covers the outer surface of the bones, by anastamosis, through the solid bone, supplied the place of the great nutrient arteries. He says that, in case of a rupture of such artery, nature sets herself to work and gets up the process of anastamosis.

He says that anastamosing is the formation of a great number of small blood vessels distributed over the bone, and that these vessels supply the part with the requisite amount of blood, sending the blood into the hard bone. But how these delicate blood vessels managed to penetrate hard bone he left impenetrably obscure. How plain did he make the subject to you?

I confess I do not understand what he means. If you do, I think you have accomplished more than most men could effect.

When I asked him how, by anastamosis, he would in aneurism supply the place of the ruptured artery, and how, in such a case, he would convey the blood to feed the process of repair through the solid bone; he said that in aneurism there *never* was a rupture of the artery, but a mere dilatation of the walls of the artery; that were the artery to be ruptured, the man would die almost momentarily.

It is, perhaps, not very material whether in aneurism the artery bursts or not, but for the purpose of testing his knowledge upon this subject, I read again from Gardner's Medical Dictionary. Of aneurisms, he says:

" *There are four principal kinds.* 1. True aneurism. 2. False aneurism. 3. Aneurismal Varix, or Varicose Aneurism. 4. Aneurism by *Anastamosis.*"

Of False Aneurism he says :

" *Traumatic Aneurism.— When all the coats of the artery are ruptured*, or wounded, and the blood, escaping into the surrounding textures, occasions a pulsating tumor, the case is said to be one of false aneurism."

From this you will perceive that Dr. Porter is about as correct us upon other professional matters. He seems to have a wonderful aptitude for disagreeing with the standard authors upon a science which makes up his profession. His disagreement is not upon some immaterial point, but upon those points which are essential, fundamental truths.

I have demonstrated by this author, that upon the subject of aneurism he is entirely mistaken, so that what he knows of this difficulty does not amount to anything. He ought not to be mistaken about so important a matter. He ought to have known that the fact was the reverse of what he testified to. If he did know better, he ought not to have testified thus loosely. We must not give credence to his professional opinions. He wished to show us how much he knew about the reparation of bone. So he tells us positively that the ossific particles are deposited at the site of fracture from the blood as it courses through the arteries.

Nature in her kindest mood, has provided that the blood shall yield a part of its constituents, and deposit particles of phosphate of lime around the fracture, where it reaches that point through (as I suppose) the *medium of inflammation.*

But how these particles can be thus deposited without perforating or opening the artery, is the question to be solved. What an idea for a sane man!!

Ossific particles of matter are dumped at the point of fracture like the Irishman's loaded wheel-barrow.

He says blood makes everything,—man is made of blood— every tissue of the body is made of blood.

Where stands Beckland and other great authors upon this subject? They are nowhere compared with Dr. Porter. Blood makes man! Blood—blood—blood! Think of that for a moment, gentlemen.

I assert, without fear of successful contradiction, that he never read any such theory in any book, ancient or modern.

We at every breath inhale the common air. Do you call that blood, too? It must be, if *blood is* and makes everything.

Take the egg; is that, too, all blood? When we expose the egg to a given heat, a given length of time, a chicken comes forth with bone, nerve, muscle, blood and blood vessels. Do you suppose that is all blood? Has not the egg all the elements which constitute the chicken, nerve, bone and every tissue? If so, how does the gentleman come to the conclusion that blood creates everything. I assure you, gentlemen, that, to my mind the proposition is absolutely and supremely ridiculous.

And, as Dr. Ludlam well says, you could not make a man out of a tub full of blood.

Moses says that man was formed out of the dust of the earth— not out of blood. Moses had no correct conceptions upon this subject if Dr. Porter is right; for upon his theory it is obvious that man was made in toto out of blood.

All that would be necessary in order to people the unnumbered worlds that float throughout the illimitable regions of space would be, to have blood occupy those realms.

What an airy absurdity! When we go back to the time when chaos reigned supreme—before worlds were formed or animal life had its origin, blood filled immensity! What gauzy speculation! He repudiates the idea that the bone cells multiply upon each other, and are pushed out from the ends of the fractured bone and interweave, and thus repair the injury; or, that bone tissue reproduces bone from materials manufactured in its own laboratory.

The great Saviour of man, it is said, declared that " men do not gather grapes from thorns, nor figs from thistles." But upon Dr. Porter's theory he would have taught that you could gather grapes and figs from blood.

When we examine closely, we perceive that everything is produced by multiplying itself. This is so both in the animal and vegetable kingdom, and what is true as to the totality of an organism is true as to each tissue of that organism. Repair or cure is properly *re-production*, or *pro-creation*.

The theory that every tissue is fed or obtains from the blood the elements of which it is composed, or which it needs to support and sustain itself, was explained by Drs. Beebe and Ludlam. And they illustrated it by the growth of wheat, barley and corn, side by side upon the same soil—surrounded by the same atmosphere, receiving the light and heat of the same sun, and watered by the same dew and rain—each, according to the wants of its own nature, as with an intelligent hand, drawing from all these sources the elements needed for the conservation and complete development of its whole organism.

They are generated—grow to maturity—reach the culminating point—they die and are reproduced in endless succession. Each tissue of the human body thus produces or reproduces its kind. It does not draw so much of material from the blood as constitutes that particular tissue; but from the elements thus abstracted it produces its BEING-CELL, and this cell lives and grows from the *elements* which the blood furnishes; not that the blood has these specific articles on hand already manufactured for deposit in case an accident should occur which would necessitate their use, as Dr. Porter teaches. The blood is to the forming bone what rain is to the growing vegetables; each must have the moisture and the simples or elements of that moisture, in order to attain perfection; but it possesses its own individuality.

Mr. De Wolf read from an author who shows that the growth or repair of the bone is consummated by the reproduction or multiplication of the bone cells. Of this scientific truth Dr. Porter did not appear to have the most remote conception. He tells you that if the elements of bone were not in the blood, it could not deposit the materials for the support of the tissue, and there would be no such thing as the repair or growth of bone. We could have no brick houses unless we have bricks. The brick house is one thing—it is an existing structure; but the elements out of which it is constructed are very different things. The brick, composed of clay, sand and water, is not a house; nor are the elements—clay, sand and water—brick; yet these elements, manufactured in a given way, make brick. When from these elements you have the brick, you still must have mortar—having its constituent elements before you can have the house. With these materials the mechanic can proceed to the construction of the house. This illustration was given you by one or both of our professional witnesses.

Now, as we have proved blood is made from chyle, yet chyle cannot be detected in blood; but of chyle as an element, blood is formed.

It is no more singular that bone should be formed from elements furnished by the blood, than that blood should be formed from the elements of chyle.

A change is made by which each tissue takes on its own form of life and structure. I believe the word chyle is from the Greek "*chulos*," signifying "*the juice.*" Chyle is formed from food, and blood from chyle, and yet no food is detected in chyle, nor chyle in blood. There is a *transmutation* of substances—a conversion of material;—and the bone cells are not blood, nor is blood chyle, nor chyle food. Each differs from the substance or material out of which it is formed, so you see that the explanation of Drs. Beebe and Ludlam are founded in nature, and they are sustained by the highest scientific research.

I cannot do anything which will illustrate this subject better than has been done by those gentlemen.

You will see from the diagram of the different cells, drawn by

Dr. Ludlam, a full explanation of this matter. Thus you see how differently these cells are shaped. The bone cell has a very different form than that of any of the others. Each form of cell has its particular tissue. Dr. Ludlam says that he has examined each cell in the field of the microscope, and that this is no mere theory, but scientific truth, well settled and defined ; that cells are thrown out in the manner as somewhat roughly sketched in this diagram of the repair of bone in case of fracture. These cells, when newly formed, are soft and yielding, and easily ruptured, even the pronation of the hand might endanger or stop the process of repair. But, although this repair might be thus impeded, it might, under favorable circumstances, still go on, and in the end, after a great length of time, become complete.

Provisional callus is very far from being bone, containing only about 3.3 per cent. phosphate of lime, but hoop-like is extended around the ends of the fractured bone, in order that bony union by definitive callus may take place. This is shown by this diagram of Dr. Ludlam, and he and Dr. Beebe have explained the whole matter to you, as known to the best surgeons of the day.

Thus much for the repair of bone under the great natural law, in opposition to this man of fanciful theories—Dr. Porter. We have shown, in relation to all his theories, that he is completely contradicted by standard authors ; and Drs. Beebe and Ludlam are most triumphantly sustained in every position they have taken by these same authors.

When Dr. Porter took hold of the boy's arm with such a flourish, and ranged out as though he was to give a lecture on anatomy, instead of testifying in a court of justice, his manner was calculated to awe you and the spectators into the belief that he possessed a vast amount of knowledge connected with the subject matter of this case. But how does he stand before you now ? How different his conduct from the unpretending manner of Drs. Beebe and Ludlam ?

But, gentlemen, the question for you to determine is, whether the boy's thumb and arm are in their present condition from want of skill or care of Dr. Pratt ? To solve this question, you will consider what were the injuries which required treatment. Were they trifling or were they severe and dangerous ? Were the wounds properly dressed, and were the dislocated joints and broken bones all properly set, or reduced, and properly dressed, or secured by splints and bandages,' and were they timously looked to from time to time? Did the flesh wounds kindly heal in about the usual time? If they did, is it possible that the bandages were too tight, when there was no death or sloughing of the soft parts. Did the broken bones unite within the lapse of eight weeks from the time the fractures occurred, and was the arm then deformed or in natural shape? Were the fragments out of place on the third of February, when old man Yeoman says they were, and that he helped Dr. Pratt put them in place? If they were out of place, was it the exercise of proper care and skill to put them in place? If these fragments were *not* out of place, but Dr. Pratt on that occasion manipulated the part to see what the actual condition was, was that want of care or skill?

If the fragments were then somewhat out of place, could they have become united by the twentieth of the same month? We have proved that this might have been, and no one has deposed to the contrary, and we have proved that union was complete on that day. No one has testified that these fractures were not properly put up; and that they were not is the sum total of their complaint, as developed by the declaration. If you find that union had taken place on the twentieth of February, then after that, did the boy re-fracture the arm or rupture the new union, by playing ball or otherwise; and after this, were the fragments put in apposition by Dr. Pratt? And did he subsequently watch the case and find that the fresh fracture had not united, and did he try to produce union by friction; and did he try this a second time upon the recommendation of other surgeons upon consultation; and up to this time was there any pretence put forth by the boy or his parents that Dr. Pratt had not treated the case with proper care and skill; and did he then and at other times insist that other means promising success should be resorted to, and was he allowed the privilege of so doing, or was the case taken from him without any cause being assigned for doing so? In short, did Dr. Pratt in any particular fail to pursue the mode of treatment recommended by the very best surgeons, and if so, wherein?

Is this arm still curable as we have proved, and has any one testified that it is not? Have they proved what it was that caused this non-union, and are they not bound to prove that the cause was want of care and skill by Dr. Pratt, to maintain this action? Clearly this is so.

You are to consider the facts in this case coolly, deliberately and dispassionately, and apply the law as given you in charge by the court. You are not to decide this case upon the score of sympathy, nor should you be led astray by the eloquent appeals of Mr. Turner, directed rather to the passions than to the judgment. You should look upon and consider the facts stoically. If you properly understand the testimony, you do not need to be out five minutes to find a verdict for the defendant.

I trust, gentlemen, that you will so decide this case that in future life you will have the pleasing reflection that you have done justice to the parties under the law and the testimony.

I tender to you, gentlemen, my thanks for the attention you have given, through the lengthy argument, loaded with some considerable repetition, which I have deemed it my duty to make, to the end that you might properly appreciate the case in all its phases. So far as I well could, I have discharged my duty, and it is now closed. When you shall have heard all the arguments and the charge of the court, in the silence of the jury-room your great duty will commence. When there, exercise that common sense of which Mr. Miller spoke, and that is all we ask.

COL. TURNER'S ARGUMENT.

May it please the Court, Gentlemen of the Jury:—It is very seldom that I approach the discussion of a case with so much embarrassment, and with so much hesitancy as I do the present one. There are several reasons why I feel thus. I remember that many years ago, after the Bunker Hill monument was finished, I climbed to the top of that monument, and with a glass took a survey of the surrounding country—the ocean and hills of New England, the little cottages which nestled there, the forests and the rocks. For the time being I felt I was lifted above the world while looking from that exalted position. That which lay beneath seemed to have dwindled into comparative insignificance. You can comprehend my feelings here to-day. We have been soaring in the fields of science far above the ordinary flights of human nature. Our minds have been so filled with the sublime truths

which lie at the bottom of creation that you will pardon me if, in
coming down to the plain region of matters of fact, I am a
little dizzy now. There is another reason why I feel embarrassed.
I have seen you farmers and mechanics, accustomed to active out-
door life, sit here for seven long days, deprived of that muscular
action and wholesome air which you have been accustomed to
enjoy, and I feel that to do justice to my client, I must occupy at
least half the time occupied by the gentlemen who preceded me.
If I do so, I fear your patience will be wearied. There is
another reason why I approach this case with fear and trembling.
I fear I have not the ability to perform my duty to my client. I
see on my right the court; before me the jury, and the court house
filled with spectators. After the wonderful display of eloquence
and science which has been brought to bear upon this case I feel
I may fail to satisfy the reasonable expectation of this large audience. On the one hand, I feel I ought to make a full speech; on
the other, that I ought not. When I see the intense anxiety manifested in this case—when I behold men and women sitting here
from day to day, I feel that I ought to follow the gentlemen
through all the intricacies of science which he has brought into
the case. But, when in imagination, that poor boy looms up
before me, he seems to say to me, You have but one object to
attend to and that is, my rights. What is there in this case? Are
the principles which lie at the foundation of the universe, and the
developments of science, all involved in this case, as the gentleman
claims they are? If they are not, why did he occupy your time for
ten long hours in the discussion of these principles. My interests are
identified with my client's. And there is another reason why I
feel embarrassed in this case. I allude to the remark of the gentleman upon taking his seat—the most remarkable one I ever
heard fall from the lips of counsel, and I have practiced some
twenty years. He told you that when the argument of the case
had closed, and the court had given you your instructions, then
no tampering would be allowed. What, has there been any tampering with you during this trial? How did he wish to be understood? Did he mean that up to the time he should give his
instructions, the jury had been tampered with; that you had been
followed from store to store; from pillar to pillar; and had this
subject discussed before you? Is that it? That, sir, is not the
way we practice law in this country. But, gentlemen, the main
question which presses upon my mind in entering upon this dis-

cussion is, whether the interests of my client require me to go on the same range of argument which the counsel on the other side have done.

The last gentleman who addressed you in a ten hours' speech of the most ingenious character, tried to lead you away from the issue, and to blot out from your minds the broken arm of this boy. In attempting to do so he has indulged in some things of a comic character. He stood up here with the gravity of a minister, and told you he was a Homœopathist, and that his father had a dog who ate bread and milk, intending by this, I suppose, to show that his father brought up his dog and his children very much alike. It was vastly important that you should know this. I have learned some new things here. Dr. Belding told us that we had an internal memory, and an external one; with the internal, he stores up certain things, like a boy with a cage filled with pigeons; one boy lets them out and the other shoots them. The external memory is the door through which the things of the internal memory are let out. Now, this story of my friend about his father's dog, has opened the trap-door of my external memory, and suggests a story to me. An old deacon in Pennsylvania, had a nice orchard and house, and was blessed with an only son, exceedingly bashful. The ladies called him awkward. The old man wanted him to marry a little fat plump Dutch girl, by the name of Stillwagon. Joe went over to see her, and set down by her side. Joe seemed to be much embarrassed. After a while, Joe looks up to Betsey and says, " Betsey, does your cats eat dried apples ?" If they had, I think it would have been a more wonderful illustration than the judge's, and I tell this story to the jury and to the people, and I trust it will be enrolled on the archives of Carroll County. But the judge put a sort of query to you which had more to do with the case than either the dog or the cat.

It was one of those wise things which lawyers sometimes happen to think of. You will remember that the fact was called out by the other side, that the father refused to give up the brace, but after talking with his wife, concluded to give it up. How triumphantly he appealed to you and asked how can you account for his refusal, unless he thought that the keeping of the brace would be important testimony against the boy. He dwells upon this a full half hour, and says that he would have burnt it up. But if they had burnt it up it might be called in question and they dare not do it. But we may answer this query by saying that the boy could not sleep without the brace, and the family did not want to destroy it or to give it up. The poor boy, when he come to have that splint taken off, his arm dangled there and he could not bear to sleep without the splint. It was more than the poor boy could bear, and the father and mother, in the goodness of their hearts, concluded to indulge him in his request to keep the splint to sleep in. The gentleman had the audacity to intimate that they wanted to keep the splint to avoid its testimony. It is perfectly cruel to do so. There is pathos in this little incident. The boy had worn the splint so long he did not know how to be deprived of it. But, gentlemen, I hardly know where to commence the review of this remarkable speech, the most remarkable one that I or any one in this house ever listened to. That it was ingenious and that he dealt hard blows, I will not deny.

But in reviewing it I will commence with aconite. I do not feel much, however, like going into a full discussion of that important medicine. Neither its history nor its composition cuts any figure here. I ask you, gentlemen, what has aconite to do with this case? Not a witness has testified that a drop of this medicine was administered to this boy, and the defendant's witnesses, who made it the great panacea to allay fever and inflammation, and to take the place of the lancet, might have saved themselves that trouble. But what do they prove? These Drs. from Chicago, say it will allay fever, check inflammation, and do away with the lancet. Now, I will tell how this struck my mind. If aconite will do all this, I ask you would it not have been better practice to have given some of that aconite to keep down inflammation, and given the boy some food? They refused to give him food for days and weeks. Why not control the inflammation with aconite, and give him something to eat? But no witness has testified the Dr. gave the boy aconite. Arnica was applied to the head, and there was some other medicine; nobody knew what it was. Why the necessity of this starving process? I think the Drs'. acts contradict their theories. I am not presenting the plaintiff's side now; I am only presenting some of the many inconsistencies of the defence. I will now take the blood question. There has been an immense amount of misrepresentation in regard to our view of the theory of the blood. I shall have occasion to refer to this question more extensively hereafter. There was one remark of Judge Knowlton, to which I wish to call particular attention. He said no author ever maintained that the blood contained ossific matter. This was his language. He did not make that assertion accidentally or carelessly, for I called his attention to it, and he repeated it. (I never made such a statement, Mr. Turner.—*Knowlton*.) I was surprised that he should make such a sweeping assertion, when, the day before, he and his colleague both read from a work admitted to be a standard work, and they had read up to the very paragraph which I propose to read ; but Mr. De Wolf, when he reached this point, for some reason, stopped reading. Now, I propose to read what he omitted, Wilson's Anatomy, page 48 : " Ossification is accomplished by the formation of very fine and delicate fibres within the intercellular substance : this process commences at the punctum ossificationis, and extends from that point, throug every part of the bone, in a longtitudinal direction, in long, and in a radiated manner in flat bones. Starting from the punctum ossificationis, the fibres embrace each cluster of cells, and then send branches between the individual cells of each group. In this manner the net-work, characteristic of bone, is formed, while the cells by their conjunction constitute the permanent areolar and Hoversian canals. With a high modifying power the delicate ossific fibres here alluded to, are seen themselves to be composed of minute cells, having an elilptical form and central nuclei. These cells attract into their interior the calcarious salts of the blood, and these nuclei become developed, as I believe, into the future corpuscles of Parkinje."

Is this a standard author ? He says these new cells throw into other new cells calcarious matter. (Very different from the deposit of ossific matter. Published). It is impossible. Where is the science now ? The underpining is knocked out. Where, then, is the superstructure which these learned men have erected ? Both Drs. Beebe and Ludlam swear this is a standard work in their college—the very book which they teach to the young men. That book says that this ossific matter is taken from the blood by these cells and converted into bone. Now, is it not possible for these professors from Chicago to be mistaken when they say that the bone does not derive its material from the blood ? If they are mistaken upon that point, may they not be mistaken upon other things that Drs. Miller and Porter and others have testified to, and who have been so shamefully abused, may they not have some little knowledge ? If these mighty men from Chicago possess so much, then there is that great question which

Mr. Knowlton gave to you and the ladies to solve, and I thought it was given more to the audience than to the jury.

I do not know whether the jury will determine whether Moses or Dr. Porter is correct. Moses has no attorney here; his reputation is to stand upon its own merits. Moses has been dead five thousand years. Why should he be dragged into court and pitted against Dr. Porter? He did this with the gravity of a minister. Now, gentlemen, I have shown you, and the gentleman knows it, and he cannot get away from it, that these professors are mistaken when they say that the bone is not derived from the blood. I have shown you the gentleman's rhetoric and eloquence is not logical, where he asserts what he did, and the books say that this ossific matter is in the blood. We will not undertake to be witty upon this point. I cannot follow him in that direction. But it did strike me that in order to get up a little laugh, he abused Dr. Porter. He said Dr. Porter told you that every thing was made of blood—that according to that theory way back in time, he should read in the first chapter of Genesis that the chaos of the great universe was a vast pool of blood; and the gentleman seemed to dwell upon it with a great deal of emphasis —"Blood! blood!! blood!!!"—as though Dr. Porter had sworn to anything of that kind. Dr. Porter swore to no such thing. He did say that the arterial system carrying the blood supplied the necessary material for making bone and muscle. That is what the book shows, and that is all there is of it.

And now, gentlemen, I must be permitted to pursue this a little further. If I had not a ten hours' speech before me, I would dare to extend my remarks; but I will do so now. The gentleman in his argument, and both witnesses on the stand, speak of the manufacture of bone and the growth of wheat from the grain. Did they not have one witness that went so far as to say that the bone was made of intelligent agents—that every cell was an agent. Well, now, gentlemen, that struck me as a very singular proposition—yet I was very much astonished, because they opened the theology of this case. This case has a theology attached to it, as presented to your minds. From the testimony and the argument of counsel, I tell you that these men are disciples of that old Pantheistic theology, that God is in everything. These gentlemen declare that the law of Omnipotence pervades everything, and they are disciples of the old Pantheistic school, which has now been resuscitated, and it is here claimed

that God, the Great Jehovah, is a permeating spirit, and that
everything is permeated by Him. The logical conclusion of this
theory amounts to this, that they believe in an independent creation—that everything has created itself. One said these little
cells are a living intelligence, creating themselves, and the other
says there is a vitalizing principle, like wheat, which caused them
to reproduce. I must be pardoned for speaking a little more
upon this subject than I otherwise should, if they had not said so
much about it.

I wish to take up Dr. Beebe's testimony. He said these bone
cells occupy the same position that the grains of wheat do—that
these cells did not draw their nutriment from the blood. The
material from which they build up this bone, he told you, was
not derived from the blood. Now, I want you to consider this
matter a little. You are farmers. Take this grain of wheat and
you will find in one end of that wheat; although it is small, a
small delicate point, you cannot see it with the naked eye, but
with the misroscope you will find there is a little delicate point
there which contains the form of the plant; you plant that in the
ground, and the atmosphere, the rain and the ground operating
upon that delicate point, it begins to draw this nutritious food
around it, and causes it to reproduce itself very much in the
same manner that the cells do. Pretty soon the stalk grows up
and produces grain. It is reproduced. It is, in other words, the
living principle which has been stamped upon nature by the
Infinite Giver. It has performed its feat of re-producing itself,
and the grain has returned to its mother earth.

Let us see. There is a covering which we call bran. It is a
nice, delicate substance, thrown around that grain for different
purposes; like the skin of the hand, it has great functions to perform. You take that bone and plant it—it will not reproduce
itself—it will not produce bone—it will not produce wheat, or
that out of which wheat will come forth. Let us take that ten
thousand bushels of wheat and plant it which does not contain
this little point, and you cannot raise a stalk.

A few years ago, an American tourist was traveling in Egypt.
On the top of one of the Pyramids he found a kernel of wheat
which had lain upon that Pyramid at the time when Moses was
upon the earth, and still back of that period it had been lying in
the darkest part of this Pyramid for thousands of years. It was
planted, and it germinated and produced wheat. I ask you, if all

16

the bones in the universe had been planted in that Pyramid, could one ounce of bone have been produced? I would like to carry this farther; but I am now testing these men, gentlemen of the jury, upon the sublimest principles of logic and science, and I will show every proposition which they have made to be false.

Gentlemen, how can bone produce itself? Can you extract from your body a bone, and by any possible process that your ingenuity can invent, will it make bone? Has it, in other words, the power of producing itself? Now, gentlemen, you must adopt the great principle that Nature's God has stamped upon man. Like the grain of wheat, under the laws which the Omnipotent has given, can He reproduce, or does He reproduce, Himself? No; not one particle of man reproduces man, and when they say that bone can reproduce itself, they say what science will not bear them out in, and what philosophy contradicts, and what God never did say. If these little cells are independent intelligences, and reproduce themselves, as the judge says they are, you may set to work here and make feet and hands. Some poor fellow in the army comes along who has lost hand or foot, and we may go to work and plant a bone and raise him a foot or hand. That is a process we have not yet learned; yet Chicago is a great city, but I tell you that this war closes before the Chicago surgeons learn to do that. Now, gentlemen, in regard to that theory, I have upset it. Where do they stand now? I say that logically, physiologically, morally,—theologically, if you please,—the whole structure has tumbled to the ground. It has not a peg whereupon it can stand. If this case is turned over to you, I believe there are twelve minds here who will say that it is so.

Well, now, gentlemen, whatever I have to say about the circulation of the blood, I will say when I open the case. The judge has labored with wonderful skill and learning, and the gentlemen from Chicago have testified with a wonderful degree of skill and learning. And here let me say I will not undertake to denounce men as fools and ignoramuses, because they do not believe as I do; because Drs. Ludlam and Beebe do not agree with me, I will not denounce them as fools. If I ever go to Chicago, I shall try to cultivate their acquaintance. I never come in contact with such men without learning something. There was an Old School Presbyterian preacher, who lived in an adjoining neighborhood, who preached every Sabbath, and I used attend his church, on account of the girls. My father did not like it, and used to threaten to whip me if I did not keep away. I liked the doctrines, but my father did not, and was determined I should hear nothing which he did not like. Just so with these gentlemen; if they cannot build up their own side they are determined to break down all others. They run down all our doctors except one, and I will tell you why they except him before I get through. I will drop the blood question now. I do not believe that chaos before creation was a tub of blood.

I now come to the subject of false joint, and here again, gentlemen, there is no misunderstanding of the testimony of the Chicago doctors; both of these professors swear positively, without a why or a wherefore, that this boy's arm is not a false joint. I take issue with the gentlemen, and if I prove it is a false joint, according to the understanding of false joints, you must conclude the Chicago gentlemen must be mistaken with all their learning. I will prove it out of their own books, which they teach the young gentlemen who go there to study medicine. I have nothing to say about Drs. Miller and Porter; their heads are as clear as mine. Drs. Freas and Bulkley are young men. Is it a fact, that under all the lights of surgery and Homœopathy, in the Chicago, Cincinnati, Cleveland and St. Louis schools, young men are permitted to graduate without being taught what constitutes a false joint? If they say they do not teach about false joints, they are lying, and I will expose them. Some of our men state it is a false joint. Among the authors they state as reliable, I will read one—Miller's Practice of Surgery, 630. Pardon me for reading more than one. I propose to read under the head of false joints :

Disunited Fracture.—"The *false* joint which results *from* disunited or *from* un-united fracture, bears no resemblance to normal articulation; there is neither articular cartilage nor synovial apparatus. The ends of the bone taper somewhat, and are rounded off; they are invested by a dense fibrous expansion, *and by a similar texture* they are joined together."

I will say here, that false joints are not always uniform, as that book says. They use this book in Chicago. Now then, what does it say ? Drs. Beebe and Ludlam told you that this was a case of disunited fracture. They said there was no false joint; but this book says there is. They admit that there is a cartilaginous substance, so that the bones will not rub against each other. This is to the joint what grease is to the wagon. Just exactly the case here. Now, then, that is all there is of it. When the bone does not unite where it has been refractured, so that the bones play upon each other, that is a false joint. I do not care to run this thing further to see whether false joints may not sometimes have ligatures. I do not remember of ever reading of or of having seen a false joint. This leads me to another proposition, and one that I was very much struck with. When the gentleman brought it out in the argument, the counsel said that instead of prosecuting this man, he ought to feel very thankful this was not a false joint. I think he ought to thank his Maker first for giving him one good joint, Dr. Pratt for giving him another. But still I am not sure that you would feel much like thanking the surgeon for giving your son a second joint at the elbow. I think that theory of false joints is pretty well answered.

I now come to review that part of the gentleman's speech where he talks about provisional callus and definitive callus. Well, perhaps, if I were delivering a lecture before a medical class, or if I were making a speech to a purely literary society, and where my scientific knowledge would be very closely scrutinized, I would go into it more lengthy. If I were going to educate you for physicians, I would go into a discussion on this subject—I would show you, probably, in this connection, what forms the bridging or scaffolding over which to carry the bone—I would first tell you that the first outgrowth or exudation had a less proportion of life in it than that which forms definitive callus, and that definitive callus has 50 per cent. of phosphate and 10 or 12 of carbonate of lime.

Much fault has been found with Dr. Porter for saying that nature has wisely provided for this callus; but it is a truth which will stand, and stand forever—that nature has well provided for the repair of fractures in the human body—not in the human body only, but in the animal and vegetable creation, and I maintain, the mineral creation also. It does in the vegetable creation.

I will now talk about something of which you know something. I have been there myself. I have cultivated trees and carried on farming. I know you know all about it, just as much as the professors do—probably more. Go out this time of the year with your axe and strike into a cherry, a poplar or chesnut, which grows very rapidly. Where it is cut there is a wound—a great fracture in that tree. This great law of nature—this wise power

of Omnipotence—you will see how the energies of nature go
to work to repair that tree. You see how the sap runs in it and
runs out. The bark you see pushing out the woody fibre, and
presently you see a great clump healed over. True, nature has
been injured in that blow of the axe ; but that wise provision of
nature has gone earnestly to work to fill in with cells and to close
up the wound. If you watch this you will see this process going
on, and that provisional callus which is first thrown out becomes
hard, just like the rest of the tree. Just so in the human body.

Well, now, these gentlemen undertook to say that nature does
not put forth any of this energy ; that is their theory, in order to
repair these damages. I apprehend some of you are heads of
families ; if you are not, if you remember when you cut your finger, or foot, as I have done many times with the axe, you will see
how earnestly nature goes to work to repair the wound—in three
weeks from that time, if you will closely examine it, you will see
the granulations taking place, and nature working as busily as she
can be—you will see a little degree of redness, and these little
cells pushing out within a week, and in a few weeks nature has
bridged over that gap, and the work is complete. But, here, the
gentlemen ran off with the theory that it healed by what he
called first intention. What of it? They say that none of these
gentlemen have explained it; that if you cut your finger and put
every vessel in place, the circulation goes right on, and you
hardly know you have been injured ; it is all healed over ; the
instrument, if a sharp one, or if from any other cause there is no
foreign matter taxing nature, the work is soon completed and the
bone will do the same. These gentlemen say they have read the
same books—which prove that bone will do this same thing, and,
not one of these gentlemen ever saw bone do that. Our friend
from Chicago, who has had 4000 cases, never saw but two cases
of the *humerus fractured*, and Dr. Miller, who has practiced surgery, never saw but three. Dr. Ludlam says he never saw the
humerus which would not unite. They say it is in Miller's Practice of Surgery, and I have referred to it, and you will
find that all the knowledge in the world is not centered in
Chicago, and here again, gentlemen. I must be permitted to read to
you the treatment of false joint. (Miller's Practice of Surgery, 669).
That is the point they come to. 657, subject, provisional callus,—
and here is what it refers to. I will show you that the reference does
not in any manner bear out the conclusion that provisional callus

is not necessary. They say that the provisional callus is not necessary to a re-union. I refer to the book and page, and to see
that it is not necessary. We find it is not so laid down. Here is
the reference, and they have failed to make their point here.

Now, gentlemen, this author does not teach that a bone ever
united without provisional callus. It does say it may unite with
but very little, and that is all there is of it :

" It appears, from the observation of Mr. Paget, that in a well
managed facture, the formation of provisional callus is reduced
to a minimum ; the exudation being thrown out almost entirely
between the fractured ends, and nature's splint being in a great
part superseded by that of the surgeon."

Knowlton says, " Read that on page 630."

" To undo the apparatus of a fractured limb, and to find the
solution of continuity in the bone still unrestored, at the end of four,
five, six, seven or eight weeks, is no demonstration of the expected
union having altogether failed. It may be that the formation of
definitive callus is yet in progress; and, if undisturbed by movement of the limb, this may be completed in no unreasonable time.
The provisional callus has doubtless failed, but in truth this is not
essential to osseous re-union. When it does exist, it is but a ferrule, or clasp, tightly embracing the broken part."

I know what I am about. He wants to refer me to the cases
of flat bones where no provisional callus is thrown out, to prove
that their doctrines are right. By the way, gentlemen, I wish to
impress upon you this fact,—in calling my attention to the treatment of these bones, it is merely a repetition of what was said
before. In speaking of the treatment of these bones, it does say they
may form without provisional callus, and refers back to the subject as *prima facie* proof of that—and when I go back to it—it
says it forms without much provisional callus.

I would read more if I had the strength and lungs to talk to
you, and you had the time to listen to it. But, take the fracture
of the skull ; if it produced provisional callus, it would produce
congestion on the brain and cause death. Nature is always right;
man may err. There is another thing which tells me that if there
is considerable motion, it takes much provisional callus to hold
it in apposition. When the bone on the head is broken, the brain
is pressed against the skull and the little veins are all around it.
If you have never examined, it will astonish you. There is no
different position which the bones can occupy. The little provisional callus which forms there is just sufficient to hold the bone in

place. Suppose there was a little provisional callus attached to the bows of these spectacles ; before the definitive callus could form, nature would throw out a provisional callus to hold the bows in place. It would be hard to conduct definitive callus without provisional callus. It is more than scaffolding for the definitive to lean upon.

He (Judge K.) undertook to say that the books say there could be no provisional callus on the femur, which has a head like the humerus, *only more so.* This is placed in a very delicate socket, like a new box skein which fits so nicely that you cannot put the blade of a small knife between them. It is so with the femur. It operates in that little socket so that nothing can intervene. It has a thin, oily substance—if it was not for that it would squeak, we should go round here with squeaking joints. Suppose, for illustration, that here was the fracture on this bone. That upon some occasion or another that part was fractured, but not removed out of the socket ; you see the fitting it to the socket so closely would not permit of callus being formed around it. The idea of a fracture presupposes a space. Can a fracture have provisional callus without space. It is like a crack in the delicate china cup which the housewife cannot discover until she puts it into the hot water. They say there cannot be any such callus. Hence, there is no room for it, for there is a fracture without a crack. If the tea cup does break there is a crack in it, or vacuum in it, I don't care how minute ; it might go down to the third or thirty-third attenuation of a hair, like the gentleman's aconite. It is there, and by the microscope can be seen. It is the same. as nature has made it—there is evidence of provisional callus here, they say ; but it was so minute they could not discover it. I remember that when my mother broke a cup, she had to mend it in the best way she could ; there was some kind of an herb which she would boil and put the cup into it ; the crack would be there, but something got into the crack and stopped it up. It was milk and leek. It was not bread and milk, I am sure. She made a provisional callus of it.

Well, now, gentlemen, I have disposed of the blood, the aconite and the provisional callus, and these were their great principles involved in this case, so far as I remember. There are some other things which some how or another have worked into this case. I don't know how ; that is, I don't know why they should, but they have got into it. There was one other subject that there was a little issue upon. The subject of inflammation. Now I shall have to read a greatdeal more than I want to, to dispose of that subject as I should like to. Drs. Porter, Miller, Bulkley, McPherson, Freas and Haller all testify that inflammation, to a certain extent, was necessary to union in all fractures, and they told you why it was necessary. They told you that in most cases inflammation was the mode that nature adopted to carry off the debris caused by the fracture. It was not absolutely essential, but they all testified that it was a system of absorption that would carry it off, without injury. Nature provided through means of this inflammation, that the old superstructure which had been broken up, might be repaired, and that nature also provided by this inflammation, a greater supply of blood; thereby making a greater supply of material for repair. I spoke of the tree where inflammation was going on, where you discovered an unusual degree of activity, in carrying the sap to the place of injury. Drs. Porter, Miller and others all agree upon this point; they said inflammation is necessary to the supply of blood to form the provisional callus. These Chicago physicians say it is not necessary; it is only a diseased state. If I remember right what I have read, it is this, that where nature does a certain thing in a certain way, we have a right to conclude this is the right way. I have a right, then, to conclude this is the right way. If by planting an apple seed a hundred thousand or million of times, it will produce a tree, we have a right to say that nature will not produce anything but an apple tree from such a seed. They have no right, then, to conclude that nature ever fails in her modes of operation. She will never produces apple leaves from oak trees. We have a right to say this is nature's mode.

And, gentlemen, if any physician or surgeon has testified that any bone is actually cured, or any fracture was ever restored without inflammation, I say they are going contrary to nature's laws. We have had six medical men on our side, and they have had three or four, and not in one single case have they ever had a fracture cured without inflammation. They have a theory that the infinitessimal dose of aconite might cure. If I should go to a college a year I might get a theory into my mind I could produce apple trees from acorns—my learning does not teach me so. Here is a witness who has had 4000 cases; every one had inflammation and resulted favorably, so far as he knew. Here is that terrible

Dr. Porter, that awful man, who stands in direct opposition to
Moses, who has practiced twenty years and never had a case
without inflammation. I conclude that inflammation is a universal and immanent force—that nature has not cut in on this uniform
rule. If Dr. Porter was a disciple of that doctrine which teaches
that God is in every thing, I do not know but I might think nature
might prove false to herself. According to that theory you need
not be at all surprised before I get through that you may see a
young lamb grow right out of that book, because it is covered with
sheep skin.

Now, gentlemen, there has been a great many things said, in
these remarkable speeches, that I may go over in reviewing this
case. I want to observe due courtesy to Mr. De Wolf. I must
notice two or three remarks which he made. He said there was
a question of outside pressure in this case, and you must not be
governed by it. Who made it, and where did it come from? I
do not know there is any outside pressure. I have not felt it.
There has been no outside pressure, but only the pocket pressure,
and which does not apply to me in this case. When I look around
here and see my client, I see a poor crippled boy, not yet sixteen
years of age—a boy who does not know twenty persons in Carroll
county, and without friends; and the proof shows that Mr. Frisby
is a poor man—that it is not three years since he removed to the
county of Carroll,–before he had fairly moved into the county,–this
boy's arm was fractured before they had got settled. I may say,
in regard to the father of the boy, that he is an ignorant man—
not a man of position; that he is a good, honest man, I have no
doubt; that he is not a man of intelligence you saw by his appearance on the stand, when they applied their science to him; you
saw he was ignorant of science. This poor boy and this stranger,
his father, who has but just become a voter, has produced no
such an outside pressure; certainly not. He has no means
of producing an outside pressure, for there is no interest
felt here for him in this trial. It is not because of overshadowing talent; but fair, common lawyers, like myself whom
you have heard make speeches before; and you have known
me before Carroll county was born. If I may be allowed the
expression, I used to haul my grub up here from the Mississippi
with an old pair of oxen, driven by myself, so you see there is no
pressure in that direction. Who has done it? I will tell you,
gentlemen, where and how it comes. I stand here presenting to

you a poor boy, without friends and without money, against the wealthiest men in Carroll county, backed up by the best talent in Chicago, lawyers and surgeons. There is where the outside pressure comes from. Look around you; surrounding us here are lawyers whom I have met for many years; men who have tried cases successfully with me. I find in this case, the defendant has not employed these, but has employed counsel of the most overshadowing ability of any in the Northwest. There he sits, that Ajax of the Northwest. He has been brought here at an expense of one thousand dollars; brought here, for what? Primarily, to sustain Dr. Pratt; secondly, to sustain a system of medical practice. Further, I look around, and I am not going out of their own circle of practice. I see a large number of medical gentlemen who practice the same system, but are not called in this case. We did not send for Dr. Blaney, nor Dr. Brainard, and the mighty lights of Chicago. We took up with Dr. Miller and Dr. Porter, this second Moses. We picked up Drs. McPherson and Freas and others, as we could gather them. They did no such thing; they did not have a single physician from the country. They go to the city of Chicago and select two of the mightiest men in that city; keep them here for more than a week to testify in a case where this poor boy prosecutes for a ruined arm. That is where the pressure comes from; there is where curiosity is excited. I remember of reading in a certain paper in the city of Chicago, why a certain convention should be held there; that Chicago was the great centre of finance, and the great centre of railroads; the great centre of commerce, and two or three other reasons why it should be held there. But really, gentlemen, until this trial took place, and I heard the speech of my learned friend, I did not know that Chicago was the great centre of intelligence, before the gentleman informed you that you would take such a case to Chicago rather than trust it to Miller and Porter—old Moses, here on the anxious seat. I am under the conviction, and I may be a convert to Homœopathy. The first proposition was, that Homœopathy was taken from the Greek, and meant that like cured like. The second was taken from Latin, and means that like produces like—that bone produces bone. But I must be permitted to tell a story.

When I was a bigger fool than I am *now*, when I was stumping it for the democratic party, there was a speaker on the other side. I hit him and he hit me. He said that Chicago was önce a great frog pond, and that you might find there all sorts of frogs, from the great bull frog down to the little white-bellied, striped-backed peeping frog, which falls in the spring rain; that when the water had fallen away it left the frogs upon the ground, and there was a terrible commotion among them and divers scrambling. When they found they could not get water, they got into a rampage and swore "Be Jabers, they were no more frogs; but dimmercrats," and ever since that they have had a great antipathy to cold water. This man says, and I believe there is some truth in it, that Chicago is a great city. The first time I visited Chicago, was immediately after the Black Hawk War. I walked over a thousand miles to see this great city. It was nothing but a frog pond then. I saw frogs there, from the big bull frog down to the little white-bellied peeping frog. Behold Chicago, rising out of the frog ponds, and look at the varieties of frogs which have been sent out here, from the great big bull frog down to the small white-bellied peeping frog. Like produce like. That is why these people are here. They knew Chicago was going to exert herself. They have come out here from their abnormal state (excuse me if that is not a surgical phrase). It is not quite fair that this state of things should exist. Is it fair, in other words, that we should be overshadowed in this way? It seems to me that the talent here would have been sufficient for this case under ordinary circumstances. It is not fair that us *country clod-hoppers*, that have tried to get along in this case, should be pushed out by these learned professors and gentlemen from Chicago. I remember when a boy, reading the translation of Homer. I would read along where the mighty armies were pressing down upon the little handfull of horsemen, that old Homer would paint the great Gods as descending and entering the hearts of the weaker party. That was the style that struck my young fancy. When I saw the feeble army struggling for the right, for God and Liberty, and I saw the Gods descend from Heaven to aid the weaker, I could not help crying.

We present you this case, of a poor boy who has been misused, and that these mighty gods of Chicago have descended upon us to carry us away. Perhaps they will succeed. I don't know what there is in this case, stripped of all its excitement. What is there in this case? On the one side we have a boy who claims he has not been properly treated by a doctor; on the other side we have a doctor, and no doubt a very respectable man, so far as I know.

I know nothing against Dr. Pratt. I have no reason to speak ill of him; no reason to say anything but what he is a respectable man. So far as feeling is concerned, there is not, in the deepest recesses of my heart, the slightest ill feeling towards Dr. Pratt..

Gentlemen, I am not related to this boy in any way that I know of, only by the common ties of humanity. I never saw these parties until they came to this court house. I saw the plaintiff only once before I took this case, and I have nothing to do with this case but to see that this boy has his rights—only so far as it lies in my power to aid him. I was astonished at the closing remark of the gentleman before he took his seat. I was greatly astonished when the gentleman told you (if I understood him right) I was a man of an affectionate nature, and to look upon me *stoically*. I think these were the words; and look upon me stoically, because I was a man of an affectionate nature. I claim to be no more affectionate in my nature than falls to the lot of humanity. You will bear testimony that I am no more affectionate than common men. When I saw that arm stripped here before you, I did not turn sick and faint at the sight. I cast my eyes over the jury and saw there this great distinction which distinguishes man from the beast, which manifested itself upon your countenances, and some of you could hardly endure the sight. Now, gentlemen, if that arm so much affected you, being entire strangers, how must it affect that mother, whose head has grown gray under this trouble?

How must it affect that father, who has looked upon that boy from day to day as he has grown up before him, and that every night when he undresses him he has to look upon that arm! How must that woman's heart bleed every time when she looks upon that distressed boy! How must that father's hopes shrink back into his heart when he beholds his son crippled for life! Then tell you to look upon me stoically. Shut out from your heart that which distinguishes you as men and look stoically upon me. I am asking no favors, gentlemen of the jury. I am not coming here a beggar at your feet by any manner of means. I am presenting to you the most outrageous case of malpractice, and yet the attorney asks you to look upon me *stoically*, or not to look upon the case with humanity. We find, from the testimony, that on the 20th day of December, 1802, this boy, with the elder brother, was coming home with a load of corn from an adjoining county. They attempted, on the defence, to prove that they attempted to run their horses—that this boy tried to run past his brother, or his brother past him. That may or may not be so, but probably is so. I don't care anything about it. It cuts no figure in this case. The boy was thrown out of the wagon and badly hurt —the right hand badly lacerated; the metacarpal bone was fractured; the head had a contusion which took a little time to cure, and the left arm was broken—how much, you must find from the testimony, because that is matter for you to find.

These people had just come into the precincts of Carroll county; they were utter strangers in the neighborhood. The proof shows they knew no doctor, and when the accident happened kind neighbors called the doctor and had the wounds dressed. It occurred near the house of Mr. Morris. The elder brother picked up the boy and tried to take him to the house. On his way to the house he met Mr. Morris, and said his brother had been killed—go for a doctor. He did not look stoically upon it, and goes for Dr. Pratt, and sent for the father. When the father got there Dr. Pratt was there. They had not commenced doing up the arm. The chloroform was sent for, the first thing to be done in the case. The father sees his boy badly wounded; he finds the doctor there. What would you have done? You would have done as he did. He says to Dr. Pratt: "Are you competent to take this case and take care of it?" Dr. Pratt says, "I am." Dr. Pratt tells him, "If you wish for any other doctor you can have him." Frisby said, "I am a stranger here, and as lief employ you as any other man, if you can do it right." Dr. Pratt assured him he could. What would you have done in similar circumstances, in a strange country, not acquainted with any doctors, the boy lying there, with his wounds undressed, and utterly incompetent to help himself? That reminds me of another thing, gentlemen of the jury. The question was not asked, what kind of physician he was. There was no question about "pathies" at that time. The only questions at all operating upon the mind of the father were, "Are you capable?" "Are you skillful?" "Are you competent to take charge of this boy?" He told him as he ought to, go on and spare no pains or expense. He felt as you would feel. If you had found your boy mutilated you would spend the last dollar you had in the world that the boy might have proper treatment. Upon that assurance the doctor goes to work and does up the arm in splints, and sets one of the Mr. Morris to make splints. Gives him chloroform. This was on

Saturday. On Sunday the boy was taken home in a wagon. On Monday or Tuesday Dr. Pratt visited the house in company with Dr. Wales. Two or three weeks after this he visited it with Dr. Wales again. He continued to visit it occasionally afterwards; and that brings me to the first great discrepancy in the testimony. There was no discrepancy as to the wounding and dressing; but in what occurred next there was a great discrepancy. One of the great things for jurors to do is, to reconcile testimony and discard that which ought not to be reconciled.

We come now to the testimony of the splint. There is no witness that has testified that this is the angular splint which was put upon the arm. There is no testimony to my mind, or would be if I was a juror, to show that this might be the splint. Now, it becomes a question of the gravest importance, as to when it was put on the arm. Even old Moses here admits, and no one denies it, that the splint is a good one. Now then, when was it put on the arm. Dr. Wales says, on Monday or Tuesday he visited the patient with Dr. Pratt, and the splint was on the arm at that time. Dr. Pratt, in presence of the parents and the boy, observed that the splint was put on at Morris's, as to move him. I state it fairly and candidly, and as favorably for Dr. Wales as I can. He swears positively that Dr. Pratt said he put it on to protect the arm, in bringing him home from Morris's. Then, according to that testimony, it was then on and must have been on at Morris's at that time. That brings me to the most disagreeable part of the case, gentlemen of the jury. It is disagreeable for me to have to take certain possitions to expose the reasons which I have for arriving at this conclusion. I must refer to the testimony, and I will state it to you, and they have it taken down in the same way. Mr. Frisby does not know. He tells us he has no recollection of it, when it was put on; it might have been put on the next day or the next week. Then his testimony does not amount to anything definite. But Mrs. Frisby's testimony is direct, that on the Tuesday of the second week Dr. Pratt came there and she sent her son to Dr. Pratt's for that splint. She swears positively that it was never near the boy until the second week. There is no equivocation about that.

Mrs. Moscript swears positively, and sticks to it, that the splint was not put on until the second week.

Harvey Frisby, the brother, swears positively that he was sent for this splint to Dr. Pratt's.

That was two weeks after the injury. I have stated it exactly as it stood on the cross-examination by one of the most able and ingenious attornies that ever visited Carroll county. That Dr. Wales could have been mistaken I cannot believe. I am as charitable as most men, and I know it is difficult for me to arrive at a conclusion which implicates any man. If I have a weakness that overrides my judgment, and which my friends blame me for, it is, that I am too charitable to believe any man guilty of perjury, and I never give it up that it could be so until it is thrust upon me by evidence I cannot resist. There is but one conclusion as regards the splints which a logical man can arrive at, and that is, either Dr. Wales has sworn to what is not true, or else these two women and Harvey have perjured themselves, and stand here before Almighty God guilty of the highest crime known to the law resting upon their consciences. There is no reason for a mistake by either. The other party will not call it a mistake. These witnesses, unimpeached, swear that splint was not on the day Dr. Wales says it was. "False in one thing, false in all," is the Latin maxim. If Mrs. Frisby, Mrs. Moscript and Harvey have sworn falsely in one part of the case, you are to disregard their entire testimony, and say in your hearts that these three witnesses stand before High Heaven with the crime of perjury resting on their heads. If Dr. Wales, for the purpose of sustaining his partner, or of sustaining Homœopathy, or any other "pathy," has falsified the truth, you are to disregard that testimony. Before the eye of the Omnipotent God, you are bound to disregard that testimony.

Gentlemen, who has falsified the truth? These three witnesses or that one? What are the probabilities that charity would say, that one man was guilty rather than two women and one man? Who committed that perjury? Humanity would admit only this conclusion.

Now, gentlemen, without delay upon that subject at this time, let us proceed a little further. Following it up, we find Dr. Pratt constantly saying that this arm was doing well for some six or seven weeks. Here, again, we come in conflict with direct testimony. Here we find Dr. Wales testifying that he and Dr Pratt undressed that arm in the presence of the father and mother;—I am not certain as to the father. They found that the boy could raise his arm to his head; that he called the attention of the mother to the fact, and that she noticed it. There can be no mistake about it. Mrs. Frisby swears that she never saw that arm raised—was never in a position it could be done. " False in one thing, false in everything," is again echoed back to our minds. Who would be the most likely to treasure it up in their hearts forever, the young aspirant for surgical honors and partner of Dr. Pratt, or that mother? Had I a jury of mothers they would answer that question very soon.

Gentlemen, you may have the good fortune to have children· I remember the degree of pride when I went home and my wife told me that our eldest had taken the first step. Show me the mother that cannot remember when her child cut its first tooth or took its first step. There is something there that is treasured up. These peculiar emotions at the first step or the cutting of the first tooth are applicable here. Think you that mother, who, for several weeks did not take her eyes from that child, would have forgotten this important fact? When the important news came that he could raise his arm, would she not remember it? I have known bad women, but I never knew one so lost to the dignities of womanhood, who would not have treasured up that fact. How much more would the mother be likely to remember it when she had wasted her own health in taking care of him—the lifting up of this arm. Look upon me stoically, but not upon that boy or mother, for God's sake. The echo comes back, " False in one thing, false in all." Did that mother lie when she told you that that boy's arm never had been raised from the time is was fractured? Did she lie when she said Dr. Wales never called her attention to it? She did, or some one else did.

There are other discrepancies in this testimony, but I shall not weary you with following it out as particularly as did Judge Knowlton. I will try this case without any ambition on my part to show my knowledge of science. On the third of February old Mr. Yeoman was there, and Dr. Pratt was there, and Mr. Yoeman, at Dr. Pratt's request, took hold of the shoulder, and Mrs. Yeoman took hold of the arm; and he tells you he thinks he pulled a hundred weight. There was extension applied, and Dr. Pratt manipulated the arm at the same time. Mr. Knowlton ridicules this idea, and undertakes to show he could not pull much.

The injury took place on 20th Dec., and this was the third of February, and ossific union had not taken place. If this had been properly set, there would ordinarily have been union by that time. The testimony shows that treatment was not proper.

The Chicago gentlemen claim, if the bones were out of place, it would have been proper to put them in place. The old gentleman who testified to this, has not been contradicted, is a respectable man, and his countenance shows him to be an honest man. There he sits, and he has as good a countenance as any of you, gentlemen, and you are bound to believe him. Dr. Pratt said pull harder. I know that is the way to make extension, for I have assisted. It is perfectly natural that Dr. Pratt should have said so. The probability is that the provisional callus, if any had formed, was broken up then, when Dr. Pratt reset the arm.

Sometime about the last of February, it is claimed that this arm was refractured. Upon this point there is some contrariety of testimony. Mrs. Frisby says that the boy came into the house and went up stairs; that she discovered there was a slight split on the side of the splint, but she interrogated Frank, and he said it did not hurt him. The testimony of the other witnesses all agree that it was not as much fractured as it is now. Did the boy refracture the arm on that occasion? If it was not in apposition on the third of February, there had not been time for the arm to unite between that and the last of February, when this took place. Young Shaffer testifies he caught his arm on the fence post, but that the boy kept on playing for some time, and did not complain. Mr. and Mrs. Frisby both swear that when they saw the splint split, they interrogated the boy thoroughly, and he said it did not hurt him. The remark that Mrs. Frisby was alleged to have made was, that she thought it hurt him worse than he pretended. She denies; and you have a right to bring your own experience to bear upon this point, to test the probability of her having said so. We know it could not have been done without being attended with pain, and no one heard him complain of pain. We find that the Morrises and all the witnesses testify he was in much pain at the time of the fracture. Mr. Morris did not mean to be understood that the boy did not complain of pain; he did complain, then. The testimony of Miller and Porter is direct upon this point, that there must have been pain, and the Chicago Drs. say there must have been some pain in case of refracture. Suppose it was refractured the second time. Dr. Pratt was there the next day following, and the parents did not conceal what the boy had done, but Dr. Pratt did not even take the

17

splints off. He said the boy had loosened the parts a little. But suppose the arm was refractured, which we deny; what was the duty of the surgeon? It was to reset the fracture. I tell you, there is a beautiful young lady in this room who broke the bone of the femur, and had it set, and fell and refractured it, and the Dr. set it again, and she soon walked around with it as before. These Drs. from Chicago say it could not be that it could refracture without pain. You have been really fortunate if you have not had some instance of this kind. These cases, however, of delayed union are mostly in the books which are written by professors in the medical institution—and occur about cities, being rarely in the country.

In this county of Carroll, which has sent one thousand soldiers to the army, there has not been a single case of fracture of the humerus, I venture to assert, which did not re-unite. If you have been in the hospitals in the cities, you would have seen men and women rotten with disease from head to foot. There you would find the miserable debauchees, and every form of vice; and there alone you would find the false joints treated of in the books. In the country like Carroll county, where the young men and women are healthy, under proper treatment you find no false joints. There is one of the miserable old fogy doctors who had never had any these cases of false joint? Where is Dr. Miller? I do not see him; if he is not here he ought to be. He has practiced surgery twenty years, and attended the birth of more than half your children in Carroll and Jo Daviess, for that period of time, and he has never seen a case of false joint. What a miserable old fogy. He has stood by the bedside of families of this county, and assisted in bringing into existence two-thirds of the children of this county. Poor old fogy! What a pity it is that your people could not have had Chicago Drs. to set the fractures. Will you not take the next son or daughter who has a fractured limb to Chicago to be treated?

Dr. Porter, he has been sometime in the West, and he has never seen any false joints since he left Baltimore. Dr. Freas has never seen a case in twelve years' practice. Dr. Haller has practiced two years and has never seen a case before. I believe you are all fogies. George Washington was an old fogy; he never saw a railroad But I think you will not take your children to Chicago to be operated upon by these Chicago Drs. I think the day is far distant when Carroll county will be blessed with that kind of life which will cause false joints like those in the city of Chicago. There is another bit of collateral testimony that comes in here in regard to this old fogy practice—which always cures. There was one thing which struck me as curious; you have not failed to notice that Judge Knowlton has the most imperturbable countenance you ever saw. Whether things go to please or displease, it makes no difference with him. I should recommend him for the next Secretary of State, for he can beat even William H. Seward in that. When I had old fogy Miller on the stand, he said he never had seen a false joint. He said he had seen one which went some five or six months, and by this friction power he cured it. If one of these big Southern bomb-shells had exploded under the Judge's chair, he could not have jumped up quicker than he did when I asked Dr. Miller that question, and objected to its being answered. He was not permitted to answer my question; the court overruled it. But why was it that that question had such remarkable effect on the Judge? Was that one of Dr. Pratt's patients? The witnesses did not say so. I cannot say so. Shall I tell you what struck me? It was that this was a case of incipient false joint, and they did not want to have Dr. Pratt's surgery examined. If it had been good they would have been proud of it. I leave it to you to judge what the motive was. Dr. Miller would not have been afraid of having his surgery examined; why should Dr. Pratt? He could have called up his friends and had them testify in this matter. Miller would have allowed these witnesses to come up, and so would old Moses. Then this case and that case are the only cases which Dr. Miller ever saw, and that one Dr. Miller cured—this is tolerable good evidence that he might cure this one. Dr. Pratt says you may take this case to any one around here or in Chicago, but Dr. Miller, because he would not do justice, because he is so opposed to Homœopathy. It struck me that when he touched Dr. Miller so lightly, and pitched into Dr. McPherson and handled him without gloves, and skinned Porter up one side and down the other, it meant something. He says Miller is a pretty good old fellow; is all right. But Dr. Pratt said, go to any other living man but Dr. Miller. Yet Dr. Miller had had a case, and it had been cured. But to return; Dr. Pratt did not re-adjust that bone on that occasion, if it was refractured, or ever afterwards. The testimony of Mrs. and Mr. Frisby, and Mrs. Moscript all concur in saying, that two weeks after that time, Dr. Pratt did say it was back to its original place, and thus all concur in saying that Dr. Pratt did continue to say it was doing well up to the time when he went down to Dr. Belding's. How did he come to go there? The testimony shows Frisby had become uneasy, and, that about the 15th of May they went to Dr Belding's and met Dr. Belding and Dr. Freas, both of whom have been witnesses on the stand. Dr. Belding says, that in questioning him, I did not state his testimony fairly. If I did not, gentlemen, you undoubtedly know which was correct. Dr. Belding says, by the way, he felt a little nervous about the shingle nails; he said it only in a joke, that he only said he would fasten the bones together with shingle nails. He likes to be witty, and I am inclined to make due allowance for everything he stated; he is seventy-three years old; he said that old head could not think as fast as he used to. I would not utter a word against him; perhaps none of us will reach the age he has attained; the probability is, that our minds may not be as well preserved as his. I have no doubt that what he told you was true, that what passed thirty or forty years ago he could remember; what two or three years ago, not so well. He could not remember passing events; and the old man Dr. Belding has not sworn to anything which affects this case one way or the other. He told you his opinion was made up partially of his own examination, and partially from the examination of Dr. Pratt and Dr. Freas. He says that if I said that his opinions were made up from what Drs. Freas and Pratt said, I misrepresented him. I said that it was in the condition as now.

Dr. Freas says he examined the arm and found no evidence of provisional callus on the arm. That he, Dr. Pratt, did not claim that the arm had ever been united. Dr. Belding says that Dr. Pratt claimed that what we call the principal fracture (which I did not think existed) had united. Dr. Freas says he did not claim that the arm ever united. It is strange that at that consultation, when everything was talked over, this was not mentioned. Freas says they did say something about the splitting of the splint, but there was no pretence on the part of Dr. Pratt that the bone had ever been united. Mrs. Belding testifies that on that occasion Mrs. Frisby told her that the boy had refractured the arm; that she had made the boy own it up, or words to that effect. Mrs. Frisby, who was the speaker, swears she never did make any such statement; that she never had any introduction to Mrs.

Belding, and did not talk to her at all. Mrs. Belding said, "I was
at your house, Dr. Pratt, a week or two ago. You told me that the
arm was united, and how is this ?" Dr. Pratt said, "It was hit;
Frank was playing ball and fell against the fence and refractured
his arm ; is that not so, Frank ? if not, how was it ?" The boy,
she says, said it was the way it was done. If this conversation
occurred, then Mrs. Frisby does not state the truth—you must
reject one or the other of these witnesses. If Dr. Pratt made
any such statement, he was mistaken. Take either horn of the
dilemma. When it comes to conflict of testimony, I have a memory as impressible as wax, and remember such testimony very
accurately. I cross-examined her upon how long it was before
this time, she was at Dr. Pratt's ; she said it was three, four, or
five weeks ; not longer than five weeks. That would carry us back
to the fifth of April. This corroborates the statements of Dr.
Pratt, to the parents of this boy, that the arm was doing well ;
he told her he was going to take off the splints soon. You must
do one or other of these two things—if you believe Mrs. Belding,
then Dr Pratt did not tell her the truth. I leave it to your con-
science, which is correct. This was no more than a month after
they claim the arm was refractured. I have given a statement
of what I call the conflicting testimony. We have three unimpeached witnesses against Dr. Wales. We have the testimony
of the mother—you well recollect it. I have shown you that Mrs.
Belding has stated what is true or not true ; you may take either
horn of the dilemma.

Having disposed of the conflicting testimony, I propose to
show the statements of these women, in regard to splints. One
swears that the angular splint went on at the time of the fracture
—and then that it did not go on for two weeks. If I had known
as much about these long splints at first as I do now, I would
have had them brought here. The testimony is not that when
the arm was first fractured, Dr. Pratt was called and dressed the
arm, and made a very bad job of it, as I think. There is a little
conflicting testimony about the thumb ; I do not care much about
it. Dr. Wales stated that the arm was done up first, and then
the thumb, and finally he stated that he was positive the arm was
done up first. I pressed him hard upon that point. We call the
two Morrises, and they swear positively that the thumb was done
up first. I want you to remember this. I now go to the bandages. One of these Morrises swears—*by the way*, when one of

these women was on the stand, one of them swears that these
splints were used—one of the Morrises says there was certain
shingle splints put on the arm, which I do not doubt. I never
tried to controvert that testimony. If we had had these splints
on the start, we would have gone into the more minute particulars. This young man says these pine splints were longer than
these, when there was nothing put on to the fore-arm to brace it.
Dr. Wales testifies that the roller was applied from the wrist up
to the shoulder. The women say the bandages came just below
the elbow. I am going to show that this testimony is true. We
call your attention to the splints. Dr. Wales positively testifies,
three or four times, that these were not the splints; if they are,
they have been cut off after they were put on. Mrs. Moscript
and Mrs. Frisby both swear these splints were on the arm when
it was undone, and that they were never cut off. Dr. Freas
noticed they were too short, at Dr. Belding's, but did not speak
of it. Dr. Wales testifies they were cut off then. If these have
been cut off, Mrs. Frisby and Mrs Moscript both swear falsely,
and Dr. Freas was mistaken. In conclusion, Dr. Wales, by
swearing that these have been cut off, tacitly admitted they
were too short. Did he tell the truth? I think we have
established our position on the subject of splints, and perhaps
these two shingle splints, which the witnesses say were as long as
this one—then measuring by the size, they may be mistaken. I
do not wish to give a false statement of it,—that there was no
other support of the fore-arm, only as it was bandaged to the
wrist. If Dr. Wales has so falsified the truth that you cannot
believe him,—that the bandage went to the wrist. This testimony shows, after the arm had been done up,—*by the way*, this
bandage should have been kept on all the time. They testify
that the arm and hand swelled, and was black and blue. If that
bandage had been on they could not have seen that the arm was
black and blue. Dr. Pratt told them to rub the arm. It would
do no good to rub the arm when the bandage was on. Dr.
Wales says it was put in a sling. They cannot find any author,
Homœopathy, Allopathy, Hydropathy, or any other pathy, but
what says the arm must be so confined as to prevent muscular
action. Some say it must commence at the finger, but most of
them contend it must commence at the wrist. These learned
Drs. from Chicago tell you why, and so do our old fogies, too—
that the muscles which affect the hand and [fingers are fastened

near the elbow; and this pronation and supination are made by these muscles. They tell you, the old fogies and the new fogies, Allopathy and Homœopathy, that if the bandage is not tight enough to keep these muscles confined, they will draw the bones out of place. I have shown that these muscles here could not be kept quiet, if the bandage only extended to the wrist, they were not tight enough, for there was muscular motion here. Mrs. Moscript says the arm was uncovered several times. If it was uncovered so often, you could plainly see whether it had properly coaptated, for every time it bowed out, the non-union could be seen if it bowed out. If it bowed out every time, it was not held in place, it was not properly set. It was six weeks after this that we find this pulling process was resorted to, as testified by Mr. Yoeman, and a protrusion of the bone. It was contracted and moved by these muscles that were not confined. Was this good surgery; not to confine the muscles of the fore-arm? I refer you to their own books—to Hamilton, this is the best book of any of them. Here again Mr. Knowlton shows his great ingenuity in arguing this case. He took a place in Grose and showed you certain plates where the bandage only extended to the wrist. He did not tell you this was the proper bandaging used with certain kinds of splints; their own books concur in stating the fore-arm must, in all cases, be confined and kept in a quiscent state. (Shows the bandaging plate which Judge Knowlton exhibited.) From their argument, we must suppose that the author argued that that was the kind of splint to be used. The diagram has nothing to do with the roller coming out to the fore-arm and up to the shoulder. If that is useful, that wants to be put on in the first place. There was no bandaging on the fore-arm, and the bone was not put in apposition, as proved by Mr. Yoeman, and the manipulation of the arm.

Gentlemen of the jury :—I thought I had said all I could about keeping that arm in place. I attempted to show that arm had not been put in place, and never been kept there. The gentlemen read from several books, the cause which prevent union, and if I were to undertake to read over again what they read, and pick out what applies to our side of the case, it would take more time and more voice than I can expend upon it. I very well see that you must be tired by this time.

These testimonies show there was no constitutional causes which could operate to procure non-union. We must, therefore, look to local causes. If you will turn to Hamilton you will find that the !practice is upon army surgery, applied to gun-shot wounds, which are much more likely to fail of union than any other case. We must conclude, then, that if this arm had been properly dressed at first, and kept in a proper place afterwards, the arm would not have failed to unite. (Knowlton.—I wish you would read the title of the book. That shows it is not a treatics on army surgery.) I have read it, and it fully sustains what I stated. .:

Now, in regard to the thumb, I have a word to say. There was a tearing of the soft part of the thumb, to a considerable extent; it was an ·ugly wound; the thumb was put out of joint, or more properly speaking, broken; at all events, the thumb was not cured. A Chicago physician said he would have been proud of it. After the outside wound had healed, he said that he should have gone to work to repair it. Dr. Pratt said he was ashamed of it. Why ashamed of it? If it was such a job that the Chicago physician would be proud of it, I should feel gratified. If, after I have closed this case, I feel I have done my duty, I know my friend Knowlton feels gratified with the effort he has put forth here. I know that the thumb was put up to suit Dr Pratt. If he was ashamed of it he did not perform his whole duty. You must take this into consideration. What was the fracture on the arm? I think the testimony of Dr. Wales has no weight. The Chicago surgeons testify that provisional callus will form around a comminuted fracture. I think no surgeon has had the sagaciousness to say that this bone would unite without provisional callus. It is where the fracture is simple, where the parts are put in proper apposition, but in cases of bones broken in many places, I challenge them, all books and physicians, to say that this has been a comminuted fracture—from the provisiona callus.

Judge Knowlton read a case of a child having a fracture at its birth. In a year that callus had gone away. I tell you that was very natural; there was not a bone in the child's body you could not have bent. It hardly passed out of a callus state and therefore, when there was a great diffusion of the callus, and flexing of the parts it was in the uppermost part of the bone formation. If this had been a comminuted fracture, it would not have thrown off this provisional callus in five months. Dr. Freas tells you that he examined the arm at Dr. Belding's in May, and no provisional callus had formed there, and the bones had rounded off, as though absorption had taken place. Was there any callus there at that time? Dr. Freas failed to see it. Dr. Freas says, from that examination he was satisfied it was a compound fracture; and there is pretty strong evidence that it was not a comminuted fracture.

Dr. Miller is one of the most skillful surgeons in the North-West. He says he has practiced surgery here and in Jo Daviess for twenty-three years, where he has had twelve or fifteen cases per year, or more. They admit he is good authority, and he states positively that he examined the arm, and that it was not a comminuted fracture; that it would have produced provisional callus and could not have been destroyed by that time. There were two surgeons who examined it within five months, and who say there was none to be found, and they were as good surgeons as we had. We are backed up by Dr. Porter, who says there is no provisional callus, and there was never a comminuted fracture, and with all the abuse they have heaped upon him, they have failed to produce a man of more science.

Dr. Bulkley, of Freeport, has practiced twelve years, and has about as good practice as any of them. He lives in my town, and I do not like to praise him too much. We think he is about right. Dr. Bulkley did not put on any airs—made a critical examination, stated if a comminuted fracture, there would have been provisional callus there.

Dr. McPherson, who did not graduate, but who attended a course of lectures, made an examination of the arm, says there is no provisional callus—that the callus would have been there if a comminuted fracture. Four surgeons state it was a compound fracture. There was no comminution. Have we not any evidence upon this subject? Have we not the evidence of that celebrated man, Dr. Ludlam, who said there was no evidence of provisional callus there, and could see no trace of compound comminuted fracture.

When I come to the testimony of Dr. Beebe I take exceptions. He pressed his arm with great force. I ask you if it would not hurt you to pinch your arm in that way? He pinched it until the boy winced. Dr. Beebe took that as evidence there might have been a fracture there. He did not say there was one; there might be. There is no one of you who would stand it without flinching. I think there are as good Drs. in this Court as Dr. Beebe claims to be. Dr. Ludlam appears to be a fine man and exceedingly skillful in his profession ; he could detect none.

Now, Gentlemen, what are we to infer? Dr. Wales merely fixed up this testimony to suit the case. If it was a compound comminuted fracture, after the warning the father gave him, not to spare any pains or expense, it was his duty to put the bones in proper place, and to see that they were kept there. If John Doe hangs out a sign and claims to be a tailor, and I take a coat there to be cut and made, and he spoils the coat, he is responsible ; and so of every profession or calling.

They say upon the other side, that the surgeon is not an insurer that the limb will heal, but he is bound to use due skill and care. The simplest form of liabiliy in law is that of an attorney in collecting a note. You come along here and see a sign out, "Miller and Smith, attorneys at law"; you place a note of a thousand dollars in their hands for collection. That sign is an assurance that they practice law. They take your note and begin a suit, file a declaration. The note is dated in 1863, promises to pay A B, or bearer, one thousand dollars, six months after date. The case comes on for trial ; there is enough in the case to warrant recovery, but when they come to try it, their papers are not right. The jury is empannelled; there is the note. The declaration is in 1853. Here is a variance, and the note is ruled out, and the judgment is against you ; your thousand dollars lost. Who is to blame? Their shingle that attracted you to the office? If I was guilty of such an act, what would you do with me ? You have lost your thousand dollars,—you would go to some other good lawyer and bring a suit against me, and recover the amount of note lost and the cost. The public has a right to be protected against frauds and malpractice. Suppose I am insolent ; your damages is lost ; the thousand dollars you put into my hands has been the means of turning you upon the world a beggar—and you are crowded as such. You would not be obliged to put confidence in such a lawyer.

Now, what would you do with the doctor? I cannot tell what is his general skill. Now you notice that we attempted to prove that the doctor was not a skillful surgeon, but the Court ruled it out. He might have treatedone thousand cases successfully before this ; and if he failed to give this case the kind of treatment which resulted in a cure, he would be responsible for the case. If you think that Dr. Pratt ought to pay damages in this case, that is why I may undertake to prove what is the general skill of Dr. Pratt. I knew as soon as I put my eye upon the countenance of the Judge that he would try to direct your minds away from the real issue, and not try the case upon the merits. You are not to enquire whether he is the most skillful or unskillful surgeon on the earth, or whether it is the most careful or negligent. You have nothing to try but the treatment of this case. The tailor to whom I took my coat, and who spoiled it, may have before and since made a thousand good coats; but he spoiled mine, and must pay for it Dr. Pratt has spoiled this boy's arm, beyond all question, and must pay for it. This is probably the last point in the case which I wish to discuss to any considerable length. Was the treatment of this case conducted right or wrong? The general hypothesis of the case was all that was put to the surgeons. What did they tell you? What did these women swear to? They said that the boy was kept for three or four weeks with no diet at all—gave him gruel, crackers and toast. The father and the women swear to this. Was that proper treatment, gentlemen. The gentleman in his argument, said it was not the quantity, but the quality. They tell you that it was the low diet, and small quantities. They say he cried for something to eat. A boy fourteen years old cried for food, because his parents dare not give it to him, because the doctor forbid them not to do it. They felt sorry for the boy while weeping for food, still obeying the orders of the doctor. But love for the boy triumphed over the mother's better judgment, and she refused to give him food. Why did not the doctor give the boy something to eat and control it by aconite? But they did not give a particle in this case.

They said the blood stood in puddles on the floor; and the quilt was saturated with it, according to their testimony. I show you from their own books, that in cases of this kind, of severe extravasation of blood, Drs. Miller, Porter and all, tell you that a generous died was required in each case. But they throw themselves upon their dignity and say that food has nothing to do with the manufacture of bone. But this blood goes from the heart down through the arteries, by which the capillaries in the bone are fed, and then back again to the heart. Now, I will see if they are consistent. I tell you they are not consistent. If the ossific matter is not thus deposited, why attempt to prove that the destruction of this nutritious foramen would delay the manufacture of bone. If it did not get any nutrition from the blood, how could the destruction of this artery delay the manufacture of bone? Answer it upon your oaths. I should like to talk about that nutriteous foramen, and this anastomosing process and vindicate these little men, Dr. Porter and Dr. McPherson. Mr. Knowlton said a good deal about Dr. McPherson saying "provisionary" callus instead of "provisional." I say there is no more learned man in Chicago than Judge Knowlton; he has studied law and medicine, and has explained almost the whole field of science, and yet he talks about a system of cross section. Cross section is a term for enquiries in surgery. There is resection, but no cross section. Shall we say he has no scientific skill because he said cross section instead of resection? He makes use of another word, and I will venture the assertion, that he uses "Worcester," because he is a Boston man, instead of Webster. He talks to you about "*tenaciousness.*" Every school girl knows better; there is no such word. I wonder if these school girls here are taught this word at your seminary. "*Tenaciousness*" is a new word, and there will have to be a new dictionary got out. Will it be really fair to try my friend, McPherson, because he said "*provisionary*" instead of provisional callus. I have shown their inconsistency in saying that bone is not derived from blood. Judge Knowlton has occupied a position on the bench, and is a lawyer and doctor, and I don't know but doctor of divinity, too. But when he presented you the egg and said it was not made of blood, he had a purpose other than the promulgation of science, when he turned and appealed to the audience and asked, "Is the egg all blood, too?" He thought he had a question which could not be answered. But how is it, school girls in Chemistry? I say it is the doctrine of Liebig, the most eminent chemist who ever lived, said the egg was all blood except the coloring material, which is iron. Chicago men will not deny this. It is taught in all the text books on chemistry which are used in the schools. How is it, then, that these Chicago men are at issue upon this point with " *Old Moses.*" I don't read that good book as much as I ought, but I recollect that when Moses was giving the law to that wonderful nation, the Israelites, and telling them what they should not eat, he said that " all these animals you may eat, but the blood of the animal which is the life thereof thou shalt not eat." Where is the issue now, between Dr. Porter and old Mr. Moses? Dr. Porter is right, or else Moses is not right. He said the iron in blood is the coloring matter. We have heard a great deal about this reproduction. How is it that this little thing, called the egg, produces the chicken? In this are little membranes laid up, and when you apply a moderate heat these become quickened, and all the materials for the future chicken are here. It is in the blood, and the heat developes it; surrounded in this little world, the shell. Neither dew or rain have anything to do with producing the chicken. All the materials of the chicken,—the flesh, the vessels of the blood, the bone the skin and feathers, are in this blood, and the heat applied to the egg developes; no matter whether from the hen or from other sources—the heat developes and arranges the materials in the egg, and a chicken is in due time brought forth to view. If these materials are not in the blood of the egg, where do they come from? Will the gentleman deny that the egg is blood? If he does I have the author here, and I will prove to you he dare not deny it. I remember how I used to do when a boy. I would take ten or a dozen pure white eggs—not blood—and put that under the hen. I might as well here state that in the yolk of the egg is blood, except a little yellow oil which makes up its composition. In about three weeks you will find a check in the shell and the chicken's bill sticks out, and in a few days a full formed chicken. It is all blood. It is fully supplied with blood. You cut its head off and it will bleed profusely. It has feathers, but not very well coated.

Where does the muscular tissue—where does the nervous tissue—where does all that beautiful arrangement come from? And where the bone? It all comes from blood. What then becomes of the theory of the gentlemen who so triumphantly asserted before you that the egg was not blood. I tell you further, that what I state is proved to be true by every book which they have furnished here. This chemistry and philosophy teach] that you can 'find blood in every substance. This book teaches it. I can prove it by these school girls in that gallery, who study chemistry, that blood is in everything which goes to make up bone. Even in the turnip there is blood, although some people say it has to draw blood out of a turnip. I challenge that man, or any other man, to refute that great German philosopher, who says that the lean meat we eat is mostly blood, only a denser form from that in the arteries. The fat is a decomposed matter; it is used for various purposes; for oiling the machinery, and to supply heat. Blood produces the bone. But how is animal heat produced? I will illustrate it to you. Take a pan of lime from the kiln in the coldest days in winter; lay on to ice, and water enters into the lime, and the whole substance is slaked; it becomes quick lime, and a burning heat is produced. Liebig, the great German chemist, says the blood is absorbed in heat.

The blood passes into a fluid state. In that state it makes animal heat. I have much respect for these Chicago men, although they do not appear to have studied these books much; they do not appear to understand how the material of bone can be produced better from animal than vegetable food. They claim the ox who is fed from vegetables has large bones; they cannot see how his flesh can produce more material for bone than the vegetables themselves. I answer, by eating the flesh of the animal. It's not by a tub of blood or a tub of chaos.

Both these gentlemen on the stand question man's being carniverous. Dr. Porter said, from the formation of teeth man was not calculated to live on either a vegetable or animal diet, but upon both. This is not Dr. Porter's theory; solely we find it in books on anatomy and physiology, by men who have written upon this subject for the last two or three hundred years. They pitched into Dr. Porter because he taught what these books teach, —that man is not made to live on either animal or vegetable diet. You remember that Judge Knowlton tried to get over it by saying his father's dogs ate bread and milk, and had bones. One of them thought he had answered me triumphantly, when I asked him if wolves had bones. He said they cronched up bones and all.

But the gentleman's testimony was more logical than his argument. I have been referred to the fact that but very little meat should be used in the South. But further North they eat fat pork or something of that kind. But his science was badly formed. That Great Creator who created everything upon this earth formed him for all climates. The elephant, the lion, the tiger, are all formed for Southern climates. But the polar bear, the seal, and various other animals are formed polar for regions. They have teeth formed for the mastication of animal food. But man is in the North, South, East and West, and has constituted him to subsist on either animal or vegetable food, or both. Less animal is needed in hot climates, and more in Northern ones. The Esquimaux revels while eating the seal and the bear oil; even a candle he would eat with a gusto.

Oh, gentlemen, when they undertake to talk to you about science and scientific truth, they do not seem to understand what is taught in the great book to which Judge Knowlton refers, that the Great Jehovah, who made man of this earth, as Moses tells you, has dominion over all these things, over the beasts of the field; over the fowls of the air, and the grass of the field. When the gentlemen undertakes to talk about science in a case of this kind, you may understand he is treading on sacred ground. I wish to read from Hamilton on Diet, but which is moee fully laid down in Grose. Hamilton says, in order to hasten consolidation, they should use a generous diet, and may resort to wines, brandy and other stimulants. Now, when a patient was in a low condition this is proper treatment. When we see the boy enfeebled by the loss of blood, they ought to have given him good, healthy died, and used this panacea, aconite. This is a very curious idea, that low diet would not injure him.

Gentlemen, I have gone over this case hastily. I debated in my mind, whether I should go into the examination of this case in detail, item by item, as the other side did. Judge Knowlton occupied one nine hours, and Mr. De Wolf two. But I have tried to present the case plainly and without prejudice. I have no personal vanity to gratify, nor professional reputation, as a speaker, to build up. I therefore concluded to confine myself to a few points in the case, believing as I did, that the condition of the arm was good evidence that the boy had not been properly treated. They have failed to show he was properly treated. This man, Beebe, who has had 4000 cases, not one failed of union. As I told you before, we did not come here begging. I have tried many of these cases, as well as Judge Knowlton, and in my whole practice there has never been so sad a case as the young lad before you, turned out upon the world without a hand to help him. The right hand crippled, the left hand destroyed. But, say they, it can be repaired by an operation—take him to Chicago and let Drs. Beebe or Ludlam cure him.

Gentlemen, when I look overy these books, I find that this resection is attended with great danger. Dr. Miller said, when the weather got cold he might attempt an operation. If this mother and this father, after nursing that boy for two years, and seeing the condition he is in, should take him to Chicago to these doctors to be operated upon, they would take him there as they would to the tomb. They would take him there with no hope of recovery. They must take him there with the design to give him up. But because we did not let them try these experiments, they say we took him out of Dr. Pratt's hands too soon. Dr. Pratt told these parents, all the time, that this arm was doing well, and they tell you they never knew otherwise until Dr. Freas told them, at Dr. Belding's.

This treatment reminds me of the New England witches. A man by the name of Wilkes discovered an infallible way to detect the witch. It was as great a discovery as aconite. When a woman was suspected of being a witch, she was sewed in a sheet and thrown into the river; if she sunk to the bottom she was an honest woman—if she did not sink she was brought out and hung, and many of the trees and posts at the corners of the streets of New England witnessed the victims of that man's discovery.

Leave that boy with me till I doctor him to death—I will take him to Chicago and have him operated on. This reminds me of a case your honor related, of a doctor who presented a bill in the settlement of the estate of A B to Dr. Jones, Dr., thirty dollars for curing your wife till she died. Now this would be Dr. Pratt's account—Chas. Frisby to Dr. Pratt, Dr., to curing the boy till he died, two hundred dollars. They should have left the boy until all these experiments had been tried. 1st. Friction. 2d. Puncturation. 3d. Resection. 4th. Ivory pegs. I have learned something new from these Chicago Drs. I thought this driving pegs was like dowelling; but I find I was mistaken. Saw off the bones, drill a hole through, and drive some ivory pegs, and wire the ends together. Is this so? Their books say so. Was there anything objectionable to Dr. Belding's driving shingle nails through? There is another way, by running down a hot iron; all these they must witness before taking that case out of Dr. Pratt's hands. I have a boy of that age; I would not leave him in the hands of such a doctor; no man of sense would do it.

How cruel it was, when they wanted to call in the best surgeon in Carroll county, Dr. Miller, he would not let them. What are you going to do with this case? If you have made up your minds that you are going to try Dr. Porter instead of Dr. Pratt, or Homœopathy or Allopathy, my talk is useless. I have no prejudice against Homœopathy—my best friends are in that school. I am not going to say that Homœopathy is a humbug, when I see such men as Drs. Beebe and Ludlam and Judge Knowlton defending it. I do not know that Dr. Pratt is a Homœopathist by anything which appears here. I am not trying Homœopathy.

I have no prejudices. I am trying a case against a respectable man who has made a blunder, a terrible blunder, by which a poor, unfortunate boy is made a cripple for life. I believe if I should meet Dr. Pratt to-morrow, he would meet me in friendship, as I certainly would him. I have a feeling of sympathy for him. Dr. Pratt has no friend in the world I have the slightest ill feeling against. I have come to this work, believing this boy should have damages ; I have tried it faithfully. If, in the start, I had had my present knowledge, I could have tried it vastly better. I have done my duty. Your duty, in part, is to be performed. How will you perform it—on your Homœopathist or Allopathist? Will you go to your jury rooms and discuss the two systems ? I will say to you, gentlemen of the jury, that these Chicago doctors admitted to you that they had a deep feeling in this case, because they said that other doctors were testifying against their system of medicine. You remember with what gusto Dr. Beebe explained the Homœopathy. He said, " I wish to remove from your minds the prejudice here exhibited toward Homœopathy." I must say, gentlemen of the jury, that these witnesses, throughout their testimony, have maintained their theory. Our doctors had a different theory than theirs ; but really, surgery means the same in both systems. Upon this ground Judge Knowlton has abused Dr. Porter, to a certain extent. He has been actively engaged in his profession since he graduated in Baltimore, some twenty years ago, and what has induced him to misuse Dr. Porter? You see that Dr. Porter was a good witness ; he understood more of this technicality of the science of man than he had the words upon his lips, and those men who came from Chicago came directly from the professional chair they had been occupying in teaching their system. As soon as I began to question their position, they would turn to you and speak of it. I think both sides enlarged upon their theories too much. They drew them out, and, as Knowlton says, you have been betrayed by it.

Dr. Porter has not taken a position he did not sustain, and that I could not find in the books. I never saw these men before they came here, and so far from abusing them, they have commanded my respect by the knowledge they have displayed of their system. If I ever meet them I will use them well.

And I do not think the Judge should come out here and abuse Dr. Porter, and other physicians who have testified here. You will find them just as good men as Drs. Ludlam and Beebe. Dr.

18

Beebe has treated two cases of fracture of the humerus, but qualified it by saying, he had the care of but *one* of the cases. Dr. Ludlam says he has *treated one.* Drs. Porter and Miller have treated several. Let it be understood, when I speak of Dr. Beebe's cases, I mean those in his civil practice. Would you not trust a fracture in the hands of Dr. Porter or Miller as soon as in care of Dr. Beebe or Ludlam? I would. *You would.*

Now, gentlemen, what is to be your verdict? The oath which you took when you took your seats in that jury box, that you had no prejudice against any system, or either of these parties, you answered under the solemnity of an oath, that you had not expressed or formed any opinion as to the merits of this case. We then took you upon trust. After that was done, with your hands uplifted towards high Heaven, you said you would try this case and render a true verdict, according to the testimony. That oath rests upon you to-night, and rests down upon you until your verdict is rendered to the Court. You did not swear that you would try Dr. Porter, or any one else—Homœopathy or Allopathy. I think we have made out a clear case. It is a matter that I cannot determine for you; you must determine it for yourselves. You must sift it for the great object it embraces. If you find the defendant guilty, the next thing will be, what amount of damages will you give this boy? Upon that point there may be diversity of opinion among you. My client's son has failed to have a good arm, in the hands of Dr. Pratt. We have no doubt, gentlemen of the jury, that by your verdict you will not do wrong to Dr. Pratt, and bring damages upon him which he is unable to sustain ; we have no vindictive damages to ask. We simply ask that Dr. Pratt shall stand the damages he has caused. We have no right to call witnesses to show the damages ; you may give one or ten thousand dollars. His arm and right hand are injured. If this be your opinion, you cannot fail to find him guilty. If guilty, you fix the amount. In estimating these damages, you have many things to take into consideration. They have argued that this may be repaired. How much is this going to cost to send this boy to Chicago to be treated ? How much must you pay him for this suffering? These are the principal questions. And when you have discharged your duty, you will have the honor of saying that you have sat for eight long days in this court house, and that no counsel on this side has attempted to persecute any one. We have been called upon to do our duty, and we have done it.

You have listened with a great deal of patience, for which you have my hearty thanks. I leave this case—I leave it feeling that I have not, in my weakness, done my client the justice I ought to have done. I feel, in parting with this case, and in trusting it to your hands, that there is much that I should have done that I have 'not done, and I give it into your hands—and I believe I leave it in the hands of twelve honest men, that will decide and meet the great argument in this case, and do justice.

www.ingramcontent.com/pod-product-compliance
Lightning Source LLC
Chambersburg PA
CBHW020855020726
47497CB00005B/1419